Steel Walls and Dirt Drops

By
Alan Black

Books
By
Alan Black

Science Fiction
Steel Walls and Dirt Drops
Metal Boxes
Chewing Rocks
Titanium Texicans (coming soon)
Larry Goes to Space (coming soon)
A Planet with No Name (coming soon)

General Fiction
Chasing Harpo

An Ozark Mountain Series
With Bernice Knight
The Friendship Stones (Book One)
The Granite Heart (Book Two)
The Heaviest Rock (Book Three) (coming soon)
The Inconvienent Pebble (Book Four) (coming soon)
The Jasper's Courage (Book Five) (coming soon)

Historical Action/Adventure
Eye on the Prize (coming soon)

Non-Fiction
How to Start, Write and Finish Your First Novel
(coming soon)

STEEL WALLS AND DIRT DROPS
Published by arrangement with the author

Printing History
2009, 2014 Copyright by Alan Black

Cover Design: Amy Black

ISBN-13: 978-1496028761
ISBN-10: 1496028767
Library of Congress Number: 1-1234311241

Dedication:

I dedicate this novel to my wonderful wife Duann; the real Chief Master Sergeant Duann Elizabeth (nee Brown) Black USAF RET.

Acknowledgements:
Thanks to the real people who inhabit these pages and have helped me visualize the characters and their stories:
Duann Elizabeth (nee Brown) Black,
John Cochran,
Clarice (Clancy) Preston,
Tammie (nee Qualls) Wright,
Brianna (nee Wright) Morin,
Bennett Beaudry
And
Richard Jackson.

Thanks to my beta readers,
Steve Black,
Duann Black,
And
Tom Brennan.
Their help and insight has been invaluable for this re-publication and correction of an old novel.

More information about Alan Black at
www.alanblackauthor.com
https://www.facebook.com/pages/Alan-Black-Paperback-Writer/259372705810

Steel Walls and Dirt Drops

By
Alan Black

CreateSpace

Chapter One

Newly promoted Third-Level Commander Hamisha Ann McPherson stepped off the space station slide-walk. She moved light and easy for a big woman, but a worried expression flashed across her none-too-attractive face. The Allied Protective Expeditionary Services (APES) normally promoted leaders from within the ranks of their existing unit. She wondered what kind of fouled-up unit needed an outside commander. Surely, a unit this size would have someone qualified with the desire to move up the command track. How bad could it be if the APES had to promote a newly minted second-level to third to fill the slot? What kind of nightmare unit would it have to be to assign a second-level who had just gotten her whole command killed on their last drop?

Her new command was a hundred meters away. She was eager to begin in spite of her mounting apprehension. The gate and guard were well within sight despite the curvature of the station bulkheads. It was a huge station and the curve was gradual compared to many smaller stations she had visited.

Misha was worried. She was not worried about her own abilities, but more than a little uneasy about what she was walking into. Distaining the use of the yellow and black striped caution handrail, she walked to the tarmac side of the Allied Mobile Space Forces (AMSF) echo deck on Heaven's Gate Space Station in orbit around Heaven Three in the Heaven System. For the hundredth time since leaving her home world of DropSix, she wondered why it was called the tarmac side. The spacecraft parked there sat snuggled into hangers around the station rings with their back ends hanging into the nothing of space. Nothing was nothing; it certainly wasn't tarmac.

She stopped in front of a view port overlooking the military section of Heaven's Gate. It was the last view port before coming to the entry gate leading to her new command. She read the small warning sign just above the view port controls. "FOD kills." Misha gave a mental shake of her head. "Vacuum-breathers!" she exclaimed. She had seen this particular warning sign posted somewhere at every AMSF base she had been on or passed through, including her own four-year tour of duty before joining the Allied Protective Expeditionary Services (APES). In all of that time, and in the eight years since, no one she asked had been able to explain why it was called tarmac or what FOD even looked like. However, since FOD warnings were everywhere, she knew she would do her best to avoid it at all costs, if she ever saw it.

Misha spun the dial on the view port controls setting the opacity level to the highest possible filter. Turning the 'dark on' changed the port into a mirror. Slowly, she smoothed her hands down the front of her light-gray dress tunic. Straightening the seams brought the tunic's blood red trim into line with the matching red stripe on the trousers stuffed into her soft-soled jump sneakers. The tunic didn't have buttons to button, collars to straighten or pockets to close, so her adjustments did not take long.

Still, Misha let her fingers linger over the red triangle of her new rank. She hadn't even had time to get used to being a second-level commander before getting bumped up another notch. Reaching third-level in the APES was quite an accomplishment for a woman who barely looked out of her teens, although she had just passed her thirtieth standard birthday. Her youthful looks were thanks to GerinAid, Delta Corporation's anti-aging drugs, more than any family inherited trait.

She smiled remembering how in only eight years in the APES she had earned her triangles. Her smile faded quickly to a frown as her fingers slid down to the row of ribbons high across her left chest. If service tradition had not required that she wear her awards and decorations, she would have shipped them home to DropSix to let her baby sister's new daughter play with the colored bits of metal and silk.

The top ribbon was the Aries Award. It sat alone on a row of its own. It took its name from old Earth's

Grecian god of war. The Aries was the highest combat medal possible in the Allied Systems. Sixth-Level Commander John Cochran personally presented the commendation to Misha. It gave her a small shiver recalling that the top commander of the Allied Protective Expeditionary Services took the time to present the award to a lowly APE.

"Presented," Misha reminded herself. "I did not earn it. I just did what I had to do, dammit! It belongs to those good APES on Guinjundst who did not come back and are gone forever. Gone," she thought. "The whole squad Gone; with a capital G. Hellfire, might as well capitalize the whole thing: GONE."

Most of the APES who dropped dirt on Guinjundst had not come home. Her own third-level commander and nine other second-level commanders died along with the rest of the unit. The Sixth had been very specific to point out that while she was a new second-level commander; she rallied the survivors and took the battlefield back from the non-human Binders. She had turned what surely could have been humanity's first defeat against the Binders into a significant and decisive victory.

In a private ceremony afterwards, the Sixth shook Misha's hand telling her the Aries Award was as much for the invaluable information she had brought back as it was for her combat record. He had tacked on her third-level command triangle with his own hand. Misha knew the information she brought back was now highly classified. She was certain no APE under the rank of fourth-level, except herself and those pitifully few Guinjundst veterans knew the real story of Guinjundst. She knew very few people in all the Allied Systems knew the truth.

Misha shook her head to try clearing the mental pictures of men and women who had not come home from that deadly dirt drop. So many APES died so she could have a pretty ribbon to wear on her chest. She would rather have her old squad back. However, she knew that wasn't going to happen. Dead is dead.

Today, as the new commander of the 1392nd, she would take leadership of a squad of ten troopers, plus gain command over ten second-level commanders, each with their own squad of ten troopers. It was a larger unit than she was used to commanding and it held more unknowns than she liked.

Misha studied her reflection in the view port taking in the whole picture. She was not shy about her size anymore, not like she had been when she had first left DropSix. She stood 6 feet 5 inches tall. That was short for DropSix. She was shorter than any adult in her family, including her mother and her baby sister. She weighed in at 325 pounds standard, but looked like she weighed less; much, much less.

She smiled at how often people had been fooled into thinking she weighed about 245 pounds. People from normal range gravity worlds sometimes underestimate the muscular density of heavy-worlders. DropSix was a 1.16 standard gravity world and over the generations the children of DropSix colonists developed a dense musculature with the heart and lung capacity to quickly pump oxygen to those dense muscles.

"Still," she thought, "if anyone is surprised at my size it is their own fault, be they training partners, dance partners, sex partners or just barroom brawlers." She chuckled inwardly at the thought of dance or sex partners. There were few of those, but it still didn't hurt to think of the possibilities.

Misha knew anyone who looked close enough would see she was from a heavy world. The eyes staring back at her in the view port mirror were almost black, with specks of bright blue, a gift from her Scottish heritage. The red rim surrounding the cornea of her eyes was a specific trait of growing up on a heavy world. It was a dead give-away to anyone who took the time to look closely.

"Not that anyone has looked that closely in a long time," Misha thought as she smiled to herself. She scanned her face out of habit. She knew she wasn't beautiful, pretty, cute or even average. Her features were

4

okay and all in the right place, but she had always felt things just did not seem to come together. She had nice eyes and a nice nose, but somehow they did not seem to meld into a pleasant and harmonious union.

"Maybe I need a new hairdo?" Her hair was jet black, cut in the standard grunt cut. She shaved the left side of her head from front-to-back and brim-to-nape for ease in attaching the control nodes in her armored helmet. This cut gave new meaning to the age-old military phrase: high, wide and tight. She cut the rest of her hair anywhere it might fall into her face or over the shaved area. She shook her head as the rest of her hair settled into place in various shaggy lengths normally hacked off whenever it got too long. It was very duty-functional, but it wasn't designed to attract members of the opposite sex.

"Well, it is time to saddle up," she said, blowing a long breath through gritted teeth. She spun the view port dial back to open view and stepped on the slide-walk for the last hundred meters to the military section's guarded gate. She was more worried about her new unit than she had ever been when facing an enemy in combat. In combat, the worst that could happen was that you died. If this unit was as snafu as she imagined, then it might be worse than dying, she might fail. She only hoped she could handle this outfit with a more delicate hand than she used in battle.

Chapter Two

Trooper One Donnellson of Foxtrot Squad frowned at the beer in front of him. It was only his second brew and it was a freebie to boot, since the owner of the beer had passed out shortly after buying the beer and was even now under the table. He really wanted to drink it, but he knew he shouldn't. Second-Level Commander Race Jackson, his squad leader, would tear a wide strip off his backside if he so much as sniffed it. It did seem to make sense not to drink too much since he was technically on duty. Then again, half of the troopers in the bar were on duty.

He thought, "Still, Race put me here to keep an eye on the slide-walk for our new third-level commander. She isn't due until tomorrow, but then Race doesn't trust anyone above second-level." Donnellson understood the feeling because he did not much trust anyone at any rank above trooper. Donnellson snorted to himself thinking about the last third-level the old ninety-second had endured. The man was a full-fledged domestic-level waste of air. No wonder so many troopers were dogging it at the Monkey Hole, on duty or off.

He thought, "Maybe I can chug this one really fast when Race isn't looking, just like I did the first beer a few minutes ago."

"Hanging dirt! There she goes," Trooper One Sigget Donnellson shouted over the noise.

Second Jackson spun around just in time to catch sight of a woman's back as the slide-walk moved her around the space station's gentle curve and out of his sight.

"Did ya see her, Race?" Donnellson asked excitedly. "It has to be her. Big woman! A damn amazon in uniform and I swear I saw the triangles of a Third. I think it looked like her pix on the vids download last week."

"Crap in the bag! Then it's probably her," Jackson affirmed.

He swung his gaze around The Monkey Hole. As usual, the barroom was crowded. It was a favorite location for APES, the ground combat troops for the Allied Systems. It was as common a bar as on any other space station catering to military clientele. There were few decorations or adornments, fewer tables and even fewer chairs along the pre-fabricated plasticine bar covering the whole length of the back bulkhead. It did have plenty of standing room. An oddity of station architecture left the ceiling little more than a gaping hole through three decks. It was completely open where the fourth wall would have been as it faced the slide-walk. That openness made it particularly popular with APES. These men and women spent most of their working lives confined to a station, in transit on troop transports, or encased in the hard-shelled APES combat suits. It was the most non-claustrophobic hangout possible on Heaven's Gate. At least, it was the most non-claustrophobic hangout that served alcohol this close to the AMSF hangers. As usual, the Monkey Hole was jammed with APES from all over the station. Most were stationed on parked spacecraft but a few were just passing through.

Race Jackson knew he and Donnellson weren't the only APES in the bar deployed on the AMSF Spacecraft Kiirkegaard. He finally spotted Second-Level Commander Takki-Homi. "Taks," Jackson shouted over the noise of the bar. "Hey, Deuce Taks! We got company knocking at the hatch."

Heads swiveled and bodies crushed toward the open space between the bar and the slide-walk. Voices shouted, "Where?" "I don't see anybody special." "Who?" "Is that her? The hero of Hydra?" It was well noised about that the 1392nd was getting a new third-level commander. What made the gossip particularly juicy was that this commander was a certified, battle-hardened hero.

Jackson snorted and shouted over the din. "Shut your frakking pie-holes. It was the Battle of Guinjundst in the Hydra Sector, you morons, and yeah it was most likely her. Donnellson spotted her on the slide-walk." He turned to Takki-Homi and asked, "What do you think, Deuce? Can we beat her back to the Kiirkegaard?"

Second Takki-Homi nodded slowly. He tapped the communications unit tagged onto his breast pocket glass-pack data unit turning their unit's comm gear on and opening up a channel. With a little luck, their new boss would not have slaved her comms to their unit's frequency. "Unit 1392: McPherson's Second Tier, listen up. This is Second Takki-Homi," Taks spoke swiftly, broadcasting to everyone in the 121 trooper outfit. "To the APE on the gate: The new third-level commander is on her way. Do a slow stall, don't get yourself in a jam with the boss, but try to slow her down. Do a triple bip warning on the comm when she gets past you. Vark, are you on board?"

Takki-Homi heard a single bip from the comm unit. The bip told him that squad leader Second-Level "Vark" Aardmricksdottir was listening and on board the transport. She knew she did not need to take mission-critical time speaking.

"Good," Taks said. "Set-to with whomever you got, no matter whose squad they're in. She's early so scramble to unshamble. Every APE not on board the Kiirkegaard is to head to the delta deck gate. Cut across the maintenance bay and get onboard through the cargo hatches. If the vacuum-heads yell about you being on their turf, just ignore them. I'll straighten it out with the load master later. Move it, APES!"

Chapter Three

Misha stepped off the slide-walk and turned toward the AMSF main gate leading to the military's principal decks.

Misha knew her uniform, boots, hair, eyes and even her teeth were spotless. She changed from her blood-red utility jumpsuit into the dress uniform just a short time ago in the transport pod coming up from Heaven Three. She deliberately delayed a hundred meters short of the gate. She had stood gate duty on many stations and knew what it was like to have any commander catch you unprepared. The delay should have given the gate guard time to spot her and be ready to greet her.

Each APES unit deployed to an AMSF spacecraft regardless of size was required to assign a trooper to the main gate. Officially, it was to vouch for APES with the AMSF guard on duty, thus eliminating the need to carry passes, authorizations or any other sort of bureaucratic red tape. After all, APES were just tenants and passengers on Allied Mobile Space Force vessels.

On a large station like Heaven's Gate, APES were deployed on any one of a dozen or more spacecraft. A lot of troopers from a lot of units would be on gate duty at any given time. Her delay at the mirror should give the troopers on duty time to sort out who she might be and which trooper should be on his feet and at the gate to greet her.

Unofficially, gate duty was designed to have a friendly face greeting returning APES. It was also a time to meet troopers in other commands, tell war stories, trade gossip, make new friends and network. However relaxed it might become, most troopers made sure the right trooper was available at just the right time so a returning APE wouldn't even break stride passing through the gate. Delaying an APE at the gate was traditionally bad form. Delaying a command level APE at the gate, even seconds and thirds, might land a lazy trooper on a punishment detail: scrubbing toilets, shuffling mobility pallets, or scraping the bottom of the combat skid plates.

Misha had no desire to start her new command by jumping down the throat of the first trooper in her unit she met. She was more than a little surprised to see that only an AMSF spacer stood to greet her. She could see small clusters of APES troopers behind the gate, many of them looking decidedly nervous. However, none of them stepped up to the gate. The spacer, a young, absolutely tiny woman, glanced behind her at the knot of troopers and shrugged helplessly.

Misha halted at the gate entrance, neither remaining outside the area nor stepping in as her bulky size blocked the gate entrance. Misha shrugged back and said, "Third-Level Commander Hamisha Ann McPherson reporting for deployment aboard the AMSF spacecraft Kiirkegaard." She handed the young woman her glass-pack. The spacer slid the glass-pack into the slot on her command board and pressed the big green 'go' button.

The glass-pack was a leaded crystal rectangle about three inches by two inches and only an insignificant fraction of an inch thick. Data was stored at a molecular level and transferred by light code at light speed. Each subset of stored data was encrypted and buried behind a maze of firewalls, thus insuring that when a user dropped the glass-pack into a slot the reader could only access authorized data for the specifically requested data transfer.

Misha's glass-pack, like everyone's, contained her whole life, private, professional and archival. It held enough copies of books, plays, and movies to stock a small planetary library. It held all of her photo-images and mail from home. It held her financial and banking records, small as they were. It also held her orders the Kiirkegaard deployment orders and the orders authorizing her to take command of the 1392nd.

Glass-packs could automatically transmit appropriate codes without inquiry or comment, but certain military traditions remained sacrosanct. Reporting to a new duty station had its own set of rules having nothing to do with any available technology. Faster than either could have requested the data verbally, the command board queried the glass-pack, which responded equally fast with the appropriate answer.

The command board's resident hologram image was a twelve-inch high AMSF General in full-dress uniform. It popped into existence and hovered a few inches above the board. Speaking loud enough for every trooper in the area to hear and in a clear well-modulated voice, it said, "Welcome aboard, Third McPherson. Proceed to hangar E-315, please." The little man blinked out before Misha could say thank you.

The diminutive spacer said, "Yes, ma'am. Let me locate your trooper." She handed Misha back her glass-pack.

Misha smiled to put the young girl at ease. "Thank you, Spacer Second Class. It is second class, is it not?"

The girl blushed. She couldn't have been more than sixteen, even accounting for the delayed aging GerinAid injection. She was obviously on her first term of enlistment and just out of boot camp. "Um, yes ma'am. It's Morin, um…Spacer Second Class Brianna Morin." The girl almost saluted, but halted her arm midway up, remembering at the last moment that APES don't salute. Instead, she started to turn to the troopers behind her. Misha stopped her.

"Spacer Second Class Morin, it is 'sir'," she said.

The girl looked confused. "Pardon me, ma'am?"

"In the Allied Protective Expeditionary Service all commanders of third-level and above are called sir not ma'am. Second-level commanders are called mister. Gender does not matter. It is hard to tell the sex of someone encased in a combat suit. It might do you well to remember that. Who knows, Spacer Morin, you may want to become an APE someday!"

"Me, ma'am? I mean, sir," the spacer stammered. "I'm way too small to be a fighter type."

Misha replied, "Well, when I was a first-year rookie, the second-level commander of my squad was just about your size. Deuce Saheed kicked my butt every day of the week. Size, just like gender, does not always matter. Now you may find me my trooper."

Misha had deliberately delayed beyond all reason and was beginning to get a tad bit peeved. If she delayed at the gate it was her business, but she should not be delayed by others. Not even a newbie rookie trooper should have been left standing this long. The girl turned and motioned frantically to a trooper lounging in a chair off to one side. The man came over, not on the double as Misha would have expected, but quick enough she held her tongue.

Misha glanced behind her. A line of APES and spacers was starting to back up, waiting their turn to gain entrance. Misha was glad she had sent all of her gear on ahead by cargo pod. At least, she wasn't carrying her bags. Still, she completely blocked the entrance to the main gate.

"Sir?" the trooper asked.

"Sir what, Trooper?" Misha asked. "Has the hearing standard been relaxed for the Thirteen Ninety-Second?" She looked the man in the eyes. In them, she saw boredom, not apprehension, not worry, not confusion, just boredom. "Are you or are you not assigned to the 1392nd currently deployed aboard the Kiirkegaard?"

"Yes, sir, it is now McPherson's Second," he said, still not motioning for her to move through the gate.

Misha bit back the growing anger. To be delayed was one thing; this was close to being a deliberate insult. The calm showing on her face belied her raging emotions. She looked the man up and down. He was a good looking, dark-haired man with the frame of an ex-athlete who did not work out as hard as he could, but still looked fit. He was older than her, but far from going gray.

She said, "Beyond any reasonable doubt, I am sure you heard me tell Spacer Second Class Morin I am that very McPherson."

The trooper started to reply, "But Trey, you aren't here officially until tomorrow and-"

Misha cut him short. "Trooper, you will call the Kiirkegaard, get the second in charge to send out your replacement, then you will escort me to the Kiirkegaard. Do you understand?" Without waiting for a reply, she continued. "You will do it now." Misha could barely keep a calm face as the man reached up and turned on his comm unit to make the call. The insult was becoming incompetence. Never had she heard of anyone shutting down their comm unit when on duty. That was the equivalent of sleeping on the job. Fuming, she listened as the man called into the APES detachment aboard ship. She held her temper in check, knowing that pounding someone in your command on the very first day would be very bad form.

"The call's in and Second Moraft is on her way," the trooper said. "It'll be just a tic, sir. I'll grab my gear and be back before they get here."

"Freeze, Trooper," Misha all but shouted through gritted teeth. "I will stand right here. You will stand with me."

"But my stuff-" the man whined.

"Trooper, upon returning to your squad, you will report to your squad's medic for a hearing exam." Misha interrupted and leaned in close to the man's face. She was a foot taller than him, so she bent slightly, causing the trooper to crick his neck upward to stare into her face. Speaking so softly only he would hear she said, "Trooper, know this: I will take no more crap, sass or back talk from you. I do not want to hear anything other than 'yes, sir' or 'no, sir'. Do not test my patience further."

Misha heard a shout from behind her, "Hey! What's the hold up? I got duty in fifteen."

Misha looked behind her at the ever-growing line of men and women waiting a turn at the gate. She swiveled her head back around to the trooper. She could sense his dismay as she stepped a fraction closer to him. Eyeball to eyeball, nose-to-nose, not a drop of sweat separated the two, she hovered over him. Neither Misha nor the trooper blinked. Her anger grew and she could see the realization in his eyes that he had pushed the wrong person.

Misha caught sight of Spacer Morin in the corner of her eye. The young spacer glanced at the growing crowd at the gate and back to the two APES.

"Um, sir?" Morin asked in hesitation. "Third McPherson? Would you care to wait for your escort inside the gate office where you might be more comfortable?"

"No thank you, Spacer Morin," Misha answered without taking her eyes off the trooper before her. "I am fine here."

"Yes, ma'am, I mean sir. But, the Kiirkegaard is way around the tarmac. And…well, the traffic at the gate?" More shouts from the line interrupted the girl.

"Yeah, move it up there." "Come on, we ain't got all day." "Hey, Beaudry! You got a new girlfriend?" Misha realized that until this moment she hadn't known the trooper's name. Not that it mattered, a person would not remain anonymous for long in a unit of only 121 people.

Taking her eyes off Trooper Beaudry, Misha turned only her face toward the girl and said, "Thank you for your concern, Spacer. I am sure that I will be fine right here. Don't worry, Brianna. Here comes the cavalry. You have done fine. Let your boss handle it. That is why he gets to wear the fancy uniforms at officer's parties." She smiled and gestured towards the hatch of the gate office. A young second lieutenant was bustling toward them.

The lieutenant pulled up short. Misha could see his eyes bug-out at the Aries Ribbon on her chest. She knew how he felt. Before she had an Aries medal of her own to wear she had only seen them on recruiting posters and then only on ancient and scarred veteran warriors.

The man swallowed, obviously nervous. "Third, we must clear the gate. I am sorry, but I must ask you to step into the holding area until we can resolve whatever is, um, what is, I mean, you know…" The man trailed off as the growing crowd behind Misha became louder and more profane.

Misha spun on her heels and faced the queue of men and women. "Silence!" she bellowed. "You will behave like adults or you will be treated as children." Smiling, she turned back to the man. "I am in no mood for more insults, Lieutenant. I am sure if we work together we can run this crowd through the gate faster than a hot knife through warm butter, if you get my drift." She tapped the man's officer tab, a single gold bar.

"Y-y-yes, ma'am," the man stuttered.

Misha shook her head in amazement. Spacer Morin hid a smile behind her hand. Misha saw the girl had the grace to blush at the officer's gaffe. Misha shot her a wink that said, 'Well, what are you going to do?' She decided she was not in the mood to instruct any more people in the manners and customs of her outfit, not even to instruct an officer of a sister service who should know better.

Misha said to the lieutenant, "Call me Third or Trey if it suits you, or even Misha. Now, shall we clear this deck?"

Before the man could respond she shouted, "All right. All APES on gate duty form a double, gauntlet style line to the outside curve of the gate. Move it!" Troopers scrambled to fall into place. Beaudry started to move, but Misha put a restraining hand on his chest. "Not yet, Trooper Beaudry," she said. "Lieutenant, if you would be so kind, form your people to the inside curve. We should be able to clear the decks, toot sweet."

Misha turned to the restless queue seeking entry. "All right, ladies and gentlemen. APES form a single line to your left. Spacers form a line to your right. Anyone who is from the Marshal Service or a civilian on official business kindly step to the holding area on your right. We will not hold you there for long and the lieutenant will personally see to your entrance."

She turned to Beaudry, "Trooper, you will take your place in the gauntlet. Admit anyone from the 1392nd, but you will instruct him or her not to leave this area. Move!"

The queue dissolved and as if by magic, coalescing into two ragged lines and a cluster of individuals in the holding area.

"Everyone is to expedite entrance," she shouted loud over the crowd noise. "Please have your glass-pack out and ready if you require documents to prove admittance. Once you have gained entrance, please move out of the area to make room for those behind you. All you APES, no yakking. Just clear the gates. Do it now!"

Misha stepped to the side and watched the lines surge forward as if a dam had broken open. The APES line was moving at double time. She nodded approval as a trooper motioned another APE to stand behind him. The man's glass-pack was in his hand waiting for review. He was obviously checking into a new command, just as she was. A trooper from his unit set him aside to get the line clear. Even seconds and thirds were getting into the act, moving quickly and encouraging the others around them. She almost winced when she saw a fourth caught up in the rush move through the line. The man smiled in approval as he went past.

The AMSF lieutenant was staring google-eyed at the rush of people. Misha tapped him on the shoulder and gestured pointedly toward the holding area at the small knot of people waiting patiently for his attention. The man rushed forward like a fish moving upstream now that he had a purpose he could grasp.

Misha felt a presence behind her and turned to face an older woman in the red utility APES work uniform with a second-level commander's X on her collar. The woman was out of breath, a true indication she had given up on her daily exercise routine some time ago. She looked old for APES service with gray streaks in her hair, GerinAid notwithstanding.

"Second Moraft, sir, reporting as ordered."

Misha said, "Mister Moraft, are you the second in charge of details today?"

16

"No, sir, that would be Second Aardmricksdottir, but she got jammed up. I volunteered to come down in her place. I brought Spakney to cover for Beaudry," Moraft said.

"Thank you, Mr. Moraft. I appreciate your efforts, but it doesn't look like Beaudry has had anything to do." Misha pointed to where Beaudry stood alone. No other member of her command stood near him. "It appears we had a trooper on gate duty when there were no members of our unit off ship. My comm unit is not channeled to the 1392nd, so if you would please call Second Aardmricksdottir to do a roster count and if necessary issue an immediate recall signal. We will not need Beaudry or Spakney on the gate if we don't have anyone unaccounted for."

Chapter Four

Misha left Moraft and Trooper Spakney on gate duty waiting for any stragglers. She herded Beaudry along the corridor passing by half a dozen ramps leading to various military spacecraft. The space around most ramps was liberally littered with crew lounging around, laughing, talking and just breathing station air. The Kiirkegaard ramp space was empty except for four armed AMSF security guards standing duty. The AMSF required a ship's guard on duty at the main hatch when in a port other than a military installation, but most captains ignored the rule on Heaven's Gate as it was about half military. Having armed guards was a bit much, but at least the Kiirkegaard's captain had not requested APES in a combat suit as back up to the guards as he might have done in some backwater civilian ports.

She slowed her march into the ship to report in, but Beaudry skittered around her and past the guards without a glance in their direction. She shrugged and followed. It was the ship captain's business if he did not need or want people reporting in and out. The glass pack in her pocket would automatically report and timestamp her entry onto the ship without any human contact.

She expected Beaudry to continue leading her to APES country aboard the Kiirkegaard. She knew from her orders the ship was a huge mothership with massive flight decks for numerous squadrons of FACs, their fighter craft. Any newbie could get lost in two turns along its twisting corridors. Beaudry seemed to slow down with each passing step. He did not appear to be lost or deliberately dragging his feet. The man just did not seem to be in a hurry to get anywhere.

Misha was not concerned about getting lost. She had been aboard dozens of AMSF spacecraft and they always warehoused their APES in approximately the same area. Besides, if she even thought about getting lost, she could pull up the basic ship's schematics on her glass pack. Specific schematics would be classified, but she would be able to get enough of a rendering to find her way to APES country. She scooted around Beaudry and picked up the pace. She could feel him struggling to keep up with her without running, but she refused to look behind her.

She found the hatch into APES country exactly where she knew it would be. The entry was a huge heavy garage style hatch that was rolled up out of the way, giving any combat suited APE access through the tall double wide hatches leading to their dirt drop chutes, to their equipment warehouse or to their special training bay. The surprise on her face turned to glaring anger as she looked at the command buildings. The prefab, mobile buildings were dropped into the area without regard to traditional order and certainly not neatly lined up. There were jagged gaps and odd angles between each of structures.

APES rental space on a ship of this size should be able to hold all of their equipment and gear if the prefab units were aligned properly. With this jumbled mess, their extra gear and supplies must be stored in another warehouse space somewhere on the ship. She hoped their secondary space was close by and had external hatches to dump their equipment with them on a dirt drop. She would hate to have to either get by without their gear or hump it into place prior to the drop.

The first room inside the hatch was the unit commander's office and day room. It was slightly off kilter and she had to slide between the ship's bulkhead and the office's steel wall to get to the hatch. Beaudry tried to beat her to the hatch switch, but she slapped it open before he could reach around her.

"Frakking crap on a crutch," she sputtered. The stench of the toilet in the back wafted out the open hatchway wrapping her in its foul cloak. The odor was unmistakable, yet it was mixed with touches of alcoholic vomit and stale month-old sweat socks. Litter, half-empty meal packs and assorted refuse was scattered about the office reaching knee high in the corners allowing only for a small path to what might have been a desk under a pile of rubbish where the path forked. One path led to the toilet area and one path blazed a trail to the sofa where a cushion lay bare. It was adorned with a small pile of human excrement in the middle.

Safely stacked in a small hastily cleared area near the hatch was her baggage. It weighted as much as she did, yet she hefted it easily with one hand. She pointed her other hand at Beaudry and then back at the commander's day office. "Clean it and don't come out until it is done. You may call for volunteers to help you as necessary and good luck with that."

She spun on her heel leaving the distraught trooper behind her. Fortunately, Alpha Squad's bay was right next to the office. It was not fortunate because of the heavy luggage as that was easy for her to manage. It was fortunate because Misha's rage was rising to a boil. She knew if she ran into any mess as nasty as her new office, she would slide into combat mode and someone or something would get broken. There was little chance of finding such a mess in the short distance between the office and her squad bay.

Misha slapped open the hatch to Alpha Squad's bay. It was a combination barracks, classroom, weapons locker, combat suit storage area, dining area, shower facility and when grounded on a planet during a dirt drop, it became a combination bunker and tank.

She sighed. It was clean and the air smelled fresh. No one noticed her entrance, they were all busy cleaning, scrubbing and making bunks. It was obvious they had heard she was on the way and were frantically cleaning before the arrival of their new commander.

Tossing her bags on the first bunk inside the hatch, she gave a low whistle to get everyone's attention. A large trooper moved from the back towards her as everyone else stopped working and turned in her direction. She did not expect or even want anyone to call the squad to attention. That was just not the way APES did things.

She held up her hand to stall the trooper before he spoke. She knew who he was, just as she knew every

APE in her squad. Their files had been required and interesting reading since she received her assignment orders. Misha kept her voice quiet and well modulated. It was the inside voice her mother taught her to use as a child. Still, it echoed from the steel walls of the huge room. "Mr. Singletary, I am sorry if my baggage is crowding whoever's gear is on this bunk. I expect to maintain traditional bunk spacing, so the existing gear will need to be shuffled to the appropriate owner's bunk." She could feel her anger at Beaudry and the state of her office beginning to cause her muscles to clench, so she took a deep breath and told herself to remain calm. Using her best after Sunday School voice she said, "Mr. Singletary, as you know, by tradition the squad leader regardless of rank is first out the hatch, first in combat, first to fight, and logically takes the first bunk. And you, as Trooper One by tradition ride drag bringing up the rear to watch over any new troopers, stragglers or walking wounded. Is that clear?"

She did a quick turn without waiting for an answer. A few steps brought her to a large wall locker that should have been hers. It was unlocked, so she slapped the panel and opened the door. She did not expect anything to be in the locker, since it was traditionally the one used by the squad commander. She did not expect it to be spotless considering the state the last commander had left his office. However, she certainly did not expect to see it stuffed full of drugs, alcohol and pornography.

Slamming the locker door closed with a bang, turning her back to the locker, she leaned against it. She could feel the heat rising in her face and spreading down her neck to disappear under her collar. She closed her eyes and clenched her teeth. She believed that what an APE did off duty was nobody's business but theirs as long as it did not affect their combat readiness. She was fuming. This was illegal and illicit contraband. It was not just on board ship and not just in APE country, but in her locker. Someone brought this crap into her house, right in the middle of her bedroom. She bellowed, spun on her heels, locked her arms around the locker and heaved.

A screech of metal wailed through the bay as she ripped the locker from the steel wall. Without consideration of who was nearby, she slammed the locker onto the deck. The unlocked door flew open and the contents spilled across the deck. She shook the locker dumping all of the remaining contents onto the deck. Heaving the locker over her head, she slammed it down repeatedly on the jumbled pile. Tossing the locker to the side, she stomped through the broken bottles and vials to what should have been her bunk. The bunk was snuggled into a box-type arrangement. When the blast shutters were in place, the bunk became a self-contained escape pod. A bunk with the shutters dropped gave its occupant a modicum of privacy and afforded a number of small spaces for an APE to store a few special personal items.

Misha pounded open the first small storage space inside the hatch. She reached a meaty hand in, dragged out and crushed what appeared to be someone's personal pornography stash. She yanked the blanket and sheets off the bed, realizing the sheets underneath were filthy and had not been changed in weeks. She wanted to gag, but it only made her angrier.

Troopers scattered as she tore through the bay, tossing out this and that, throwing gambling paraphernalia, boxes of tobacco, bags of drugs and even old-fashioned nudie photos on the deck. She yanked open lockers, locked or not, stripped bedding from bunks, and threw unopened bottles of tile cleaner into the shower area, splashing odd colored liquids into places that were previously virgin to their touch.

Without seeing who belonged to what, she yanked open a locker and grabbed a double handful of contents. She squeezed and shook the contents, feeling something delicate snap between her fingers. She threw the contents onto a pile on the deck with everything else.

She stopped. Misha realized the locker she had just torn into had been neat and orderly. An eye for care and precision arranged everything. Glancing at the pile on the deck, she saw a silver-colored flute twisted and broken in the mangled mess. The name Ottiamig was neatly stenciled on the locker hatch along with the number 8.

She looked around and spotted Trooper One Singletary. "Get this place cleaned up. Do it beyond inspection standard. Dot the I's and cross the T's, Trooper. Do it now and do it fast."

Chapter Five

Trooper Bennett Beaudry jabbed the scrub brush around the toilet bowl and muttered, "Bitch! She got no right to put me on punishment detail. She isn't even the commanding third yet. Bitch still doesn't even officially take over until tomorrow."

He looked around at the single-seater latrine and through the open hatch into the empty APE commander's day office. He damned the rest of his squad for not responding to his request for help.

It was not the first time Beaudry had been in the command office. Third-Level Commander Hamilton Cans, now retired, had often called in Beaudry, but not for disciplinary action. Beaudry had a particular talent for reciting lewd jokes and limericks that amused the commander when he was drinking, which even Beaudry would admit, was much of the time this past year. Beaudry had been fond of Trey Cans and not just because Cans hadn't ever put him on punishment detail. Cans did not put anyone on punishment detail. He was fond of Trey Cans in the same way a dog sometimes returns to its own vomit.

Beaudry turned back to the toilet bowl. "Bitch! Bitch! Bitch!" he said as he jabbed the brush around the bowl with each invective. The toilet was self-cleaning, but the cleaning solution tank was bone dry and seemed to have stopped working. He had to get the toilet clean before the toilet could keep itself that way and he would probably have to get a new series of gaskets to replace the old dried-out ones for the solution tank. "And damn Cans, too! Least he coulda' cleaned up his own pigsty before he left."

Third Cans had retired in the saddle a year before actually taking his leave of the service. He filled the commander's slot on the organizational chart, but did as little as possible to get by. He left the day-to-day operation of the unit to the seconds below him. He neither oversaw any work nor cared about its completion, unless it might affect his retirement pay. He

24

left the day office in utter disarray, leaving personal items and official document packs scattered among the discarded half-eaten meal packs, bottles and general debris of the drunk and slovenly.

Beaudry hadn't minded the mess when he was sitting in it, drinking with Cans. But, he could not understand how it had gotten this bad, this fast. After all, they had only been deployed on the Kiirkegaard for a month. The office had not looked near this bad when they had power-jacked its mobility pallet base into the spacecraft's locking deck plates.

It was the same office Cans inherited upon his promotion to third in command of the 1392nd. All APE equipment was designed to move with the unit. Every barracks, office and storage area was completely self-contained and built on a powered combat specification skid plate. The skid plate was shaped specifically to the office and designed to clamp into dozens of different AMSF spacecraft deck configurations.

Like the office, the entire 1392nd was completely self-contained. The design and build of each prefab barracks, storage shed, weapons locker, repair shop and even their mini-hospital for sick call was for rapid deployment on mobility pallets with their own power skid plates, armor and weapons compliments. APES units went into combat fully outfitted with everything necessary for a quick dirt drop. They touchdown on a planet prepared for any type of hostile action or when long-term deployment if the need arises. Someone had coined the phrase 'dirt drop' years before in describing how APES units appeared to poop out the back end of a spacecraft for the drop into planetary atmosphere. The name stuck.

During Cans' last thirty days of service, he retreated into his office and only came out once for his own retirement ceremony. Sixteen other APES had put in their time and retired along with Cans. Six of the sixteen were second-level commanders, leaving the unit drastically short of experienced seconds and drying up their pool of long time veterans.

Trooper Beaudry would have joined them if he could, but he only had forty-four years in the APES. Those years plus his four years in the AMSF still left him two years short of a full pension. He was beginning to regret not taking a reduced stipend for retirement. A few troopers voluntary quit the APES because of Can's command. Many other troopers opted for transfer to other units.

"Damn it, Cans! It's your fault I gotta clean up your mess," Beaudry growled to himself. "But that bitch is gonna pay for putting me here. It's her office now. She should clean up her own space. Yeah, she's gonna pay…"

Chapter Six

Trooper One Singletary watched Trooper Four Peace DeLaPax poke a long tapered black finger into the ragged hole of the barrack's steel wall. DeLaPax shook her head in wonder. "Did you see the size of her arms when she ripped that locker out of the wall? Whooeee! She stripped the screws out, heads and all."

"Yeah? So what?" asked Trooper Two Jem Li Park from across the barracks. "So she's got muscles. She doesn't scare me any." He dumped a dustpan of broken glass into the trash chute. "Besides," he continued, "we had it good before she got here. Trey Cans left us alone. Hell, we were his squad and he didn't even come into the bay anymore."

DeLaPax said, "True enough, Jemmy Li. But, the good times are over. Don't mess with this one. She isn't like Trey Cans ever was." DeLaPax shook her head.

Singletary was in Cans' squad for almost twenty years. He did not think Cans had ever been strong enough to rip a locker off the wall. For that matter, he didn't know anyone able to do it.

DeLaPax motioned for a couple of other troopers to help her move the locker back into place. She grunted with the effort; a small trickle of sweat slipped down from her black kinky hair and slid along her smooth skin that was only a shade lighter than her hair.

She said, "Jemmy Li, you may be sierra hotel with that old-style Korean Karate, but I don't think you want to tangle with our new squad leader."

Before Park could reply, Singletary said, "All right, knock it off. We don't have that much time to get this barracks back into inspection order. And we gotta do it right this time." He motioned to DeLaPax, "Peace, you take the new guy, what's his name, Ottiamig?" He glanced at the tall man. "Yeah, I'm talkin' 'bout you, numb-nuts." He pointed a finger at DeLaPax, "Peace, you take oh-my-gods with you to the repair shack. Get a hand welder and put that locker up permanently. Bring back a vacuum cleaner, too. We gotta get all of this glass up off the deck. No more half measures got me? Cans is gone. We got a new boss and we do it her way." To himself he added, "For now."

Singletary looked around at the barracks mess. It looked shredded from one end to the other, like a small whirlwind had blown through. Personal effects, uniforms, and bedding were scattered every which way. Six Able Squad troopers were picking their way through the mess. Four members of the squad were still missing, presumably dockside, having either not heard or ignored Second Takki-Homi's first call or Aardrmicksdottir's second broadcast recall.

When Third McPherson's gear had arrived earlier, Singletary as trooper one of Able Squad sent it to the day office. He hoped she would take the hint from Third Cans example and move in there. Singletary heard she had been escorted directly to her office upon boarding the Kiirkegaard. Instead, she carried her gear from the office and threw it on the first bunk inside the hatch. It was the only bunk not double stacked. That had been his bunk, since Cans moved out. McPherson had burst into the room just when the squad had almost succeeded in making it somewhat presentable. It was obvious she was angry before she blew in through the front hatch. She reminded him politely that the last bunk was his. She explained quietly and very politely she expected traditional bunk arrangements.

Traditional meant trooper two would get a bunk in the next stack down the line from hers. Since she was a third-level commander, there was no trooper three in Alpha Squad. Just as in a squad commanded by a second there was no trooper two or in a squad commanded by a fifth there was no trooper five. In McPherson's squad, trooper four took the bunk above trooper two, and so on down the line. All the bunks were aligned down one steel wall, interspersed with their combat suit racks. Lockers, showers, and toilet stalls lined the opposite wall mixed with tables and reader ports. That left Singletary at the tail end of the barracks. He was stuck bunking in the back with the FNG, newbies and tranferees. FNGs and newbies always screwed-up because they did not know any better. Transferees were always screw-ups because they were screw-ups to begin with and someone was dumping them from their squad to get rid of a problem. After twenty years in this squad, Singletary much preferred to bunk near the veterans. Some of these men and women had been with him for much of his 1392nd Alpha Squad tenure. Some were close friends, like Park. Some, like DeLaPax were not friends, but she was a veteran and he trusted her to watch his back in combat, both in bars and on dirt drops. He did not trust any frakking new guy.

He blanched at the memory of McPherson losing all semblance of politeness when she opened the door to what should have been her locker. Inside she found his stash of alcohol, drugs, gambling paraphernalia and pornography. When she tore the locker from the steel wall and sent it sailing across the deck scattering disks, bottles, vials and pills, she wiped out almost a year's worth of inventory. That would put a severe dent in his special pension plan. His Apes and vacuum-breather customers were either going to go dry for this trip or they would abandon him if they found other suppliers.

McPherson's inspection of the squad barracks left nothing uncovered. Fortunately, she hadn't bothered to ask who owned what contraband. He wasn't going to volunteer that information. Everyone else in the squad knew the stuff was his and if they knew what was good for them, they wouldn't say a word. She slowed down only when she had accidentally smashed Ottiamig's flute. She stormed out ordering everyone to clean the barracks to the jot and tittle.

Chapter Seven

Misha stood in the middle of the APES training bay. She could not believe her senses. The huge open bay area was a jumble of mobility pallets, shipping containers and scattered litter. After the clean planetary air of Heaven or even the filtered air of Heaven's Gate Station, the training bay smell was almost enough to make her wretch. It smelled of stale sweat, moldy cheese, flat beer and a few really strange and unidentifiable odors.

Standing around her in a rough semicircle were her ten second-level commanders. Misha was sure some of the unusual odors were coming from her direct reports. That was not surprising. Until a few moments before, all of her squad leaders except one had been off duty, whether officially or not. APES worked hard and APES played hard. She refused to let their drunken state inflate her already exploding horror and anger at the condition of her new command.

Misha stared at the assembled group. Bleary eyes squinted back at her. She tried to size them up, but it was too early in their relationship to gauge anything by looks alone. The red utility uniforms gave her no clues. The only distinguishing mark was the X insignia of a second-level commander on their collars. She looked slowly at each of their faces. It didn't take long for her to realize each of her squad leaders had more time in service than she.

Second-Level Commander Moraft was the woman she had met at the gate. Even taking into account GerinAid anti-aging, Moraft looked as if she was well over the fifty-years time in service required for minimum retirement. The youngest looking of the group was a tall blond woman who, in years only, was still Misha's senior. Age, just like size and gender doesn't matter in command. Misha wore the triangles.

"Okay, ladies and gentlemen. Who is the senior second?"

"I am, sir." Moraft spoke. "I am Second-Level Commander Theda Moraft of Bravo Squad."

"Thank you, Mr. Moraft," Misha replied. Her whole command was down loaded onto her glass-pack. It included every piece of official data, bureaucratic detail and file image available for each APE in her unit. She recognized each of her seconds, although her whole command would take a little longer. But, she believed letting them introduce themselves would give her time and insight to get to know each one.

"Who is Mr. Aardmricksdottir?" Misha asked. Even though she had practiced pronouncing the names, she stumbled over the last name. She was not able to fathom how to pronounce the second's first name.

A tall blond woman raised a hand. "Sir, I am Second Aardmricksdottir. I want to apologize for Trooper Beaudry at the-"

Before she could finish Misha cut her short. "I do not want to hear apologies from anyone. I am not in a forgiving mood, so save them for later. Mr. Aardmricksdottir, do you have a recall count?"

"Yes I do, sir. It isn't pretty," the woman answered. "And it's Vark."

"Pardon me, Second?" Misha replied.

Aardmricksdottir replied with a shy smile, "My name is a handful. If the Third pleases, call me Vark. It's a nickname but since my real first name can't be translated into Standard English, Vark will do. You know: Aardmricksdottir slid to Aardvark and onto Vark. It's a short progression and easier on the tongue."

Misha smiled back inspite of herself. "All right, Vark. However, I do not ever want to hear the phrase 'not pretty'. I heard too much of it as a child." She could hear her father telling her how a little self-depreciating humor always set the other side of the negotiation table at ease. It put your opponent at an easy state of relaxation to use for an advantage. This may not be a negotiation, but she needed to put these seconds back on their heels. She nodded at Vark, "Please get station security to locate our lost lambs. Have them dragged back by force if necessary. As you are the officer of the day, your squad is on duty. Get your communications

31

technician in here to channel my comms unit to our outfit's frequencies and code specifications. Who is next senior to Mr. Moraft?"

"That would be me, sir. I am Second-Level Suzuki Takki-Homi of Charlie Squad. Taks is good for me, if it pleases the Third."

Misha continued, "Thank you, Deuce Taks. Good. And who is next senior?"

No one spoke. Moraft and Takki-Homi both started to speak, but Misha waved them off with a quick gesture. Misha clapped her hands loudly and shouted, "Too late dammit!" Startled glances confirmed she had caught them as their attention drifted. It was just as her father had predicted. The humor caused them to relax just enough for her to slap them back to the present.

She continued in a calmer voice. "Hypothetical situation: we are in combat, I am dead, both Seconds Moraft and Takki-Homi are out of commission. Your lack of understanding about your own command structure has just killed this whole outfit. And people, with the Binders creeping into our backyards, we can't afford to lose even one more trooper through stupidity. Come on! You are in squads that are in alphabetical order. How difficult can it be?"

A tall, thin second looked as if he had just lost focus. She stepped forward and leaned into his face. Nose-to-nose, she shouted. "Can't happen? Or you just don't care?" The man blanched through his already pale skin. Misha spun back toward the group.

"Okay, people. I know you have heard nuggets of info about Guinjundst passed through the grapevine and those lurid tales on the newsnets. Guinjundst was not just an accident or a fluke. Some very bad stink happened there. We lost a lot of good troopers because we were not as ready as we could be. We didn't adapt as rapidly as we should have. Some seconds lost their place in the chain of command. A flash of hesitation in combat can snowball into a shit storm of epic proportions.

"Other than Moraft and Takki-Homi, who knows who is next?"

"I do. I am Second-Level Race Jackson, sir. Next would be Bilideau, then Portland and then me. And Trey, just in case no one else has said it: welcome to the 1392nd. I, for one, am glad you're here."

Standing next to Jackson, Takki-Home made a small circle with his thumb and forefinger. Pressing it tightly to his lips, he generated a loud smacking noise. He winked at Misha as he nudged Jackson in the side with his elbow.

Jackson sputtered, "Dammit, Taks! I am not kissing up. I mean it. We got to get off the crapper. We got to get loaded for bear. And we got to get into this war. I didn't join the APES to garrison some backwater dust ball with a third-level commander who has gone civilian. I lost a brother and two cousins on Guinjundst. It ain't gonna happen again if I got anything to say about it."

Misha could see some heads nodding in agreement, a few heads nodding as a political gesture and a few heads nodding as if they had heard it all before. "I agree with Mr. Jackson. It is time," Misha said. She held up her glass-pack. "First things first, I have engagement orders from The Sixth John Cochran, through Fifth IvanYetta Vaslov to my immediate supervisor Fourth Kema Wallace Ottiamig. We are to deploy to an undisclosed planetary destination on the AMSF T/E-716 Kiirkegaard. Lieutenant Colonel William Park Britaine in command of the Kiirkegaard will brief me on our designated target planet once we leave the Heaven System. The 1392nd, McPherson's Second, is to then commence deployment onto the surface of said planet to engage all known and unknown enemies and hostile forces. We have dirt drops on our agenda. That is combat. And we are not ready to handle a girl sprout's picnic much less warfare.

"Get your people squared away. Get it tight, cold and in numerical order. Get your squad bays sorted out. And ladies and gentlemen, I do mean rigid and organized, not just pretty on the surface. Then get your people in here to spit shine my training bay. This place is a disgrace. The air in here may belong to the spacers, but we have to breathe it. Get our own environmental techs on the air scrubbers, both in the bays and in this sewer. General inspection is in one hour. That is fast, so kick it into overdrive."

Chapter Eight

Misha reached out her hand to Lieutenant Colonel Britaine as he stood to greet her. She was startled to find him so attractive. He was only a few inches shorter than she was with shoulders just as broad as hers. She tried not to stare, but she would have given her left hand to have hips as slim as his. His eyes were startlingly bluish-grey under a wild mass of dark hair. She almost winced under his careful appraisal, wishing she had a more classic look about herself. Heavy-worlders rarely entered inter-planetary beauty contests. She knew she couldn't even pass the nomination round for a beauty pageant on DropSix, and those pageants were less about beauty and more about the speed and accuracy with gutting sheep.

Britaine said, "I am Lieutenant Colonel William Britaine, Commander of the Kiirkegaard. Welcome aboard, Third McPherson."

Before Misha could answer a paper airplane sailed between them. "Hey, Muffins, don't hog the new girl. Introduce us."

In spite of herself, Misha blurted out, "I am Third-Level Commander Hamisha Ann McPherson, Colonel Britaine. I have just taken over command of the 1392nd Allied Protective Expeditionary Service deployed aboard the Kiirkegaard."

Britaine's smile seemed to glow back at Misha, "Really, Third-Level Commander Hamisha Ann McPherson of the 1392nd Allied Protective Expeditionary Service, we don't need to be so formal out of earshot of the crew, do we? Call me Bill or even William, if you have to, but Colonel Britaine seems to be a bit formal among fellow officers, don't you think?"

Misha glanced behind him at the spacers in the Colonel's office. There were half a dozen men and women in various chairs lounging about. By their collar insignia, she could tell they were all officers, each with a set of pilot's wings over their left breast pocket. Even the man with the medical insignia on his collar had wings on his chest.

The man who had thrown the paper airplane spoke up, "Billy or Willy, huh? Sorry, McPherson, but we call him Muffins for reasons I am not at liberty to explain. So, what do we call you, darlin'?"

Britaine said, "Nuff, Digger. Hamisha, isn't it?" He pronounced the first syllable as if it were a part of a cured pig's butt, not the proper DropSix pronunciation with the long a.

She was used to having her name mispronounced, even though she had pronounced it correctly just seconds ago. She replied diplomatically, "Misha is fine, sir."

Britaine nodded and pointed around the room at the assembled officers, "Digger Paradise is my XO. These others are Skunk, Waterboy, Tinker, Spanker, Aces, Puke and Nuke."

Misha was not surprised to see the names given did not match the names on their uniforms. Pilots and FAC crew used nicknames, often vulgar and offensive, rather than their given names. She had seen this on other AMSF spacecraft. Her first four-year enlistment had been with the AMSF in flight intelligence where she interacted with the spacecraft command and FAC jockeys.

Britaine continued, "Puke is Doctor Richard Dimms, our esteemed fight surgeon. You are welcome to call upon his services as needed, although I do believe you have your own medical staff for the rest of your people."

"Yes, sir. I have not been able to meet with all of my people yet, just my seconds. However, according to my organizational chart, we are sufficiently staffed for most medical problems. Does Dr. Dimms have a staffing problem that precludes inter-service medical attention? I am sure my people could lend a hand."

"No, quite the opposite," Britaine flashed a brilliant smile at her. "Puke has got an excellent staff. We find that on the Kiirkegaard it works best for Puke to handle mainly FAC crews, plus a few other select officers like yourself as ranking commander of your forces. He has a competent staff to handle the rest of the officers and crew. It helps to split the duties up for more specialized care."

Britaine stepped to the hatch of his office and bellowed, "Spacer, coffee in here." He turned back to Misha and said, "Or would you prefer another beverage? No? Well, if I recall Third Cans mostly carried his own drink."

Misha heard sniggers from one or two of the officers in the room, but she decided to ignore it. Inter-service rivalry was as old as military service itself. However, she was surprised to see more than one officer roll their eyes or make a face behind Britaine's back. She wondered if the facial expressions were directed at Britaine or because he mentioned Cans. It made her feel more confident to think that Britaine might not be as well liked by all of his crew as everyone pretended.

Britaine smiled. "From what I have heard of you, Misha, you are just the gal to whip his old bunch of mud crawlers into shape. About your seconds, you will find your predecessor was a bit lax about them. It seems he let them run loose. Please don't get me wrong. I am not about to tell you how to command your people. That is your business."

She said, "Third Cans may have been a bit lax about a few things, sir, but, I can assure you my seconds and I will get things in order well before we drop planetary." Before she could say anything else a master sergeant brought in a tray with coffee and condiments.

Britaine said to the man, "Spacer, why didn't you bring us some donuts or cookies from the officer's mess? I know they have them. And get a haircut, too. Dammit, man! At least try to look good even if you aren't any good at your job."

Misha was aghast, but kept her face neutral. Spacer was a generalized name for the lower third of the nine enlisted ranks. It was never used on a sergeant or above. Sergeant was a title reserved for the middle three ranks. Proper military courtesy was to call a master sergeant by his full title of master sergeant, a senior master sergeant was a senior master or simply senior, and the top enlisted rank was the chief master sergeant or chief, an exalted and rarefied position. Calling a master sergeant a spacer was an insult that any enlisted man would not let pass if voiced by another enlisted. Misha could see no change of expression in the master sergeant's demeanor. She wondered, "Surely the colonel knows the rankings of his own service."

Britaine continued, "Now, Misha. Your seconds are sort of like our enlisted noncoms or sergeants. So, I would appreciate it if you kept them out of officer's country unless they are on official business."

Misha said, "Sir, I am sure you know we consider all APES to be enlisted. We don't have officers at any command level."

"Tut tut, Misha, we know that is the APES official propaganda, but we also all know differently, don't we? The cream always rises to the top. And on the Kiirkegaard, we like to separate the cream from the milk."

"Excuse me, sir. But-"

Britaine interrupted with a smile, "Don't worry, you'll get the hang of it soon enough. Besides, I don't think you will be deployed here very long. We can get to your engagement orders quickly. As I said before, Third Cans was a bit lax. I believe we did not start off on the right foot here, Misha." He gave her another of his dazzling smiles and continued. "I don't want to come across too harsh on our first day together, but my people tell me that you came aboard almost four hours ago. Why is it that you are just now presenting yourself to the vessel commander?" Before she could answer, he continued as the smile slid off his face. "No, please don't interrupt. I really do think we should adhere to military courtesy between services. I am the captain of this vessel and its senior officer. I realize you are not of FAC crew caliber, but surely even APES report in when deploying to a new command. Perhaps you could explain yourself to me and my staff."

Misha looked at Britaine and his assembled staff. She wondered if he was joking or serious. The return looks she got from the men and the women in the room varied enough to not provide any clues to Britaine's sense of humor. She was sure some of the officer's expressions were well practiced poker faces.

"With all due respect, Colonel-" Misha began.

Britaine snapped back, "Whoa! Hold on there, APE. I truly hate it when I hear a sentence beginning with 'all due respect'. It is an inevitable indication that I am going to hear something I don't like. Are you certain you want to continue in that manner?"

She began again, deliberately keeping her temper in check, "Yes, Colonel Britaine. With all due respect-"

Britaine held up a hand for her to stop and said coldly, "Enough, girl. Let me make this clear to you. This is a direct order. No embellishments, no 'with all due respect' excuses, no extenuating circumstances. You will come to attention as befits who I am. You will apologize for your discourtesy to me. And yes, I see your fine pretty little ribbon on your chest. Giving an Aires medal to a ground pounder is like feeding fine earth caviar to an enlisted man." He looked over his shoulder for his officer's agreement.

Misha slowly counted to ten, very slowly. Then looking Britaine directly in the eyes, while remaining at a comfortable at-ease stance, she counted to ten again. Inter-service relations were often strained, but she was sure relations on this craft would get real tense if she pounded this arrogant cretin. She was even pretty confident she would come out ahead if she took on this whole bunch of flight weenies in unarmed conflict.

Most of all, Misha decided she was not going to kowtow to this petty tyrant. She had met his type many times before. They called themselves flight jocks. They were men and women who would take their tiny and deadly fast attack craft (FAC) into one on one space bound dogfights against an enemy FAC or even larger transport craft or motherships like the Kiirkegaard. To Misha, it was crazy work. Sure, she fought inside a tin can, much like FAC jocks, but she fought sensibly on the ground in an atmosphere where if, gods forbid, something goes wrong, at least she could breath.

As a rule AMSF promoted pilots into command positions and pilots promoted other pilots who in turn promoted more pilots. Many command level officers continued to fly their FACs into combat. They left control of their motherships to junior ranking flight crew, often rotating control to give them each the experience of commanding one of the large spacecrafts they called trash haulers.

A FAC jock's rally cry was "If you ain't a pilot, you ain't shit.". This seemed to fly in the face of logic. It caused many of them to treat their mechanics, engineers, and weapons technicians as serfs or second-class citizens. It was the height of foolishness to insult, even by omission, the very people your life might depend on when you went into combat. She decided it would be prudent to never get into a small craft piloted by Britaine. It might not be safe due to equipment malfunctions of the preventable sort.

Misha thought briefly about her earlier rampage through the APES held parts of the craft. It might have ruffled a few feathers, but she knew the main difference was that she and her fellow APES would be going into combat together. She knew an AMSF technician could easily leave a valve turned the wrong way or a button unpushed, then calmly go to lunch after launching a FAC off the flight deck, all without any damage to themself. Most AMSF personnel Misha met had too much pride in themselves and their service to do such a thing. However, if a FAC jock insulted and pushed the wrong enlisted person, it would be a long walk back to the mothership, with very little scenery to take their mind off the nagging lack of oxygen in space. Misha met more than her share of this type of officer in her time in AMSF intelligence.

Misha decided to let Britaine stew in his own juices. Her father taught all of his children to argue, haggle, negotiate and generally verbally twist their way through most conversations. She had never been very good at negotiation, but one phrase she remembered very clearly. She could even hear her father's voice as he shouted 'the first man to speak loses'. Besides, in this case it seemed to be much more prudent to remain silent than to draw blood.

She continued to stare at Britaine in silence.

Finally he said, "Well?"

Misha smiled at him and replied, "Pardon me, Colonel. Did you ask something?"

"You know damn good and well I did, McPherson. I command here. I will not be insulted on my own spacecraft."

"Colonel Britaine," Misha said, still smiling, "I may be a new third, but I am not ignorant of our respective service's contracts. I agree you are in command of this vessel. Without a doubt, sir, I agree."

She stepped toward Britaine, moving quickly to break through his physical comfort zone. Misha didn't know where the man was from. If he was from one of the crowded worlds, he might have only a few inches of personal space. If he came from one of the agricultural worlds like her home planet of DropSix, he might have come to the AMSF with a bubble space of four or five feet. That much space would be greatly whittled down over the years of spacecraft service. However, she had never met a FAC jock who didn't get uncomfortable when pressed physically, at least when they were sober. She was pleased to see a flash of concern in his eyes.

She said calmly, "I have a copy of the APES contract with the AMSF for this deployment. It has been attached as Exhibit 11 of my orders. It is in my glass-pack. Do we need to review them, sir?"

Britaine's eyes hardened, "So you are a barrack's lawyer, McPherson?

"Hardly, Colonel, it is just that I am not ignorant of my rights and responsibilities." Misha stared into his eyes with as much control as she could muster. "Our agreement states clearly you are in command."

"See there, McPherson." The man was positively gloating.

"However," she said as if she hadn't been interrupted, "our agreement does not place me under your command nor does it place me on your organizational chart with a few minor exceptions. That would be to repel boarders, assist in a mutiny, or for emergency battle damage while in space. Furthermore, Colonel, my orders are to report to you when my command is present and available for transport. My orders clearly state I have until tomorrow at 17:00 standard hours to report, at which time you will provide my command with transportation into a combat zone. End of relationship."

She continued, "I did stop by today as a courtesy call. I would prefer to have an amicable relationship with you and your officers, Colonel Britaine. But, if that is not the case, then I can persevere while you take the 1392nd to our destination." She smiled sweetly, knowing everyone in the room knew she had just called an AMSF Colonel a glorified bus driver. Britaine's face was red as he tried to control his temper. Misha could see he was struggling to hold his tongue.

She said, "Colonel Britaine, it does seem I have interrupted your staff meeting and perhaps I have been remiss in starting our relationship off on the wrong foot. May I suggest we start over fresh tomorrow after I have assembled my command?" Without waiting for Britaine's response, Misha spun on her heel and was out the hatch. She held her temper, but at a cost. Internally she was boiling. Something or someone was going to get hurt if she didn't work out soon to blow off some excess energy. Still, she hadn't expected to hurt someone as quickly as she did. She slammed full force into a man coming in the opposite direction down the hallway. He was sent sprawling out before her on the deck with his civilian clothes in disarray.

"Ow," the man said quietly as he looked up at her. "Slow it down a bit, young lady. I am just a tad too delicate for this kind of meeting, at least without the proper introductions."

Misha would have walked on with only the briefest of apologies if the man had not been smiling. Instead, she did something she always hated herself for doing. She blushed. When she blushed, it was a bright red from the tips of her ears to the nape of her neck or even further depending on the situation. Blushing was an unfortunate side effect of a heavy-worlder's ability to pump copious amounts of oxygen-rich blood into their dense musculature. Combined with Misha's pale skin, a left-over from her Scottish heritage, she almost glowed in the dark.

She offered the man a hand and pulled him to his feet. He was a smallish man, almost a foot shorter than her, he was very slightly built, not skinny, but more of the wiry type. She was glad to note she hadn't damaged him, seeing as she was twice his size.

The man said, "Sergeant Gan Forrester of the Allied Marshal Service. And you must be the vaunted Third Hamisha McPherson? I am pleased to meet you."

She said, "Sergeant Forrester, please accept my apologies. I wasn't watching where I was going."

"Well, it only seems fair that you put me on my keister. You tore through the APES like a whirlwind and from what I just overheard in Britaine's office you stirred up a shit storm in there with the AMSF. You might as well try to do some damage to the Marshal Service, too. Make it a clean sweep for the day." The man smiled up at her. "Well, Third, I don't seem to be damaged beyond repair. No harm, no foul."

"Thank you, Sergeant."

"Please, call me Gan. And you prefer to be called Misha if what I read in the news is correct. Well, Misha, perhaps we can get together before this little cruise is over. I would love to hear about Guinjundst, that is, what you can tell me about it. I understand the secrecy and all of that. Military history is sort of a hobby of mine."

Misha said, "I don't know how long the 1392nd will be aboard the Kiirkegaard, Gan."

He smiled, "Longer than I will, I would guess. I am going on a little field investigation in the Gagarin

System. It's not so much an investigation as it is a little boondoggle for me. It is a like a paid vacation. It's kind of a reward for me having the least errors in the productivity reports over the past year. That's me, just a good little data pusher."

Misha turned to go, but the man continued unabated. "Since you are heading on past the Gagarin System, we will have a few days before the flight takes off, plus it is three jumps to Gagarin, even for military spacecraft."

Misha's comm unit emitted a quiet bip and broadcast, "Third McPherson to the main hatch."

Forrester sighed, "Well, I would love to stay and continue our chat, but it seems you are needed elsewhere and I have to go face Colonel Britaine now that you have stirred him up. Thanks for that, by the way." He smiled, turned and headed into Britaine's office before Misha could respond.

Misha was almost at the main hatch before it occurred to her that Sergeant Gan Forrester knew more about her destination than she knew. She wondered how the little man knew so much about her when she had only been on board a few hours. Or was it longer? She shook her head, thinking that it was going to be a long transport to wherever it was they were going. Wherever that was, she was going to have to do a dirt drop when she got there. That would mean she would have to stuff her command into combat armor, strap onto skid plates, jump out hatchways and slide through the atmosphere of a hostile planet to engage an enemy. She knew that much about her mission. She may not know where or when, but putting combat boots on the ground was what APES did.

Reaching the main hatchway, Misha saw the diminutive form of the young spacer from the station's principal gate. She brushed past the AMSF main hatch guard and greeted the girl.

"Brianna. Thank you for taking on this little task for me. I appreciate it."

Brianna smiled, "It's my pleasure, ma'am. I mean, sir. I am sorry it took me so long, but I had to wait until I got off duty to get to the shops."

Misha smiled back. "Did you have any trouble finding what I need?"

"No, sir. Only…" The girl's voice trailed off.

"Only what, Brianna? I won't bite your head off."

"I found what you asked for, but I think it was probably a bit more expensive than we thought. Um, I kind of took a hit in my savings account getting it for you. I've never bought anything like it before. I hope I did okay."

"Hand me your glass-pack." Misha said. She took the device from the girl and tapped the two glass-packs together making a cross connection. Whistling through her teeth, she said, "You are right, Brianna. This is a bit more expensive than I thought, too. Well, never mind, you get what you pay for. And a girl's gotta have what a girl's gotta have." She punched in the financial codes to transfer funds from her account to Brianna's. She didn't mention the extra ten percent she authorized for her time and trouble. Favors for friends were one thing, but she did not want to overstep bounds with someone she just met.

Brianna said, "Third McPherson, may I ask you a question?"

"Of course," Misha handed the girl's glass-pack back. "Only we are not on duty now and since I had you running all over the station on personal errands for me, why don't you call me Misha. All of my other friends do. Ask away."

"Yes, sir. How do I get to be an APE?"

"Good question. I can see you have been thinking about it. Well, finish your four years in the AMSF. That is first." Misha went on to explain to the girl how all APES must complete at least four years with another military or paramilitary service: the Allied Mobile Space Force, the Allied Marshal Service and even some planetary ground forces or police forces from some larger cities qualified.

APES service was strictly voluntary. A person could do what APES do if they could pass the mental and physical requirements of another service. What the APES did was combat; wherever and whenever called upon to do so by the Allied Systems. Every APE fought from The Sixth-Level Commander John Cochran down to the newest rookie. In the APES, most combat training was on-the-job training. You became a veteran if you survived. If you didn't survive, the APES would send a letter home to your family with an insurance settlement check.

All APES maintained secondary and sometimes tertiary duty qualifications. The design of each squad was to be self-contained and self-supporting; having their own medical staff (medic, doctor or psychiatrist), cook, skid plate expert, quartermaster (scrounger), armor repair technician, records specialist, weapons technician, expendables (ammunition) supply clerk, general supplies clerk, power specialist and intelligence/linguist. All commanders require secondary duty qualifications outside of the command structure. A fifth-level commander might also be a general supplies clerk and thus functionally report to the quartermaster, the cook, or any other position depending on the situation. Many commanders did come from general supplies as that specific secondary duty offered an individual a wide understanding of most squad functions.

Many old-timers have more than one secondary duty due service time and changing interests. Additional duties are an individual choice to be tackled on their own off duty time. Each such duty merits extra pay. Each APE also has training in some spacecraft system: environmental, gunnery, power-room systems, tactical, intelligence, small craft or fixed-wing operations, etc. Since many APES come from the other services this is normally a matter of expanding on previously learned skills.

Misha explained that every commander regardless of rank commands his own squad. A fifth-level commander (a fist) or The Sixth himself commands a fighting squad of ten troopers and goes into combat. By tradition, a commander's own squad is never handpicked, no matter how high his rank. It is comprised of any remaining members of the squad he commanded as a second-level. Over time, he gains replacements. Randomly assigned replacements come from existing available troopers or new recruits. Commanders who foolishly lose a high percentage of their squads are regarded unfavorable for higher advancement.

Ten troopers and one commander form a squad. These eleven people constitute what is organizationally the first tier. A second-level commander (a deuce) is in command of most squads. This is the most basic APES unit structure. Any squad unable to regain full strength during a regeneration phase is folded into another short squad or if severe shortages occur, they are disbanded to fill other squads. Commanders must fill a slot in the organizational chart. Any commander without a slot is re-organized downward or if the need arises, moves upward into an open slot.

A third-level commander (a third or trey) directly leads a squad of ten troopers and also commands ten second-levels. Each deuce is in charge of a squad of ten troopers. These 121 people constitute a second tier.

The fourth-level commander (a quad) leads a squad of ten troopers. This is affectionately called a quad squad. The fourth directly oversees ten third-level commanders. These 1,331 fighting troopers form a third tier. Often times a unit this size or larger does not have its people located physically on the same spacecraft, station, planet or even in the same region of space.

A fifth-level commander (a fist) leads a squad of ten troopers and supervises ten fourth-levels. These 13,310 men constitute a fourth tier.

The sixth-level commander leads a squad of ten troopers and also directly commands, if the APES were fully staffed, ten fifth-level commanders. These 131,100 men constitute the fifth tier.

Misha told Brianna that her command was in the first fifth. It had to be as there had never been two fifth levels in all of APE history. If a hundred and thirty-one thousand APES in combat armor could not do the job, then it couldn't be done. She also pointed out that her command was in the third fourth tier, plus the ninth third tier and the second second tier, otherwise known as the 1392nd.

She explained that no APE is, was, or ever will be drafted or inducted against their will. Nor will they be kept in the service unwillingly. The only exception is that an APE cannot quit when on deployment or during regeneration phase. Even taking on replacements during a deployment is not normal as it can affect teamwork.

"So," Misha concluded. "There you have the short course in APEery. Still want to join up?"

Brianna nodded. "Only it sounds like I can't get assigned to your squad even if you would have me."

Misha smiled. "I would trade for you right now if I could. I would rather have heart than size any day, but it just does not work that way. Tell me the truth, Brianna: are you having problems where you are now? Because, if you don't like military service in the AMSF, then you surely will hate being in the APES."

"Oh no, sir. I like it fine, but...well, you know. Sometimes it's just not enough. Plus, I saw the way you handled the crowd at the gate. I never saw anyone take control like that. I mean, I have always been somebody else's little."

"Excuse me?" Misha asked. "You're a 'little'?"

Brianna smiled, "Yes, sir. You know, Daddy's little girl and Mother's little helper. My older sister Danielle is in the AMSF. She's a captain now. She got me assigned to this safe little job on the gate because I am her little sister. I don't want to be a little anymore. I want to do."

Misha said, "I know. Believe me, I know. You finish your time in the AMSF then find any APE commander and enlist with us. In the meantime, find the oldest noncom you can in your outfit. Get their advice, listen to them and learn from them. Ask them who to go to for training in hand-to-hand combat. I assume you are already learning a martial art form as part of your duties? Good! Also, pick a specialty: if you like cooking, then cook. If you are good at physics, begin to learn power mechanics. Don't waste too much of your time in bars and at parties. By all means, play and have fun, just don't make it a time-consuming habit. And if I can ever do anything, you contact me. I've already downloaded my address into your glass-pack. You write and let me know, hear?"

Brianna said. "Yes, Misha, I hear. I'd like to write to you. Thanks, you don't know what this means to me."

Misha said, "I mean that now, that's an order. You write and let me know how things are going."

Chapter Nine

Misha stepped into the training bay where all of her squads had assembled. She had ordered an inspection for one hour and she had lost all of that hour. First she spent too much time with Britaine, then bumping into that weird little man Forrester, and finally she spent way too much time with Spacer Morin. However, she realized the time she had spent with Brianna had brought her back to why she had joined the APES in the first place. It cleared her head and she felt ready to tackle her new command. As ragged as it was, it was now hers to mold, form and shape into a fighting unit.

Unfortunately, she might only have a week or so to pound this group into some semblance of a fighting unit before dropping in combat mode on some hellhole of a planet. Fully twenty percent of her troopers were APES rookies headed for their first dirt drop. Six out of her ten seconds were new commanders, although each was a veteran trooper.

Each squad clustered into rough groups with the clusters scattered around the training bay. Troopers squatted or sat on the deck as the mood struck them. Most were chatting among themselves, although the tension in the room was almost palpable. Her squad had assembled near the hatch.

Trooper Singletary saw her enter the room and shouted, "Commander on deck."

Before anyone could make a move to stand, Misha called out, "As you were." The APES were not an outfit that held to a lot of the old-style rigorous military traditions. No one marched about. No one saluted. No one ever jumped to attention and formations consisted of milling about in the general area of the meeting. Still, it was polite to stand when a higher-ranking APE entered the room.

Misha said, "Okay people. I am sure most of you know who I am by now. But, in case you have been asleep, or you have just joined your squad for the first time, Third Cans is gone. Enough said about him. Got me?"

Misha nodded at the chorus of 'roger that'.

"Good. Deuce Vark, are we all present?"

"Yes, sir," Aardmricksdottir called from the back of the training bay where her squad stood. "Some of us are going through a rough detox, but physically we are all here."

Misha nodded. "For the record, I am Third-Level Commander Hamisha Ann McPherson. As of today, I have taken command of the 1392nd. I am given to understand that a high percentage of the 1392nd are rookies. So, in case you haven't figured it out, I will tell you, this unit has been a shithole. And that ends now. There are to be no questions, comments or suggestions, unless I ask for them. I am not in the mood to go into combat with a group of mush-for-brain clowns. I am not in the mood to die on some gods forsaken unnamed planet because someone in this room has had their head stuck where the sun don't never shine." Misha momentarily paused before continuing. "We are now under deployment orders. If you expected to get a transfer or to retire, then tough luck, that pig has gone to market. We are in this together. From this point on we get it right and we get it right the first time.

"Ladies and gentlemen, the first order of business is to correct an error I made. Trooper Tuamma Ottiamig, where are you? Come up front, trooper. You come up here too, Trooper Singletary."

A very tall, slender young trooper from Misha's squad stepped up. "Tuamma Ottiamig, sir." Singletary stood quietly next to the young man.

"Very good, Ottiamig," Misha smiled to put the man at ease. Speaking so everyone in the training bay could hear, "Upon my arrival today I stepped into what should have been my squad bay. Instead, I stepped into enough Treemer crap to fertilize my Grandma's garden for years to come. If you have ever been around when a Treemer lets loose you would know why the locals on New Nippon call them gas-gaggers. I found contraband,

51

including smut, snuggles, snifflers and snowberries. Said contraband has been rendered less than useful. I believe Trooper One Singletary can verify the entire stock of goods has been properly destroyed?"

"Yes, sir," Singletary replied in a carefully modulated voice.

"Good. I don't know who those items belonged to nor do I care. Everyone understand me, clean this garbage out before any of the seconds or I find it. Woe betide the fool who thinks he knows a better hiding place than I or your seconds. Please return to the squad, Trooper Singletary."

Misha continued. "Further, I found items, both legal and illegal stored in breakable containers. People, this is a mobile unit, emphasis on mobile. We will drop our mobile squad bays into combat with us. They will become bunkers, pillboxes, tanks and personnel carriers. Have you veterans forgotten combat?" Misha shouted, "No breakables, dammit. I don't want to be walking around on broken glass the first chance I get to climb out of my combat suit. Clean it up and I mean clean it up everywhere."

In a calmer tone, Misha said, "In my haste to dispose of the aforementioned items, I damaged a musical instrument belonging to Trooper Ottiamig. I wish to rectify that error." Misha handed the Ottiamig the box Spacer Morin had bought for her. The young man unfastened the buckles and brought out a brand-new flute.

"Sir," he stuttered, staring at the flat shine of the platinum instrument. "This is too nice. It is much better than the one that was broken." He looked up at her and said quietly enough so only Misha could hear, "I don't expect any special favors because of my family connections."

Misha replied just as quietly, "Trooper, we both know that your Uncle Kema is my direct supervisor. I don't give a fart in a windstorm about that. It doesn't have a thing to do with it. I broke the old one. I got you a new one as good or better. I take care of you. You take care of me. Uncle Kema can take care of both of us as he sees fit."

Misha changed her tone loudly enough so everyone could hear. "Please note Trooper Ottiamig's new flute has an unbreakable case. I don't know how much longer we have at Heaven's Gate. Get the right kind of case if you have legal items you don't want broken. Ask your second if you don't know what type of case to get. That is what they are there for. However, all passes are canceled, so you will have to order it over the net and get it delivered. We have a very short time before we leave station, so put a rush on it. Throw the breakable out or put the item in permanent storage if you do not have or cannot get a case.

"Everyone fall out to your squad bay for immediate inspection." Misha stepped sideways away from the hatch to let the rush of bodies sweep past.

Chapter Ten

Misha sat quietly in the back of Kiirkegaard's main briefing room. The room was full of AMSF officers and a few senior enlisted men and women. Britaine was at the dais shuffling through data on his glass-pack, apparently waiting for precisely 1700 hours to begin the mission briefing.

Misha didn't mind the delay. It had been grueling since her speech in the training bay. No one in her command slept while she completed inspection after inspection. She inspected squad bays, munitions lockers, general stores, medical supplies and every piece of APE equipment she could find. A flood of down-checked items and gig tickets buried her new unit.

She demanded perfection from her seconds who in turn demanded perfection from their squads. Misha knew there were grumbles over some of her nitpicking, but she knew even the slightest mistake, missing item or bolt out of place could cost a life. Misha had called a general work stoppage while she went to Britaine's briefing. It would only be a few days before this unit dropped into combat, but it wouldn't matter how ready they were if her troopers were too tired to fight.

Misha watched the clock on the bulkhead slide to 16:59:59. Britaine cleared his throat to speak, but before he could get a word out, Misha jumped up and shouted, "Colonel Britaine, Third-Level Commander Hamisha McPherson of the 1392nd Allied Protective Expeditionary Forces presents her command as ready for deployment." Satisfied she had met the conditions of her AMSF contract, Misha sat down. Britaine was fuming. Misha stifled a chuckle. She knew it was childish, but if the man wanted to fight with her, then she would give him a fight. She would not belong in the APES if she was inclined to be any other way.

Britaine's voice cracked with anger at his first word, but he spoke clearly. "Thank you, Third McPherson. I am sure the entire spacecraft is relieved to know you are all accounted for. However, the rest of us have other considerations on our minds."

Looking theatrically around the room, dropping his glass-pack into the slot on the podium, he called up a view of the Heaven System. The podium generated a flat holographic image like a marker board or a slide screen hovering in mid-air. Marked on the view was the name of each planet, moon and base. A large red arrow pointed toward the fourth moon of the eighth planet in the system.

He said, "In order of activity, the Kiirkegaard is to assemble at Heaven System Point 17A to join a flight wing under General Gurand. Assembly is to be completed for departure in four days. However, each spacecraft has been ordered to reach 17A as quickly as possible. I have already alerted operations to prepare us for departure ASAP. For mission security reasons, I have ordered communications to shut down all outgoing traffic." Britaine reached up and tapped the holo-image. The podium registered his hand's interference with the image surface and signaled his glass-pack to call up another view. At first, the view encompassed all Allied Space and its buffer zones. A large blue arrow pointed to the Heaven System. A red arrow pointed to a system in the buffer zone between Allied System and the neighboring Tartar System.

"Altec," said Britaine. The name blazed into red on the view. "This is our destination. Normally, Altec is only three jumps from Heaven. But, because of operational security, the flight wing will make four jumps to allow us to enter the Altec System from other than a direct line of flight." His glass-pack rotated the view, showing four quick successive jumps into the target system.

Britaine continued, "From 17A, it is four days to the first jump. This will allow time to clear heavy traffic around Heaven Three and give the flight wing time for form. We will have one day between each jump through the C1973 and C201 unpopulated systems. Each of these jumps will require no less than one-day standard to regather the wing before the next jump. We will then have a very short delay in the Gagarin System to drop off our Marshal's Service passenger, Sergeant Gan Forrester and wait for the remainder of General Gurand's wing to arrive from various locations. The time delay in Gagarin is unknown, but it is one quick jump to Altec after that.

"At Altec we will deploy the ground forces aboard Kiirkegaard onto Altec Four and then the real work of taking on any space bound Binders found in the system will commence." Britaine smiled in Misha's direction, so she smiled back. He wouldn't get to her making digs about the work given the APES. He had just told her she had at least nine standard days to work with her new command. That was more than she had reason to expect.

Britaine said, "Update your glass-packs on the relevant Altec info. In conclusion, I have already ordered the flight office to prepare for 17A departure."

Speaking into the comm unit on the podium, he said, "Flight office? Execute take off now."

Misha shouted, "What? Dammit, Colonel." She tapped her comm unit and all but yelled, "1392nd, prepare for flight departure now." She barely got the words out of her mouth before the spacecraft lurched backward, tilted rapidly and then seemed to lurch forward. Normally, the antigravity units could adjust and smooth the ride, but operations must have dialed them down so they could feel the motion. Almost everyone in the briefing room was seated and felt no more than a little bumpiness, but a female chief master sergeant standing in the back of the room was knocked off her feet. She scrambled up without a word and dusted herself off. A nearby junior-grade major started to get to his feet to help the chief, but she waved him back down.

From the panicked looks and frantic calls, it was clear Misha had not been the only officer or senior enlisted who had not been let in on Britaine's plans. She wondered if the man was this uncommunicative with everyone or if he enjoyed being the only one in the know. Not telling your own officers about such a move was likely to get people hurt.

Misha knew most of her APES were sacked out because of the work stoppage and probably wouldn't even wake up. Even so, she also knew the armor repair techs had decided to use the training bay to disassemble and repair a few of the massive combat suits. It was likely to be a mess with pieces scattered everywhere. And anyone not sitting or lying down would be tossed around.

Britaine smiled, "What's the matter, McPherson? I thought APES were always prepared. Besides, our contract only specifies I have to give you notice of departure. It doesn't say how much notice, does it?"

Misha smiled back coldly, "Not a problem for me, Colonel Britaine. It is your vessel. It is your business if you want to treat it like an amusement park ride."

Chapter Eleven

The rest of Britaine's briefing was the dry dull business of various departments reading through canned speeches about department preparedness. She was only interested when the female chief master sergeant and the junior-grade major from intelligence tried to give an update on possible Binder activity in the Altec System. Britaine listened with ill-concealed impatience through the major's portion, but cut the chief short in mid-sentence. He ended the briefing with a command to put anything else on the general command net for review later.

Misha headed toward her day office. She intended to make use of what little downtime was left to read through any deployment orders and the attendant data blizzard that normally followed. Just as she was passing the AMSF medical bay, Gan Forrester stepped through a hatch. She avoid knocking him to the deck again only by quick maneuvering on both their parts.

"Damn, Misha," he said with a smile. "We've got to get our schedules coordinated. You seem to be making a habit of trying to knock me on my butt."

Misha smiled back. "They didn't build this transport with much elbow room for petite women like me. Are you coming from medical? No damage from our first collision, I hope?"

"No, no, no. I am bruised, but I'll live. It was my own fault anyway. I should have been watching where you were going. I was helping a crewman who slammed into a bulkhead when we left the station. It is just a broken collarbone. We do not have a very happy bunch of spacers on this craft. There seems to be quite a number of bumps and bruises with a few broken bones here and there."

"Really? I know Britaine didn't give the APES much warning, but I would have thought he would have at least alerted his own crew."

"I haven't quite figured our good captain out. I may be wrong only having known him for a short while, but he seems to like the sense of power that comes from being the only one who knows what is going on. It must be more than a little frustrating being subordinate to that man. Still, I am sure if Britaine told his own crew, then your boy and girls would have picked it up through the rumor-net. You have got a couple of good second-levels on your team. I hear that Jackson and Takki-Home regularly sit in on various enlisted crew briefings. Besides, as commander of the ground forces, you have access to any broadcast Britaine issues to the crew."

"Excuse me?" Misha looked puzzled. "I know I am a new third, but I don't recall hearing that in any of my training."

"Oh, it isn't quite official. It really is an old backdoor trick from the early glass-pack programming days. Call up crew orders for any spacecraft you are assigned on and use pass-command control slash alt A. You'll learn anything the crew learns. It sometimes takes a ton of reading, but you would be surprised what information gets dumped into open cyberspace."

"Sergeant Forrester-" Misha began.

"Gan, if you please," he interrupted.

"Gan, I am heading to my office. You just earned yourself a free cup of coffee."

"Can I get a rain check? I promised to stop by the intelligence shop after the command briefing to meet with Buzz and the Chief. By the way, weren't you intelligence during your AMSF tour?"

"You seem to know entirely too much. What gives?"

"Oh, nothing, my dear, it is just what an old data pusher remembers reading in the newscasts. Hero of Guinjundst and all of that, you know."

"No. I don't know. I've seen and read most of the drivel spouted about me. I don't remember any mention anywhere about what I did with my time in the AMSF."

Forrester smiled, "Well, what do you know?! Huh, I must have read it somewhere. I'll let you know if I remember where, is that okay? Anyway, with your background, you should stop by and meet with the intel pukes on this craft. They are the best duo outside of the Marshal's Service."

"I will do that, Gan. Thanks, but I need to spend some time with my squad."

"Ah, such are the pressures of command. Well, Misha, look me up if you have some time for a real sit-down meal together. I would like to hear your side of what happened on Guinjundst. I'll take you up on that free coffee, but I am buying the food. I have seen what you APES call rations and thanks, but no thanks."

Misha laughed, "I know what you mean. They are meant to keep you alive, but not fat. How about lunch since it is almost lunch time? I do have a few questions for you, too."

Forrester cocked his head sideways, like a bird checking out an unusual bug, "Lunch would be great, but I have been led to believe you will be dining with Britaine and his staff." At Misha's puzzled expression, he said. "Well, I am sure the invitation is in the mail. Let's plan on lunch tomorrow?"

Misha said, "You are one strange man, Gan. How do you know about my lunch schedule for today?"

Forrester waved a dismissive hand, "Like I said, I am just a data pusher. My job is to gather information, collate it and put the reports together. I happened to see the mess steward's lunch list. It's no big deal. It is posted on the net. And by the way, I wouldn't mention finding AMSF data on the shipnet to too many AMSF officers if you know what I mean."

"All right, Gan. I'll buy that for now. Look, tomorrow morning I have scheduled unarmored hand-to-hand combat training and evaluations for my command. Stop by our training bay and we can do lunch together."

"Great," Forrester replied. "May I stop by early and watch? I am just a passenger, you know, so I don't have any other duties to get in my way."

"Better yet, come by even earlier and you can work out with us. It would do you good. I promise not to pit you against someone too tough."

"It is a deal for tomorrow morning. What time?"

Misha smiled. "Well, I am sure you will be able to find that out on your own. I will see you tomorrow morning."

Forrester pointed a finger down the corridor behind Misha. She turned and watched the approach of a pair of Kiirkegaard's security forces. The two stopped before her and came to attention.

"Sir," a sergeant, the shorter of the two, said, "Captain Britaine extends his compliments and requests we escort you to the captain's mess for midday meal."

Misha nodded, "One moment, please." As if speaking into the thin air Misha continued, "All seconds and Trooper Singletary?" The glass-pack relayed the comm quickly and she received a chorus of responses to her query. "Mr. Moraft, run a quick damage assessment on our takeoff. Comm my glass-pack with the data as it becomes available. Security rotations go into place per SOP. Everyone not on security takes down time. We will have at least nine days before the drop. That is not much time, but we need to be fresh when we get there. I will want bright and shining faces in the training bay tomorrow AM." Misha heard a chorus of 'roger that' from her comms. She continued, "I will be dining with Colonel Britaine for lunch. Good will among services and all that crap. Singletary, you make sure it is down time in our squad."

"Roger that."

"I mean down time. I don't care if they crawl into their bunks with each other, but if they do, then the blast shutters go down and so does the noise level. If someone is sacked out, I don't want to hear they were awakened because someone was having a loud personal conversation with the gods. Got me?"

"Yes, sir. You don't care how we relax, just so we don't disturb anybody else."

"Correct and keep it within regulations. Plus, I will be back shortly for some sack time of my own. So, if someone is inclined to gripe about their new squad leader, send them somewhere else."

"Sir?" Misha could hear the smile in Takki-Homi's voice. "You don't mind if we complain, just so long as you don't have to listen to it?"

"Taks," she replied. "It is every grunts right to complain about life, death, taxes, crazy family members, squad members, the size of the member between their legs, and heaven forbid, even their own squad leaders. I expect to hear all complaints anyone wants to share with me. I just don't want to hear it while I am trying to get some sleep. Comprende, tovarich?"

"Oui, mein fraulien. I stand corrected."

"Anyone else? No? Okay then you APES take your down time like grown-ups before I change my mind." Turning to the two Security Spacers, Misha smiled. "I am sorry for the delay, gentlemen. I had to check in with the team first. Please lead the way. So, are you two my escorts for this little jaunt or are you my guards?"

Neither man smiled, but the sergeant said, "Sir, truth be told, I don't really care which. If I have to call in a squad to drag you to see the captain for your private little get together, that is what I am gonna do and I don't care whether you like it or not."

Misha halted in mid-stride. "Excuse me?"

"Sorry, sir, if we could continue on to the captain's mess, please. I meant no disrespect."

"The hell you say. You meant to be disrespectful, but I don't give a rat's ass about that. Why should you care about what goes on between Britaine and me?"

The man looked ready to bust, but just shook his head.

"Come on. Give it," Misha demanded.

"Right! Like you care!" the tall spacer spoke bitterly.

"True enough, spacer," Misha nodded to their surprise. "I may not care, but on the other hand, I might. I won't know until I hear what is eating at you two. This is just between us working stiffs."

The sergeant blurted, "All right, dammit. You sort of pissed off the old man. I don't thank you for that. Look, you've been around long enough to make third, so you know shit runs down hill. Well, we live deep in the valley. And the hilltop on this spacecraft is shitty enough that it makes us valley dwellers ready to build a raft just to float away at the first opportunity."

"Roger that, Sergeant. I apologize. Please lead on." Misha couldn't help but wonder what kind of officer would treat his people with enough disrespect to engender such a hostile attitude.

All too soon her escort delivered her to the captain's mess. It was a corner of the officer's mess with temporary walls. Already seated was a group of officers, each with pilot's wings. Misha nodded to the steward as he gestured towards an open chair.

Shortly after Britaine's grand entrance, Misha found herself listening to a first lieutenant lecturing her about vectors, azimuths and target acquisition. All of which was common knowledge to anyone who had ever fought in an APES combat suit. However, she let him ramble on and on as listening was easier than participating in small talk. And so what if the lieutenant was condescending in his tone? At least, the food was good and the wine was excellent, although she would rather have had a decent cold beer.

Colonel Britaine interrupted the lieutenant's spiel. "Third McPherson?" he asked. Misha could hear his voice grate as he tried to sound pleasant. "I hear you have been doing a bit of house cleaning?"

"Yes, sir, we just had a few items to clear away before our destination. Speaking of clearing away, I would like to request the use of some of your cargo crew to assist in clearing our training bay. It seems that some excess items have been dumped there instead of a cargo hold."

"Well, Misha. We don't normally allow shop talk at the dinner table."

"I am sorry, Colonel. I thought your question about my housekeeping chores was an invitation to discuss business."

"Perfectly understandable, since this is your first meal with us, we will let it slide this time," Britaine said.

"First meal, Colonel?" she asked.

Britaine smiled, "Of course. It is traditional in my outfit to have all staff officers dine together at least once each day. Although you are probably the lowest ranking officer on the ship, you are in command of the ground forces. So, I would expect you to attend our lunches. It would improve our relations, don't you think? After all, we are going to be in bed together, so to speak, for the next few days or so."

Misha blushed at the snickers around the table over Britaine's carefully couched sexual innuendo. She noticed the young lieutenant next to her had the grace to blush and look away.

"Colonel, I am not sure I understand your reference," she said.

"Come now, Misha. Surely, a little inter-service cooperation would help to pass the transport time. A charming young lady like you could do worse for herself than getting to know me better or even some of my staff for that matter."

Misha couldn't tell whether the man was being sexually suggestive or just trying to bait her. She decided it was best to let it drop. "Colonel. As much as I have enjoyed your meal and the charms of this intelligent lieutenant, I must pass on your invitation to dine with you regularly."

Britaine's face clouded rapidly, "Once again, Misha, you have misunderstood. I didn't offer an invitation. Dining together is a tradition I expect to be upheld. I made an exception for that pig you replaced because I wouldn't have him at my table. You may be rude at times, but you will attend."

"No, Colonel. I will not. Once again," Misha said mimicking his own words, "You misunderstand me. I don't take your orders. APES tradition says I eat with my squad."

"McPherson, are you determined to continue with your insubordinate attitude?" he all but shouted.

"Colonel Britaine. I formally request you address me properly as Third McPherson from this point forward," Misha spat out the words. "I don't care if you see me as rude, uncouth or ill-mannered. I cannot be insubordinate to you because I do not report to you or anyone else in your chain of command. And further, I don't care if you respect me or not. I am going into combat with my squad in just a few days. I do care that they know and respect me. APES tradition is for squads to eat together. Got that, Colonel Britaine?"

"You can't talk to me like that in my own command. I will report your attitude to your commanders before the end of the day," Britaine shouted.

Misha felt the sudden rush of adrenaline pumping into her system. She felt the same rush in combat. It was more than a surge of energy. It was a calm feeling of power where each action seemed to slow down. Had she and Britaine been on opposite sides in battle, he would have been dead and dismembered before he could have finished his last sentence. The rush also seemed to slow her thoughts where each idea became clear and each thought became precise.

"Colonel Britaine," she smiled like ice. "Report away as you see fit. Now, what about my request to get help clearing the training bay?"

"Clean it yourself if you want it cleaned up. My people have better things to do than cater to a group of dirt worms."

"Colonel, if you please, when you report on my attitude, please include a reference to your contract adherence failure regarding the training bay maintenance. Britaine stood and started to speak, but Misha interrupted, "And Colonel, if you think that you can make me to bow to your petty little tyrannies, then you have made another mistake. You can bully and insult your own people, but not me or mine. You just drive the bus, Colonel. Leave the real fighting to us."

Chapter Twelve

Misha awoke with a start. She could feel the sweat soaking her skivvies and her hair was plastered flat on her scalp. Pulling an arm free from the twisted sheets she reached up and slapped open her bunk's blast shutters. The sounds of the squad bay had been a quiet murmur easily drowned out by the white-noise generator. Now sounds flooded into her bunk. She could hear Ottiamig's flute playing a quiet little tune, general laughter and the sounds of a card game going on somewhere in the back.

The nightmare that had startled her awake returned as a vivid memory, not unlike a bad meatball sandwich eaten way too late at night. The nightmare was more memory than random dream sequences. It all came flooding back much clearer than dreams ever did. She was once again the newly promoted Second-Level Commander Hamisha Ann McPherson fighting for her life on Guinjundst.

As a new second, she did a quick mental review of her squad. It was about her thirtieth time running through the list, but it was her first time in command during actual combat. She was nervous, even though everyone knew this was a milk run, a cake walk or as easy as a two-dollar curb-crawling whore on New Las Vegas. Her combat suit fit her like a second skin. All of its tell-tales were reading in the green. The massive shell of armor and ordinance was working as well as a human could make a machine function. All of her APES were where they should be.

Misha had spent her whole APES career in the squad she now commanded. Eight of the troopers had been with her since her first day in the APES. She had trained with them, eaten with them, gone on liberty with them and they watched each other's backs in combat. They were already a highly trained fighting unit when Misha was promoted, replacing Second Saheed who retired to take a job as a civilian security consultant.

She had been promoted above veterans with many years more seniority. Misha was pleased to learn her promotion over those veterans was at the insistence of those same veterans. Every combat experienced warrior anticipated today's action against the Binder to be mild. Easy or not, she was thankful Jackson wanted to give her time to get used to her suit's newly uploaded command functions in substantial action. Earlier in the mission briefing, Third-Level Commander Richard Jackson told his seconds that he expected the battle on Guinjundst to be more of a training exercise than an actual combat situation. Binders were not much of a threat against the heavily armored APES. Misha wanted to be ready anyway since people died in wild ass hairy combat, in milk runs and even from slipping in the shower. Dead was dead and she wasn't going to take any chances, whether the enemy was Binders or a bar of soap.

Binders always attacked straight into the APE lines, so it was mostly a matter of what lasted the longest. Would the APES run out of ammo first or would the Binders run out of Binders? Since a combat suit could process raw dirt and rock into ammo, the Binders rarely came out on top.

Binders were odd little creatures. They looked more like living tumbleweeds than any animal. They came in all colors and sizes. They seemed to be all arms and legs that rolled, twisted and turned so no one knew which was their front or back, or even if they had fronts or backs. Their body, or their head, or whatever it was they called it, was in the center of the mass of twirling arms, legs, hands or whatever they were called. All of their sensors were at the end of their arms, along with bundles of tentacle-like fingers or toes, depending on your point of view and the Binder's own orientation.

Binder hardware was non-metallic. They had developed a plant-based technology that few xenobotonists or xenoagrologists had come to understand. No human scientist could duplicate Binder technology. It was only speculation on how such a technology could have developed into a space going civilization. Their ships were fairly easy for humans to capture, but they died quickly without their Binder handlers to keep them alive.

Little was known of the Binders other than what could be gleaned from the remains of a battlefield. Captured Binders died rapidly. Humans hadn't discovered much about any Binder language, written, spoken or mental other than a few seemingly non-random symbols on various flat surfaces. Humans hadn't discovered any permanent space stations. Humans hadn't discovered the Binder's home planet. Humans hadn't even discovered why the Binders insisted upon attacking well established and well defended human systems.

The first human and Binder contact was deadly to humans. But, that was because the humans had been unarmed farmers. The Binders swarmed by the hundreds using energy weapons from long distance, hard thorny-like projectiles fired from close range, and a myriad of cutting weapons for hand-to-hand combat. In fact, one early surviving farmer claimed that when the Binders moved into close combat, they looked like rows upon rows of whirling harvesting combines. The name stuck since humans also hadn't discovered what the Binders called themselves.

A Binder, no matter how it was armed, was no match for a human in a hard-shelled combat suit. None of their weapons, projectile or energy, could penetrate the armor. The most damage they could inflict was for a large knot of Binders to swarm over a suited APE and hold him down until other APES could rescue him. This was cause for serious ribbing at the expense of the unlucky APE who found himself buried under a squirming pile of Binders. The normal APES anti-binder combat strategy was to line up and lob explosives or to use skid plates to hover over them dropping hand grenades or high-explosive shells until everything was dead.

Misha, Kosimov and N'Guakkano were all newly promoted second-level commanders. The commander gave the easy positions to the least experienced of his second-level commanders. Jackson ordered Misha's squad to cover the right flank, sending Kosimov's squad to the left flank and N'Guakkano's squad to protect the rear. This put the unit in a square approximately seven kilometers to a side, with all their mobility pallets arranged inside the square. The rear and flank positions should have been cushy assignments. He designated the squads in the front line as acting artillery. The remaining squads were to use their skid plates to hover over the attacking forces, dropping explosives and generally expending ammunition with an APE's usual wild abandon.

Jackson placed his ten squad unit in a flat area facing a series of high ridged hills. The Binders encamped to the far side of the hills. There were dozens of passes through the hills. He used his unit to plug the largest pass. Around the APES was clear ground with small, but steep sided hills on each flank that should funnel the Binder's main attack through the big pass and allow the APES to concentrate fire into the Binder's mass. Not being a stupid man, Jackson deployed his unit in a standard box formation, in case the Binders deviated from their normal attack pattern by spitting their troops and coming at them from more than one direction.

Misha deployed her squad along the flank as ordered, linking Mendo to the front line and Loranzo to the rear guard. She sent Bambi and Boozer up on skid plates to provide squad air cover and to relay a tactical overview. Each trooper was strapped onto his skid plate, but she grounded everyone else.

It was a warm day with a slight wind; a nice day for combat and a good day to kill something. Since Guinjundst had a breathable atmosphere, Jackson did not order face shields sealed. The time for sealing up would be when the Binders got close enough to tangle with in hand-to-hand action.

Misha was watching her squad's activities while keeping one eye on the front line action on her suit's display. It necessitated her closing up the suit to get the full effect of the heads-up display and tactical relays. Everything seemed to be going like velvet. There were no warnings that things were about to start going horribly wrong.

She saw the flash of a Binder energy weapon highlight Boozer's skid plate on her HUD. At that range, it would not do any more damage to Boozer than give him a medium-sized sunburn and only then if he was naked. Boozer's preferred state was nude, but on the battlefield instead of being naked he was encased in armor twice the size of a normal human. He might get a rosy glow on his cheeks from the Binder's flash if he had his faceplate up.

Boozer didn't shrug off the effects of the energy weapon as Misha expected, instead his skid plate flipped end over end. It drove him straight into the ground. His combat suit would normally have withstood the force causing only a few minor jests by the rest of the squad. However, Boozer's face shield was up. The skid plate pushed him face-first into the ground and down a dozen feet, packing dirt and rock into his suit, crushing him into a small squished mess at the bottom.

Almost at the same time, a Binder pod burst over Bambi's skid plate. The pods were not a serious threat to armored humans. The worse thing a pod could do is clog up one of the intake valves on the skid plate. It would take a dozen pods going off all at once to ground a skid plate. Nevertheless, Bambi's skid plate slewed sideways. It slammed through the squad's line, knocking men and women a dozen different directions. Misha used her suit's power to kick free of her skid plate and bounce to Bambi as she shot past her position. A quick twist of the manual override on the skid plate and Misha grounded it. Bambi slumped to the ground in a metal heap.

Within seconds, Misha sent a situation report to Third-Level Commander Jackson and ordered Severin and Yamara to dig Boozer out of the ground. She called Pushkin the squad's medic to give her a hand with Bambi and ordered everyone else to get back to position. Almost as an afterthought she ordered the squad to stay off their skid plates.

Although a combat suit weighs near three and a half metric tons, the servos in Misha's suit flipped Bambi onto her back. Bambi was bleeding profusely from her mouth and nose. Her eyes had already begun to glaze over when the convulsions hit.

The APES combat suit is designed to encase an APE and amplify every muscle twitch and movement. This allows an APE to jump higher, run faster and kill quicker than most people can think. Lack of movement discipline can send a suited APE bouncing around the terrain like a lopsided rubber ball on amphetamines. Bambi's convulsions threw Misha a hundred yards to the rear before she could react and compensate.

"Pushkin. Dammit, get to Bambi. Now!" Misha shouted over the squad comm-link. She bounced back up and leaped on top of Bambi's suit. By design, there is no external off switch on a suit. However, all command suits have an emergency override. Misha ordered Bambi's suit to shut down, run diagnostics on all physical systems, pump any appropriate medicines into Bambi, and shut the face plate.

"Pushkin, where the hell are you?" Misha shouted. She knew shouting did not help amplify her voice any more than normal speech. It just seemed like the thing to do.

There was no answer.

She checked Pushkin's telltale on her HUD. He was in position on line, but not moving. Quickly scanning his vitals, she realized he was ill. All of her squad was beginning to red line.

"Face shields down now!" she shouted. Not waiting for a response, she hit her command suit override and shut down every face shield in her squad. She flashed another sitrep to Jackson, but did not receive an acknowledgement.

"Misha?" a voice sounded in her ear.

"Deuce Goober? Is that you?" she asked. Second-Level Commander Aric Gubicza's squad was on the front line.

"Yeah. What the hell is going on? Where's Jackson?" Goober asked.

"Dammit, Goober. I don't know. He's supposed to be up on the front line with you. We need to order all suits sealed up. Now! I think the Binders have started using biological or chemical warfare," she all but shouted, trying to keep her voice calm yet forceful.

"I can't order that on the unit net for the whole unit. Where's Jackson?"

"Goober, at least get your squad to shut face shields. I don't know where Jackson is now. He was supposed to be with you. He isn't reading on my HUD or on the TAC map. Are your sensors reading him? Who is next in line if he is out of action?"

"I don't know. Suzuki or Chang is next in line, I think. Check your HUD. Suzuki is not reading on my HUD. Park shows as red-lined. What do we do?"

"You are senior to me. Order all suites sealed," Misha said.

"Who is in the chain of command after Park?" Goober said. "I don't think it's me. I don't want it to be me. I don't know. Get off the line, whoever you are. Let me think. I don't know."

"No time, Goober. Order it done."

"Can't do, Missy. No time for all of this jibber jabber, I'm gonna go fishin'."

Misha realized the second was incoherent and babbling. She toggled her communications to broadcast. "Hostile air! Listen up, people. Everyone in Jackson's Second, seal your suits immediately. Run your diagnostics for bio and chemical contamination. I say again hostile air, seal up now! Ground all skid plates."

Misha bounced to her squad line. Bambi's telltale was still showing as active, but it was redlining fast. "All troops, tag your suits to me, now! Stand your line."

Misha expected to be swamped with signals, but only a handful of lights blinked on her HUD. She overlaid the signals on a battlefield map. There was a cluster of three lights from N'Guakkano's rear guard.

One light was from Kosimov's squad on the other flank. Nothing was showing on any of the other squads.

She tagged the tactical map with Jackson's last known position. It was in the center of the original line of combat. "Okay people. Check your tactical displays. Keep your face shields in place and keep your skid plates grounded. Bounce to the position I've marked on your TACs. Be ready and loaded for bear. Weapons hot!" Misha shouted as she used the suit's muscles to cover the distance in a ground-eating run.

"What the hell is that?" a voice shouted in Misha's ear.

She checked her command displays to find out who spoke. It was Ng from Kosimov's squad, the first APE to reach the front line.

"Hold on, Ng. We're almost there," Misha responded.

She skidded to a stop a few hundred yards down the line from where Ng stood. Checking her HUD, she could see a trace of red arching over the Binder's front line as the enemy rolled forward. There were indications of additional pods launching harmlessly against the armored APES. Flashes of red were washing over Ng as the Binder energy weapons targeted him, apparently without effect. No other APE was moving. None of the APE skid plates originally tasked to hover over the Binders was visible.

"Hit your magnification, Deuce," said Ng. "Check out their front line."

Misha cursed herself under her breath. She should have thought of that. She spun the magnification up and caught her breath. "What the hell is that?" Misha unconsciously echoed Ng's earlier comment. "Never mind, don't answer."

The three APES from N'Guakkano's squad hit the line, bunching up next to Misha.

"Spread out. On the bounce. We don't have much time to get our act together," Misha said. She silently cursed herself for having called them to bunch up in the first place.

"Are we bugging out, Deuce?" Ng asked.

"No, dammit! We don't leave APES behind," Misha spat. She wanted to add dead or alive, but she kept that to herself. Besides, she was pissed and wanted to kill something.

"But, Deuce," Ng complained, "You saw what is coming, and they're coming fast. Are we supposed to fire into that?"

"Shut up, Ng and stay off comms unless you got something important to say. You'll fire when and where you are told to," Misha ordered. She checked her HUD noting the names of the new arrivals. She didn't have much to work with, but each of the three new arrivals from the rear guard was a long-time veteran she knew from exercises and multi-squad assaults. Only Ng was a rookie.

"Okay, Rodriguez and...damn, both Rodriguez, I need prisoners. I want that and that and that." She tagged specific individual targets on the TAC map from the enemy front line. "And if you can, get that big red son-of-a-bitch just back of their front lines. Preferably alive, but anyway you have to. Stash them in the first APE mobility box you can get to. Mark the bunker as used so we know where we shoved them. On the bounce, Rodriguez, both of you."

"Roger that, Deuce," both voices answered; one male and one female. Two combat suits bounced forward toward the front lines in giant leaps.

"Weapons hot, Troopers. Take it down if it isn't one of the four tagged on the TAC, leave only a small slick spot for their mamas to mourn over," Misha shouted. "Ng and Papadoropoulis, cover fire for the Rodriguez duo. Lob explosives to the rear of the enemy's front. Pour your mass drivers into their flanks. Ng fire into the left flank and Papa fire into the right flank."

"Papa here, Deuce. Suggestion?" His voice punctuated by small clicks as he opened fire with his suit's weapons.

"Go, Papa. Let's not stand on ceremony." Misha began dropping high-explosive rounds from the ammo racks built into the back of the suit into the Binder ranks. She vaulted straight upward about sixty feet using the muscles of the combat suit. She arched rounds into the Binders on the way up and the way down. She could feel the slight recoil as each round left the tube located over her shoulders. She swung each arm in front of her and triggered the mass drivers. She was firing hundred round bursts of inert material. It was shot at speeds that cut through a dozen Binders before striking their hard body mass and ripping huge holes in said bodies. Any other hit on a Binder might rip off a dozen arms or legs, but that would not be enough of a loss to slow down their forward movement.

Papadoropoulis said, "Deuce, we can use the squad bays as bunkers and mobile tanks. There are too damn many of these for just the five of us."

"But, there are not enough of us to effectively man the mobility pallets and still remain mobile. We need to be free to fire and pull back. We need to keep from being surrounded."

"Right, but our mobility boxes are weaponized and we can put them on automatic. Hell, Deuce. Give me two minutes and I can drop them all in the middle of that mess out there and set them on random rapid fire."

"Automatic? How do you do that?" Misha asked. "Never mind, you can show me later, when we get out of this. Do it, Papa."

"Roger that," he said.

"Juanita Rodriguez here," a female voice said. "We got your prisoners. Two each. We are heading back toward the central drop point."

"Papa," Misha said, "Tag a bunker to stash the prisoners."

"Juanito Rodriguez here," a male voice said. "Are you sure you want them alive? It wouldn't be much of a problem to make them otherwise."

"No, let's keep them alive if you can. I think we are going to have plenty of dead ones to look at. And tie them up, sedate them, stuff them in a locker or wrap them in duct tape if you have to. Get back up front fast."

All the while she spoke, Misha fired into the oncoming ranks of enemy combatants. Finally, the soft chunk and recoil of the high-explosive tubes quit. The suit's HUD showed ammo chambers were empty.

Ng shouted, "I'm out of ammo. Gods help me, I'm out of ammo."

"It's okay, Ng," Misha said calmly. "They can't hurt you if you stay sealed in your suit." She silently hoped it was true. Who knew what other unknown weapons were in their hands if the Binders were using bio and chem warfare for the first time? Plus, there was the uncertainty that came with the new prisoners; what the hell was the deal with them?

Misha called to Ng, "Okay. Ground yourself." Misha's mass driver's quit firing with the sickening klunk of an empty weapon's chamber. She was talking to Ng, but it was as much to herself as for the rookie. "Get your feet down, dammit! Think calmly. Remember the mass drivers fire junk mass. The suit can collect it for you and convert as you fire. Remember it can use dirt and rocks, but you've got to get your feet down and stand still for it to work. Do it." Upon contact with the ground, she felt the suit vibrate and begin to sink down as the ground gave way to the suit's conversion process.

"But they are almost on us. We'll get overrun. I can't see. Where did all this fog come from?" There was an edge of panic in the rookie's voice.

"Stand where you are, Ng or I will hunt you down myself. It's not fog; it's just dust from the suit as it chews up dirt and rocks to reload your ammo. Open fire. Use your HUD's infrared to see. Papa, how is it coming?"

"I am setting the first few to auto now. Give me a minute," Papadoropoulis said.

"Roger that. No rush. Ng and I can handle this. Right Ng?" There was no answer, but Misha's TAC display showed his mass driver shooting streams of green from his position. The front line of the enemy had collapsed and the main body, a united mass of Binders, was pouring over the dead bodies of their own front line as if the piled remains were no more of an impediment than a small mound of sand.

"Damn," Juanita Rodriguez said.

"Speak up, Rodriguez," Misha said.

"It is nothing serious. One got away while I was stuffing the other in a locker. Juanito got him and put him away. But, I think we broke that one."

"I don't care right now. Get back up here if they are secure," Misha commanded.

Juanito Rodriguez spoke. "Hey, Deuce. If you need ammo, we can get it from our guy's suits. Your suit can do the over ride command and pop them open."

"Thanks for the suggestion, but I am about to start tearing them apart with my bare hands. They are getting a tad bit too close. Get up here as soon as you can. Papa?" Misha involuntarily ducked as a Binder threw something at her. She jumped out of the hole her suit had dug and bounced high.

"Ng. Get moving. Bounce around. Don't let them swarm over you and hold you down," Misha said in mid-air. She could see her suit react to energy beams and her HUD showed groups of pods bouncing off her armor. But, it was doing little or no damage.

She came down in a small cluster of Binders. She lashed out with both hands, slicing through arms and legs to slam into the central body mass. She whirled on her left foot and sent her heel crashing into a knot of the Binders swarming at her.

A second leap took her off the ground and over the Binders. Even in the brief time her foot had been in contact with the ground the suit had converted enough mass for a short burst. She sprayed the ground under her feet.

She landed with a slight jolt taking the impact on her knees. Flexing, she jumped again, not upward but in a shallow arc, aiming toward a group of Binders. Instead of landing on her feet she curled into a hard ball and crashed into the group, rolling and smashing dozens of the enemy into tiny blobs of goo. She somersaulted into a crouch and shot forward again crashing into more

Binders. But, the enemy was relentless and completely disregarded any damage to its own soldiers. They continued to chase after her like a pack of puppies after a bouncing ball.

"Papa?" she shouted. "It's time to do your magic."

Papadoropoulis said, "Ten seconds to impact. We have mobility pallets airborne now. Get to clear ground. All ammo to auto-expend at grounding. We will have horizontal fire in three seconds."

Misha caught sight of a falling squad bay that had just become an automated killing machine. She shot from under a pile of Binders and jumped upward toward the falling machine. Twisting, she curled into a hunched knot of metal and collided with the squad bay in mid-air. On contact, she uncoiled and used the bulk of the machine and her suit's muscles to leap hundreds of meters to a clear zone behind a small hill on the right flank.

She could feel the vibrations through the ground as the mobile bunkers became automated weapons and fired with buzz saw ripples. She flipped to her feet and set the suit to loading mass driver ammo as she tried to check the ridge of the hill for enemy troops, check her HUD and check her TAC display all at the same time. Ng's telltale glowed yellow. He didn't clear the killing zone.

"Ng," Misha said in a calm voice although she wanted to shout. "Set your suit to static. Go dormant. Set your meds on high. Hang on. We will get to you."

There was no response from Ng. The three other APES' telltales glowed green.

Misha called out over the comms, "Can anyone get to Ng?"

"Negative." "No." "Sorry, Deuce."

"Okay, Ng. You hold on, buddy. We'll get there soonest."

Ng's telltale stayed yellow and didn't dip any farther toward red.

Misha thought, "Maybe the suit kicked in enough meds and he is out of it."

The ground continued to rumble and shake as the automated systems blasted away at the Binder troop mass. The squad bays held a limited amount of ammo and would soon be little more than dead boxes scattered about the battle field, but the weapons bay and storage lockers held an incredible amount of high-explosive rounds.

Suddenly, the TAC map beeped. Masses of enemy troops were working their way through other passes and rapidly closing to firing range. The TAC map showed them as clusters of glowing red symbols flowing forward like a flood after a dam break.

"Okay, troopers, it looks like we have more company coming. Check your TAC maps. Papa, how much longer will this barrage keep up?"

"It will be a while yet, Deuce. I dropped a couple of ammo storage bunkers in there that can blow out for another five or six minutes."

"Okay. Keep them at the main force. Move them back to the original drop point if any of them run dry. That way, the Binders won't have anything to hide behind out there. Can you drop a couple of empty boxes next to Ng? I don't see that the Binders have anything that can get to us if we are sealed up, so maybe he got hit by friendly fire. A couple of boxes would give him some protection from the other guns."

"Roger that, Deuce. Good idea, I should have thought of that," Papadoropoulis said.

"Rodriguez, both of you, bounce to these two hills I have marked on your TAC. You should still have almost a full load of H.E. You will be in a position to lay down a cross fire on the closest group."

"Going, going, gone," Juanita Rodriguez said.

Misha watched their telltales streak toward the designated areas on her TAC. They might be able to get out of this mess if the Rodriguezs could take care of the second group, if Papadoropoulis's trick with the bunkers wiped out the first batch before the third group reached them, if there were no other groups of Binders sneaking up on them from out of nowhere, and if the little bastards did not have any other bio or chem tricks up their non-existent sleeves.

"Papa, keep at them, but don't expend your suit's high explosives until the automatics run dry."

"Okay, I could drop one of the armories into that third group of Binders coming through the hills. Whadda ya say?" Papadoropoulis asked.

"Negative. Good idea, but it looks like it will be photo finish whether you run out of ammo here first or whether you run out of Binders. It may be close, but I think we can squeak through this thing if my timeline reads right," Misha said.

"Okay, Third McPherson. You are the boss."

"Nothing is coming my way now. I've got to re-arm with H.E. I am going to work my way back to our lines and scavenge what I can. I am sending the override to all suits, so everybody reload as you can."

Misha reached their original front in three low-level bounds, barely skimming the surface of the planet, keeping well below the ridge lines and out of the bunker fire. The first APE suit she came to was lying on its back with the face shield still open. Blood and sores covered the face inside the helmet. The lesions seemed to have something growing out of them; small green wiggly shoots of some kind. She toggled the HUD display until she matched the suit number to the telltales. Even without the suit confirmation she knew the APE was dead.

Misha hit the command override to shut the face shield. She reached underneath the body and with a grunt that was more for the sight of the APES face than for the effort, she flipped it over to uncover the backside. She commanded her suit to unlock the magazines for the high explosives' storage. She sat down on top of the dead APE and she attached her H.E. feeder tube to the other suit's discharge tube. The soft chunk of machine to machine feeding began. While it was filling, Misha grounded her feet to allow the mass-driver to convert dirt and rocks to top off her ammo storage.

"Rodriguez team, report." The TAC map showed a rapidly shrinking number of Binders and a steady stream of fire from two green blips.

"Juanito aqui, hefe. This is just like the shooting range back home."

"Si si, hefe, Juanita here," the female Rodriguez responded. "We can finish this off about the same time as Papa gets done, but we will be completely out of high explosives."

"Can you finish with mass drivers and not expend your entire H.E. load?" Misha asked.

"Negative" and "No, too many. H.E. takes them down a lot quicker. Plus, we don't have to be so careful in our aim and with H.E we can bounce around and stay out of their direct line of fire."

"Okay. Do it quick. We've still got more company coming."

"Papa, get to Ng as soon as you can," Misha ordered.

Papadoropoulis replied, "All done here, Deuce. The field is clear and I am heading toward Ng now. By the way, have you sent a sitrep to the boys upstairs?"

Misha would have slapped her forehead, except she wouldn't have felt a thing inside her helmet. She should have already sent a situation report to the AMSF for their information and for relay to APES Command.

"Dammit. I forgot," she said. "Uplinking now."

"No sweat, Deuce. We've been a bit busy," Papadoropoulis said.

"Thanks for the reminder, Papa. I am ammo'ed up. I've got six telltales showing APES down but still in their suits. I have marked them on our TACs. Get Ng back to the squad bay where you stashed the prisoners. Then help me check vitals on these guys. And Papa, they ain't pretty, so make sure they are sealed up and you stay sealed up too, hear?"

"Roger that."

"We may have a short breather before the third mass of Binders gets here, but don't get too relaxed. Take on max reload. And everybody stay sealed up until we can get through decontamination. I have notified the AMSF to stay out of the atmosphere until we can get a decon team to clear the area."

"Oh, hefe," Juanito Rodriguez groaned in mock pain. "That could take days."

"I know. Listen, team, I don't know what we got hit with here, but we can't afford to spread something nasty to the rest of Allied space..."

Misha allowed Alpha's squad bay on the Kiirkegaard to swim back into focus as she took a deep breath. She stopped the memory playback, looked around, shook her head and rattled the living nightmare from her mind. She kicked her feet loose from the covers and swung her legs over the edge of her bunk.

She knew how she looked and didn't care. All the leadership manuals said you should occasionally show your people your human side. "Well," she thought. "You don't get any more human looking than this."

The flute music stopped and she looked down the squad bay. Ottiamig was peering around his bunk with a questioning look. He held up his flute and wiggled his hand back and forth from the wrist. It was the combat hand-signal for 'okay?'.

In response, Misha smiled back, pumped her fist up and down and slid her flat hand ahead, the signal for 'forward.'

Ottiamig's signaled back, 'roger, will comply'. He smiled and ducked into his bunk. Soon the soothing sounds of his flute filled the room again.

Misha hung her head in her hands reflecting on the memory that forced her awake. She knew that once upon a time many combat veterans' bad dreams were misdiagnosed as the result of post-traumatic stress disorder. That was spot-on accurate for a lot of combat veterans, but it was not always the case. Medicine, specifically combat medicine had since learned post-traumatic stress disorder wasn't what affected many veterans. Studies proved some individuals became addicted to combat, to the adrenaline rush, to the charge and challenge of war. Then, in times of peace or peacefulness, the body reacted to their addiction and the resultant lack of adrenaline to feed the veteran's addiction. In effect, the lack of combat stress induced adrenaline sent the veteran into a type of withdrawal.

Misha's little argument with Britaine had pushed her addiction to the edge, giving her a fitful sleep, an uneasy feeling something was wrong and most of all a sense of not fitting in with the world around her. But, she knew, as did many combat veterans, without her addiction she could never force herself to go back into combat. After all, what normal person would throw themselves into danger, seeking to kill or be killed time after time?

Medical science also progressed enough to develop a non-addictive synthetic substitute to ease days and nights like this one. All Misha had to do was push herself off her bunk and get a pill from the ditty bag stashed in her locker. Instead, Misha sat on her bunk in her squad bay aboard the AMSF Kiirkegaard holding her head in her hands and analyzed the events of Guinjundst, replaying it all in her head again trying to make sense of what went wrong.

She, Papa, and the two Rodriguezs made short work of the remaining group of Binders. They had trapped them in a high walled canyon and used their high-explosives to bury the Binders under tons of rock and rubble. An AMSF spacecraft picked up the squad bay with the injured and their prisoners. Only Ng and one other APE would survive. Misha was left on the planet with Papa and the two Rodriguez. It was a long week trapped inside a combat suit with nothing to do but carry the dead to the up point, until a decontamination team could finally clear them.

Misha shook her head at the memory. Pushing off the bunk she stood and stretched. She glanced down at her timepiece and decided since it was only a couple of hours until time to get up, she might as well stay up. Since she wasn't going back to bed, there was no reason to take a pill to ease her combat anxiety withdrawal. She might as go stir up trouble.

Chapter Thirteen

Marshal Sergeant Gan Forrester stood in the training bay watching the chaos around him. He was breathing heavily after barely surviving a dozen assaults in hand-to-hand combat training. Trey McPherson left him at the mercy of Charlie Squad's Second Takki-Homi.

Forrester had wanted to spend time with McPherson's squad. She interested him, but she explained that Second Takki-Homi's squad was the most complete veteran team. They would be able to integrate him with the least disruption to their training schedule. He did not have a logical argument against her reasoning. He would just have to try to get her cornered at another time.

Second Takki-Homi tapped Forrester on the shoulder and said, "Watch Able Squad." He pointed to McPherson's squad.

"Watch what?" Forrester replied.

"Trey McPherson is setting up a free-for-all within her squad. It is a good way to evaluate both the martial arts and physical fitness levels of a team."

"Is she any good?" Forrester asked.

"I don't know. She looks more like a weight lifter than a fighter, but she moves like a cat. A big, angry cat, at that," Takki-Homi said.

"Yeah, I noticed that," Forrester said. "So, why do a free-for-all?"

"As you may know each APE comes to the service with a martial arts style of his own choosing. This type of evaluation pits each style against a bunch of other styles. It doesn't point out if one style is better than another; instead it shows who needs additional training," Takki-Homi explained.

"Okay. But, I always wanted to ask; why require a martial art form to join? It's not like you guys fight bare handed."

"True enough. But, we don't usually have years to train in the use of a combat suit. Mostly, we get stuffed in a real suit in a combat situation with only a few hours in a tri-wave simulator and just a couple of hour's suit practice time that is little more than ambling up and down the training bay. Knowing a martial art form helps the recruits with their physical discipline and muscle control." Takki-Homi pointed to a squad who appeared to be resting in reclining loungers with helmets on. "They are using the tri-wave sim with specific integrated training modules. I am sure you used them in school and probably in your training for the Marshal's Service."

Forrester nodded, "Yeah, but all of them were individual modules, where we went through the live-action scenarios and came out learning the prescribed courses of learning. I have never been hooked into an integrated system. How does it work?"

Takki-Homi shrugged his shoulder, "Damfino. You might ask Trooper Ortiz. She is our squad's repair tech. All I know is that we go in, get linked, spend anywhere from a few days to a week or so in combat situations and I come out knowing more about my team, my suit and combat than I went in. Plus, after day's session, I will somehow be able to read and write French. And just like magic it all takes place in about an hour. And you ask me how does it work? Damn, Gan, it could really be magic for all I care. It works. If it doesn't work, then I call Ortiz to fix it. What more do I need to know?"

Forrester said, "I get all that. I grew up on Heaven Three. Every school on the planet has the tri-wave sim. Of course, we learned things like math and science, instead of fun simulations. We always got dropped into some dry historical era, you know?"

Takki-Homi nodded, "I know."

"May I ask a personal question?" Forrester asked. "I get that combat simulations are standard, but the second part of a tri-wave is the download into the brain of some course of learning. Do you get to choose the course of learning that gets crammed into your head along with the live-action simulation? I mean, why not learn APE approved subject like suit maintenance or even how to repair the tri-wave simulator? I would think APES would want to learn something service related. Why would you come out knowing French?"

Takki-Homi laughed, "Reading French is service oriented. Didn't you know that I am Charlie Squad's cook? I have some French cookbooks that tomorrow I can read in their original. Today I can't. You'd be amazed at what I can do with APES standard rations."

Takki-Homi continued. "Okay, I think Able Squad is ready to set-to."

Forrester watched as one of the troopers in the squad shouted, "Go!" He expected an immediate clash, but the free-for-all began so small it was as if no one moved. Subtle movements showed here and there with the individuals moving around sizing up each other's skills before striking.

"Watch carefully," Takki-Homi said. "I am willing to bet the tall black kid makes the first contact."

Suddenly the young man lashed out with a foot aimed at a short Asian man's head. But, the man's head wasn't where it had been. The Asian whirled, grabbed the extended foot and drove the black man into the back of a skinny white woman. Bodies began to spin, strike, hiss, grunt and hit the deck. Once a person was knocked to the deck, they rolled to the side and stood, out of the contest.

A wild melee ensued. Forrester watched in fascination as McPherson deliberately leapt into groups and clusters of fighters; jabbing, punching and throwing bodies around with raging abandon. She seemed to lash out in all directions at once, without any apparent style or gracefulness. All too soon it was over. McPherson stood alone in the center of the group having defeated all comers.

"What kind of style is that?" Forrester asked. "It just looked like she was using wild street fighting."

"I've seen it a few times, but never done that well," Takki-Homi replied. "It is called Bào Dòng. That is old Earth One Mandarin for mayhem. Bào means explosive, huge and sudden. Dòng means movement and chaos. It is a word that actually used to be used for riots or melees. As a martial art, it doesn't have any such thing as belts, levels or ranks. It is a matter of win or lose, get better or keep getting beaten. No holds barred and no pulled punches. They use any object at hand as a weapon in offensive movement in all directions at all times. It also blatantly steals moves from all other known martial arts styles. No apparent grace or fluid movement, no ritual or fancy outfits, just all out wanton destruction and devastation until no enemy is left standing to oppose you."

"Damn," said Forrester.

"Damn indeed," replied Takki-Homi. "It works if you have the right attitude."

"I see it works for our Third McPherson."

The two men turned as a voice called out. "Yo, Taks, who is your new friend?"

"Second-Level Commander Race Jackson, Foxtrot Squad. This is Sergeant Gan Forrester of the Marshal Service," Takki-Homi said introducing the two men.

Jackson nodded at Forrester. "Training with the big boys today?"

Forrester smiled back, "No, just Taks' squad. It looks like your new commander is the big boy today."

"Damn straight," Jackson said. "You guys see her moves? She must be hell on wheels in a combat suit."

"Yeah, a hard act to follow," Takki-Homi said.

"Hard or easy, follow it is. With the hero of Guinjundst in the lead, it is payback time for those Binder bastards," Second Jackson said.

"Hey, Deuce Taks, how did you know who would strike first in that free-for-all?" Forrester asked.

"Rookies always do. It's a guarantee if it is a confident rookie. And most of the time they end up on their butts. Now, Sergeant Forrester, it is time to put you on your butt."

Chapter Fourteen

Misha cursed under her breath. She knew deep down that she was in the tri-wave simulator and had been for less than an hour of real time. Every sensation was being fed into her brain through the connectors around the shaved part of her head. Electrical relays or not, everything felt real, smelled real, and even tasted real. She knew from the uncomfortable pressure across her midsection that the plumbing in a combat suit was uncomfortable and that she had been attached to the suit for too long. She had itches she hadn't scratched in what seemed like hours. It felt like three days sealed into the armor with the face shields in place. All she wanted was to brush her teeth. She could taste the scum build up. She swore if someone figured a way to improve dental hygiene in combat armor, then she would have their baby, whether it was man, woman or those weird Altan Thumbtaskers.

"What did you say, Trey?" DeLaPax asked.

"Nothing, Peace, I was just thinking out loud, I guess," Misha said.

"Must be thinking too loud, Third," Singletary said. "I agree this is a bitch. So, why do we have to stay sealed up? I mean, all the scans show clean air with no biological or chemical contaminates." Almost as an afterthought he added "sir."

"You are and you will stay sealed up until I say so. And we are doing it because I don't trust the Binders to use biological and chemical juices that our suits can detect. All suits received the new software upgrades after Guinjundst, but even that doesn't guarantee the Binders haven't come up with something new."

After a few more grumbles, Misha said, "All right, APES. That's enough. I have spent a week in a suit and it didn't kill me. This little outing won't kill you either, unless you get distracted. Our HUDs aren't showing enemy contact, but we know they are around here somewhere. Chill and get icy cold, people, we've got work to do. Slezak, take Ottiamig, use your skid plates and move to the ridge I have marked on your TAC maps. Keep a low profile."

"Roger that, Third," Trooper Aimee Slezak replied. "Come on, rookie. Let's move." The two slid along the ground like surfers on some unseen wave. Their skid plates were four-foot metallic discs sliding effortlessly through the air at grass top level.

"Park, you and Bear Cutler scoot to these points. Juarez and Metzler move to the points on your TAC maps. That should give us an open line of sight across all cardinal points. On the bounce troopers, as the quicker we locate the enemy the quicker we can go home and get out of these suits. Everyone, keep your skid plates low to the ground. Let's avoid being spotted by the enemy."

Misha mentally ticked off her troops. She had just paired off three veterans: Trooper Six Aimee Slezak, Trooper Two Jem Li Park, and Trooper Five Miguel Juarez with rookies Trooper Eight Tuamma Ottiamig, Trooper Seven Bear Cutler, and Trooper Eleven Oouta Metzler. More importantly, she had split up those three veterans from Trooper One Singletary. The four seemed almost joined at the hip. She was sure they formed a core of one problem subset for the 1392nd. She did not like putting rookies with troublesome troopers, but she did not have any other choice.

Ottiamig might not want favoritism because of his family connections, but the tall man did come from a family with a deep history of service to the Allied Systems. He was probably a better trooper than the veteran Slezak. The only other veteran she had was Peace DeLaPax, a tall stunningly beautiful woman. DeLaPax always seemed to be smiling and was supremely confident. That left the rookies Trooper Nine Israel Steinman and Trooper Ten Tammie Qualls. Both APES were exceptionally weak, neither given to extending themselves beyond what was required.

Using the squad wide communication net Misha said, "Okay, APES. Everyone set your scans to the maximum passive range. Let's see if we can pick up some sign of where the enemy is hiding without giving our position away."

Misha checked the tell-tales of her squad on her HUD. Everyone seemed to be dragging a bit, but not enough to order meds. Qualls was showing some dehydration. Misha knew some rookies took time adjusting to the fact that their water supply was usually recycled from their own waste and sweat.

Misha toggled her comms for one-on-one. "Tammie, you had better drink some more water. You need to get another three liters down before sunset." Misha heard the trooper sigh, but saw the water consumption level start to inch up.

Misha toggled her comms again. "Slezak, is that all the farther your passive scan can set? Crank it up, trooper. Max it out."

"Roger that, Third," Slezak replied.

Misha watched the comm channels. She did not want to become one of those commanders who listened in on personal chatter among her troops, but she did want to see the activity levels. A four-way comm between Singletary, Slezak, Park and Juarez had been going on way too long.

Misha said. "Okay, troopers. Let's cut the chatter and-"

Before she could finish, Ottiamig interrupted on the squad channel. "I have hostile markers at the edge of the TAC, Charlie 16 by Whiskey 354. I have hot marks!"

Misha checked her TAC. Ottiamig updated the map with his scan data. It did indeed look like a large concentration of Binders, crawling up through the canyon between Slezak team and Park's teams.

"Good job, Tuamma," Misha broadcast. "We should be able to squeeze them together and take them in the canyon."

"Trey!" Ottiamig shouted in excitement. "They aren't moving like Binders. Look at this scan. They are bouncing forward. They are moving like humans in combat suits."

"What the hell is that?" Singletary asked. "Slezak, what kind of scam are you trying to pull?"

"I am not doing anything, honest. Check the scans, the kid is right," Slezak said.

"Okay, Third. What gives?" Singletary demanded. "Are we linking up with another squad? I thought we were the only APES here?"

Ottiamig said, "It is not just a squad. That looks like we got almost a dozen squads in armor."

"Can the chatter, you APES. Slezak, can you read IFF?" The Identity: Friend or Foe was an active scan and would alert the new contact to her squad's presence and let any enemy know who was there.

"Roger, blipping now. Oh, shit! We are taking fire. Damn, get me out of here," Slezak shouted.

"Stay put. I can't analyze what I can't see. Tag your signal to the squad net. Tuamma, confirm under fire from APES," Misha said. Her HUD interpreted the incoming fire at Slezak and Ottiamig as red streaks with definite overtones of angry.

"Yes, sir, it is max range for mass driver fire. We aren't taking any damage and won't for a minute or two yet. But, I don't think they are APES. Check this magnified image," Ottiamig said.

Misha stared at the visual. "What do you think, Singletary?"

"The kid is right. That ain't our suit configuration. Look, the legs are too long and the arms are too short," Singletary replied.

"Sir, DeLaPax here. That is an Orion Confederacy suit. I've seen scans on them in the armory repair bay."

"Are you sure, Peace?" asked Singletary.

"Damn right. I am an excellent armor repair tech. I know my scoobies. They are more mobile than our old v 2.0A, but they are not as well armored. Our mass drivers will punch a hole through two at a time, if we can get close enough," DeLaPax said.

Misha used the conversation between Singletary and DeLaPax to lay in a new battle plan. She quickly uploaded it onto Able Squad's net. "Okay, APES. I have a new tactical plan. Follow what is on your HUD. Break into teams one, two and three as marked. Slezak and Ottiamig, hold there until I give the word."

"Come on, Third," Slezak whined. "That is going to expose us to more fire. Hell, that puts us in H.E. range."

"It is barely within H.E. range, Aimee," Misha said. "I don't see any indication they have skid plates. Your skid plates will move you out of range before you get hit. You are the bait. We need you to draw them in and draw their fire until we can catch them in the open. Now enough chatter people. This isn't up for debate."

Misha watched as Singletary slid his skid plate along at grass top height as he moved into position with Park and Cutler on the left flank. Qualls skirted wide to join up with Juarez and Metzler as they scooted up the back of a sloping hill on the right. She wasn't happy about using skid plates after Guinjundst. But, she had been assured that Bambi and Boozer, infected with Binder biological and chemical agents, drove their plates into the ground on Guinjundst and not the other way around.

A single comm request blipped on her HUD. It was Singletary asking for a one-on-one. She toggled her comm unit.

"Okay, Singletary. What's up?"

"Look, Third. Are we supposed to fire on humans? I mean, we are not at war with the Orion Confed, are we? Besides, there are too damn many for one squad to handle. That must be a full second sized unit."

Misha toggled her comm to the squad's open channel. "Okay you APES, our IFF marked the incoming suits as hostile and they fired at us. I don't need any more justification than that to shoot back. We are going to draw these A-holes into a trap and pound them into mush."

De Le Pax shouted, "Incoming, check your upside, eleven o'clock high. I am reading what looks like rocks with those weird Binder markings."

"Hold your positions, APES," Misha commanded. The trajectory of the incoming was definitely unguided.

The signal showed it to be native chunks of rock. Sure enough, there was evidence of Binder activity. Peculiar and unreadable vegetation marked the edges of the rocks. The rocks were arcing toward them as if tossed from a long distance away, yet still coming in suborbital.

"Slezak and Ottiamig, take off now. Lead the hostiles to us," Misha ordered. "Team one, keep it cold you APES, and stay in position." They would expose her ambush if they moved to avoid the incoming rock barrage.

Misha watched the indicators on her HUD grow closer as the rocks curved toward her. She felt the ground complain as large rocks and boulders began to rain out of the sky. One rock the size of a two-seat flitter smashed into the ground a few meters from her. The shockwave flipped her thirty meters before she plowed back into the dirt. Keeping as low as she could, she crabbed backward to the crater caused by the rock's impact. Now she had cover.

She heard a high-pitched scream over the comms. It sounded like Qualls. However, checking her command HUD, she saw a large boulder hit Steinman. His telltale on her HUD showed severe damage to his legs. They were probably crushed. Even a hardened combat suit can only provide protection from some levels of damage. These rocks were coming down with less than terminal velocity, but they were hitting the ground with force enough she could feel the ground quake and churn.

"Hold steady, APES." She hit the command override on Steinman's voice comms. She checked his vitals. He was still alive, but the suit had automatically sealed off his legs and pumped him so full of meds that he was unconscious. She noticed Able Squad medic Cutler's comm signal also logged in to check on Steinman. Misha thought, "Good check for a rookie. I need to remember to give him an attaboy."

Misha was tossed out of her crater with the thump from another near miss. She ducked back just in time to miss being smacked by Slezak's skid plate as the trooper zipped past. Ottiamig dove off his skid plate as it shot by. He flew into Misha's crater. Without a rider to guide it, his skid plate slowed to a walk and furrowed its way into the ground.

"Welcome to my hole, APE," Misha said.

"My, my, my, sir. I do love what you have done with the place." Ottiamig's voice cracked in a smile.

By way of reply, Misha called, "Hostiles in firing range. Team one, fire at will. Make sure you use plenty of tracers, so they know where we are. Keep them bunched up and coming through that little valley. Shoot any high bouncers moving up the slopes of the hills. I want them coming straight at team one. Teams two and three, check fire until they are well and truly cornered."

She stepped up to the edge of the crater and opened fire with high-explosive rounds that fell on the rear of the Orion troops. It had the effect of pushing the Orions forward into her mass driver fire.

Ottiamig took careful aim with his mass driver at an individual target. The figure blew backwards and crumpled to the ground. Misha toggled her comm for one-on-one with him and slapped the side of his helmet to get his attention.

"Negative, rookie, this isn't sniper school. Open it up. Fire controlled bursts of one to two seconds. Shift and fire again. Point at clusters, don't aim."

An H.E. round exploded in their faces, knocking both Misha and Ottiamig backwards into the hole. Misha could not tell if the red was the HUD interpretation of hostile fire or the explosion itself. She rolled with the blast and came up on her feet. Bounding forward she targeted the back side of the enemy troops and let loose with another barrage of return H.E. She sprayed the oncoming forces with a long sweeping burst of mass driver fire.

Misha's suit showed no damage. She quickly checked Ottiamig's vitals. His telltales didn't show any extensive damage, although he appeared to be in distress.

"Tuamma, report," Misha ordered.

"Sir, can't breathe. It feels like someone is sitting on my chest. I've got to open up to breathe."

"That is a negative, APE. You stay sealed. You're okay. Get on your feet. You can breathe if you can talk. We need your firepower." She reached down and grabbed his suit. With a grunt, she set him upright and tossed him onto the crater's lip. "Shoot, APE. Or they might as well bury us in this hole."

Ottiamig rolled into a prone position in the grass just outside of the crater rim and began firing controlled bursts. Misha nodded. He would do all right. She shot a barrage of electro-magnetic pulses, comms and heat jammers skyward.

Misha could see by her HUD that team one was pouring fire into the advancing armored enemy, but at this distance, they were barely making a mark. She recognized both mass driver fire and H.E. coming from Slezak's position. DeLaPax was also pouring fire into the opposing forces. Only Steinman wasn't firing.

"By the numbers team one, sitrep," Misha ordered. "Command is fully operational." Although her HUD showed her the location and status of each APE from all three teams, she wanted to hear from each trooper.

"Trooper Four DeLaPax, still firing. No damage. I have half magazine of H.E."

"Trooper Six Slezak, same-same, Third."

"Trooper Eight Ottiamig, I got a dent in my chest, but I am still loaded for bear, sir. My mass-driver ammo is showing low."

"Ottiamig, get back in this hole and on your feet. Set your suit to convert dirt and rocks to ammo. Move it, APE!" Misha shouted.

Misha didn't hear from Steinman. "DeLaPax, are you close to Steinman?"

"Not now, sir. I was when he got hit. Huge rock just smashed his legs to liquid. I think the suit sealed him up."

"Yes. He is medicated and his vitals are still not red. He will be fine if we can get dust-off out of here in the next day or so."

"They're almost on us. Damn it, Third. Do something!" Slezak shouted. Misha could hear the rising panic in her voice.

The enemy forces channeled neatly into the gap between the two hills. Misha knew either the enemy commander was an idiot or his suit didn't have the scanning capabilities to detect her trap. Either way she was not going to leave a wrapped present under the tree.

"Singletary and Park, you may open fire at your discretion, but listen APES, I want team one to snag at least a couple of prisoners out of this mess. Other than that, leave nothing but a brown streak in the dirt."

Singletary's team two opened fire on the left flank of the enemy and Park's team three opened up from the right. H.E. rained on the enemy forces blowing wide gaps in their ranks.

"They are starting to fall back," Park shouted.

"Team two, push at 'em," Misha shouted. "Watch your cross-fire zone. Team three, go airborne. Team one, move into them, I want those prisoners."

Misha bounced up from her crater and shot forward, putting all her momentum into a loping motion, hugging the ground. In the middle of one leap, an explosion pushed her feet out from under her. Two more explosions rocked the ground around her. She hit the ground rolling and came to her feet. Her HUD highlighted the explosions in green.

She launched herself forward again and crashed into the collapsing enemy front. Bodies scattered and broke as her more powerful armor impacted against the Orion suits. Misha's HUD tagged an Orion suit. It was emitting a high volume of comm traffic. It was broadcasting with enough power to push through her still active jammers. Logically, this must be a command suit, or at least a communications suit. She sent another barrage of jammers skyward.

She plowed her way through the enemy forces. Two suits reached out to grab her arms, while a third suit swung a hand carried mass driver muzzle toward her chest. Misha kicked her right foot forward. The foot impacted on the stock of the weapon and sent it sailing away.

She continued the kick on upward and slammed her boot heel into the faceplate of the man. Then, taking all the weight off her feet, she crashed to the ground on her back, breaking the grips on her arms. Rolling onto her shoulders, she whipped her feet into the mid-sections of the two men next to her. The man on the right collapsed backward as his armor buckled. The man on the left rolled with the kick. He leapt into the air bringing both feet together to come down onto Misha's helmet. She rolled. Instead of rolling away, she rolled into the man. When he came down his feet caught the edge of her twisting armor, knocking his feet out from under him. Misha, still on the ground, whipped her left leg around and impacted against the enemy soldier's helmet. Even through the armor, Misha could feel the blow. The helmet's inferior armor collapsed.

Misha flipped to her feet. She located the enemy command suit by her HUD's targeting and dashed after it. The enemy was in full retreat. She dove forward, becoming airborne. Her shoulder hit the torso of her target, driving him to the ground.

"Teams two and three, go airborne, pursue and destroy, except Trooper Cutler. Team one, consolidate any prisoners. Everyone meet back at point one minus one K south in twenty-five. Do not take any longer, or we will leave you behind," Misha ordered. "Cutler, find Steinman's locator on your TAC. He needs a medic. Call if you need assistance."

"Hey, Trey, I grabbed two prisoners," DeLaPax called over the comms. "Do I get to keep them both?"

"Good job, APE. Slezak, Ottiamig, prisoners?" Misha asked.

"Ottiamig here, sir, I grabbed one, but he is pretty busted up."

"That'll do. If he lives and if we can peel him out of his suit, we can see what Doc Cutler can do for him," Misha said.

"I am negative here, Third," Slezak reported. "Uh, mine just died on me."

"Roger that, trooper. Grab a hold of one of De La Paz's captures. Let's get them to the rally point."

Twenty-five minutes later, Able Squad stood at one kilometer south of point one. Misha did a mental tally. Only Steinman was seriously injured. Cutler said the man was stable, but needed to get to a med-bay to treat the leg stumps or the new legs might not attach. There was only so much physical trauma their combat enhanced med-nanites could repair.

A few troopers, including Ottiamig and herself had bruises, but when you are inside a suit, bruises don't show, so they don't matter. Three skid plates were non-functional due to the rock bombardment. The vitals on Slezak's suit were showing some redlining of non-critical systems. That is non-critical unless you are in combat and need them. They had three and a half prisoners.

Misha would have to keep a double dose of comm jammers in the air to block the prisoners from sending signals until they peeled them out of their suits. They also seriously depleted their stock of H.E. All in all, a very good outcome against ten to one odds.

"Sir, can I ask a question?" Ottiamig asked over the open squad comms.

"Sure, fire away, trooper." Misha was glad to see he used the open comms instead of the one-on-one comm with her that was available. It showed he wasn't shy about asking questions. And if you don't ask, then you don't know. This way on open comms everyone might learn.

"Why one kilometer south of point one? Why not just go to point one?"

"Good question. Anyone else want to field this? No takers? Okay, you APES, it is because it was raining rocks at point one. Does anyone know where those rocks were coming from? It sure wasn't these dung-for-brains grunts in the cheap off-the-rack combat suits. Whoever was throwing rocks knew where we were. One kilometer moved us far enough to get out of the rain. And south? Well, that was just the first direction that came to mind."

Misha continued, "DeLaPax, peel these cretins out of their suits without too much damage. I want to send them back to HQ for intelligence review."

"Roger that, Trey. What about any bio or chemical reaction on the prisoners?"

"It's their stuff if there is any here. I would call that poetic justice," Misha said. "Besides, scans don't show anything, so the best next test is on human subjects. We can go back to breathing something besides canned air if they live. However, we will still stay sealed up until we get to the squad bay for complete scans."

Misha continued. "We have to get the prisoners out of their suits to shut down their comms. We can't take them back to drop point with us if we can't peel them. Anyone tracking them would eventually locate them because of the dead air around our jammers. The quicker we get them peeled, the quicker we get back to drop point and into our bunkers.

"All right, you APES. Let's use standard squad stagger for movement and move by the numbers," Misha ordered. "We don't leave any of our equipment, or any captured Orion equipment behind. Double up on skid plates. Let's get this show back on the road."

She toggled the command switch deactivating the tri-wave simulation. One second they were fighting on an unnamed backwater planet in combat that felt, smelled and tasted as real as any action. The next second the squad lay in reclining lounge chairs in the training bay.

Misha checked her time and sighed wearily. The past three days took less than forty minutes. However, the whole ordeal felt as if it took three days worth of energy and she needed a rest. "Even so," she thought, "I still need to brush my teeth. Nevertheless, first I've got to take down Slezak."

Chapter Fifteen

Misha felt drained from the tri-wave sim. Last night's sleep had been fitful and it had been a rough morning. She pushed her entire unit almost to the dropping point in the past six hours. Each squad had run physical exercise where the seconds tested and probed for weakness. She insisted as many squads as possible spend time in the tri-wave simulators. Each trooper checked and rechecked, fitted and refitted their combat armor.

Only recently, she ordered the squad leaders to send their cooks off to prepare lunch. Her squad's cook was Steinman. He was still a bit shaky from having 'lost his legs' in the sims, but he looked eager enough to get back to the kitchen. The rest of the unit was humping excess cargo to the proper holds.

She saw Sergeant Forrester sitting on the deck by the hatch. She had been watching him off and on throughout the day as Second Takki-Homi's Charlie Squad ran him ragged. She even noticed Takki-Homi took him with his squad through the sim training. She smiled at the memory; Forrester came out of the tri-wave sim pale and sweating, but with a smile and eager to do it again.

Misha expected their cooks to call lunch break at any moment. Even though she remembered her lunch date with Forrester, she didn't need a shower as everyone smelled like fresh sweat. She planned on having him sit with her squad for lunch. Steinman's record indicated he was exceptionally well gifted in the kitchen. But she still had one task remaining before any break for lunch.

"Slezak, come here a minute." Misha waved the woman over to a quiet corner.

"Yes, Third, what can I do for you?" the woman said.

"I ran a computer check of our time in the sim. In fact, Trooper Slezak, I ran it twice. I will also tell you that I am recording this conversation on my glass-pack."

"I don't understand," Slezak said with more than a little unease.

"I think you do, Trooper Slezak. I suggest you request legal counsel now. No? That is fine by me. We both know you just tried to frag me in the sim."

"No, I didn't. It was an equipment malfunction. I documented that for the record. You can even check the suit logs for the damage. You can't prove anything else," Slezak whined.

"Oh, but I can. Slezak, you are stupid on three counts. Point one, I would accept the excuse of an equipment malfunction on one H.E. round, but you fired three. Your suit would have warbled a friendly fire alarm after the first round and shut down. You had to manually toggle the firing switch for each round. Point two, the computer timeline shows your suit took damage after you released the rounds. Point three, you tried to frag me in a sim? Are you that much of an idiot?" Misha said.

"It isn't real anyway. It wouldn't have really killed you. It's just a game," Slezak said.

"I believe we must amend your count of stupidity to four. People die in sims, trooper. They have for years. Ask Steinman how it feels to have your legs crushed. It is true very few APES die because of our physical conditioning. Our hearts are strong enough to take the stress. It is also true that there is abundant statistical data to bring you up on charges of attempted murder."

"Third McPherson?" a voice called from across the training bay.

Misha held up a finger to ask the voice for one minute.

"You just don't get it do you, Slezak? You're redlined as of now. Confine yourself to solitary in the squad bay. Post the order in writing on your bunk. Anytime, and I mean anytime, another APE is in the squad bay, you are to remain sealed in your bunk with the blast shutters down. Do it now." She stood watching as Slezak headed out the side hatch toward the squad bay. Misha thought she saw Slezak and Singletary share a passing glance, but it was furtive enough she couldn't be certain.

She turned to see who had called her. Standing by the hatch were the two spacer security escorts from before yesterday's dinner. Certain it was more bad news, Misha shook her head as she went to the hatch to greet them.

"Have my hall monitors come to visit?" Misha said.

"Not quite," said the short male. "Colonel Britaine requests that you meet him at 13:00 hours for a late lunch. He sent us to make sure you attended and didn't get lost. Get the meaning?"

"Yes, I think I do," Misha replied. She turned to Sergeant Forrester. "I am sorry Gan, but it seems I have been summoned again. I have to beg off our lunch date. Whatever his reasons, I do have to talk to Colonel Britaine. Besides, I hear you really should check out Deuce Taks cooking."

After a silent and tense walk, her two escorts delivered her to Britaine's office instead of the officer's mess. They bracketed the hatch and stood at ease.

Misha shook her head in wonder and pushed the comm button on the office hatch. A small chime sounded and the hatch opened silently. She stepped across the threshold and into the office.

The room had been reset as a dining area for two, complete with a table cloth, lit candles and what looked like real china table service. Any desk or office cabinets that might have been there were missing, probably shoved into a connecting room behind one of the other hatches. A bottle of wine was chilled to a perfect one degree Celsius in a crystal bucket; the neo-ice sparkling a deep electric blue.

Growing up on DropSix, Misha's family ate on banged up metal plates with common stainless steel forks and spoons. Hunting and work knives were used at family meals instead of table knives. Meals were raucous times with everyone talking at once. Food was not passed; it was grabbed. Rolls were tossed, whether they were buttered or not. Laughter and wrestling matches broke out with equal commonality. It was a fun, family time.

However, Misha's mother taught all of her children a variety of customs and manners for many different types of societies. She knew that in polite society, you didn't talk with food in your mouth and you chewed with your mouth closed. She knew which fork was for shellfish and which spoon was for the sorbet. She knew that on Camden Prime you ate snails with your fingers and on New China you ate snails with tiny trident-like forks. She knew a spitlaise was a fine wine from the fourth harvest of grapes in the western European region of Earth One and a frostaire was a really crappy wine from any harvest on Gastalt. Britaine was in for a surprise if he meant this lunch to be intimidating.

The only person in room was the same master sergeant Misha had seen on her first day aboard. He apparently served as Britaine's steward. She nodded to him and gave him a quick smile.

"If it pleases the Third," he said, pulling her chair out and gesturing her to her seat.

"Thank you, Master Sergeant," she said. "I presume my host is delayed?"

"Yes, Third, he should be along in about..." The man consulted his glass-pack's time piece, "ninety seconds."

True enough, in ninety seconds Britaine stepped into the room. He smiled broadly at Misha as she stood to greet him. He waved her back into her seat. "Good afternoon, Third McPherson." He sat opposite her and dismissed the steward with a wave of his hand. "I thought it might be best for us to meet alone and put some air under our wings to give our relationship a bit more lift.

"I agree, Colonel. We do not have much time together, but I believe we can spend that time for our mutual benefit."

"I am glad you said that, Third. I know we just had an unfortunate clash since we are both powerful people. Who knows, we may both be on the Kiirkegaard for a long time," Britaine said. "Wine? It is a strong, heady vintage from the Australian Compact Sector. From the New Queensland region, I believe." He tapped his glass-pack signaling for the steward.

Misha smiled. "I have heard produce from the Australian Compact was considered contraband, so I am eager to see what they have to offer."

Britaine smiled, "Well, rank doth have its privileges."

Behind Britaine's back the Master Sergeant's eyes rolled upward and he quickly turned his head away from Misha's glance.

Britaine filled her glass and said. "I offer a toast to the Allied Systems and to new friendships."

"To the Allied Systems and to new friendships," she replied. Silently, she added, "Whoever they may be."

The master sergeant quickly served their meal and silently disappeared. Misha enjoyed the food despite having to listen to Britaine's monologue about his career. She only needed to add a "hum" or "ah" occasionally to hold up her end of the conversation.

While the meal began to wind down it was obvious Britaine was not. He continued to ramble from one self-aggrandized heroic tale to the next. Misha dabbed her mouth with her napkin, placed it on her plate and waited patiently for an opening. Finally, Britaine took a break for air.

Misha quickly interrupted, "You know, Colonel. I could sit and share war stories for hours on end. I have enjoyed myself immensely. But, I was wondering if I could seek your advice?"

"Certainly, that is what I am here for," he smiled.

Misha thought to herself, "I am sure that is what you think. I wonder why he really asked me to lunch." She had a brief visual image of Britaine's hands sliding softly over her naked skin. With a quick shake of her head, she cleared the picture from her mind. Yes, he was gorgeous and he might be fun in the rack, but he was an arrogant prick. The sex wouldn't be worth the problems. She thought, "I doubt if he is looking at me as more than another notch on his flight stick."

Misha smiled at Britaine, "I am planning on working my APES as hard as I possibly can."

104

"Good for you," he applauded. "They need a bit of shaping up."

"Yes, Colonel, they are a good bunch of people, but we do have a long way to go. I can only push them in APES training so far. I am not worried about their physical conditioning. For the most part, that seems to be from very good to excellent. I don't want them to go into mental overload before we get to our destination."

"Yes, I can see how that might be a problem with your people," Britaine nodded. "I can make our library and game rooms available to you as a diversion, if that would help?"

"Well, Colonel. I am not sure I am worried about recreation at this point. We don't have that much time left. I do not want to leave my APES with much free time, but I don't want to keep pushing training sessions and inspections on them all day every day. I would like to request permission to integrate my APES with your spacers on a time permitting basis. This would allow my people to use some of their secondary and tertiary skills. Many of them transferred from the AMSF to the APES. This should keep them mentally active, but off of their normal duties. Keep them from going stale, as it were."

Britaine looked thoughtful, "Well, I can see how that might benefit your people, but I don't think so. I don't want to be blunt, but my crew doesn't need any ham-handed grunts mucking about. Present company accepted."

Misha smiled sweetly and nodded.

He continued. "I hope you understand. My officers and I have built a highly trained war machine. I am sure your people may have been, shall we say, adequate when they were with the AMSF. But really, that may have been ten or fifteen years ago, or even more. And I am sure you know if they were any good with the AMSF, then they would not have left to become a grunt, right?"

Misha continued smiling sweetly, "Thank you for lunch, Colonel. It has been very enlightening. If you will excuse me, I do have to go baby sit my children."

Britaine, oblivious to the sarcasm in her voice, stood to show her out. Misha felt his hand slide along the small of her back as he guided her to the hatch. She adjusted her uniform slightly, giving it a small tug to dislodge his hand. She smiled at how nice it felt in a creepy sort of way.

Chapter Sixteen

AMSF Master Sergeant Twiller Bruce, the Colonel's steward bumped into APES Second-Level Commander Rice Bilideau, Dawg Squad's general supplies clerk. They were alone in one of the Kiirkegaard's storage holds.

"Well, Beans," Bruce said. "It sure seems like your new boss and the OAIC have finally made a truce."

"OAIC?" Bilideau asked.

"Yeah. You know: Old Asshole in Charge, that serious waste of an officer's uniform, Old-Scrotum-For-Brains, Britaine."

Bilideau looked thoughtful. "The last word I heard was they weren't getting along."

"Crap!" Bruce said. "That must be a cover for what is really going on. I tell you they just had one of Britaine's quiet, intimate lunches. And you know what I mean by intimate, right?"

"Yeah, I heard he ran our Deuce Vark through one of his lunches. It was a lunch that lasted all afternoon. She came back all smiles and cheery, you know. But, he must have got what he wanted and dumped her fast. She got blocked out of the officer's country faster than a thick turd gets stuck in a plugged toilet," Bilideau said.

"Her and every other thing with female DNA on this bird," Bruce agreed.

"Except that old chief master sergeant you got in intelligence. What's her name?"

"You mean Chief Brown? Yeah, I think he's scared of her. Hell, most of us are scared of her. She's tougher'n sun soaked shoe soup. Her nickname is Dead-eye and she got the name on the gun range. I know Britaine thinks with his dick and it is may be hard to tell but I don't think he is that stupid."

Bilideau nodded, "So, how come you think he dicked McPherson? And why the hell would he? I mean, she ain't much of a looker."

"I don't know about that. She is attractive enough in her own way," Bruce said.

"Yeah, like my dog's butt!" Bilideau grimaced.

"Hell's bells, grunt. I've been Britaine's steward for almost a standard year now. He would boff her for no other reason than the challenge. And I saw them come out all friendly and smiling. I've seen it before. Man, he even put his hand on her ass in front of his security goons. Yeah, he tapped into her goodies for sure."

Chapter Seventeen

Forrester shook his head as the young spacer walked away. As always, he was amazed at the amount of information he could gather just by wandering the hallways and indulging in a bit of gossip here and there. He was certain eighty percent of all gossip had a truth at its roots, and fully half of all gossip dealt with mission or command-related issues.

It only was a few hours since McPherson's lunch with Britaine. Already the rumor and propaganda machine was generating its usual swill about their tryst. "Not that I care," he tried to tell himself, but he caught himself at his own lie. He wasn't jealous even if it was true. Forrester just liked Misha. She was almost too good for her own good. She had great potential. It would be a shame to see her command collapse because of a mistaken affair with a jerk like Britaine.

Forrester knew the enlisted crew hated Britaine. Britaine's fellow officers didn't hate him, but universally distrusted him. In the past, Britaine burned too many contemporaries in his climb up the promotion ladder. The hatred, resentment and wariness were almost palatable.

Contact between spacers and APES was limited, but on a spacecraft, even one this big, it was impossible to hold back any rumor this juicy from spreading into both camps. Forrester was sure he was not the first person outside of the AMSF who heard of what supposedly went on between Britaine and McPherson. As a matter of fact, Forrester already heard the story three times, each time with differing details.

When Forrester pressed this last spacer about whether it was rumor or truth the man had replied, "It's gotta be true: where there is water someone is gonna get wet."

Forrester doubted whether McPherson had been seen buttoning up her uniform as she left Britaine's office. He doubted it for two reasons. One: he didn't think she was that foolish or careless. Two: APES uniforms don't have buttons.

Still, he intended to hunt her down. He might find out a bit of truth if he could be tactful enough. Forrester wasn't an incurable gossip. He long ago accepted himself as a true died-in-the-wool analyst. He would worry at a problem or a puzzle until it unraveled revealing its secrets. McPherson was definitely a puzzle.

Forrester found McPherson in her day office. She was sitting with her feet on the desk scanning rapidly through data on her glass-pack, flashing images against a blank bulkhead. The room was now spotless since her predecessor had left. He could see she hadn't added one iota of clutter to the room. It was bare and clean as if no one had ever used it. No personal items were visible.

Forrester tried an old fashioned knock on the hatch frame.

Startled at the sudden noise, Misha looked up. "Well, Sergeant Forrester. Are you here to beg off of this afternoon's training? Did Charlie Squad run you through the spin cycle, already?

Forrester smiled. "Actually, I wanted to thank you for the time your people gave me. Taks is a very instructive man to have around."

"Yes," she said. "Not too instructive, I hope. We don't want all of our APES secrets leaking out to the Marshal Service."

Forrester laughed, "It is nothing like that, I can assure you. After what you put me through this morning, I am not sure I want to know about any secrets if you have any of them."

"I am sure you've heard the first day of training is always the hardest. Well, that is hogstuffings; the first day is always the easiest." She smiled. "Keep on coming, Gan. We will make an APE out of you yet."

"We will not make an APE of me at my age, child. However, I will try to keep up with you folks for most of this trip. Lord knows I can use the exercise." He patted a non-existent paunch.

"So, Gan, are you on a mission or did you just wander by my office for a social call?"

"A little of both and some of neither," he replied. "You know how we Marshal Service guys are; we're always spreading rumor and propaganda."

"Ah," Misha said. "My lunch with Britaine has hit the gossip circuit?"

"Well, now that you mention it, I do seem to have over heard a thing or two," he said.

"It was lunch, a bit of idle chatter and some minor business discussions. It was nothing more; end of story," Misha said.

Forrester frowned. "I am not trying to get into your personal business, Misha. No, don't interrupt. Just accept this bit of advice from a nice meddling old man. Britaine doesn't have a good reputation with women. Be careful of him. Nothing has to happen for people to think it happened. It is old advice, but try to avoid the appearance of anything wrong, okay?"

"Not okay. It is none of your business. Nothing happened between Britaine and me," Misha caught herself blushing. "Dammit, Gan, look what you made me do."

"That is an interesting shade of red." He smiled trying to ease the tension. "He is a pretty sort of fellow, isn't he?"

Misha's blush deepened. She looked for something to throw at Forrester.

"Easy, Misha," he laughed. "I believe you. Nothing happened with Britaine. I didn't believe it when I came in here. I am just passing along what I heard. He isn't a very well liked commander and that is putting it mildly. You could get hurt by association."

"Your warning is taken, mother. Do you want me to clean my room and do my homework, too?" she continued. "Hey! Have you had much time on skid plates? We are giving our rookies training this afternoon at 15:00 hours. Be there?"

Chapter Eighteen

Second Jackson looked at the seven newbies gathered around him, four from his Foxtrot Squad and three from Second Portland's Easy Squad. McPherson also saddled him with the sergeant from the Marshal Service.

Jackson thought, "Not a bad bunch of rookies. Hell, I've seen worse." He said loudly, "Damn sorry looking bunch of FNGs, I swear I haven't seen a worse looking bunch of numb-nuts in all my years. But, maybe you ain't hopeless. For that matter, even if you are hopeless, it doesn't matter. We are in this together, got it?"

A rousing chorus of 'roger that' answered him.

"You!" Jackson shouted at a trooper. "What are you?" She was a short woman from Easy Squad.

"Trooper Nine Sheila Ramirez, I am Easy Squad's medical technician," the woman shouted.

Jackson shouted back. "No. Dammit. I didn't ask who you are. I asked what you are. You are a combat grunt; a malevolent, unpleasant killing instrument. You are one bad ass, tough s.o.b. You are infantry in the Allied Protective Expeditionary Services. You are an APE. You are armored infantry. You are armored, mobile infantry. There is heavy emphasis on mobile and extra emphasis on hostile."

In a calmer voice he said, "Everybody got that? Everybody fights. Ramirez, you are a med tech second and an APE first. Everyone in this bunch is a rookie, a newbie. And you will be a rookie until and if you survive your first combat dirt drop. We will seal you into your armor, strap you to your skid plate and drop you out the ass end of a cargo pod into the atmosphere of a hostile planet. Upon hitting the surface you will engage the enemy and you will kill it. That is what we do. Are there any questions?"

Without waiting for a response he continued. "Deuce Portland has taken all the veterans from Easy and Foxtrot. I got the rare privilege of showing you the ins and outs of the skid plate. Pay attention to what is going on around you. You are not mindless robots. If the government wanted robots, they would have built robots. Instead, they wanted you. You're cheaper to build and replace, I guess."

Ramirez said, "Yeah, and easier to fix. I oughta know." A smattering of nervous laughter died quickly under Jackson's glare.

"True enough," Jackson said, "But our suits are designed to take damage our bodies can't. And what damage our bodies do sustain, Ramirez will fix. Ain't that right, trooper?"

"Right, Deuce. If you break it, I will fix it. I am good at it," she replied.

Jackson nodded. "That is fair enough. Look, people, Third McPherson took you rookies from your normal squad structure for one reason. That is training on your skid plates. We are a mobile force. Our bodies may be conditioned to run fifty kilometers in a day and fight at the end. Our suits let us run five hundred kilometers in a day and fight at the end. But, our skid plates let us ride five thousand kilometers in a day and fight at the end, plus they give us air superiority. They give us high ground. So, we gotta learn to use them and use them right. I know every one of you has had tri wave simulator direct feed education in the operation and handling of the skid plate, everyone except maybe Sergeant Forrester. You have the control operations embedded in your muscle memory. Plus, everyone in this group, including Sergeant Forrester has spent time in the sims practicing operation of the skid plates. You have all spent time in the saddle, as it were."

Jackson continued, "My job this afternoon is to show you some tricks. There isn't much we can do in this squad bay, due to space limitations. We are going climb aboard, so be careful. Pay attention to what is going on around you."

Jackson frowned at the group. "This is a serious exercise. It may seem like a kindergarten recess game, but in about a week or so we are going to follow Third McPherson onto some unprocessed mud ball. We are going to get our payback from those Binder bastards for what they did to our brothers on Guinjundst. If we aren't at our best, if we can't do our best, then the Third can't use us to kill those frakking weed eaters. Nothing and nobody is going to get in my way, understand? So, you will get good from the ground up. Are there any questions yet?"

There was a determined silence from the group.

Jackson nodded. "All right, APES. Your skid plates are grounded in place. Get on them."

Suddenly, he shouted, "Keep them grounded and powered off!" In a normal tone of voice he continued, "Good. We are going to play Simon Sez. Follow my movements and do exactly as I say when I say it. The key to skid plate operations is control."

For forty-eight minutes Jackson called out command after command. The group before him swayed and twisted with him, some catching on faster than others. With their skid plates off and grounded it looked like a modern jazz dance group practicing some weird aboriginal mating dance. Each movement they practiced could send a skid plate racing, dipping and swirling around the sky.

Much to Jackson's surprise, he was unable to shake Sergeant Forrester from the routine. The marshal met every one of Jackson's moves, even down to the irregular finger twitches. "Damn," Jackson thought. "Taks said he was good, but I didn't bite. He doesn't look like much, but he is a tougher nut to crack than I thought."

"Take five, APES," Jackson finally shouted. "Hydrate or die! Water up, APES."

Jackson turned to watch the activity around the squad bay. Second Portland was working the veterans of Easy and Foxtrot Squads though a series of vigorous exercises. He did a quick check on his veterans in the group. Trooper Four Dashell had a tendency to slack off if he wasn't being pushed, but Portland had his number and was riding him hard.

All around the training bay there were groups of veterans and groups of rookies. The seconds were pushing everyone hard. He spotted Third McPherson in a far corner with the veterans from Able Squad and Vark's Joker Squad. A small rush raced through his system when he saw McPherson. He was surprised to find he was getting sexually excited just watching her. Jackson shook his head to clear it. He knew she wasn't the prettiest thing around, far from it. Sexually, he knew he would rather be with Deuce Vark. He looked around until he spotted the tall blonde woman with a group of rookies. "That is one fine looking babe," he thought. He looked back at Third McPherson. "No comparison. And DeLaPax is with her. Man, I would kill for a piece of that action." He looked over his shoulder to check on his group of rookies. "Hellfire," he thought. "I think even Ramirez would be a better lay than the boss." He turned back to watch McPherson. He wondered if her being the boss must be what was yanking his crank. Other women might give him sexual pleasure, but Third McPherson was going to give him revenge on the Binders and the thought of that was what was giving him a woody.

He continued watching McPherson as she put her group of veterans into a circle. She put Trooper Beaudry from Joker Squad and Trooper Juarez from Able Squad in the middle. At some signal he couldn't see from his vantage point, the circled APES attacked the two troopers. Beaudry and Juarez were quickly overwhelmed and went down. He could see McPherson nodding and patting the two men on the back. Beaudry gestured wildly with his hands, obviously showing her what he had done wrong. McPherson grabbed Beaudry in a headlock. She laughed and rubbed his hair with her knuckles. She then spun him around and a well-placed boot pushed him back into the outer ring as the circle reformed.

Jackson said to himself, "Nuggies! I haven't seen someone getting nuggies since I was twelve."

"What was that, Deuce?" Jackson turned to see Forrester standing next to him.

"Nuggies, Sergeant Forrester." He pointed into the direction of McPherson. "The boss just gave Beaudry a nuggie and then kicked him in the butt."

Forrester smiled, "I take it that is not usual conduct for APES?"

Jackson smiled back. "I should say not. I don't know how she knows, but the big sister act is the perfect approach for Beaudry. He is kind of the loner type, you know. Doesn't seem to fit in, even after, what, maybe forty years in the APES. He has got four times as much time in service as Vark. But, Vark got the promotion to Joker Squad second, not him. For that matter, Spakney's got a ton more time than Vark, but who the hell would want that piece of shit for a commander? Hell, I'd follow Vark into combat just to watch her ass swing and sway."

Jackson pointed. "Hey! Check this out, I think she is going to take her time in the barrel."

As the two men watched Misha and Trooper Putinova stood in the center of the circle. Putinova was a petite blonde woman from Joker Squad. At the signal, the circle appeared to collapse as the veteran troopers rushed the two. Misha grabbed Putinova around the chest and whirled about. Putinova kicked with her feet, flailing at any unprotected head, arm, or chest. Two troopers were knocked off their feet and rolled out of the melee. Misha spun Putinova around so the two stood back to back. Misha spun sideways, slamming into two troopers trying to force an opening on Putinova's flank. The force of her drive knocked both troopers to the ground and out of the exercise. Putinova quickly leaped onto Misha's back and vaulted upward, coming down into a group of troopers. None hit the ground, but their planned assault was broken before it began. Misha grabbed Putinova by the uniform collar and yanked her into place so they again stood back to back. The circle of troopers hesitated and watched for an opening. Misha stood on the balls of her feet, arms outstretched, like a wrestler while Putinova slid back and forth from one foot to the next in a rhythm that only she could hear.

Jackson said, "Teamwork Sergeant Forrester. She is teaching them teamwork. If she and Putinova work together the others will have a rough time taking them down. They will have to work as a team to do it."

116

The two men watched. The attackers feigned a rush from the flanks and then a group drove into Putinova, overcoming her and swarming over Misha. Bodies were tossed and thrown about. No one, no matter how well trained could stand up to the mass rush of half a dozen APES. Misha went down momentarily. She jumped up laughing and slapped the back of Trooper Park of Able Squad who had put her down. Park shrugged it off, but Jackson could see that it hadn't settled well with the little man that he hadn't been able to do it alone.

Jackson saw Misha turn away quickly. Even from this distance her face flushed red. Almost anyone else would have thought it was the rush of activity that pushed the blood to her face, but he had been watching far too closely for that. Initially, he thought it was Park's silent rebuke of her compliment that embarrassed her, but he saw her eyes glance up. He looked up at the observation gallery overlooking the training bay. He could see Colonel Britaine smiling down at her.

"Damn," he thought. "What is that martinet doing down here with us working stiffs? Aw hell, he wouldn't tell anyone why he was watching us even if he had a good reason for being here. That man plays it closer to the chest than industrial-strength pasties on a double-d stripper. Shit, those rumors about him and McPherson must be true. Well, I don't give a rat's patootie. She can play with fancy boy all she wants to, but she is mine when it's time to go to the dance." Jackson turned back to his lounging rookies, "Okay you lazy APES. Back up on your skid plates. We got too much work to do without you lollygagging around all afternoon."

Chapter Nineteen

Gan Forrester stepped back onto the skid plate shaking his head quietly. He saw Misha's reaction to Britaine and Jackson's reaction to the whole thing. Plus, he had mixed reactions of his own. It was true Misha was a young woman with needs; it shouldn't be anyone's business where she found comfort. Plus, it was Britaine's command. He could go anywhere on the spacecraft he wanted. But, didn't the man have enough sense than to show up here? He suddenly realized it would be up to Britaine's usual standards to deliberately start rumors about McPherson. Then when she failed at her first command, he would be justified in his previously stated opinion that she wasn't up to command standards.

Second Jackson shouted, "Get your mind on your job, Forrester."

"Roger that, Mr. Jackson. Sorry."

"Don't be sorry. Be right," Jackson bellowed. "The next exercise is a bitch. We power on our skid plates, lift off and hover, I repeat, we will hover. No one is to go above one inch over the deck; one inch, no more no less with no side-to-side movement. I have manual override logged in through my glass-pack on everyone's skid plates. Excess movement and you fail. I will ground you. This calls for serious muscle control on your part. Lift off now."

Forrester tapped the up switch and rocked back slightly on his heels. The feeling was much the same as he had experienced in the tri wave sim earlier this morning. It wasn't so much feeling that the skid plate was moving, but that the skid plate was standing still and everything else was moving. He couldn't tell how high he was hovering. One inch was not very elevated and there were no shadows to give him a clue. He ducked his head quickly to see if he could gauge the distance. The skid plate slipped sideways with the movement. He banged into another trooper.

"Sorry. Sorry," Forrester apologized. He steadied himself and tried to calm every muscle, demanding

118

nothing move. He was out of position from where he started. Even so, as he eyed the rest of the rookies, he noticed a number of them were already grounded. The rest of his group was no longer in neat little rows. Out the corner of his eye, he saw Second Jackson gesturing wildly at a trooper whose skip plate was hovering about four feet up. He could barely hear Jackson as the second tapped his glass-pack, dropping the trooper to the deck with a crash.

Jackson shouted, "One inch. Get 'em down, you APES."

Forrester thought he had been low. "Okay," he said to himself. "Lower. Ease it down until we are almost touching. Lower…lower…lower…" He felt a thump. He immediately thought he had gotten too low and bumped the deck, but then he realized he was laying flat on his back, staring up at the ceiling.

"Ground 'em, now," Jackson yelled. "Sergeant Forrester, what the hell are you doing?"

"You know, Mr. Jackson, I am not sure. It seemed like a good time to take a break."

Trooper Ramirez's face appeared over his own. "I am sorry, Sergeant."

"About what, young lady?"

Jackson guffawed, "'About what?' he asked. Ramirez knocked you off your skid plate and then ran you over with hers. Get it back up, man. You've got to set an example for the rest of the children."

Ramirez stuck out her arm, "Hand up?"

"Well, thank you Trooper Ramirez," Forrester said. "But it seems that my arm isn't quite working up to normal parameters."

Ramirez knelt down next to him and ran her fingers down his arm. When he winced with pain, she said. "Sorry, Sergeant Forrester. Damn, I'm a medic; I am supposed to fix people, not break them."

Second Jackson said, "Come on, you two. Play time later. Let's get to it."

"I broke his arm, Deuce," Ramirez said.

"Damn, Ramirez. Okay. Get him up and fix him up. You're a med tech, right?"

Forrester looked up to see Misha approach. He smiled up at her.

Smiling back at Forrester she said, "I see that you have found a new way to mess up my training schedule."

"Yep," Forrester said. "I thought maybe Trooper Ramirez needed additional time to practice her medical training."

Misha nodded. "Maybe so, but it looks to me like she needs more practice on her skid plate. Don't you agree, Mr. Jackson?"

"I do indeed, sir," Jackson replied.

"Gan, do you think you can survive a walk over to the Kiirkegaard's sick bay? Yes? Good. I will escort you myself. That would leave Deuce Jackson and Trooper Ramirez to their training. What do you say?"

Forrester found himself nodding. Ramirez helped him up by his other arm. He was surprised to find himself a bit dizzy.

"I am sorry, again, Sergeant Forrester. I don't know what happened," Ramirez said.

"Not to worry, Sheila. I'll heal, not as fast as you APES with your combat enhanced nanites, but I will heal." He turned to see Misha patting Jackson on the back and smiling.

"Good job, Jackson," she said. "At least, when you broke one, it wasn't one of ours." Before the man could protest, she smiled. "Kidding, Race. I am only kidding. You are doing a great job. We don't have much time left and I can see you are making good progress with the time we have. You've got no complaints from me."

She turned to Forrester. "Ready?"

Forrester followed along behind her, but when he caught up with her in the hallway just beyond the hatch to the training bay, he said, "I can make this trip myself. I do know where I am going."

"That's all right, Gan. You make a good excuse for me to take a break without huffing and puffing in front of my troops."

Forrester tried to think of another way he could make the trip to sick bay on his own, but he was unable to come up with an excuse. He needed to make a trip to sickbay to meet with someone, but it would be difficult for him to touch base with his undercover contact if Misha was with him. Nothing came to mind. He would have to deal with things as he could.

Someone called to them as they stepped into the sick bay, "Sergeant Forrester, looks like you got a bit banged up. Playing out of your league?"

Forrester smiled wanly, "Dr. Dimms, I believe you have met Third McPherson."

Dr. Dimms smiled, "Why yes, I believe we met when you first came aboard, didn't we?"

Misha nodded. "Yes, sir, and we met again at the Colonel's table."

"Well, McPherson. First, you take on an AMSF commander and then you physically abuse a sergeant in the Allied Marshal Service. What's next, a full-scale assault on your own troops?" Dimms asked.

"Enough, Puke," Forrester said. "It wasn't her fault. I wasn't paying attention and got my arm broke. It is my own fault. Misha was just polite enough to escort me here. So, can you fix me or not?"

"Sure, sure. Don't get your skivvies in a twist. I'll get someone to fix you right up. Rezzi, front and center. Busted arm from the looks of it." Rezzi was a very small woman with large dark eyes, olive skin and black shiny hair.

"Come on, Puke," Forrester said. "You're the doctor, can't you fix it? Nothing personal, young lady, no offense." He smiled at Rezzi.

"None taken, sir. Doctor, I do have all of those HQ reports that have to be re-initialized and encrypted," Rezzi replied.

"Nonsense," Dimms said. "Medical Technician Staff Sergeant Jèsusa Rezzi is one of the best we've got. There is nothing I can do for a broken arm that she can't." Dimms left before anyone else could get a word in.

Forrester smiled at Rezzi. "Well, I guess it is just you and me, doll."

Rezzi laughed, "Watch it, old man. I could always set this arm crooked." She turned to Misha. "Thanks for bringing me my patient, but I can take it from here."

To Forrester's dismay, Misha said, "I will stick around with Sergeant Forrester if you don't mind. Just to make sure he is okay."

Rezzi said, "I can assure you that he is in good hands. I'll take care of him like he is one of my own."

"I can wait," Misha said with finality.

Forrester smiled, "Okay, ladies. Let's not get in a catfight over me. There is enough of me to go around."

Misha laughed, "The hell you say. There isn't enough muscle on you to make a decent meal for a petite woman like myself."

Forrester laughed back, "Ah, so I see that your tastes do run to larger men. Say AMSF officers?"

Rezzi looked up from her work and frowned.

Misha missed the look on Rezzi's face as the blood rushed to her own face. She tried to turn away, but Forrester grabbed her with his good hand.

"Sorry, Misha," he said. "That was a bad joke."

"Not funny, Gan. I told you nothing was going on between Britaine and me. Besides," she glanced quickly at Rezzi, then back to Forrester, "this is not the appropriate forum to discuss that anyway."

Rezzi said, "Don't mind me, I am only the help. I do my work and do my time. What goes on in officer country is for others with better minds than mine to decipher."

"See there, Misha," Gan said. "It is just as if we were alone. Anyway, if Britaine isn't interested…or interesting, what was he doing watching you work out in the training bay?"

"I didn't say he wasn't interested," Misha said. "I am just telling you that nothing is going on. You'll have to ask him if you want to know what he was doing watching APES train."

"Well, he wasn't watching APES train, Misha. He was watching you. Besides, I don't hear you saying you aren't interested in him."

"Gan, it is a good thing you are already in sick bay, because you are about two seconds away from needing more medical attention," Misha said.

"Whoa, people," Rezzi said. "I just fixed the one broken arm. Let's not have any more."

Surprised, Forrester said, "Done?"

"Yep, all fixed. It should be solid in about four days so don't stress it too much. Now get out of my sick bay. I've got real work to get done."

Chapter Twenty

"Hey, vacuum head!" Trooper Dashell, the Foxtrot Squad med tech called out. "Have I got a deal for you!"

The spacer looked up from the counter. "What, APEShit? You don't got nothing that I need. Besides you got your own supplies. You don't need to be dipping into the Kiirkegaard's medical storage."

"Nah, it is not that kind of a deal, junior." Dashell said. "I hear that you've got a box of Orion Confed blue smokes?"

"Yeah, so what? They ain't illegal, just hard to come by."

"I know, I know," Dashell said. "I just thought we might make a trade."

"Yeah, like I said, you ain't got nothing I want."

Dashell smiled, "Leave us not be hasty. I hear that you might be in the market for Binder technology?"

The spacer looked up quickly. "Well, I might be. What have you got?"

"A scythe; it is even battle chipped." Dashell said.

"Really?" The young man's eyes light up. "Maybe it is from Guinjundst?"

"Nah, I can't lie to you, kid," Dashell replied. "Nothing is coming from Guinjundst. Anybody tries to tell you different is a liar. Everything was quarantined, classified and sent to intelligence for review."

"Yeah," the spacer said. "Everything but your new boss; I thought maybe she snuck something out."

"I doubt it. Security is pretty tight on that one. So do we have a deal?"

"Why not? If our bosses can get together, then I don't see why we can't."

"Yeah? What have you heard?" Dashell asked.

"Well, just between us, I don't usually spread gossip. I got this first hand. I was delivering medical supplies to the sick bay. McPherson was in there with that Marshal Sergeant. They were talking about Britaine. She blushed like a school girl every time he mentioned

Britaine's name. I couldn't hear it all, but I did hear her say she was interested in him."

Chapter Twenty-One

Able Squad's Trooper One Gates Singletary cursed just loud enough that only Park, Juarez and Slezak could hear him. Not that he cared. The only other APE in the squad bay was that whiner Steinman.

"Come on Steinman. Move it! Don't you have somewhere else to be?" Juarez yelled across the squad bay.

"Shut up, Miguel," Slezak said. "For all we know that little weasel will run straight to the bitch."

"He won't if he knows what's good for him," replied Park. "Besides, what would he have to tell her? That we are talking loud. Wooooo, I'm scared."

Slezak said, "All right for you, dipwad. But, I am under house arrest, remember? I ain't supposed to be out of my box. You might get a slap on the wrist for talking to me, but, I would get put in the stockade."

Singletary nodded. "Yeah, yeah, yeah. Zip it up all of you." He shook his head. "Damn, I hate these combat jump lock downs. They always give me a headache."

"Yeah, you and every other creature with human DNA. Quit'cher bitchin'," Park said. "We ain't got much time."

"Yeah, all right," Singletary agreed.

Singletary thought that it has been a long lockdown for such a short jump. The AMSF bastards decided to use these jumps to practice combat entry into a simulated battle. All he knew about it was that it required all personnel to be strapped into their stations. For the APES, this meant they were strapped into their bunks with the blast shutters in place. The engines pushed to the maximum speed in normal space; then without warning the spacecraft would snap into sub-space, spin and roll for twenty or thirty minutes, and snap back into ordinary space. Since it was a combat insertion and might mean a high probability of enemy presence, the flight crew would run a computer-generated random flight pattern that would cause the spacecraft to tumble, twist and turn just barely within the

126

limits of the inertial dampers and anti-gravity systems. For an AMSF squadron or wing combat insertion, multiple spacecraft computers linked into a real-time network to avoid collision with the friendly spacecraft. The flight crew would retake control only after the automated targeting systems assessed any possible enemy presence.

"Now with this damn headache that bitch McPherson got us volunteered to stand at AMSF stations," Singletary complained. "I quit the AMSF because I hated standing station on spacecraft."

Park smiled, "Hell, Gates. There ain't nobody here but us chickens. We all know you left the AMSF one step ahead of a court-martial because you were running their quarter master's supply room like your personal garage sale."

Slezak nodded, "Yeah. You got to agree that the APES let you scrounge a bit more creatively-"

"Or at least, Cans did," Juarez interrupted, seeing the look of irritation on Singletary's face. "McPherson seems to have a different attitude. And anyway, how the hell did she get Britaine to agree to us standing watch? Everybody knows he thinks ground troops are a waste of military spending."

Slezak nodded, "All I can say is she must be better in the rack than Vark. I can't imagine it, but it must be true."

"The word is he refused her request the first time on us standing stations and she had to ask him twice. But, it doesn't matter how," Singletary said. "Maybe we can use this time creatively, push for a few contacts to replenish our lost stock. Since we are only getting assigned as bottom-rung assistants on the first watch, we'll have to be careful. First watch is where all of their best crew gets put. Some of those guys are pretty gung-ho and on the up-and-up so watch yourselves. That bitch McPherson may have dumped our inventory, but she didn't take us out of the game, got me?"

Everyone nodded their agreement.

Singletary continued. "Miguel, I hear that Dashell from Foxtrot made a new trade contact in the med storeroom. Talk to him and see what the deal is, find out if we can get in on whatever he has cooking. And Jem Li, your old AMSF station was fighter bay maintenance. I know you've got some side connections with Ivanov and Jacobis over there. Push 'em on whatever inventory we can turn for them, got it? And Aimee, dear stupid little Aimee."

"Ah, come on, Gates. Get off my back," Slezak said.

"In a tri wave sim? What the hell were you thinking? Never mind. We can't do a thing about it now. You'll probably get down checked for this upcoming op, but she can't make any serious charges stick. She might force a transfer on you after that. Shit, if you had been a bit smarter, we could have used you to get some cameras dropped into a couple of the AMSF women's bays. I never understood why those prudes separate the sexes and then build special private comfort rooms to let them get back together. Anyway, I got a guy in the AMSF who would pay big bucks for the right pictures of the right female spacer, or you could have got some of your AMSF girlfriends to do some amateur porn gigs for us. Never mind, it's a done deal, just get back in your box."

Chapter Twenty-Two

Misha stepped through the hatch into the intelligence vault. It was called a vault because it was more like a bank safe than any normal room aboard a spacecraft. The hatch was a meter thick with massive tumbler locks and deadbolts as wide as her arm. To gain entry, she buzzed through a dedicated and hardwired intercom. She had her glass pack scanned and knew as she stepped through the hatchway the security devices physically scanned her for weapons, recording devices, hidden cameras, and dozens of other items not allowed in the vault. The hatchway automatically transmitted a signal to glass packs, shutting them down upon entry. From her duty tour in AMSF intelligence she knew the bulkheads were packed with high tech counter surveillance gear. No scan could penetrate into its interior and any effort to do so would trigger ear-shattering alarms throughout the craft.

Misha was surprised to see Gan Forrester sitting on the corner of a desk. How he had found a clear space on the desk to park even his small posterior would be an hour-long program on the popular video show 'The Universe's Unanswered Mysteries'. Piled high on the desk were glass-pack readers, hyper projectors, stylus highlighters, 3-D scramblers, coffee cups, used lunch trays, an assortment of tiny spacecraft models and a very bizarre assortment of Plasticine figures representing a militaristic group of what looked like wild boars in battle armor with weapons. Forrester and the female chief master sergeant Misha has seen earlier at Britaine's pre-mission briefing were playing a mock battle with the figures. Both were making weird and quite impossible noises. A junior-grade major sat facing the two, while scanning through a glass-pack, completely ignoring the Plasticine carnage threatening to engulf the chief's desk.

Without turning around the chief called out to Misha, "Come on in, Third McPherson, and shut the hatch, you're letting the flies in. Gan, you lying sack of civilian sheep shit, I just killed your commander and you know it."

"Yeah, yeah, yeah. That's what you think." Forrester looked up at Misha and smiled. He tossed her the figure he held. "What do you think? Should we recruit these guys to fight the Binders for us?"

Misha turned the figure over in her hands. It did indeed look like a semi-intelligent pig of some kind, wearing armor with odd weaponry stuck out at every angle. "I don't know this species. But, it looks like there would be serious gaps in their armor. I don't recognize the cannon this man… er, pig… um, whatever it is carrying. Who are they?"

"Relax, Third," the junior-grade major spoke without looking up from his reading. "Those are just some of Dead-eye's toys. Children's toys. You know how silly some chiefs can get in their old age. They are the P.O.O.P.; Pigs Out On Patrol. You can get them at any station exchange in the toy section."

The chief smiled, "Yep, I got the whole set." She stood up and stretched out her hand to Misha. "Chief Master Sergeant Elizabeth Brown, intel's NCOIC. And that is Major Junior-Grade Hiero Krandiewsky. We call him Buzz for short. We let him think he is the head intel puke around here. And you know Sergeant Forrester, I believe?"

"Yes, Chief," Misha smiled. "You don't know how relieved I feel to be back in an intel shack. I think that outside of APES country, this is the only room on an AMSF craft that I feel comfortable in."

"That's not surprising. If you felt comfortable out there, you probably wouldn't have made a good intel puke," the chief said. "I pulled up your personnel files when we got Colonel Britaine's authorization to let you guys play with us. It looks like you were pretty good at intelligence work, for a beginner."

"Thank you," Misha said. "I believe Major…um…Buzz called you 'Dead-eye'. Should I call you that or Chief Brown."

"Shoot, child. It doesn't matter either way. Try it with just Chief. That seems to work fine for most of us. Besides, Dead-eye is more of a joke than a serious nickname," the chief said.

Forrester replied, "That is not what I hear. Word is that you are deadly with a hand weapon."

Chief Brown snorted. "Right and that does me diddly-squat. I am a pure bred intel puke. Who am I gonna shoot? Buzz or maybe some annoying Marshal's Service sergeant? Even if we got boarded, I wouldn't be given a handgun. We would lock ourselves in this vault and hold up until the APES either saved the day or the ship blew up."

"Still," said Buzz, tossing down his glass-pack and looking up for the first time. "You earned the nickname on the firing range." He pointed to the bulkhead behind the chief's desk. A paper target with a human silhouette was stuck to the bulkhead. There was a small cluster of bullet holes inside the center heart ring, a very small cluster of bullet holes in the center of the head, and a very, very small cluster of bullet holes in the groin.

"That is some impressive shooting," Misha said.

"Yeah," said Chief Brown. "That is why I keep it stuck up there. It keeps the lower-ranking intel pukes in line and it seems to have a calming effect on the raging childishness of some of our FAC jocks. But, it is just a piece of paper with holes in it."

"Yes," Buzz interrupted. "But, they are holes you put there from twenty-five meters out with an old-style .45 caliber hard projectile weapon."

Forrester said, "I have shot those things on our range. They have recoil and enough of a kick to break your wrist. If you can do that kind of damage with them, you would be twice as dangerous with a needler or a driver."

"Nope," Chief Brown said. "It's just a hobby, a talent, a skill to be so admired I will be adored by those beings lesser than I. Speaking of which, Buzz, what did you do with Jimmy?"

"Sent him off duty, why do you need him for something?"

"Majors!" Brown said with mock exasperation. "You can teach them chain of command until you are blue in the face, but they still think they are in charge. Why pray tell, Major, did you send Jimmy off duty?"

"Damn, Chief. I thought we talked about it. With Third McPherson here, we didn't have enough for him to do. I thought he might as well fill in on third shift. Sergeant Sticks will punch him through some more on-the-job training."

Misha said, "I am sorry. I didn't mean to cause any disruption when-"

Brown interrupted, "Nonsense, glad to have you here. We shift people around all the time. Normally, Colonel Britaine wants only the best personnel on first watch, then the next best on second and the dregs on third. But, we kind of mix and match here in intel. When we do our final jump into Altec space we will pack this vault with everybody we've got handy. But, until then we could have handled a bunch of you APES."

Misha smiled, "Well, it seems that I am the only one in my outfit with AMSF intelligence experience."

Forrester laughed, "Doesn't that say something about the intelligence level of APES?"

Brown glared at him. "No, Sergeant Forrester. It says something about the intelligence level of our AMSF intel people. It means we are smart enough to stay away from where we could get killed. Present company excepted of course, Third McPherson."

"Call me Misha, please. No offense, trust me. I caught all kinds of spacer flak when I first joined the APES. My AMSF commander thought I was nuts and the NCOIC wanted to lock me up until I changed my mind."

"Smart people," Buzz said. "I would have sent you off for a psych eval. Your record looks too good to let you go easily."

Brown nodded. "I would trade you right now for some of these nitnoys we got saddled with. Still, you will only have a few days with us, and we are almost fully staffed, so I am afraid there isn't much to see and do. I hope you understand I have most of our major Altec campaign tasks assigned to my regular people."

Misha smiled. "Sure, I understand. I don't want to be in the way. No offence, but I was looking for some extra work for my people so that they can keep busy. I don't want them worrying about the upcoming drop and I did not want to assign them extra duty without me doing it as well. That would be a bad example."

Forrester said, "That makes sense. You are pushing them pretty hard with their training, but it is a new command. It doesn't take much to shift morale."

Brown nodded, "True, all too true. Misha, if it is busy work you are looking for, I can bury you for all time to come. Your records indicate that you rate 1A on communications analysis, right? Well, we got a pile of that with your name on it."

"Great. I am ready when you are, Chief."

Forrester said, "Hey! If you guys are going to actually do something, then I am going to get out of here, before you put me to work."

Brown snorted, "Doing what? I already have someone to empty the trash."

Misha and Buzz laughed while Forrester looked on in mock hurt.

"I am crushed, Chief," he said.

"Yeah, I can tell. Now get your skinny marshal's butt out of my vault and let us do some real intelligence work." They all laughed as Forrester stormed out of the vault and with exaggerated force tried unsuccessfully to slam the vault hatch behind him. Buzz turned back to his glass-pack reading.

Misha said, "Oh, Chief, before I get started, can I ask a question?"

"Sure, Misha, fire away."

"Funny you phrase it that way, Dead-eye," Misha smiled. "I know the AMSF requires all officers and NCOs to be proficient in old-style slug throwers. What I don't get is why? I mean, hardly anybody uses them anymore."

"Ah, good question, Misha. It is just history and tradition. And like most traditions, it bears little connection to reality."

"Not true," Buzz said, not looking up. "Handling a needler is a no-brainer if you can shoot a .45 with accuracy."

"True," said Misha, "But, why not train on what you are going to use. And you said it yourself: chances are you wouldn't ever get issued a weapon."

Brown leaned down and popped open a lower drawer. She pulled out a handgun, dropped the magazine into her free hand and checked the chamber for a live round. She tossed the handgun to Misha. "I did say we probably wouldn't get issued weapons. I didn't say we wouldn't have them if we needed them. That is a fully functional replica of a 2119 Smith and Wesson .45 caliber semi-automatic handgun. The Kiirkegaard's manifest lists it in my personal affects for entertainment purposes."

"Okay, Chief. But, why not keep a needler handy?"

"History, Misha. The AMSF is a direct descendent of Earth One's North American Air Force. They were originally only atmospheric aircraft, but they eventually moved into the upper atmosphere and from there into satellite control. It was a short jump to commanding spacecraft."

"I was in the AMSF for four years. Nobody ever told me that."

Chief Brown smiled, "It was a short four years. We have a lot of history and tradition our founders brought with them from their old forces. That was almost eight hundred years ago. Pilots are a superstitious lot. Some changes may never come."

"Great. That tells me why it is called the tarmac. That is tradition, right?"

"Yep. That was what atmospheric pilots called the area where they parked their fixed-wing aircraft."

134

"One more question before I let you put me to work. What is FOD?"

Brown laughed. "That is a secret we usually don't let anyone in on until they reach at least an E-7 pay grade. F.O.D. is Foreign Object Debris. It used to mean any trash that might get sucked into an atmospheric craft's air intake and wreck the engine. Now it is a reminder to watch for things that don't belong. You know, keep your eyes out for what is unusual. And what is unusual might be dangerous or deadly. Now, are you ready for work, young lady?"

The next few hours passed so quickly Misha completely lost track of time. She took all the readings from the last jump. She analyzed, categorized them and wrote a mission report on each one. She completed all except one that baffled her.

Misha called out, "Hey, Chief?"

"She left an hour ago, Third," Buzz answered. "Got a problem?"

"Not really, Major, I have dumped the comms analysis mission reports into your database."

"All of them?" Buzz sounded surprised. "Hell, it would have taken anyone except Chief Brown or me about a week to complete that load. It's a big squadron out there, must be a ton of communications going on."

"Yes, Major. But, most of it is pretty routine except I got one that I can't read. I am not sure if it even qualifies as comms."

"Well, better safe than sorry. I'll buzz Chief Brown to come back and take a look. If the meantime, show me what you got."

Misha called up the unusual reading. It was out of the range of standard familiar communications. The data analysis module ruled out all known human protocols as well as all previously recorded alien communications, specifically noting it did not conform to any Binder recordings.

"Looks like space static to me, Third," Buzz said.

"That is what I thought at first, but I have never seen static so consistent in tone and tremor. Plus, it died too fast. It didn't fade away, it was just no longer there, you know?"

"Well, Third. I think you have sat at that console for too long. Maybe you should show Chief Brown what you got when she gets here and then go take a break."

"I don't know, Major. Something isn't right with this."

"With what?" Brown said as she came through the vault hatch.

Misha explained the readings and her concerns again. "I know that I sound overly paranoid, but…" Her voice trailed off with a shrug.

"Paranoid is good," Brown smiled as she flashed through a readout of Misha's completed reports "The rest of these misreps are fantastic. You do good work, Misha. When you get done playing warrior with your APE buddies, you come see me. I will put you back in intel."

"Thanks, Chief."

"I got to say, Misha that I am a bit intrigued by this comm signal. I'm not sure we have enough info to puzzle this out…yet. Let's see if we can do something to scrounge up a bit more data."

Chapter Twenty-Three

Colonel Britaine looked at the two men standing before him. He shook his head. It had to be that damned APE McPherson again, not to mention that pain in the ass Chief Brown. He was amazed at the massive amount of information those two women had gathered on the system their squadron was cruising through. The next jump was still many hours away, but he would have to delay his jump for days if he was to read every piece of this data.

McPherson and Chief Brown had even queried every other spacecraft communications collector in the squadrons. Most of the other intelligence offices hadn't yet completed their mission reports. But, he doubted that Chief Brown would have trusted their misreps to report such unusual activity. The woman was a professional paranoid.

"Dammit," he thought. "I wouldn't have relented and let the APES into operations functions if I had knew it would put those two together. Still, this might be one more nail in the coffin of that uppity grunt. Why couldn't that frigid bitch be an airlock maintenance tech? All it would take is be one quick mistake and poof." He knew he had to control himself. She would self-destruct soon enough or her luck would run out when she went dirt side on Altec.

Over half of the misreps from the other eighty spacecraft didn't report this or any other unusual activity. Most of the other reports that did show this activity listed it as static or garbling caused by solar flares or sunspots. Only about ten percent listed the communications as unknown or marked it for further study.

Chief Brown was convinced enough to classify the data on an official report. She then badgered Major Krandiewsky into taking the report up the ladder to Colonel Britaine.

"And now," Britaine thought, "that office weenie is up here badgering me about this. Plus, that Marshal

Service data pusher hasn't been any help. I call him in here to back me up and he is so non-committal he's useless."

Britaine said, "Nothing. I don't see why this is even officially classified. Look at these other misreps. Major Krandiewsky, are you going to tell General Gurand that a grunt, a ground pounder, is better at intelligence gathering than his own command staff intelligence officers? I sure as hell am not."

"I agree, Colonel. I wouldn't want to tell them they missed finding important data. However, if Chief Brown is right and there is something out there, we should find out what it is," Krandiewsky said, emphasizing it was Brown who was pushing for more data. "Surely a couple of probes might get enough data to show if there is anything here or not. It wouldn't take a lot of probes. We have enough readings from other comm collectors for a good triangulation on a possible point of origin."

"Might? Maybe? Possible? No, Heiro," Britaine said, not realizing he mispronounced Buzz's real first name for the hundredth time. "There is not enough data here to go on an empty space chase just to prove something doesn't exist. Sergeant Forrester, don't you agree?"

"Well, Colonel. As you say, there is not enough data here to make a determination one way or another. Third McPherson does have a knack for the unusual, sir. More data might be indicated," Forrester said.

Britaine, despite his attempts to control his emotions, colored at the mention of McPherson's name. "Spoken like a true bureaucrat. Sorry, Sergeant Forrester, but the AMSF is an action-oriented force. We don't jump at shadows. Neither does the APES. Maybe Third McPherson isn't as suited for command as some would believe. Dismissed, Gentlemen."

Chapter Twenty-Four

Chief Brown frowned, "Where the hell is Buzz? It's been an hour. I doubt if it was worth a cold early-morning fart to send that report up to Britaine. He may be a damn good man to have in a dogfight, but he wouldn't know what to do with real intelligence information if it came up and bit him in the butt."

"Well, Chief," Misha said. "We do what we gotta do. What the higher ups do with what we do is their business."

"And that is a lot of do-do," Brown said.

The vault hatch opened. Krandiewsky and Forrester popped through the hatch and closed it behind them. "Good afternoon, ladies," Forrester said. "Been busy I see."

"Gan, what are you doing back here?" Misha asked.

"Britaine called me in to consult on your discovery. Sorry, Chief, don't get riled up. It wasn't my idea," Forrester held his hands up defensively. "And yes, Buzz put forward the info as viable data. He didn't burn you on the report."

"Of course I didn't burn your research," Krandiewsky said with a hint of hurt in his voice.

"Oh, hush, Buzz," Brown said. "I never thought any such thing. What did Britaine say?"

"What could he say?" Krandiewsky replied. "There isn't sufficient data and it's probably sunspots. That's how General Gurand's flag intelligence staff reported it."

Brown snorted, "Flag intel. Ha! Those political pukes couldn't intel their way into the mess hall without an empty stomach to lead them."

Misha said, "Okay, Gan. What do you think?"

"Well, I don't know. I will agree there were some strange readings that we can't round peg into a known round hole. But, so what?" Forrester said.

"The 'so what' is that we are running a huge squadron operation, Sergeant Forrester. I don't know about you Marshal Service guys, but if you ain't paranoid, you ain't intel. This makes the hairs on my neck stand up and mambo," Brown said.

"All right," Krandiewsky agreed, "Something was out there. The Third did a damn good job of picking it out. I'll make sure that it's noted in the daily logs. But, I don't see what else there is to do about it. Chief, reset your communications collectors to check for the signal throughout this system until we jump and then watch for it after the next jump. We can't do anything more without additional data. Does that make sense?"

"Yes, sir," Brown replied.

"Do you agree, Gan?" Misha asked.

"Not my call. Sorry, I am just a Marshal's office bureaucrat," Forrester said.

"Sorry?" Brown said. "It damn well is your call. I know you have the security clearance to see everything we do. Personally, I don't see that you have the need-to-know levels. But, that isn't for me to say. It is your call since Britaine asked you in on this."

"Okay, okay. I agree with Buzz. We don't have enough information to make a valid diagnosis on the signal. Britaine agrees. He doesn't see the need to bust his chops asking the general for permission to send out an expensive horde of deep-space probes looking for something that might be a solar flare. And frankly, Colonel Britaine does not appear to be the type of officer who would share the information even if you get enough data."

Brown nodded, "We live by data and we die by data. Okay, Misha, I'll get some people to keep looking. Later, we can see what we can put together. I assume you are planning on coming back? We didn't work you too hard on your first day?"

Misha laughed, "No. I appreciate your letting me get in here. Except for a bit of frustration at not getting this puzzle solved, this has actually been quite restful."

"Hey, Chief, you should go to the APES training bay if you want to watch Misha really work," Forrester said.

"Not me," Brown said. "I break out in hives if I even see someone else sweat."

"Gan, don't you have somewhere else to be?" Misha said. "Why is it that every time I turn around I am bumping into you?"

"Maybe you're just clumsy?" Forrester asked innocently. "Besides, I'm just hitching a ride on the Kiirkegaard. Britaine has me bunking with a couple of second lieutenants. So, where else am I going to go? I can't work out with your guys all the time. I'm liable to get killed. Your APES broke my arm last time. What would be next? And I can't just hang around the intel shack doing nothing."

"Damn right," Krandiewsky said. "You and Chief Brown get to telling old war stories and nobody gets any work done."

Misha nodded. "Tell you what, Gan. Since I owe you a small favor for the broken arm, why don't you move into my day office? It has a bunk set up and it might give you some privacy. I will code the hatch and the dataport for you."

"I don't want to push you out of your office," Forrester replied.

"It's not a problem. I don't think I'll be using it much in the next couple of days. You're getting off where…Gagarin system? I can live without a private office until then. I'm not going to be using the sleeping quarters even after that, so be my guest," Misha said.

Brown said, "Okey-dokey, that's settled. Misha, you might as well get out of here. Go take a nap or something. We'll work on collecting more anomalous data for later study. I'll call you if something hot shows up."

Misha said, "Thanks, Chief. Thank you, Major. I don't think sleep is in the cards right now. Maybe a little time in the training bay would help. Do you want to work out some, Gan?"

Forrester laughed and waved his cast, "I still have a broken forelimb. It should take another few days to get this cast off and get healed from the last beating you put me through."

Chapter Twenty-Five

"Second Aardmricksdottir, what is the problem?"

Vark clamped her jaw shut. It was not that Third McPherson was yelling at her, but more the tone of disapproval in her voice. In fact, she would rather have McPherson yelling at her. They were in the training bay. All the other squad's armor repair techs stood out of earshot. Vark was thankful for that. At least, the others couldn't hear if she had to endure getting chewed out.

"Sorry, Third-"

"Sorry don't cut it, Vark," McPherson interrupted. "I don't want to hear sorry. I know you have a sorry squad with some very sorry troopers stuck in some sorry old armor, but you are a second-level commander now. You are also the senior armor repair technician for the whole unit. How sorry are you going to be when we drop dirt into combat and people die because this armor isn't ready?"

Without thinking, Vark spat back, "That they get what they deserve for not taking care of their own gear." She froze thinking, "I didn't say that out loud, did I? Oh, stupid, stupid, stupid." She watched McPherson's face cloud up and turn a bright red. "Oh, gods!" She thought. "She is going to blow. Keep your trap shut, Aardmricksdottir. You are smarter than this. No…maybe I'm not." She said, "I didn't mean to say that, Third. Really, it just slipped out."

"Look, Deuce," McPherson said. "I know what you've got in your squad. And I know what some of the other squad leaders have to work with. We are all in the same boat. They are ours. We will fix the people. But, we can't fix them if they can't survive combat, right?"

Vark looked puzzled, "Fix the people? They aren't machines. I can fix armor. I got some good people in my squad. Let me get rid of Beaudry and maybe two or three others. I can do something with this squad if I can get some good replacements in here."

"What makes you think we'd be getting replacements?" McPherson asked. "You think we're going to pass our problems off to someone else? Not a chance, Second. You are stuck with Beaudry until he decides to leave or he gets shipped home to mama in a box. And that doesn't mean you run him off, get me? He's a good man and could be an asset to this outfit."

Vark couldn't believe her ears. She heard McPherson reaming Beaudry on her first day here. Surely, she didn't think that screw-up was worth saving. "Seriously, Third, Beaudry is not only bad, but he is a bad influence on a couple of other rookies in Joker Squad, especially Yorkvina and Dallas. Combined with Putinova, it is a mess."

"Yes, Second, but it is your mess. You deal with it."

"Come one, Third. I know you're new at command, but you can't believe that textbook crap about leadership," Vark said incredulously. She thought, "Oh, gods! Why is my mouth in gear? Shut up, girl." But, disregarding her own advice to herself, she said, "Everybody knows that you're going to burn Slezak for trying to frag you in the sim."

"What everyone knows or thinks they know isn't important here, Second. I will tell you this: Slezak has been red-lined for this upcoming op. I haven't determined what I'll do with her after that. But, whatever the punishment, I will not, repeat not transfer her out of this squad. She is my problem, just as Beaudry and Putinova are yours and by extension, mine as well. Got me?"

Vark nodded, "Yes, sir." She started to apologize, but managed to clamp the words off.

She almost stumbled backwards when McPherson stepped forward to within inches of her face. She had lost all of her physical inhibitions in her time with the APES, but this Third was so imposing she felt threatened.

"Now, Second Aardmricksdottir, once again: what is the problem with getting our armor repaired?"

"Sir, we need more hands. This is not an excuse, just a fact. We have had such a high influx of FNGs that we're not meeting up with the retrofit demands. Plus, the seconds who retired let a lot of maintenance slip. The armor in Joker Squad is pretty good, but that's because I took care of it myself. Look, Third, I'm not whining, but I wasn't responsible for the armor in those other squads until a couple of weeks ago. Now suddenly, instead of just eleven suits, I've got 120 plus suits."

"True, Second. And last week I only had one life to worry about. Now I've got 120 plus lives riding on my decisions. I can't fix your time line, but I can get you more hands. Use the quartermasters, expendables clerks, med techs, general supplies clerks, intelligence techs, and even the cooks. Most of those will be untrained hands, but they will do the unskilled labor that will free up the other techs."

Misha continued, "You said you were having big problems with the camouflage hide-and-seek sensors, right? Well, those units are very similar to some of the comms modules. You should be able to use your communications specialists to check those out."

Vark knew she should just say 'yes, sir' and shut her mouth. She even told herself to keep her mouth shut. She said, "Are those the same hands you promised Park for help in repairing the skid plates, that you promised Bill…Colonel Britaine as part time help in operations and that you're working half to death in the training bay?"

McPherson smiled coldly, "You know, Second, I think you're right. You are a second-level commander, what do you propose to do about it?"

Vark wanted to slam her fist into her own forehead and shout "Think! Think! Think!" Instead, she shrugged and said, "I don't, Third. I've got other troopers over there who have been repairing armor for years. DeLaPax should be senior, not me. She has been repairing armor for longer than I have been alive. I don't know about you, sir, but I would ask DeLaPax what to do."

"Deuce, you have the rank. You have the responsibility of command. If DeLaPax wanted to be senior, then she should have requested command track. She didn't and hasn't been promoted. You did and got the rank. You have to use it. Besides, DeLaPax has enough problems with Able Squad's armor without worrying about everybody else's."

Vark started to say something, but McPherson stopped her with a wave of her hand.

"Further, Deuce, I agree you have a lot of experience in that bunch. Use it. They know who they can use from their squads and who will be a hindrance. Work with Trooper Park from Able. Split up the people you need. I want armor and skid plates in spit-shine shape. But, armor takes precedence, got me?"

"Yes, sir," Vark said knowing she would hate working with Park. The slimy little cretin was always trying to cop a cheap feel or get her cornered somewhere. She wondered if she could delegate that to DeLaPax. No, that was not what she was told to do. She didn't deserve to get chewed out by the new Third. She hadn't been responsible when those other squads got messed up. "And someday," she said to herself, "I have got to learn to keep my mouth shut."

McPherson said, "Good. Get 'em fixed and get 'em fixed fast. We can sleep when the enemy is dead. Now get started. And send me DeLaPax for a minute."

Chapter Twenty-Six

Misha nodded to herself as she watched Vark walk away. She was pleased Vark wasn't shy about speaking her mind, which made Vark a good second-level commander. She made a mental note to make sure things went as smoothly as expected.

She wasn't looking forward to confronting DeLaPax about the state of Able Squad's armor, but Misha knew it had to be done. She liked the tall, beautiful trooper. DeLaPax's sense of humor always seemed to make a tense situation a little bit lighter. However, armor was life and death.

"You needed to see me, Trey?" DeLaPax asked as she walked up.

"Yes, I did. You're Able Squad's armor repair tech and frankly, the status of most of the equipment sucks like a vacuum through a tiny straw. I wouldn't suit up in most of that crap, so it's a good thing I brought my old armor with me."

"Yes, sir," DeLaPax smiled. "It sucks a ninety knot wind."

Misha was surprised, "This isn't a smiling matter, trooper."

"Yes, it is, sir," DeLaPax grinned. "I'm sure you don't find the state of our equipment more deplorable than I do. But, it is fixable and I will have it ready for drop. And I mean all of it. Look, Trey, I could give you excuses about bad leadership, lack of parts, stolen tools and equipment. That doesn't matter, because I don't see that as an on-going problem, do you?"

Misha didn't know what to say. She shook her head no.

DeLaPax said, "It looks bad. And I know that you've got to chew my tail out, even though I don't see this as my fault. But, I have to go into combat in this armor, too. It will be right."

"Okay, trooper. I'll buy off on that for now. I don't want to come across as rock-hard, but I don't have time with this outfit to do it any other way."

"Well, Third, I'm not sure you would know another way. Do you?"

"What the hell does that mean, trooper?" Misha spat.

DeLaPax laughed. "Easy, boss, we're on the same side. Try calling me Peace. Trust me; it'll make you feel better. I'll still call you Third McPherson since we've got to be military and all of that, but we girls need to stick together, right?"

"DeLaPax," Misha started and then stopped, "Peace. Yeah, you're right. It feels better. Dammit, I call you over here to get on your case about lax equipment maintenance and you won't let me. What am I going to do with you?"

"Just smile and make the best of it, boss. The good news is that I am an excellent friend to have. The bad news is that you don't have enough friends to go around. Whoops, Trey, I can see what you're thinking. There are to be no special favors for Peace DeLaPax. I mean it, you're still the commander and I am just a grunt. You lead and I'll follow. I am just trying to say that if you're leading, you won't have to turn around and check on me. I'll be right behind you."

"All right, Peace. I'm going to trust you on the armor. Work with Second Aardmricksdottir to get the entire unit up to standard. She is a good second. She just needs some experienced backup on this one, got me?"

"Sure, Trey, I am surprised you two are getting along so well."

"What do you mean, trooper?" Misha asked with a hard edge to her voice.

"Take it easy, boss. Damn you're touchy. What happened to calling me Peace? Besides, I thought you already knew. Maybe you don't really want to know. Never mind, forget I said anything."

"It is too late to forget, Peace. What gives with Second Aardmricksdottir? I thought she liked me well enough."

DeLaPax shrugged, "Well, it seems you are succeeding with an old boyfriend of hers, where she failed. And it was a pretty public failure at that."

"Peace, I don't have a clue what you are talking about," Misha said.

"You really don't, do you? You need a friend for girl-talk more than anybody I ever met," Peace laughed.

"Girl-talk? Peace, I never could get the hang of that even with my own sisters on DropSix."

"Sisters! I can't do girl-talk with my sisters, either. There is way too much history there. Are you sure you want to hear this? Yeah, you need to whether you want to or not. Vark had a quick fling with Britaine. One long lunch in his office and then it went to dead silence between them."

Misha said, "Okay, he got what he wanted and she didn't. What has that got to do with me? I am not having a fling with Britaine."

DeLaPax looked surprised. "No? Well, that's not what the rumors say. Vark got her pride hurt. You hurt her pride again when it appears you're lasting longer with Britaine than she did."

"Peace, I am not having anything of any kind with Britaine, except what is required to get us to our combat location. I don't care what the rumors say."

"I believe you, Misha. Maybe Vark will relax a bit now that we have rumors of you and Forrester as well as you and Britaine."

Misha was surprised. Not about the rumors of her and Forrester, she was already becoming numb to such gossip. She was surprised DeLaPax had used her first name. She would never have dared calling a second or third by their first name. But then, she wouldn't ever have dared to discuss their private lives with them either.

"Maybe I am wrong about Vark. She is a stand up APE. Britaine is just a bit of a sore spot with her."

Misha's comm unit beeped with an incoming call. "Peace. Just get the armor fixed. And thanks for the heads up with Vark. I'll talk to her when I get the chance." She tapped her comm unit as DeLaPax walked away. "McPherson here."

"This is Second Watch Commander Major Chang. Please meet me in corridor A16, Post 32. Chang out."

"Now what?" Misha said to herself. She remembered Chang from her first meeting with Britaine. They called him Waterboy. He was a tall and lanky with the look of a man born and raised in space. She half jogged through the corridors. Fortunately, all AMSF spacecraft used the same numbering sequence. She soon found herself in a section of the craft she had never seen. Turning a corner she almost crashed into a knot of people. A cluster of spacers blocked off the corridor from her direction and stood facing a small group of APES. Misha said in a loud voice, "Clear a path, please."

The spacers near her turned and seeing her APES uniform, stood still, many of their faces twisted with hostility. An average-sized spacer with three stripes stepped into her path, blocking her route. He spat at her, "Fu-" Before he could finish his first word, her hand shot forward and grabbed his uniform collar. With a twist of her wrist, she lifted the man completely off the deck.

"Pardon me, spacer," Misha smiled pleasantly. "I missed what you said. Would you care to repeat it?" A silence slid over the crowded corridor.

A voice boomed out, "APES! Prepare to engage." Misha recognized Second Jackson's voice.

Misha shouted, "Can it, Jackson. Stand down."

A second voice shouted, "Security to my location on the double." Misha didn't recognize the voice, but guessed it was probably Major Chang.

She set the spacer's feet back on the deck. She smoothed the front of his uniform. With a soft pat on his chest, she said, "There, spacer. That's better. Now, may I have a clear path, please?"

The hostility level didn't decrease, but the spacers opened up the corridor allowing Misha to move into the area between the two opposing groups. She found herself standing alone in the center. Misha turned sideways so as not to appear to take sides with either group. She spotted Chang standing at the forefront of the spacer group. "Major Chang, how may I be of assistance?" Misha asked, keeping her tone as pleasant as possible.

"Clear a path! Clear a path!" a group of security forces pushed their way through the spacers and came to a stop in front of Misha. A second group halted behind the small cluster of APES. Misha noted that all the security forces were armed, but so far the weapons remained holstered. Misha looked at Chang and raised her eyebrows in question. The man was raging in anger and frustration.

"Listen, you APE. I don't care if you are Britaine's current whore. If you can't control your animals, then I will."

A growl rose from the APES. She held up a quieting hand. The security forces wouldn't have time to draw their weapons before her APES tore them apart. For that matter, in this tight corridor, if they did draw and fire they were as likely to hit their own forces as APES. "Major Chang," Misha said emphasizing the man's rank. "I suggest you rethink that statement. I would prefer, as I am sure you are aware, that I prefer to be called Third McPherson. I am quite positive being called anybody's whore is not acceptable."

"I don't need to rethink anything. Security: arrest every APE in this corridor," Chang shouted.

Misha bellowed, "Everybody freeze." She was not surprised when her APES froze. She looked back at Chang to see the man was boiling. She held her right hand up in the air. It was the hand signal her father had used when he demanded silence and immediate obedience. She was surprised when the security forces froze and silence slid over the whole mob. She thought, "I wonder how long I can hold them this way." After about fifteen seconds, she said to Chang, "Major?"

"All right, security, belay that order."

"Thank you, Major Chang. If you let me know what the problem is I may be able to help clear it up without anyone arresting anyone."

"Come on, Trey! These vacuum heads-" Second Jackson started.

Misha didn't let him finish. She spun on him and held a quieting hand up to his face. She said softly, "Not one more word from any APE until I ask. That includes you, Mister Jackson." She locked eyes with Jackson and held his gaze until he looked away.

Misha said, "I apologize for the interruption, Major Chang. Would bring me up to speed on this situation, please?"

Chang spat, "Your APES have been rude, discourteous, insubordinate, and their actions border on sabotage."

"Those are serious charges, Major," Misha said.

Chang stood facing her with his fists clenched. "Yes, they are. And I mean them. Are you saying it didn't happen? Are you calling me a liar?" he shouted.

"No, sir. I would just like the specifics made known so that I can file the appropriate charges." She held up a forestalling hand to Jackson. She shook a warning head at him. "Nothing, Second Jackson. Say nothing."

"Major Chang?" she asked. "Please elaborate?"

"No. I will elaborate at their trial."

"Major Chang," Misha said calmly, "I understand your anger. Believe me; I know how you feel about my outfit and me. But, I am obligated at this juncture to point out that I cannot, and it's not that I don't want to, but I cannot turn them over to you for trial without knowing the circumstances of their sabotage and having the evidence presented."

Chang seemed to calm a bit, "Well, yeah. But, don't forget about the insubordination and discourtesy."

She smiled. "Well, Major, I am sure there has been enough rudeness to go around. As for the insubordination; that is an APES offence. I won't be able to turn them over to you for insubordination. I would like to, but our mutual contract specifically says I can't. However, with your testimony, the APES will be able to punish them. Sabotage is a different matter. Would you care to fill me in on the details now or would you prefer to clear out any uninvolved persons?"

Chang calmed down a substantial amount. He looked around as if for the first time, realizing he had almost caused an inter-service riot. Misha knew he had backed himself into a corner. He couldn't back down without causing a loss of face in front of his own crew.

Chang said, "Second Jackson and these troopers refused to follow our S.O.P. in re-aligning the cargo hold."

"I see. Go on," Misha said.

"Well, I am in command on the bridge and ordered a balancing of the cargo holds. Specifically, the mess your people dumped in there from the training bay. I mean, it is a mess. It is disgusting with stuff just piled all over. I demanded that all items be secured properly."

"I see. Second Jackson, are the items secured?" Misha asked.

"Yes, sir, each pallet is interlocked with its component pieces. Nothing is going to move."

"Dammit," Chang shouted. "That is not what I meant and you know it."

Misha said, "Yes, Major. Perhaps when the AMSF says to secure something, it means they want it put in its proper place. When an APE says something is secured it means it has been captured and is defensible, that it is immobile and protected. Just as the Marshal Service says when they want something secured, it means that they want to lease the item with an option to purchase. Perhaps we just have a communication gap?"

"No. He knew exactly what I meant," Chang pointed at Second Jackson.

"Mister Jackson?" Misha asked.

"Yes, sir," Jackson nodded. "I know what he wants. I wouldn't do it before and I still won't let him proceed."

"See!" Chang shouted. "Insubordinate. And those containers are stacked willy-nilly all over the cargo hold. They are stacked every which way. They could break loose and tear a hole in the hull if we have to maneuver quickly. That is deliberate sabotage." He had a smug look of success on his face.

"Mister Jackson?" Misha asked.

"Sir, all the containers and bins in question is our mobility equipment. They are stacked and locked into place with tensors at full strength. The gear is stacked per APES squad use, with each squad's equipment stacked with the rest of that squad's equipment. Major Chang wants them stacked according to size and shape, completely disregarding their functional needs as combat mobility equipment."

Misha said, "Major Chang, your charge of sabotage stems from the fact that these goods could break loose because they are stacked with a smaller container under a larger container and look completely unbalanced. That they could tear a hole in the hull if they break loose, is that correct?"

"Yes, isn't that enough?" Chang replied.

"Actually no, sir." Misha said. "They are currently held in place by combat strength tensors. It would take a direct missile hit to tear those containers loose from the deck. Our tensors have four times the strength of the Kiirkegaard's deck tensors. I must agree with Second Jackson about moving the gear from their standard APES configuration. I must point out our contract says this equipment is and must be stored according to our requirements."

"But it is sloppy. Just like the rest of you APES," Chang said.

"Actually, Major. It just looks sloppy. They are grouped as needed by our squads when we drop onto a planet. Each squad's equipment is dropped together. If it was stacked any other way, we would have to sort through the containers to find what we needed. That would be unacceptable under combat conditions in a hot landing zone."

Chang looked around at his dwindling cluster of spacers. He realized, as many of them had, that he was fighting a losing battle. "Well, Second Jackson was rude and uncommunicative. He should have told me what his objections were instead of just refusing my commands. And he called me a vacuum-breather. That is disrespectful to my rank and position."

"Yes, Major Chang. Name-calling and disrespect of rank are distressing," Misha said pointedly. Chang's face flushed. "Perhaps we can do without the security forces at this point, sir?"

Chang nodded and waved at security. They melted away. "At the very least, I demand a formal apology."

She turned to Second Jackson. "Mister Jackson, were you rude and discourteous to a flight officer of this crew?"

"Yes, sir, I was." Jackson looked sheepish.

"Mister Jackson, I expect my seconds to be more diplomatic and understanding in inter-service cooperation," Misha said.

"Yes, sir," Jackson nodded.

"Mister Jackson, you will immediately record a formal apology to Second Watch Commander Major Chang. You will specifically note any and all name calling that went on in this corridor. You will also note the exact time and place of the incident and all insults give and taken. You will attach a copy of all relevant time periods as copied from your glass-pack. You will copy Colonel Britaine and me. You will transmit your apology immediately.

"Oh, I am sorry, Major Chang, we do seem to be in the middle of your second Watch. Are you supposed to be on the flight deck at this time?"

Chang looked stricken. Misha could see he just realized that not only had he lost the argument, but that copies of him calling her Britaine's whore would be sent to his boss, and that he had left his post in the flight office for an extended period of time. He turned and dashed down the corridor speaking rapidly into his comm unit.

Misha ordered, "Everybody scatter back to wherever it is you are supposed to be. Jackson, you stay put."

"You showed him, Trey," Jackson said when they were alone.

"Shut up, Second. This is hard enough taking over this command and going into combat on such short notice without you screwing around with the spacers. Try to be diplomatic next time. And I am serious about that apology."

"Come on, Trey. He was riding me from the top."

"I don't give a rat's ass, Mister Jackson. You had better learn control and discipline. I don't have time to mediate childish disputes, got me?" Misha said with a cold edge in her voice.

"Yes, sir. Point taken. Sorry," Jackson said.

Chapter Twenty-Seven

"Hey, Deuce Jackson," Trooper Wilderman from Dawg Squad said. "She reamed your butt out good in front of the vacuum-heads."

"Yeah, so what?" Jackson said. He was seething inside. He didn't like anyone talking to him like he was an idiot. Now this loser Wilderman was getting on his case."

Wilderman said, "So nothing? You just took it like a little mamma's boy."

"Shut your hole, Wilderman. I wouldn't take that crap from anybody but McPherson. And do you know why, you puke? I will take it from her because I lost a brother at Guinjundst. McPherson kicked ass at Guinjundst and the next time we drop dirt, we are all going to kick some Binder ass; you included. You understand, or do you want to continue rubbing sandpaper across my bad side today?"

"Roger that, Mister Jackson. Understood," Wilderman backed away.

"Listen, pencil dick," Jackson shouted at the retreating trooper. "She could march me naked, painted purple into the high court chambers on Heaven Three and I wouldn't give a damn as long as she leads me to where I can kill them weed-eating sons-of-bitches."

Chapter Twenty-Eight

Gan Forrester looked around the APES commander's day office. The front room was furnished as an office with a desk, two straight back chairs and a dataport. There were no pictures or personal items of any kind in sight. The backroom was a bedroom. It had a wall locker and a standard APES bunk with blast shutters. The bathroom had a shower, toilet and sink. It was actually so small that the toilet inset into the shower. A voice behind Forrester startled him.

"Convenient, isn't it?" McPherson asked. "You can sit while you shower."

"And spotless, too," he replied. "I didn't hear you come in behind me. I hope you don't mind; I decided to take you up on your offer and move in."

"Please be my guest or rather the guest of the APES," she said. "I just had it cleaned and sanitized. The last occupant left behind a mess."

"I hope I won't be putting you out?" Forrester asked.

Misha shook her head. "I won't be using this often enough to matter until we drop dirt. Then I expect to be rather busy in here."

"Really? You're planning on taking your office with you?"

"Actually, Gan, you are standing in the middle of our mobile combat command center. Right now, the locks have it clamped to the deck plates, but it is sitting on its own combat skid plate. The whole room drops out of the back end of the Kiirkegaard along with the rest of us and all of our other gear. It is automatically targeted to drop onto our LZ." She tapped her knuckles lightly on the steel walls. "These walls are armored steel, not at all like the composite bulkheads of the spacecraft around us. It is not pretty, but the armor here could hold against a whole squad in APES quality armor. So, it is a good thing you won't be going into the Altec system with us, because I'll need the room back by then."

"This is really a nice double function design. I'd like to go on to the Altec System even if it means giving up my private accommodations. Just for a bit of sightseeing, you know. But, the big bosses tell me that I can't go that far," Forrester replied. He thought he might be able to work something out to go on to Altec after he conferred with his contact on Gagarin. He stored that thought away for later. The Binders pulled something new on Guinjundst besides using biological and chemical warfare. Whatever that something was APES command was keeping it very close to their collective chest. The Marshal Service would like to know what it was. Still, if he couldn't get any information from Misha between Heaven and Gagarin, then he wouldn't get much more going on to Altec. His contact on the Kiirkegaard would have to fill him in on what went on in Altec.

Forrester said, "So, you really are bunking in the squad bay? Doesn't that lack a bit of privacy?"

"Yep. However, the squad bay gives me more privacy than I had growing up. Sure the APES sleep in the same room, but each bunk has blast shields that work very effectively as privacy screens. The toilet and shower stalls have some exceptionally durable locks. Believe me; nobody sees anything that I don't want them to see."

Forrester smiled. He could imagine what would happen if someone were to try something with this woman. He could see why some men, and women for that matter, would be tempted to try. He admitted that she wasn't the most beautiful woman in the Allied Systems, not in the classical sense of beauty. She exuded a powerful presence, though. Sometimes power offered more attractive appeal than mere physical features. He could see why this woman challenged Britain. Britaine had charm. McPherson had a raw sort of charisma. He said, "Whatever the reason for the offer of the bed, I appreciate it. Lieutenant Holdgren snores loud enough to wake the long deceased, and AMSF bunks don't have those nice blast shutters to cut the noise."

"Just one tiny little thing, Gan. Keep it clean. The last tenant before me left it in somewhat of a mess."

Forrester nodded. He had met Third Cans briefly when he came aboard. The man actually asked about a second career with the Marshal Service. He had also heard Misha had sent Trooper Beaudry back three times until he had the room spotless to her criteria.

McPherson smiled, "Oh, by the way, Gan, the rumors about Britaine and me must be dying down. The rumor is that you took me away from him; that you and I are doing the wild, horizontal hanky-panky."

"What?! I haven't heard that."

"What's the matter, Gan," McPherson smiled sweetly, without a touch of sweetness in her eyes. "Not as funny as when you were teasing me about Britaine, is it?"

"Who the hell would think you'd have anything to do with an old man like me? That's silly."

"Not as silly as Britaine and me. What's the matter, Gan? Aren't I good enough for you?"

"Wait. It's not that. It's just that…well…how the hell did that rumor get started anyway? Look, I'm sorry. Maybe I shouldn't move in here."

McPherson shrugged. "Nope, go ahead and move in. The damage is done. Besides you might want the privacy for your other girlfriend."

"Pardon me? What other girlfriend?"

"Come on, Gan. I am not a Marshal Service investigator like you, but it only took me fifteen minutes to track the rumor back to its source."

"Wait a minute, Misha. I am not an investigator. I just shuffle data at the headquarters building."

McPherson just looked at Forrester.

Forrester cursed himself thinking he must be getting sloppy in his old age. Of course, he knew Misha was not your average knuckle banger. She was much smarter than most people gave her credit for being. That was why his boss had assigned him to contact her. Still, a rumor might bring them closer together; give them the chance to struggle against a common rumor and forge a personal bond. Maybe it would be a good thing. He looked at Misha looking at him.

"Okay, I am not admitting anything," he said. "I do like a puzzle as much as the next guy. But, Misha I do have to tell you that a rumor might cause me problems."

"Yes? And rumors have been so good to me so far, is that it?" she asked.

"No. I'm sorry, that is not what I mean. Look, I'm married. Okay? A wife may not hear everything that goes on in her husband's life, but rumors like this can hurt. So please tell me where this rumor came from?"

McPherson nodded. "I didn't know you were married. Sorry, I wouldn't have kidded you about it. I tracked it back to your little friend in sickbay. Remember that med-tech Staff Sergeant Jèsusa Rezzi?"

Forrester sighed in relief. "Okay, that one. Good. I can fix that."

McPherson smiled, "Well, I'm glad you're happy. Can you fix the rumor about Britaine and me? As it stands right now, the whole spacecraft, for all I know the entire flight wing, thinks that I'm sleeping with both you and him."

McPherson's comm unit beeped. "Third McPherson here," she said.

"This is Colonel Britaine. Please meet me in your training bay as quickly as possible, if you please."

Forrester watched Misha roll her eyes upward. He wondered what Britaine was up to now. At least, he wasn't asking for another private meeting. That might be a good thing. On the other hand, meeting with him in front of other APES might damage her command more than another unsubstantiated rumor.

She frowned, "On my way, Colonel."

Forrester asked, "More problems?"

"I won't know until I get there. Unless you know something you aren't telling me?"

He laughed, "We don't have time for what I know that I'm not telling you. We will have to meet sometime over dinner and swap secrets. Is that a deal?"

"Not a chance, Marshal Forrester."

"Maybe for a little pillow talk after?"

Misha laughed, "After? No, not after, Gan. Maybe over, as in over my dead body."

"Now you are talking, girl, at least I have a chance. You let me know where and when."

"I don't know. Let me check with my calendar and your wife."

"You sure know how to hurt a fragile ego, don't you? Seriously, I won't move in if you think it is a bad idea."

"No, Gan. You move in here. Wear it in good health. It's a bad idea for me not to know where you are. This way, I can keep an eye on you."

Chapter Twenty-Nine

Misha stepped into the training bay. She thought she was seeing a replay of the earlier confrontation between Spacers and APES, except this time, there were spacers laying about the deck, attended to by spacer medical technicians. There was also a large contingent of security forces, but this time their weapons were drawn, loaded, cocked and aimed at her troops. Instead of that wimp Chang, Colonel Britaine stood in the middle between the two groups.

"Colonel Britaine?" Misha asked. She didn't really want to know what had happened. She thought, "Why me? Why can't I just go off in quiet and kill somebody like I am trained to do?" She saw Second Race Jackson stood in front of the APES...again. She thought that if he had caused two incidents in one day, she would have to take drastic action. Red-lining Jackson for the upcoming operation would be action she could ill afford at this point in their preparation. She wasn't the only one that couldn't afford to lose a good second, the unit as a whole couldn't afford it. She hadn't wanted to red-line Slezak. She needed every able-bodied veteran she could get. Losing a second would be a serious problem. Losing a well-liked second would hurt morale as well as damage their combat effectiveness.

Britaine snarled, "While you were off with your Marshal Service boyfriend, I had to come down here during my off shift. I thought I told you to get control of your unit?"

Misha said nothing.

"Don't start that silent treatment crap with me again, McPherson. Speak up. And remember this; I am not as easy to push around as Waterboy." At her blank look, he explained, "Major Chang. Because of you and your troops, I am now going to have to discipline a good FAC pilot just before I need him in combat. Because of a disagreement with a grunt, I am going to have to ground a man whose training and career have cost the AMSF millions of credits. That wouldn't have happened if you had been able to control your unit and if you hadn't ordered an official apology."

She waved her hand around the training bay, "Colonel, at this point I don't have a comment on either what went on earlier or here. As to what went on earlier; that is over and done with. My report has been completed and filed. As for what went on here; I don't have enough information to make a comment."

She turned to Jackson. "Second Jackson, were you involved?"

"Yes, sir. But not how it looks."

Britaine interrupted, "How it looks is that your troops jumped my crew and tried to dismantle them."

Misha replied, "Yes, Colonel. I agree. That is how it looks. However, I am sure that since we are two reasonable and intelligent people, we should be able to use our working relationship to get to the bottom of this. Don't you agree, Bill?" She smiled at him, actually fluttering her eyelids. She placed one hand on his bicep and gave his muscle a gentle squeeze.

Misha was surprised at herself. She had always made fun of her younger sister GeLeann when she did such girlie things. Gee was a flirt who got her way at every turn with any man in the room. When Gee batted her eyes, smiled and swished her tail, men would rush to her aid. Gee had used those tricks to get Misha out of a jam. Misha's father, by family arrangement, contracted her engagement to Packet Skeller. Arranged marriages were the norm on her home planet, where only males inherit and females advance simply by marital connections. Unmarried females become the labor forces.

Packet would have been a good husband. He was her older brother's best friend with a large and wealthy homestead in the McDonald Highlands. He was a good man who had treated his first wife well. He was a widower with a small son. This proved that he could father sons and this was of great importance on DropSix. Heavy-worlder men have daughters at a rate of four to one due to the effects of gravity on their testicles.

The first accepted recognition that excessive gravity force affected offspring's gender came in the twentieth-century air forces on Earth One. Jet fighter pilots had a higher tendency toward daughters due to high G maneuvers than the general population. On DropSix with high gravity the constant norm, the rate of sons to daughters changed drastically. Fortunately, it was not enough of a change to make the planet uninhabitable by humans. Many societies would have accepted multiple marriages, but the majority of DropSix's population descended from the ancient Scots, whose sense of morality would not condone polygamy. Instead, their society adjusted to arranged marriages and a vast female work force.

Misha didn't dislike Packet, but she couldn't bring herself to marry him. She couldn't explain why to her parents, Packet or even herself. All the Skeller Clan was as angry as Misha's own father was at her for breaking the contract. Her sister Gee flirted with Packet for days on end until he relented and took her to wife instead. Misha knew the marriage made GeLeann happy and she would make Packet happy.

Still, it surprised Misha to use the same tricks her sister used. She was even more surprised when they worked on Britaine.

He said, "I suppose we should get the full story before we go off with our guns blazing. Right, Misha?"

She smiled sweetly, even through the bitter taste in her mouth, "Yes, Bill. If you think that's best?"

Britaine turned a cold eye to her second, "Sergeant Jackson, continue."

Misha stopped her eyes from rolling upward. She made a quick hand signal for the APES to stand fast. She didn't want any APES reacting to Britaine's insult to Second Jackson. She doubted Britaine or his spacers saw her hand movement. If they did, she was sure they would not get its meaning. No matter what the AMSF thought, APES were seconds or deuce and did not react well to hearing sergeant.

Misha nodded at Jackson, "Second, please report."

"Yes, sir. Trooper One Sigget Donnellson of my Foxtrot Squad is the senior weapons tech for the unit." He pointed at Donnellson, held in place by three other APES, who in turn had weapons pointed at them by security forces. "He was meeting with the other weapons techs about the upcoming dirt drop. You know, getting everything in order and all of that. He wanted to make sure the new guys had their act together. Anyway, when I came in to check on them, I had to pull Trooper Donnellson off those three spacers." He pointed to med-techs giving assistance to three men. "There were some other scuffles, but the rest was just pushing and shoving."

"Pussies!" Donnellson shouted.

Before Misha or Britaine could respond, Jackson spun about and planted his fist deep into Donnellson's face. "Shut your burger hole, Sigget," Jackson spat the words into his face. "One more word, boy, and I mean one more small word, and I am going to shove you into your suit and weld it shut. Then I will just leave you there. Got me, Sigget? Do you get me, damn you?"

Donnellson nodded slowly, blood oozing from a cut on his lip.

"Mister Jackson," Misha said. "I think we can do without more violence at this point."

"Sorry, sir, but that wasn't violence. That was just to get his attention, wasn't it, Siggy? Did I get your attention?" Jackson said.

"Yeah, Race. I got ya," Donnellson nodded. "Sorry, Third. I guess I screwed up. I kinda lost my temper."

Britaine interrupted, "Kind of screwed up? I should say so. Look at those men. Are you going to tell me you did that by yourself?"

"No, sir," Donnellson said. "Mostly they got in each other's way. But, yeah, I guess it was me."

Britaine said, "What could possibly possess you to attack three innocent men?"

Misha said, "Sir, suppose we ask these men what happened and why they were in the APES training bay

166

in the first place before we decide guilt or innocence. Please?"

Little by little, it came out. Donnellson and the other weapons technicians had been running through schematics of the new mass driver intake feeds when a dozen spacers sauntered into the training bay. The spacers appeared confident. There were twelve of them and only eleven APES. The APES had known what the spacers didn't. The spacers were effectively outnumbered two to one.

A low-ranking spacer spoke first. "Man, it sure smells in here. It smells like my daddy's pig farm."

Donnellson replied, "Strange. It didn't use to smell that way. Juarez, did you notice a change in the smell?"

Miguel Juarez of Able Squad sniffed their air and said, "You know, now that you mention it, I did notice a change. Hey! Can you vacuum-heads fix the air recyclers in here?"

Kranich of Bravo Squad said, "Play nice, people. Can we help you, gentlemen?"

One of the spacers replied, "Help us? I don't think I've ever needed help from an APE."

Kranich replied, "Hey. Up until forty-five days ago, I was in the AMSF just like you guys. I was a four striper, a gunnery command sergeant on the Durango. There isn't any need for hostility here."

"Shut up, you!" a spacer shouted. "You may have been a spacer at one time, but you are no better than a traitor or a deserter now."

Kranich shook his head sadly.

"Are you going to take that crap, Kranich?" Juarez said.

"Yep, I am just going to consider the source and let it go," Kranich replied.

Another spacer said, "Chickenshit! Just like all you others."

By this time, both groups of men stood face-to-face. Fists clenched and blood was running hot.

Donnellson stepped forward, "Enough already. We've got work to do. You vacuum breathers move on out."

A trio of spacers stepped forward to meet him. The tall one said, "Yeah, we ain't leaving until we get a look at your new boss. We hear she's a slut who likes to take on AMSF officers and even a marshal or two. We wanted to know how she felt about taking on a few enlisted men."

Donnellson launched himself forward. He was a typical APE veteran, physically at his peak. GerinAid kept his body a youthful twenty-five. Combat nanites kept him as healthy as medical science could make him. And after three decades of martial arts in both practice and in actual combat situations, the trio of spacers saw only a blur. It was a blur whirling around them like a tornado on steroids. All three men threw punches at Donnellson. None of the punches connected.

Second Jackson arrived in time to literally pick Donnellson up off the men and throw him across the deck. The three men wouldn't move again until the med techs carried them off to sick bay.

Misha shook her head at the story. It seemed rumors about her were at the heart of the issue again.

"Colonel Britaine. Bill," she said. "I apologize. My man threw the first punch. Whatever the provocation, he should not have resorted to violence. You have my sincerest apology."

"That is very gracious of you, Misha. Thank you," he smiled. "It does seem there may have been some provocation, and my crew may have been where they didn't belong. I can assure you that you will receive a formal apology from the spacer who insulted your honor."

"An apology is not necessary, Bill. I am not offended by what small minds think of me," she smiled sweetly.

Misha turned to Second Jackson. "Mister Jackson, please have Trooper Donnellson escorted to your squad bay. We will have to consider if he is red-lined for the next dirt drop. Don't argue with me, Race. I can't do anything about it. He attacked. He was the aggressor. I don't want to lose him any more than you do, but we don't have a choice, do we? We will make time for a full review of the incident before exercising punishment, if any."

Jackson said, "No, sir. I guess we don't have a choice."

Britaine spoke, "Excuse me a moment, Misha. I want to see to my crew and get them out of here."

"Yes, of course, Bill. I'll be here when you need me," she replied.

Misha turned back to Second Jackson. "And Race, you are on the edge yourself. I do not condone seconds striking troopers for any reason. We will be discussing that, I can guarantee it."

"Wait a minute, Third," Donnellson shouted. "Race didn't do nothin'. I won't press charges. Hell, I was just protecting your honor. It's those damn vacuum suckers who should get strung up, not me."

Misha replied, "Trooper, what makes you think that I need that kind of protection? You validate their insults by your actions. Plus, I don't need you to press charges against Second Jackson. He publicly struck you."

Jackson nodded. "She's right, Sigget. What I did wasn't any better than what you did."

He turned to face Misha. "I will red-line myself, Third. You have my apologies."

"Negative, Second Jackson," Misha said. "I don't have a choice but at least to red-line Donnellson until we do a review of this mess. However, we'll hold on the rest for review. We just need to get a review scheduled before the upcoming dirt drop."

Misha looked over at the rest of the APES gathered in the training bay. A large number gathered with the weapons techs to watch the proceedings. She spotted Trooper Juarez in the crowd. She called him over, "Juarez, who is the next most senior weapons tech. You?"

"No, Third. The next in line would be Golf Squad Trooper One Na'aranna. She is almost five years senior to me. I am next after her," he replied.

"Trooper Na'aranna?" Misha called out. The woman trotted over to her. "You are now the senior weapons tech for McPherson's Second. Get your group together and get back to work. I don't want to drop dirt on Altec and find out I have a H.E. launcher that jams up when it gets hot. Do you understand me? And Trooper, make sure you check with Second Jackson to find out who Donnellson's backup is for his squad."

She turned to the rest of the watching APES. "Since you don't have anything else to do, everybody who has an even trooper number is to report to Second Vark to help with armor repair. I don't care if you're trained in it or not. Everyone who has an odd trooper number is to report to Trooper Jem Li Park for skid plate maintenance. Move it APES."

Britaine spoke in her ear, "Misha. I'm sorry to do this, but I am going to restrict your unit to the confines of APES territory. I don't want them mixing with my crew anymore than is absolutely required. Don't you agree?"

"Yes, Colonel, perhaps you are right. Maybe I made a mistake on insisting they mix their duties."

"Well, I'm not the type of man who says I told you so, but maybe next time you'll listen when wiser heads offer advice."

"Yes, Colonel, maybe I will," Misha gritted her teeth, but smiled sweetly at the man.

"Oh, present company excepted, of course. Please feel free to make yourself at home on my spacecraft." Britaine smiled brightly and left the training bay trailed by his crew.

Misha turned to face a pair of security forces. One was a tall, gangly woman and the other was a short very muscular man. Both spacers looked nervous.

"Spacers, may I help you?"

"Sir, Third McPherson," the woman stuttered. "Bill and I, I mean Sergeant Williams and myself…I am

Spacer First Class Molinna. Anyway, we…well; I guess we want to apologize."

"Exactly what are you apologizing for, Spacer Molinna?" Misha asked.

"Well, I guess you are getting a raw deal. Bill and I were down below when that ass…I mean, Major Chang tried to run his number past you. And we both agree that…um, in spite of your thing with Muffin, I mean Colonel Britaine, you are getting the short end of the stick here," The woman's voice trailed off.

Misha looked at the man. She said, "Is that right, Sergeant Williams?"

"Yes, Third McPherson. I agree. You handled yourself very well. Both Mo and I have been very impressed. I also have to admit I'm a little more than impressed with your Trooper Donnellson. He made dog meat out of Barret, Ortiz and Wang. That trio has been bullying people since they came aboard. I'm not sorry to see they finally met someone who wouldn't cave under their crap."

Misha smiled. "Thank you both. I don't see where you have reason to apologize, but I'll accept it none-the-less. I don't imagine I will get an apology from anyone else."

"We just wanted you to know that not everyone on the AMSF side of this bucket of bolts is against you," Sergeant Williams said.

Chapter Thirty

MISHA WAVED at Chief Brown as she stepped into the intel shack.

Brown waved her over. "Morning. Evening. What time of the day is it anyway? Never mind, have a sit down or did you just drop by for a look-see before locking down for the upcoming jump?" The woman's eyes were red rimmed, but they sparkled with intelligence and good humor.

Misha smiled at the older woman. "You've been running on coffee and diesel fumes for a while, haven't you?"

"I think it has been nothing more than coffee fumes. How can you tell? Don't be fooled by the bags under my eyes. They come naturally. Maybe, it's my wit and charm. I'm told that I am very pleasant when I've been working too long. Right, Buzz?" Brown said.

Buzz blew a razzberry in Brown's direction. "She hasn't been off duty since we called her back in to consult on your anomalous comm reading."

"Yeah, but I've been busy." Brown wiped her face with a mentholated wet nap. She wadded it up and tossed it at Buzz. "What am I going to do, leave all of this delicate intelligence analysis for you amateurs?"

"Watch it, Dead-eye," a voice shouted from across the room. "Buzz is packing heat."

Misha saw a spacer crouched down behind a desk in the back corner. The spacer was a small, blonde woman who spun quickly about and sprinted across the room, sliding headfirst to crouch behind the comms collector console. Misha saw a weapon in the spacer's hand.

Misha jumped backwards, spinning sideways, she looked for a weapon, but nothing was handy. Before she could launch herself into deeper cover, Brown stood up, snapped her wrist forward and as if by magic, a pistol appeared in her hand. It looked almost like a needler, but it was wrong somehow. Buzz stood and whipped his weapon up. Before he could get a bead on Brown, she put three rubber bands into the middle of his chest. Misha gawked as the woman rapidly shot two other male spacers as they popped up from behind Buzz's desk. Each man went down as if at a shooting gallery. Neither man got a shot off. A second later, a barrage of rubber bands shot through the air as the female spacer unloaded her weapon at the men.

Misha could see Brown's gun still had a dozen rubber bands cocked and ready for fire. As she watched, Brown quickly pulled three rubber bands from a breast pocket and reset them on the gun.

Brown smiled at Misha, "Tactical reload." She twirled the gun around her trigger finger and dropped it smartly into a holster at her hip. Turning to the female spacer, she said. "You were a day late and a credit or two short, little sister. I appreciate the warning, though."

Buzz said, "We'd have done better if Ricky hadn't been off duty. Clancy, where did you come from?"

Brown smiled. "You may have done better, but you'd still be dead. I figured you for an ambush today, so I put Clancy in the corner to watch you. She's been hiding there since you three went to lunch. Come on, Buzz. You don't think I would have figured something was up with you three whispering and having special meetings all day? Besides, you almost gave our guest a heart attack."

Buzz nodded, "I expected her. I figured she would be enough of a distraction to allow us to score a win. I guess not."

Clancy picked herself up off the deck where she had been hiding to ambush the men, brushed imaginary dust from her trousers, and tapped open her glass-pack clipped to her uniform blouse. She said, "Code Six-Shooter. Alpha team 3, B team 0; update, shuffle, reset and download."

Brown turned to Misha. "It's a tension breaker, which is sometimes necessary on long ops with little downtime. We keep a running score." She pointed to her reader on the desk. A small clock had reset itself for 135 minutes. "We have a little over two hours standard

173

before anyone can attack again. The glass-pack sets a random time lapse. That keeps the game from getting stale. Furthermore, you can see A and B team members have changed. Otherwise, Clancy and I would be unbeatable. She isn't much of a shot, but she is a nice distraction, especially when it has been a long op and these hairy legged swine get their hormones raging. Damn, I am rambling a bit, aren't I?"

Clancy laughed, "Yeah Chief, you sound a bit punch drunk."

Brown nodded, "In any event it is good to see you back, Misha. As the word going around says, you have been pretty busy with yourself."

Misha said, "I will agree. It has been anything other than uneventful. I hope you don't mind if I drop by. I wanted to spend the next jump with you."

Buzz spoke up first. "We will be glad to have you. Do you want to sit at the comm collector and run the analysis for us again? I had Cuffs assigned to it, but he really should be off duty now."

Cuffs spoke up, "No. I really should be a civilian and back at my old job with the D-Tel Corporation on Veta Prime, but nooooooo, you convinced me to reenlist and then dragged me out here into the ass end of nowhere."

The other male spacer said, "Yeah, and I should be rich and incredibly handsome instead of just fantastically charming."

Clancy laughed, "And pigs in hell want ice water to wash their wings."

Brown said, "Enough, children. Misha, do you want the job or not? You're going to be working if you are spending the jump with us. No hiding out here just to dodge work somewhere else."

"Yes, Chief. It beats being locked down behind the blast shutter in my bunk," Misha replied.

Cuffs said, "Bunks sound like heaven to me. I am oh-fficially, out of here."

"Chief Brown, may I ask you a question?" Misha asked.

"You just did. Do you mean you want to ask another one already?"

"Yes, that is what I meant in the first place. Anyway, Buzz seems to let you run a pretty loose intel shack," Misha said.

"Sorry, but that is a statement," Brown said. "Where is the question?"

Misha sighed. "Okay. Why such a loose shop? It doesn't seem to match with the rest of Colonel Britaine's command style. I haven't seen any camaraderie between officers and enlisted like you share with Buzz."

Brown nodded. "That's all too true. I like a loose shop. It took us a while to unpucker Buzz's ass, but he's learned to like it too. This is a very smart bunch of people. As for Britaine, he sees what he wants to see. And all he sees from us are the pre-mission briefings in the flight room and training briefs at the education center. I don't think he has set foot in the intel shack since he's been in command. This style of management may not work for every AMSF department. I'm sure it would never work in the APES, but it works for intel. It keeps us fresh and open to new ideas like your anomaly. You are planning on looking for it again?"

"Yes, Chief. That would be my plan, if you don't mind?"

"Mind? No, I insist. If you don't look, I will. I want your eyes glued to the comm collector array blips. Watch for any patterns in real time. Don't worry about the squadron chatter. The collector will put that in the can for us, but you might spot something that a machine would miss."

"Roger that, Chief," Misha said. "What do we know about the system we're jumping into?"

"It's just like the one we are in. It's uninhabited and uninhabitable; a complete waste of vacuum, if you ask me. That's what intrigues me about your anomaly. There is something there that shouldn't be. We have a jump coming in fifteen, so get situated and comfortable. Strap into your chair tight. General Gurand has ordered the squadron to do another combat insertion, so it should be another rough jump."

Misha sat at the comm collector console. The chair she was in was the same Mark 19D Crash Couch she remembered from her AMSF tour of duty earlier. Each buckle and strap felt familiar, as did the console's arrays and displays.

She thought about the anomaly off and on throughout the day. She played with the data in her head and then put it away, only to pull it out again later. She was sure there was a matching pattern there, but they were stuck somewhere in the back of her head. The sounds were not meshing comfortably with some stuck memory key. In truth, Misha would have preferred to endure a jump strapped into her own bunk. There she could stretch out and close her eyes. With the crash couch, she was tossed about and her movements restricted, plus there was still a nagging cramp in her left calf muscle that had bothered her for years that she blamed on this very style seat.

The jump itself was spectacularly dull. It was like riding the same roller coaster a dozen times in a row. It was the jinking and twisting the Kiirkegaard went through during the combat reentry that kept things lively at the communications collector. All the spacecraft in the squadron began blasting automated and manual data in an almost continuous stream immediately upon system entry.

The automated signals would emit status of their own spacecraft, position and disposition of any other squadron spacecraft in its general area, and any unidentified or enemy spacecraft detected. If the automated systems did not detect any enemy spacecraft, it would say so; repeatedly and loudly.

The manual systems emissions were the crew. Bridge operation personnel would send data streams containing information on status of their own spacecraft, position and disposition of any other squadron spacecraft in its general area, and any unidentified or enemy spacecraft detected. If the crew did not detect any enemy spacecraft, they would say so; repeatedly and loudly.

The main difference between the automated and the manual systems was that every so often a manual signal would be lost when the spaceship jinked. It would dart off in a random direction causing the crew member to lose her breath, his train of thought, or their lunch; depending upon the constitution of the individual involved. Jinking was a deliberate attempt to confuse any enemy targeting systems. The inertial dampers could completely eliminate any feeling of movement, but humans rely on a certain amount of movement to keep their internal bearings from going completely haywire, causing some very strange psychotic episodes.

Misha found the jinks more of an inconvenience than discomforting. Her heavy-worlder heritage included a strong inner-ear alignment and an elevated tolerance for sudden high gravity movements. She watched the collector arrays between jinks, searching for the anomaly. She fed the data perimeters into the system and set it for an automated search. She knew there was little chance of spotting it before the collector's automated systems alerted her to its presence. She was right.

A small beep cut through the air and the collector array switched to a visual pattern approximating the sounds from the anomaly. Something tickled her brain just at the edge of discovery. The Kiirkegaard jinked. Its gyrations caused even the automated systems to lose the anomaly. The spacecraft settled back into squadron formation, but the signal was gone.

Misha saw the pattern clearly in her mind's eye. She knew what she was seeing was of Binder origin. The sound's visual pattern from the collector array was a perfect match to what Misha had seen on Guinjundst. It was an exact fit to the green vegetation markings along the sides of Binder energy weapons. Although she couldn't fathom their purpose, to her it was positive proof of Binders in Allied Systems space.

"I got it," she shouted. Any response was lost as the spacecraft jinked again and was covered by the sound of someone retching into a waste can.

Chapter Thirty-One

Misha left the intelligence office with a sense of mixed satisfaction. From an intel point of view it was a good shift. Everyone agreed with her assessment that the anomaly was of Binder origin. Even General Gurand and Colonel Britaine admitted as much. No one, computer or human, could match the signal to any known Binder activity. Even so, the after-action reports, the on-line meetings and the flurry of comm traffic took her away from McPherson's Second for far too long.

She relied on her seconds and her own Able Squad's Trooper One Singletary to get the unit on track for the Altec dirt drop. Misha flashed a comm to her unit between meetings and urged them to greater efforts. She knew they would fight Binders in Altec. However, true to AMSF form, a deep classification rating covered the Binder signal incident. She was unable to mention it to her troops.

General Gurand decided to jump into the Gagarin System with only a twenty-four-hour delay. A flurry of probes failed to turn up any spacecraft. That may be because space is fairly vast and somewhat empty. There may not be many places to hide, but a spaceship lying dormant can hide in plain sight. The probes may not have found anything because the ship issuing the signal had bugged out before the AMSF could get their act together and launch that flurry of probes. Where the signal had come from would remain a mystery for a while. What the signal meant was also a very dangerous unknown.

Gurand decided he needed to notify AMSF headquarters and the Allied Systems government about the new Binder signal. This required sending a spacecraft to the rear through the last two jumps. He ordered Colonel Britaine to dispatch two Kiirkegaard FACs to Heaven's Gate. The Kiirkegaard would move with the squadron through the next jump into the Gagarin system and stop off at Gagarin Four to drop off Marshal Service Sergeant Forrester. The FACs with their two men crews were small enough and fast enough to endure the multiple jumps, send a message, pick up a reply and double jump back. A FAC required only minimal downtime between jumps for the flight crew to adjust. They might even make it back before the Kiirkegaard jumped into Gagarin if they pushed it. In any event, Britaine would wait for his fighters to return before ordering the Kiirkegaard to follow Gurand's squadron from Gagarin and into Altec space.

Despite the AMSF classifying the Binder signal as deep secret, Misha decided to forward the details to Fourth-Level Commander Kema Wallace Ottiamig, her immediate supervisor, with a cc attachment to all of her up-line commands. As an intelligence specialist, her message was automatically routed to the head of APES intelligence, a fifth-level commander in the second tier. All the messages were encoded and sent with the FACs for transmission once they entered the Heaven system.

APES intelligence would combine the new data with every other piece of available Binder activity. A retransmission would be quickly downloaded to all APES as relevant tactical data. She was certain when she received the report back through the intelligence filters that it would bear little or no resemblance to the data she sent forward. Misha was confident of this because such a signal would not hold much significance for ground troops. None-the-less, it was still a gratifying intelligence find. It was particularly satisfying that an APES intelligence specialist located and identified the signal when the AMSF intelligence technicians could not or would not.

Screams of pain and howls of anger assaulted Misha's ears as she stepped through the hatch into the APES training bay.

Chapter Thirty-Two

Men and women in various degrees of sweat, pummeling, pounding and pouncing upon one another, immediately surrounded Misha. She smiled as a particularly loud bone-crunching crash echoed around the metal bulkheads. Those were the sights and sounds of warriors preparing for battle. Her warriors were preparing for her battle.

"Third on deck," someone shouted.

"As you were," Misha replied before anyone else could react. "Know sweat: know success. Get to it, you lazy APES."

A heavy weight slammed Misha's back, pushing her forward into a knot of APES. She recognized Second Takki-Homi as he tried to wrap her into a headlock. She bent rapidly from the waist, throwing the man into the small cluster of APES. Twisting sideways, she saw Trooper Ortiz of Charlie Squad slide into her legs, grappling to buckle her knees. Another Charlie trooper, Amossitta Riffler, threw herself at Misha's chest in a cross-body block.

Misha turned. She knew she was going onto the deck face first, but before Riffler made contact, a second body slammed upward across the trooper, knocking her sideways, sending her spinning off like an airplane propeller gone haywire and out of contact with Misha. Ottiamig, of her own Able Squad, quickly locked Riffler into a submission hold only a second after Misha dropped her full weight onto Ortiz's slight frame. Misha drove the point of her elbow deeply into the woman's solar plexus. The air whoofed out of Ortiz's lungs and she patted the deck in submission.

Before Misha could roll off of Ortiz, Takki-Homi slammed into her body followed by a pile of Charlie Squad's troopers. Able Squad troopers quickly followed them and a wild melee ensued that was over all too fast. She was pinned to the deck plates. The only damage she could manage to inflict on the Charlie Squad attackers was minuscule. She admitted defeat as Charlie repulsed

Able's rescue attempt. She patted the deck plates signaling her surrender. "Great way to greet your commander, Second Takki-Homi," she said with mock severity.

Takki-Homi laughed, "No sweat: no success. It was a fair fight except Charlie outnumbered Able by eleven to seven, counting you. We beat you mainly by surprise. You let yourself get sucked into an ambush, Third. Shame on you."

"Great! Just great! That is really going to do wonders for my combat image." She looked around the training bay. Everyone was engaged in hand-to-hand combat training each squad pitted against another. Looking over her own squad she noticed Singletary, Juarez, Park and Slezak were missing. She expected Slezak's absence as she was still confined to quarters. She also noticed Ottiamig was bleeding from a split lip. She looked pointedly at Able Squad's med tech, Trooper Cutler and with a finger directed his attention to Ottiamig. Cutler nodded, grabbed his medical kit and moved to attend the slight cut.

Nodding nodded at Second Takki-Homi, she said. "This is a good group exercise. Your idea?"

"Nope," he said. "Theda, I mean Second Moraft likes us to train this way all the time."

"Well, remind me to compliment her," Misha said. "It looks like it really engenders teamwork among the squads."

Takki-Homi shooed both squads back to working out before he spoke. "I am sure she would be pleased to hear that, Trey. But, the truth be known, she really likes to practice this way because it allows her to hide in the crowd. Look, I am not one to rat out another second, but Theda lets far too many things slide, including her physical exercise programs; that and her whole squad's readiness. I just thought you ought to know."

"I appreciate the heads up, Taks. I noticed those same things myself."

Takki-Homi shook his head. "Sorry, I guess didn't need to say anything."

"You'd better. Just because I saw this doesn't mean I will see everything you see. Don't you dare go silent on me, Deuce. I think we are getting ourselves into a whirlwind of trouble on this drop and our outfit isn't near as ready as we should be."

"Yeah, well, I guess you better hear this too. There is quite a bit of grumbling about that," Takki-Homi hesitated.

"Go on," she ordered.

"A lot of the veterans have been complaining that you're spending what precious little time we have left with the AMSF instead of your own command. Truthfully, I've wondered about that myself," Takki-Homi said.

"Something went down in intelligence. It's not a cover when I say that I can't really tell you right now about what went on. AMSF and APES classified a lot of what is happening. I promise I will let you know as soon as I can."

"I hope that's before the excrement hits the oscillating wind device," he smiled.

"I promise you this, Taks. I'll let you and every member of this unit know every piece of information you need before we drop dirt on Altec, whether the information is classified or not. The big bosses can court-martial me later if they don't like it."

"That is fair enough for me. Can I pass your promise on to the other squad leaders?" he asked.

"I'll do it myself." Speaking into her glass-pack, she gave the code to transmit a copy of her conversation with Taks to all seconds. "Satisfied?"

"Always was, Trey," Takki-Homi smiled.

"One other thing before we get back to grunt work; I notice we are missing a few troopers." She let the comment hang in the air as it was more of a question than a statement.

"Well, Deuce Vark is gone down to the armory. They still have a stack of new schematics to download into the suits. Don't worry; she will have us ready in time."

"The timeline has changed, Deuce. The AMSF just shortened their jump schedule. We don't know how short yet, but we've lost some time."

"Don't worry about Vark, Trey. She is new on the job as a second, but she is a solid trooper. She will have us ready. Let's see who else is missing…, well, Golf Squad is missing Trooper Na'aranna. She is running last minute checks as the senior weapons tech. I checked on them a little while ago and they're ready to lock and load; just a few last-minute details. I was told Juarez is with her and that Park may have had some issues with Able Squad's skid plates. I also heard word that Singletary had sick call. You remember about Slezak, right?"

"You are being pretty vague on Juarez, Park and Singletary, aren't you, Taks? 'Was told', 'may have' and 'heard that' are all word modifiers you just used to tap dance around where my people are. What are you trying not to say?" she asked. She was determined to ignore his question about Trooper Slezak, because she clearly remembered Slezak and still had yet to determine if she were going to red-line the veteran for the dirt drop. Still, she did not look forward to having a trooper at her back who had an inclination to frag her in real combat. She stared at Takki-Homi until he replied.

"It's your squad, Trey. It's not my place to say."

Misha said, "It is your place to say if I ask. And if I recall, I just did ask, so spill it."

"I dropped by to talk with Na'aranna before coming over here. She hadn't seen Juarez and hadn't asked or needed his help. And if Singletary took sick call, why doesn't your med tech Cutler know about it? Park? Well, him I don't know about. In truth, there are half a dozen APES missing all told. I don't know why. Sorry, but it didn't occur to me to ask. I'm sure most of them, maybe all of them, are legit."

"And Able's missing troopers are not legit? That's what you're saying?" Misha asked.

"Don't know, Trey. There's nothing I heard that I'd stand up and testify about, you know?" Takki-Homi shrugged.

"Roger that, Deuce. Thanks for the heads up," Misha smiled in response. "I'll check up on it."

Takki-Homi pointed over Misha's shoulder at a small group of troopers waiting to get her attention. The group consisted of troopers from a half a dozen different squads. Takki-Homi smiled and shrugged.

She smiled and shrugged back. "It looks like we need time for a question and answer session. Round them up for me if you would Second. Let's air some dirty laundry."

Misha much preferred a direct, take-it-or-leave-it type of briefing. She hated Q&A ever since she was a know-nothing rookie FNG. She felt it took time away from her training or study time, not to mention sleep and free time. Now, being in command, she also hated the sessions because she never knew the answers and always had to refer the questions up the chain of command to her third. She still hated Q&A for no other reason than habit.

After everyone sat on the deck, Second Kranitchovich of Hotel Squad stood. He appeared to be a tranquil second and so new at the job he was almost in mint condition with packing grease still on the moving parts. Misha was surprised to see him volunteer the initial question. She thought it was a good thing for a second to ask the first question as it might help to forestall the really stupid questions some troopers liked to ask just to hear themselves talk.

"Sir, I am Second-Level Commander Stanley Kranitchovich of Hotel Squad," he said.

Misha stifled a smile and nodded in recognition. She was sure he knew she recognized him. She was glad he announced himself, it might set the precedence for other questions. She easily recognized her whole unit now, having studied the unit records and attempted to speak to each second and trooper in the command. But, it was always good to get the name of who was speaking for the glass pack recordings.

"Third McPherson, I have been approached by spacecraft crew more than once about leaving the AMSF and joining the APES."

A flurry of voices told her Kranitchovich had not been the only one approached with such questions. She wondered if the two AMSF Security Force personnel that had come to her earlier had intended the same question, but had not gotten to the point.

"Go on, Second Kranitchovich, I am sure there is more to your question."

"Well yes, sir. Please don't misunderstand, but the word is that you and Colonel Britaine have, well, um…" the man's voice trailed off.

Misha blushed, but smiled coldly at the man. "I believe the word is that we are doing the parallel polka, the old bump and grind, the bed sheet sandwich and putting the salami to the Swiss cheese. Is that your question?"

"Well no, sir, I just didn't think it would be best for my question to get back to Colonel Britaine. I sort of promised the spacers that I wouldn't get them in trouble with their commander, you know?"

"I can see your dilemma; I give you my word that everything said here will stay here. I know I am new to this unit and most of you don't have any reason to believe I am trustworthy. But, Fourth-Level Commander Ottiamig trusted me, so I guess that will have to do."

"Yes, sir. It'll do for me. Those spacers came to me because they at the end of their rope with Britaine. I mean, Colonel Britaine. They just can't stand working for him anymore and they'll do just about whatever it takes to get out from under him. They're even willing to switch to the APES to do it. I want to know what to tell them."

"That is an excellent question, Deuce. Can I take it from the rest of you this is not an isolated incident? So be it. Okay, we do not try to pirate spacers while deployed on their spacecraft. So we cannot, I repeat, we cannot actively seek to recruit. We can talk to them if they come to us, is that understood?"

A chorus of 'roger that' rang out.

Misha continued. "Everybody in this room knows there are two kinds of commanders. There are the ones you like and the ones you don't. With patience, you can outlast the ones you don't like. Let's make it our standard tactic to try to impress on everyone who asks that they should try a transfer within their own service before jumping to the APES. Try to dissuade them by giving them a hard line about APES life if they are insistent. You shouldn't have to go far for examples of how unpleasant our chosen career field can be at times."

Laughter rang out as troopers shouted their favorite gripe: communal bedrooms, no home life, poor pay, bad food, etc. Misha let the unit gripe for a minute or two, then she held up her hand for silence. "I see you all get the drift of such a conversation. Basically, troopers, we don't want them in the first place if you can talk them out of joining the APES, got it? And tell them to look you up after this deployment, if they still insist. Understand?"

In the midst of the 'roger that' responses, Misha heard someone say something about 'Muffin's little muffin.' Others heard the remark. She could see people looking around. A couple of second-level commanders shot questioning looks at their troopers. She noticed the troopers shake their heads in the negative. She decided her best option was to pretend she hadn't heard the remark. That was not to be.

"Sir, Second Theda Moraft, Bravo Squad and that is your question of the day. What about the rumors of you and Colonel Britaine?"

A second voice shouted out, "And Forrester?"

Misha looked out over the unit. "Quite a group of gossips we have here. I'll be as transparent as I can about this. I am not, nor have I ever had, a sexual relationship with either Colonel Britaine or Sergeant Forrester. I am trying very hard to maintain a working relationship with our transportation's commander. Such a relationship is not easy, nor is it made easier by rumors and gossip. I like Forrester, as do many of you. I understand Second Takki-Homi had Sergeant Forrester over for lunch. Taks, are you sleeping with Gan?"

Takki-Homi laughed, "Not on your life, Trey. He ain't my style."

Moraft continued. "But, you've spent time alone with Colonel Britaine. Also, Sergeant Forrester moved into your private bedroom."

Misha nodded. "That's true enough on both counts. But, I haven't had sex with everyone I've ever been alone with, Second Moraft. And neither have you. The Colonel is in command the spacecraft that we need to get to Altec. We can't walk through the vacuum of space to reach the enemy. We need him, whether we like him or not. As for the other, well… Sergeant Forrester is a nice man. I offered him the use of the bedroom adjoining my office. That is all I have offered and all he has taken. You may believe it or not." Misha looked on as the unit fell silent. She thought she could have handled the question better, but didn't know what else to say. How can anyone prove something didn't happen? "Other questions?" she asked.

"Sir, Trooper Three Beaudry, Joker Squad. How come you're spending so much time in spacer intelligence rather than getting ready for Altec? I mean we're down here bustin' our nuts and you're setting up there chatting and having coffee with your vacuum sucker buddies."

Second-Level Caution of Kilo Squad shouted, "That's enough, Beaudry."

Misha held up a hand, "It's okay, Deuce. Trooper Beaudry was a bit crude in his presentation, but he does have a valid question. As a matter of fact, he is not the first one to ask that exact question." There were a few surprised looks around as she continued. "To answer this question, let me ask you a few questions first. I see Na'aranna our senior weapons technician has just joined us. Trooper Na'aranna, I understand you've been working very hard getting our weapons up to speed. Is that correct?"

Na'aranna said, with a touch of pride, "Damn right, sir. I just did a down check of the systems and we're ten points above standard. We are ready to rock and I will take on the first yahoo who says different." She looked around defiantly.

Misha hid a smile. "That's superior work, Trooper Na'aranna. I'm very pleased to hear it. Convey my thanks for a very good job done to Trooper Juarez and the rest of your team."

"Juarez, sir?" Na'aranna said. "I haven't seen him all day. I checked Able's weapons myself. Where the hell do you think I've been?"

Misha smiled coldly, "I see. Hence the question on the table: why am I not here to know that Juarez wasn't where he was supposed to be?" She noticed Second Aardmricksdottir hustle into the room through the main hatchway. Misha nodded and smiled at the woman. "My next question is for Deuce Vark. What have you been doing for the upcoming Altec dirt drop?"

Vark nodded. "Working every pair of hands I could get to bring our armor up to snuff. I can't say we will exceed standards by the time we get to Altec, but we will meet those standards and be ready to kick ass."

A ragged shout led by Second Jackson rippled through the crowd. Misha was pleased to see the unit reaction. It may have been a ragged shout, but it was definitely the beginning of good combat morale. She was also pleased to note Aardmricksdottir had been following the question and answer session on her comm unit. Her response showed she heard Trooper Na'aranna's answer about weapons repair exceeding standards. Misha knew a lot of commanders kept running tabs on their units through open communication links on their glass-packs. Personally, she agreed with those commanders who thought it was a serious violation of privacy in a service that was already too short on privacy.

She kept her own squad communications link open through Trooper DeLaPax. She would have preferred to keep a link to her Trooper One, but she wasn't ready to tackle Singletary yet. She knew she would have to announce to the unit she would be recording, not for compliance to any APES regulation, but for her own sense of ethics. So if, as she suspected, Singletary was back in the contraband business, she would have to give him notice she suspected him.

Misha could set her comm unit to search for certain words and phrases used on any of the 1392nd's open comms. All related signals would download to her glass-pack for analysis, allowing her to check specific conversations without having to review hundreds of hours of casual chatter. She could also gather any conversation spoken within the sound range of any glass-pack that might be open. Most troopers and even a few commanders would be surprised at the audio pickup range of the average glass-pack. However, any trooper could shut down his glass-pack at any time. Many troopers, herself included, never bothered to shut their glass-pack off. It made a very handy recording of everything for future reference. She was impressed early on in her APES career that the old military adage of CYA was important. You never know when, what, or which piece of information could Cover Your Ass. Plus, as a commander, leaving her comms open would allow anyone in the unit to call her at any time of any day. She believed that open comms of some kind was a necessity of command. She could, for privacy, shut off any out-going transmission.

"Thank you, Deuce Vark. The word I hear has been very favorable. I'm told you are doing an excellent job and I couldn't be more pleased."

Vark smiled and nodded her thanks.

"My next question," Misha said. "Has everyone here read the pre-op briefings on the Altec System, the dirt drop and the updated info on Binder actions that your squad's intel specialist put together?"

Another chorus of 'roger that' rang out.

Misha said, "Where does that information come from? I'll tell you. Your squad's intelligence specialist collected, analyzed and collated the raw data. Some of

190

the information comes to us through channels from APES command, as well as from the Marshal Service, the AMSF and any other place we can get information. A lot of raw data is gathered during our dirt drops. Information your squad's intelligence specialist gathers in this upcoming dirt drop may shorten the Binders war. It may even save your life in the dirt drop after this one.

"I can't share with you exactly what has gone on in the AMSF intelligence shack, but it was important information that APES command needed to know. I don't say this to brag, but without our APES support this very significant piece of information might not have been found. And I say our support, emphasis on 'our' because I couldn't be free to take time as an intelligence specialist without APES like Trooper Na'aranna and Second Vark doing their jobs so well." Misha looked around as the crowd grew silent again. She thought she could have handled that answer better, but she hoped everyone got the point that it was all about teamwork

She saw Troopers Singletary, Park and Juarez slide in through a side hatch and it interrupted her thoughts. She pointed her index finger at Singletary causing every head to swivel toward the trio. She locked into eye contact with Singletary refusing to break contact until he looked away. The three tardy troopers sat on the deck at the rear of the crowd.

Misha said coldly, "Do we have any other questions? Now is the time, Troopers."

A tall trooper stood up slowly. The woman glanced at Singletary, cleared her throat and said, "Yeah, well...um...why give a Marshal Service sergeant the only single bedroom in APES country unless something extra is going on? Shouldn't it be ours to use? Maybe we could share it on a rotating basis."

Misha recognized the woman both from her files and from training. Before she could speak, Second Vark shouted, "Putinova, that question has been answered. Do you have crap in your ears or were you just not paying attention? Sit down."

Misha smiled and held up her hand. "Thanks, Deuce Vark." She gave Putinova a hard stare "I think there might be a real question in there somewhere."

Putinova shot a questioning glance at Singletary. Singletary refused to meet her look, but made a very slight shake of his head.

Misha saw the message pass between the two. "Trooper Singletary, get on your feet," she ordered. Putinova started to squat on the deck, but Misha shook her head, pointed a finger at the woman and gave the combat hand signal for 'stand in place.' Putinova froze. "Trooper Singletary, do you have something to add to this question?" she asked.

"No, sir."

"No? It seems to me that Putinova thinks you have a particular interest here," Misha said.

"No, sir, I am just trying to pay attention. I don't know what Greggoria, um Trooper Putinova is getting at, except that...well, we could all use a private bedroom every now and then. It would be nicer than, um, you know, doubling up behind blast shutters that are in the same room as everybody else," Singletary said.

"I see," Misha said. "What about using Kiirkegaard's comfort suites?"

Second Moraft stood up, "Sir, by order of Colonel Britaine, we can use the suites on a space-available basis. That means we can get one if the AMSF isn't using it. That doesn't seem to happen. Ever."

Misha nodded. "Second Moraft, do you know what our contract with the AMSF says about our use of those suites? No? Find out and report back to me. I would suggest you read section nineteen, paragraph a213. Still, that does bring us back to the situation with Colonel Britaine, doesn't it?"

Putinova emboldened by Singletary's repeat of her question and Moraft's reinforcement said enthusiastically, "Yeah, I mean, if you don't want to use the bedroom in the day office, maybe we could raffle it off or maybe rent it out on a rotating basis..." Her voice trailed off when she realized Singletary was frowning at her.

Misha nodded. Anytime money changed hands, there was a possibility someone could skim or siphon some of it away. Any lottery or game of chance could be rigged. She could see Singletary was looking for new sources of extracurricular funds and had been looking at Putinova to front his question. It appeared that the woman cut a corner too fast and did not time her question in sync with Singletary's plans. Misha said, "Shall we hear your question again, Trooper….?" She let the name dangle in front of the woman.

"Oh sorry, sir. I forgot. I am Joker Squad Trooper Four Greggoria Putinova. I only asked about using the day office bedroom for APES use."

"You really only asked one question?" Misha smiled coldly. "I heard three questions. Suppose we hear them again." She pulled her glass-pack out of her breast pocket, waved it pointedly and ordered, "Repeat and broadcast to all 1392nd members the question at hand."

Her glass-pack and one hundred and twenty-one other glass-packs blasted out Putinova's voice. "Yeah, well. Why give a Marshal Sergeant a bedroom in APES country, unless something extra is going on? Shouldn't it be ours to use? Maybe we could share it on a rotating basis?"

Misha let the questions hang. She thought, "There. That will serve as a warning to Singletary and everybody else that they might be recorded. It may cause him to drive his conversations under wraps." Still, she knew many people didn't realize that as much information could be gathered from what is not said as there is from what is spoken aloud. "Question one: why did I give our only private bedroom to someone other than an APE…unless something is going on between Sergeant Forrester and me? Is that correct, Trooper Four Putinova?"

Putinova stuttered, "No, no…um…I didn't mean to imply something, I mean, nothing improper between you and him. I mean…" Her voice trailed off.

Misha let the silence stand for a moment. "Yes. I believe that is exactly what you meant to imply, Trooper. That question was asked and answered already." Misha now had positive proof she hadn't done a good job of answering the same question earlier. Now she had to deal with it again. She stared into the upturned faces. "Look, people. I can't control what you think of me. I have no way to prove nothing is going on between Sergeant Forrester and me. I offered him the use of the room as a kindness. It is a kindness that someday may come back to us with dividends. Sergeant Forrester's billet is with a pair of AMSF second lieutenants. That is a fate I would not wish upon anyone, so I invested that room as a favor."

She suddenly grew angry. "Think what you will of me, but do not think of me as an idiot." She knew her face was now flushed. To many people, it might look like she was blushing, but it was a rush of anger that fed hot, oxygenated blood to every muscle in her body. Misha slowed her breathing and tried to calm down. She held her hand up for everyone to 'freeze.' The 1329th froze, not a muscle moved.

Finally, she calmed herself enough to trust speaking without hearing her voice break with emotion. "If you believe Forrester and I are lovers, then think on this: only an idiot would place a higher value on a relationship with a lover than with her squad. We go into combat together. I depend on each of you to protect my back as I will protect yours. Do you honestly think I would put a higher value on any man whose sole contribution is shoving his penis between my legs? Dammit, I may be desperate, but I'm not that bad off."

Misha looked at Singletary again. "Trooper, you seem to have an interest in this issue. I will ask you: do you think it might be advantageous to have a Marshal's Service sergeant owe you a favor?"

Singletary smiled and nodded. "Yes, sir, it would be a better thing for some of us than for others."

"True, Trooper. Now, sit your can on the deck. No, not you Putinova, we still have your questions on deck."

"Um, that's okay, sir. I think I understand now," Putinova said. She glanced nervously at Second Aardmricksdottir.

"Thank you, Putinova, but we will hear the answers none-the-less. Shall we?" Misha asked with mock sweetness, that fooled no one. "This is an open Q&A. I'm sure Second Aardmricksdottir will not hold your questions against you. Seconds will not punish any honestly asked question. I emphasize honest. Do we need to hear your recorded questions again? Or do you trust my memory? Okay. Question two: 'shouldn't it be ours to use?' Question three: 'maybe we could share it on a rotating basis?' Both are good and valid questions, Trooper.

Misha continued, "Question Two: it is not ours to use. It's mine to use or not, as I see fit. When, and only when we dirt drop, does it becomes ours. It then becomes the 1392nd mobile combat command center. Until then, it's my office. Got me? Right now, I believe a good inter-service relationship is important at this juncture of the Binder War."

She looked around the bay and said, "Number three: we could indeed share it on a rotating basis. That's an outstanding suggestion for future consideration. However, think about this. We have a deployment from Heaven's Gate to Altec that should take about nine days. Surely, you can contain yourselves for a week and a half. Prior to my taking command, many of you were deployed on or around Heaven's Gate for almost two months. I know from the 1392nd records most of you took advantage of private rooms on Heaven's Gate at one time or another." She looked pointedly at India Squad's Trooper One Aggie Raza. Raza had logged into a private room almost every night during the two-month downtime. Each night, it was with a different partner or partners. "Some, more times than others." Misha blushed at her own comment.

Trooper Raza smiled and winked back as she took a ribbing from some of her squad mates.

Misha said, "Also, our rookies had recent use of private rooms during transfers. Finally, in the time between our leaving Heaven's Gate and our arrival at Altec, more than ninety percent of you would have never gotten the use of that room, even if we started from the lift off on day one. Who would want to volunteer to be a part of that ninety percent?" She nodded at Putinova, who sat gratefully down on the deck. Misha still hadn't been able to explain herself as well as she had hoped.

She desperately wanted to finish this session and go ask Sergeant Forrester what he might know about the events on Guinjundst. The man knew more than he was telling. A favor or two might loosen him up. Misha had a fleeting thought that if she were a different kind of person, she might sic Raza on him to shake some information loose. Still, she couldn't explain even to her own unit about what had happened on Guinjundst. Not yet anyway, APES command needed verification. She didn't know why the equipment and bodies she gathered on Guinjundst did not constitute valid confirmation, but that was not her call.

She returned to her answer, hoping to clarify her comments. "A ten percent use rate of the day office is not a fair distribution. On top of which, I don't know how many of you would have the energy to do more than sleep there, even if you won a lottery." A ripple of laughter swept the room as Raza waved her hand vigorously." Misha smiled, "Raza excluded, I don't know how anyone would have found the energy for anything more strenuous than sleeping. I know I've been working your tails off since I got here trying to get this unit up to specs."

Beaudry stood again amid groans from a dozen troopers. Misha understood their feelings, it was turning into a long day for everyone. She couldn't remember when she had last slept. People were tired, hot, sweaty, and a hard deck plate was not the most comfortable seat. Beaudry asked the question she was dreading to hear again. "Third, that brings us back to my earlier question, why aren't you down here working with us to get ready instead of hanging with your spacer friends, if you don't think we're good enough?"

Second Aardmricksdottir stood with her hand up to be recognized. Misha nodded to her.

"Asked and answered, Beaudry," Aardmricksdottir said. "The Third said you were protected by honest questions, not by repeating a question you should have known the answer to in the first place."

Beaudry whined, "Yeah, Deuce, but Able Squad isn't half together as some of the others."

Aardmricksdottir shouted, "Able Squad is not your concern, Trooper. You're in my squad. That is Joker Squad. I have to rely on Trooper One Spakney to keep things moving when I'm working as the senior armor repair tech for the whole unit. Deuce Taks' Charlie Squad doesn't fall apart when he stops to cook for them because Gaineretti jumps in to take over. Third McPherson should be able to lean on Trooper One Singletary. Beaudry, suppose you ask Trooper One Singletary why Able Squad is not up to your expectations? Go ahead, dammit, ask him."

Beaudry sat on the deck. He mumbled, "Never mind, sorry I asked."

Aardmricksdottir didn't want to let it go, but Misha waved her down.

"Other than questions about the upcoming dirt drop, does anyone have anything else to add? No? All right, you APES. We're all more than a little tired and we only have a few hours before our next jump. I'm going to call for a general inspection within the hour." There were more than a few grumbles echoing through the bay. "Sorry, people. Such is the life of a caged APE."

"After the inspection, I want everybody on a twelve-hour downtime. That's everybody. Cooks included so toss out a pile of snack packs for anybody who gets hungry." She smiled at the loud cheer. "I am sorry to say any sack time will be interrupted by a combat insertion jump. I know I can't sleep through those things, so I realize that most of you can't either. Get strapped in if you do go down for sleep. We may not have much time to check each bunk for sleeping troops before the Kiirkegaard jumps. We're too close to a dirt drop to have to red-line anyone for broken bones resulting from getting tossed around during the jump and combat insertion." She smiled again at the grumbles. Strapping yourself in to sleep was uncomfortable because it kept you from turning over in your sleep. Still, it was necessary because Britaine had not published his jump schedule. The captain seemed to have a pathological aversion to sharing command information with anyone, even with his own staff and crew.

"One last thing APES, at the end of those twelve hours we are going to run every squad through the tri-wave sim again." More grumbles echoed throughout the training bay. "Now get out of here and do that inspection so we can get some sleep."

Chapter Thirty-Three

Able's Trooper Ten Tammie Qualls let out a sigh of relief. Third McPherson had just begun the general inspection on her combat suit when a call took her away.

"Saved by the bell again, Qualls," DeLaPax called out with a laugh.

Again, Tammie questioned her decision to leave the Heaven Three Police Department. She remembered fondly her quiet position in the communications systems department. She might not have left if it hadn't been for that a-hole of a supervisor. She shook her head at the memory of her boss's insistence on carrying on a sexual relationship with her. No matter how many times she went to bed with him and how many times she tried to break it off with him, he wanted more.

She remembered thinking communications with a police department couldn't be much different than communications in an APES outfit. How wrong she was! Not only was she responsible for managing the communications data stream, she was also required to know how to repair and set up the equipment. All of that while she was wearing a combat suit, shooting deadly weapons and killing living creatures. She almost had a panic attack the first time she was inside a tri-wave simulation combat scenario. She only survived by knowing in the back of her mind that it wasn't real. She didn't know what she would do when she had to shoot at something live, even Binders. It was true she had learned Jujitsu with the HTPD, but it was nothing like APES training. This was harsh, brutal and more physically demanding than her old boss had ever been.

Then there was this commander. McPherson scared the bejeezus out of her. Tammie knew she was more scared of Third McPherson than she was of whether or not she could kill Binders. The Third was like a rock: cold, hard, and unmovable. Tammie would have sworn her combat equipment was up to APES standard operational procedures, but she almost fainted when McPherson popped open panels and dug into the guts of the suit. It was brand new armor. She hadn't even put any personal markings, decals or paintings on it like most of the veteran's suits in the bay. It was bright and shiny without the slightest dent. It should have been out-of-the-box perfect.

Tammie smiled weakly back at DeLaPax. Saved by the bell was right.

DeLaPax stepped over to her. The tall, beautiful woman patted Tammie on the head. "Let's take a look at this suit, rookie. Let's see if we can figure out what the boss was looking to find, shall we?"

Chapter Thirty-Four

Colonel Britaine smiled at the assembled officers. All of his flight crews were in attendance, plus that APES bitch. He extended a charming smile in her direction and nodded. He thought if he could keep her in her place until they dumped them out on Altec, then he could wangle a way to get her unit deployed to another spacecraft for any return trip. Assuming she survived combat. His smile grew at the thought of McPherson's impending death. That would solve all of his problems with the insolent bitch.

The only person he had been unable to contact was that foolish old bureaucrat from the Marshal Service. The senile data pusher had shut off his comm unit. Even those idiot second lieutenants he had set to watch him hadn't seen Forrester. Well, he would show up in due time, after all, you can't get lost on a spacecraft for long.

Britaine stood until the room grew quiet, then nodded in satisfaction. Things were going very well indeed. This latest bit of intelligence was quite a coup for him. He had shown General Gurand that his intelligence staff could out do the General's staff. He thought a few kudos, attaboys and pats on the back would be appropriate.

"Ladies and gentlemen, as most of you are aware, we gathered some significant data during the last series of jumps about a possible Binder presence in our space. The first order of business is to give our collective congratulations to Major Junior Grade Hiero Krandiewsky of the intelligence office." Britaine clapped his hands and smiled broadly when the applause spread among the flight crew.

Krandiewsky smiled back, his face blank as if he had decided it was still not a prudent time to tell Colonel Britaine about mispronouncing his first name or to mention that it was Brown and McPherson who were responsible for the actual discovery and analysis of the anomaly.

When the moderate applause died out Britaine continued. "No further signal or analysis has been forthcoming, but we can rest assured that Hiero will stay on top of it, and he will be a credit to all of us. Command doesn't expect any repeat of this Binder signal in Gagarin space, but we will be looking anyway. Right, Hiero?"

"Yes, Colonel, we will find it if there is a repeat of the anomaly," Krandiewsky said.

Britaine nodded as if he expected nothing less. "This signal does have merit; however, it demands further investigation. We need the answers here. That may be made more difficult by the fact the signal hasn't been heard a third time, correct? I want it to be us, if anybody finds the answers to this puzzle, understand?"

Krandiewsky replied, "Yes, sir. We will do the Kiirkegaard proud."

Britaine continued with his briefing. "Secondly, General Gurand agreed it was best to send this information to the rear to AMSF command by the most expeditious method. The Kiirkegaard is the spacecraft of discovery for this information, so it fell to us to provide two FAC to translate back to Heaven's Gate. Those pilots have returned in record time. That in itself is such a notable achievement it is being recorded in the pilots' files. I am sure awards and decorations are in the works."

The four pilots stood and waved as the crowd shouted both congratulations and blew razzberries. General laughter and back patting was rampant. Britaine was pleased. It was pleasurable to see excellent actions rewarded. They were young pilots, it didn't take much to encourage them and make them happy. Britaine could see their bloodshot eyes, drooping muscles and the spider web of broken blood vessels across their faces. A quick series of jumps would take a serious physical toll on the healthiest of pilots. The junior most pilot could barely stand, but her brethren valiantly held her upright. She was obviously suffering from cramps and nausea. Britain wasn't worried. They were young. Puke and his medical team could fix such minor ailments in short order. Their feat made it easier for him to stay up with to the rest of the squadron. He might be able to jump into Altec only a few hours behind that old fool Gurand if he could dump off the Marshal Service sergeant quickly enough. That would show the powers that be that he was fit and ready for promotion to a squadron command or even a wing of his own. He smiled broadly at the thought that things were going exceedingly well, despite having to baby-sit that APES bitch, McPherson.

Britaine said, "That is all. And a job well done, people." He saw McPherson stand up to leave. He could see the puzzlement on her face, knowing she was baffled as to why he had called her to this meeting when it was apparent to everyone she didn't have anything to do with the information at hand.

He called to her, "Third McPherson, I have one small thing for you if I could see you for a moment." He turned to the crowd drawing around him. He smiled; giving the crew one of his knowing smirks and said, "I am sure you could give Misha and me a moment alone." When she stepped up to him, Britaine put a hand gently on her shoulder. He barely controlled the shudder at touching her, but he managed a smile. A warm smile in return was his reward. He thought, "Poor ugly thing; desperate for the touch of a real man. If I can't put her in her place one way, then I'll do it another." He applied a small amount of pressure to her shoulder and turned with her so their backs were to the still crowded room.

Britaine took a small leather packet from his breast pocket. The packet had the APES symbol embossed on the cover. Inside was a glass-pack. He slipped it into her hand with the same sly maneuver he used in grade school when passing notes to the girls. As his fingers released the packet, they slid up her hand to dangle suggestively against her bare wrist. He could feel her noticeably quivering with excitement at his touch.

She smiled sweetly at him and slid the glass-pack into a side pocket. He smiled back knowing he had her in the palm of his hand. The bitch was putty in his hands. All he had to do was string her along until she left his spacecraft. She would prove she was as unfit for command as he had already reported, if he could keep her off balance until she self-destructed. He smiled into her eyes. "Thanks for coming up, Misha. I was sure you'd find it instructive to sit in with us. Just between us, I know you were a big help in the intelligence office. I'm sure you know I didn't mention it because this crew needs a morale boost. I know you understand?" He squeezed her elbow softly.

"Thank you, William. I'm glad I could be here. I did learn a lot," Misha smiled back.

Chapter Thirty-Five

Misha checked her six in the corridor on the way back to her day office. She was completely alone. She stood still and shuddered deeply. She asked herself how any person could be so self-absorbed not to notice how he gave her the cold nauseating shivers. "Still," she had to admit, "he is pretty. Wonder how good he would be in bed? Maybe if he had a personality transplant, with something nicer like a male DropSix lowland warthog in heat. No, I am not that bad off yet. I'll have to penalize myself with extra time in the training bay for such thoughts."

Misha shivered again and rounded the corner into APES territory. Her day office was the first hatch down the side corridor. She needed the data reader embedded into her desk to decipher the codes on the glass-pack she had been given. Since it was the middle of the day, she didn't bother knocking. Surely, Forrester would have the bedroom hatch closed if he was sleeping.

Forrester wasn't alone. He was sitting next to Kiirkegaard's Med-Tech Jèsusa Rezzi. They were side-by-side as close as two people can be without embracing. Upon her entrance, the woman flinched and started to slide away. Forrester put a hand on Rezzi's knee to stop her movement.

"Well, Misha," Forrester said. "I'm sure you know this is exactly what it looks like." Rezzi began blushing through her dark, olive skin. It flushed a deep red in contrast with her black shiny hair.

Misha replied, "I'm sorry to intrude. It doesn't matter to me what it looks like." Despite her words, she knew her face belied her emotions. "Besides, isn't the line 'nothing was going on and it's not what it looks like'?"

Forrester said quickly, "You need to let me explain."

Misha interrupted him. "No. I'm not the one who deserves an explanation even if this is my office. It is not my business."

Rezzi said, "Please, Third let me explain. No don't interrupt. Gan is just trying to protect me. He knows what it would not do my career any good to be seen with him; at least, not on this spacecraft. I know it's a double standard, but officers can sleep around with whomever they choose. Enlisted, specifically female enlisted, are supposed to restrict themselves to other spacers. It's like we are some kind of property or something."

"Like I said," Misha answered. "It's not my place to judge or to hear your confession. Who you associate with is your business."

Rezzi pleaded, "But, if Colonel Britaine finds out that I've been meeting with Gan, I could catch hell."

Misha grit her teeth. The room was silent as she counted to ten.

"Why does everyone assume I would run to Britaine with every little piece of gossip that falls my way? Even if I was sleeping with him, and I am not," she said pointedly. "I still wouldn't run to him about every trifling." She looked at Forrester. "It isn't me or Britaine who needs an explanation. I'm not a prude. What you two do is your business. It is none of my concern, but tell me Gan, are you sure that is everyone who would care about you sleeping around?"

Forrester started to speak, "Jèsusa has been a close family friend for a long-"

Rezzi stopped him with a hand over his. "Third McPherson, I think I know where you're going. I will say this: I know Gan is married. I've known his wife longer than I have known Gan. I can guarantee she wouldn't have a problem with us being together, certainly not when we are both so far from home."

Misha said again, "It is not my concern." But she thought to herself, "Why do I care? Maybe I am just a bit jealous? Me? Yes, I am and I should be ashamed of myself." She shook her head and said, "I'm sorry. I may have been acting a bit judgmental. I guess I've come to like Gan and I didn't want to see him make a mistake."

Forrester sputtered a laugh.

Rezzi flared, "So, you think that being with me is a mistake? Who the hell do you think you are, lady?"

Misha held her hands up in surrender, "I give. That's not what I meant. I mean…well, maybe it was. Please accept my apology." She couldn't help thinking this conversation hadn't gone as well as she would like. Forrester was sitting there laughing, being no help at all and this little spacer looked like she was ready to come at her tooth and nail.

Rezzi flashed, "I won't be back here if you don't approve of me. Sergeant Forrester, give my regards to your wife."

Forrester's laughter strangled out. "Hold on, Rezzi."

Misha held out her hands, "Hey! I've said I'm sorry. I know I didn't say it well. I am sorry I interrupted you two. I am also sorry I acted like a prude and was overly judgmental. I stand by my offer to Sergeant Forrester for the use my day office and the private bedroom. I won't retract it. Who he invites here is his business and it'll not go beyond these bulkheads."

"Well…" Rezzi relented and sat back down. "I guess none of us handled this as well as we should."

Misha thought, "Not me. Here I am trying to get information from this Marshal Sergeant, and I insult him and his mistress. That is good work, Misha; you might as well have stayed on DropSix and had babies." She said to the two, "I really need to use the data reader on the desk for official business. I hate to jump on your case and then have to chase you out for a bit, but the message is encoded and probably classified. Please use the bedroom. The hatch doesn't have a lock, but I promise not to disturb you in there."

Rezzi said, "I am sorry, too. I seem to be a bit hot tempered these days."

Forrester laughed, "These days? You don't give yourself credit enough. Misha, this woman is a fire-breathing temper machine. You should see what she did to the best man at my wedding when he got drunk and grabbed her ass."

Rezzi laughed, "Drunken fool. He should've known better. I did light into him, didn't I? Third McPherson, I thank you for the offer of the bedroom, but I do have duty shortly so I should go."

Misha said, "Gan, this glass-pack data was delivered by the FACs sent back to Heaven's Gate. I think Britaine was looking for you. He may have a packet from the Marshal's Service for you. He was angry he couldn't comm you and he complained pretty loudly about you having your comm off. Guess we know now why it was off, don't we? No. Don't say anything. That was a bit catty, wasn't it? Sorry you two, I will try to get this out of my system soonest. Now get out of my office. I got work to do."

Once Forrester and Rezzi left, she hit the seal bolts on the hatch slamming them in place. She slid the desk chair along the deck track and sat at the desk. She pulled the glass-pack out of the case and dropped it into the reader. It was set for voice recognition. She spoke her name and rank.

"Fourth-Level Commander Kema Ottiamig here." The man's regal image floated into place above the reader. He smiled and winked at her. Misha smiled back even though she knew it was just a recording.

"Quad Kema, good to see you again," she said quite unnecessarily.

Fourth Ottiamig continued as if he hadn't been interrupted, "I send the regards of Fifth Vaslov. The Fist said specifically she wants a rematch with you on the martial arts mats when you get back to Heaven Three. And next time don't whip up so badly on the woman who is your boss's boss. That is not good office politics." He smiled brightly at her out of his holo-image.

Misha smiled back. She remembered the match well with Fifth-Level Commander IvanYetta Vaslov. The Fist and Misha did quite a bit of damage to each other. Vaslov, Ottiamig and she knew bad politics or not, it was even worse in combat training to pull your punches. It would lead to muscle memory betrayal during actual combat. Misha never pulled her punches and both commanders knew it.

Ottiamig's continued, "I have been ordered to take second-tier units 1390th, 1395th, and the 1397th of the 139th third-tier on deployment by another route to the Altec System. My quad squad is deployed with the 1390th per our usual configuration. FYI, the remainder of the Third Tier command has been redeployed as follows; the 1393rd and the 1398th are being sent forward to the Gagarin System as backup for the Altec Expedition, plus the 1391st and the1396th are being deployed to Heaven's Gate as deep reserve. I am not at liberty to discuss the placement of the 1394th or the 1399th. Their location holds no bearing on the Altec Expedition. We are scheduled to reach Altec in concert with Gurand's squadron. This is possible because the AMSF command originally thought a roundabout route to the system would increase the chances of taking any Binders by surprise."

Ottiamig frowned, furrowing his brow. "With your discovery of the Binder signal in two Allied Space systems, we cannot be sure Gurand will take the Binders by surprise. The AMSF decided to strengthen the commitment into Altec by sending in a second flight wing by a more direct route. The Sixth agreed and is sending the additional second-tier units under my command. Your 1392nd will link with me ASAP.

"Sorry, Third McPherson, I know you were expecting your first official independent command, but that will have to wait. The way you handled Guinjundst proved to all of your command that you have what it takes to lead. This is no reflection on you."

Misha wondered if it should be a reflection. She was pleased to know that a more experienced commander would be responsible. She was also glad she was alone in her office. She was sure the relief on her face was evident.

"One last thing, and this comes directly from the Sixth himself, good job on isolating the Binder signal. Stay on top of it. We need to know what they are up to and how far they have gotten into Allied Space. Report any findings on this by any means necessary. Let your people know about the Binder signal and any significance you attach to it. The AMSF wants this signal to stay classified, but the Sixth says, and I quote: 'we don't care'. This is a good indication that we will find Binder activity in Altec. We want our people prepared, not guessing in the dark. Keep the Guinjundst events under your hat for now. At least until we get secondary confirmation. The Sixth also wants your input in your next report on how or if this signal ties into what happened on Guinjundst.

"Unofficially, you have my nephew in your squad. He is my youngest brother's boy. I was very concerned when the assignment into Third Can's squad fell to him. I don't know what stroke of fortune put him in your hands. Please note that I am not asking for special treatment. Quite the opposite, push him hard. He has a lot of promise. He has my natural and superior skill as a warrior." Misha could see the laughter in Kema's eyes. "However, he has my Brother Jimmy's lazy streak. Jimmy is a Deuce in the 1151st. I would be appreciative if you kept me up to date on his progress, simply as a matter of courtesy. There are no favors asked or given, comprende?

"That's it for now, Third. You take care and we will link up soon." Ottiamig waved a hand and disappeared, like the Cheshire cat leaving his smile until last.

Misha dropped her glass-pack into the second reader slot and ordered a copy of the message dropped into her official files buried behind a dozen firewalls and safety pass-codes. She then ordered the reader to wipe and destroy all data on the glass-pack and she pocketed the blank glass-pack. She might as well give it to Qualls for reuse in the squad's communication supplies.

She compiled a brief report containing all information on the unit transfers, the AMSF reconfigurations and the Binder signal data. She broadcast the report to her unit with a copy to her files for transmittal to command at the first opportunity. As a courtesy, she cc'd Colonel Britaine, Chief Master Sergeant Brown and Gan Forrester. She also made a mental note to ask if Chief Brown could tell her what 'cc' meant.

Misha was sure she would be learning from the best if she could get Chief Brown to teach her how to kick her people's collective asses into high gear. She didn't want to kick ass, but to kick it up a notch and kick it into overdrive. Still, whatever the outcome she was in the mood to kick someone and her own squad was just about all that was left unless she took on the whole spacecraft.

Chapter Thirty-Six

Misha's intention was to restart her squad's general inspection where she had left off earlier. All of her seconds had reported their inspection results. There were quite a few down checks and gigs, but overall they were good ratings. Her own squad had done much better than she had expected. It was almost perfect. Still, she liked a hands-on approach, whether it gigged her troops or offended her seconds. Whatever her intention, someone was going to get angry at her. Mentally, she shrugged knowing it was that kind of month.

Earlier, she had been inspecting each trooper's armor and weaponry. She was not concerned with the typical military spit and polish inspection criteria. Her objective was combat readiness. She didn't care if it was dirty as long as the dirt didn't interfere with the item's effectiveness. In truth, most of the veteran's combat suits had a haphazard mixture of graffiti, scratches, smudges and combat tattoos. Misha had been inspecting Quall's suit when she received the call to join Britaine's briefing. Then the jump warning alert sounded causing another flurry of activity further delaying her inspection. After Qualls, she had only Metzler and Singletary left to complete.

Taking up where she left off, Misha stepped up to Trooper Tammie Qualls's suit locker. She smiled as she noticed someone had been puttering around inside the H.E. launcher controls and had repaired the small glitch she had seen earlier. Qualls stood quietly to the side as Misha dug through the various suit systems. She could see a slight sheen of sweat begin to glisten on the young woman's upper lip. Misha mentally shook her head. Qualls might make a good trooper some day, but she had to toughen up. She rattled too easily. Misha popped open the suit's comms compartment. Everything was in order as one would expect for a comms tech. The slot for the glass-pack, extra comm gear, IFF signal relay, squad channel ID relays… she froze.

Slowly Misha looked at Qualls and said, "IFF."

Qualls looked confused, but snapped to quote the APES manual. "Sir! Yes, sir! IFF is Identity Friend or Foe. It is a broadcast...?" Qualls's voice trailed off as it became apparent Misha wasn't listening. "Third? Is there something wrong?"

Misha replied and slapped her hand on her forehead. "Wrong? Have you ever put a jigsaw puzzle together?"

"Jigsaw, sir?" Qualls asked. "Sure, we used to do them all the time as kids. Doesn't everybody?"

Misha clasp her arms around the trooper and laughed. "Yes, on every human planet we do jigsaw puzzles. You know the feeling you get when you put in the last piece of the puzzle? Well, you just did that for me."

Misha turned to the rest of the squad. "Singletary, finish the inspection on Jigsaw here, on Metzler, and just for good measure run a check on Slezak's gear, too. I know you just did it, but do it again. DeLaPax, since you are the senior armor repair tech, do an inspection on Singletary's suit and then check mine. Peace, do you have the 1392nd's override and lockdown codes for all the lockers or do you need me to cycle open Slezak's and mine for you? Got it? Good. Something has occurred to me that I have to take care of before the next jump."

Misha closed her fist and pumped her arm up and down, "Good inspection, APES. We are looking excellent." She realized she still had an arm around Qualls's shoulders. "You too, Jigsaw, this has been a good inspection." She gave the woman a squeeze of encouragement and then let go.

She tapped her comm unit to broadcast unit wide "McPherson here. All right, APES. Check your glass-packs for newly downloaded comms and intel reports. I downloaded some new data. Furthermore, the AMSF has gotten a data dump from Heaven's Gate, so there should be mail from home. I want you to check your intel reports first before you check with Mama to see if the cat had kittens."

Misha hurried through the hatch and down the corridors to the intel shack. She avoided the elevators and bound up ladders. When she heard the alarm to prepare for the jump into the Gagarin system, she turned her hurried jog into a sprint, shouting at spacers to clear the way.

The jump alert sounded one hour before everyone needed to be strapped down. That was plenty of time to reach her goal safely and get belted into a jump position. It should be enough time to fill in the intelligence crew, notify the Kiirkegaard's command center and get notification to the rest of the squadron. When an obstinate knot of spacers blocked her way, she blew them to all sides as she barreled through them.

The vault hatch to the intel shack was shut and locked. Misha hit the buzzer and banged on the hatch panels. She knew banging on the panels could not be heard from the inside, but it made her feel better.

"What? Who? Oh, Third McPherson. Sorry, we're locked down for jump. Better get to your bunk." Spacer Clancy's perky blonde holo-image appeared on the intercom.

"No can do, spacer," Misha shouted with excitement. "Get this hatch opened quickly and get me a direct line to Britaine." She banged on the hatch with her fist near the visual input node. The pounding fist caused Clancy's holo-image to involuntarily duck. "Chief Brown, are you in there? Get me in quick. I've gotten a handle on the anomaly."

The hatch made a few banging noises and slowly rotated open. Misha grabbed the vault hatch and all but tore it out of the hands of the two male spacers. She spun and slammed the hatch shut behind her.

Clancy shouted across the room, "Hey! When we get ready for jump that hatch automatically closes. We can only open it by hand after that. This had better be good."

Misha smiled and said, "Nice to see you too, Clancy." One of the spacers from the hatch was heading back to the comms collector. He apparently vacated the crash couch there to help open the hatch. She hooked her thumb at him. "Find another seat, junior. That one is mine."

The man whined, "Hey, what gives? And the name is Cuffs not Junior."

Misha sat in the seat and began buckling in. Cuffs stood behind her looking bewildered.

Chief Brown said, "Listen to the lady, Cuffs. Find a seat. Use the astrometrics console." She looked up at Misha. "This had better be good, grunt. This is no time to be playing who's the boss."

"I know. We've got fifty minutes until jump. Run the Binder signal anomaly again. Just do it, Chief. Buzz, get us a line to the command and control center and see if you can get them to wangle a line to Gurand."

Krandiewsky said, "I can get us a line to the flight operations office, but Colonel Britaine won't take a call from intel this close to jump."

"Not even if we can show him that the Binder anomaly is an IFF signal? The Binders didn't have drones or probes in Allied space; those were scout ships expecting a Binder fleet to show up. Why else would they send an IFF signal toward an incoming fleet?"

Cuffs said, "Come on McPherson, everybody knows the Binders don't use any signals we can recognize. They haven't used anything we can tell is an IFF signal."

Misha called up the last two signals, laying them side by side on the visual display. The base signal, while different was obviously the same pattern of rapid inquiry then pause.

Krandiewsky called out, "Kiirkegaard flight operations on line, Third."

Brown said, "Okay McPherson, I see the pattern you've got." She had duplicated the communication collector's visual display of the two signals on her desk's monitors. "But, what makes you think this is IFF?"

Misha called out to Krandiewsky, "Put it on the speaker, Buzz. Turn the volume up. She dropped her glass-pack into the data reader and called out a series of codes.

Over her shoulder, she spoke, "Chief, I am tagging the standard APES identify friend or foe signal on the overlay next to the two Binder signals. Even taking into account the species differences, this is amazingly similar; too similar to be anything else. Please tell me I am wrong?" She shouted into the air. "Flight ops, prepare to receive data."

Chief Brown said, "It's too similar. It looks like it is human in origin. Cuffs is right, as far as we know the Binders don't use IFF routines. I know it is Binder, but it reads like human."

Misha cursed under her breath knowing she was close to disclosing classified information. Chief Brown was right, but it didn't change the situation. "Maybe the Binders took a page from our operational actions. I can't say yet, but it shouldn't matter." In the background of the intel shack she could hear Brown cursing the signals.

"Major Krandiewsky, please relay this signal to the operations office, ASAP," Misha said. The tone of her voice left little doubt it was a command even though she used the word please. In every respect, the Major out-ranked her and she knew it. But, she decided due to the time factor she would act now and take the flak later for being rude to a sister service senior officer.

A voice from Flight operations boomed over the speakers, "Intel, what the hell are you doing? Get this crap off our screens. We have to jump in forty minutes."

Misha ordered, "Shut up and listen. This is a visual display of Binder signals collected in this and the last system the squadron was in. I believe that this signal is IFF. Patch this data through to-"

The voice shouted, "Shut up? Who do you think you are telling to shut up, spacer? This is the Executive Officer, Major Paradise. Identify yourself."

"This is APES Third-Level Commander McPherson. If the Binders are in system and sending IFF, then they are looking to meet up with a fleet of their

216

own. Patch this data through to General Gurand and get Colonel Britaine on the line."

"APES Commander? McPherson, you don't cut any ice with me, I don't care who you think you are or who you are sleeping with. I don't take orders from you," Paradise said.

Brown spoke up. "Major Paradise, this is Chief Brown. I think the Third is right. We may have a problem here."

"Think? May have? Major Krandiewsky, what kind of a shop are you running down there? Get this shit off my screens." The XO disconnected the line with a thump.

"Sorry, Third," Brown said. "I could have handled it better from my end."

Krandiewsky spoke up, "No, Chief, this is my fault. Third McPherson doesn't have any official status here. We should have our ducks in a row before making any calls."

Misha nodded. She knew she should have handled the call better herself. "That is your decision, Major. But, if we do have a specific enemy incursion into Allied Systems, then we are just about to jump into what? Do you know? I don't either, but I know enough about combat to know we shouldn't be moving forward and leaving the possibility of an enemy force at our back."

"Maybe you should have brought this to our attention earlier so we could have had time to investigate. You put us in deep kimchee with the XO. I am not going to put my career or the reputation of anybody in this office on the line based on an unconfirmed theory," Krandiewsky said. "Please get out of my shop, now. You have about thirty-five minutes to reach your bunk for jump."

Misha stood quietly. She pulled her glass-pack and dropped it back into her pocket. She was fuming, but she maintained her calm as she waited for Clancy and Cuffs to cycle the hatch open.

She stood in the empty corridor. With only thirty minutes to jump, everybody would be at their duty stations or strapped into their bunk. It would take only a few minutes to get to APES territory. Still, she thought, it was only a few minutes more to Britaine's command and control center. She would not have time to get back to her bunk before the jump if she went to the CNC and she might be trapped in a corridor for the jump if she couldn't get past spacer guards or locked hatches. The inertial dampers would keep her from turning into jelly, but she could take damage banging around loose on metal bulkheads.

She turned and raced down the corridor to CNC. As she ran, she called all of her seconds and Singletary, filling them in on as much of what was going on as she could. She also told them to roll into a stand-by mode as soon as the jump sequence ended. She skidded to a stop in front of the CNC hatch. It was locked in the open position. A lone spacer was already strapped into his crash netting by the hatch. It was a standing unit. He had locked his needler into a side flange to leave his hands free to strap himself in tightly, making him effectively useless. Misha nodded as she bolted past him and into the room. Everyone was in the final stages of buckling down. She spotted an empty crash couch three consoles from where Colonel Britaine sat staring at her. She wasn't surprised to see every eye in the place was on her.

"Ten minutes to jump, Third," Britaine said. "I do say that this is very unusual, but you had better strap in quick. We will resolve what you are doing here after the jump."

She sprang toward the couch and began strapping herself down. She looked around at the group of officers in the center. Their faces reflected everything from open hostility and anger to disgust. She even noticed Britaine's normal insincere smile had turned sour.

"Colonel, I apologize for the intrusion," she began, "but I have information on the Binder anomaly that you and General Gurand should know-"

Britaine interrupted. "Be quiet, Third McPherson. In addition to your unbelievable rudeness in coming here, you are about to divulge classified information.

218

Not everyone in this room is cleared for that information."

"Sir, I understand that, but this may be critical data," Misha insisted.

"Not another word, McPherson. You are not in my command, but you have intruded, uninvited, into a restricted command and control center. You have undone yourself. Be silent, Third. And if you are quiet enough, the noise you hear will be your career dissipating."

Britaine spoke into a comm unit. "Security to the CNC as soon as possible after the jump and be prepared to take Third McPherson into custody." He looked coldly at her. "Be armed and prepared for resistance."

A voice said calmly, "Jump in nine minutes."

Misha gritted her teeth. There was nothing else she could do until she could get to someone who would listen. She was confident Britaine couldn't damage her career too badly. He might be able to get her busted back to common trooper, but that wasn't her biggest concern.

She thought about the signal. Chief Brown was right. She dropped her glass-pack into a reader and called up the signal data for further review. The signal was definitely of Binder origin, but it had human fingerprints all over it. It was Guinjundst all over again. She hoped this time the outcome would be different.

The Kiirkegaard launched into the jump with a lurch forward and a slow spiraling crawl. A jump wasn't so much an action as it was inaction, but it didn't feel that way to a human body. The spacecraft jump point generators punching a hole through a fold in space caused the lurch. The spiral was the spacecraft corkscrewing through the hole. In reality, the craft didn't move. Space folded and wrapped itself around the spacecraft. The human body reacted to the change in space itself and to the changes in relative speed. A spacecraft could not exit into new space at the same speed it left the old space. Internal spacecraft inertia could slam a human body to mush in a fraction of a second, but with the use of inertial dampers, a body felt the jump like it was a quick atmospheric change accompanied by a twisting of light, all mounted on an out of control amusement park ride.

Misha watched the visual displays in front of her. She was at a command module configured with a variety of displays. With the proper sequence of commands, she would be able to view the status of each departments. As they were practicing a combat insertion, the majority of the screens were set to show communications, other wing vessels and any possible enemy spacecraft.

Upon hitting normal space again, Misha stared as multiple SOS signals from the planet and dozens of spacecraft flashed across her screen. Holo-images appeared, cried for help and blinked out. One image was of a civilian claiming to be the planetary governor of Gagarin demanding protection. His signal faded, replaced by a woman who said she was a cargo-hauler commander calling for assistance to repel boarders. Her signal didn't fade, but ended abruptly in a flare of light only to be replaced by another call for aid.

Another screen showed hundreds of spacecraft in the Gagarin system. A dozen spacecraft were clearly marked by the computer as Binders. The system colored them a glowing red. The Kiirkegaard's IFF system marked all human spacecraft as green or blue. Green was the color given to AMSF spacecraft and blue was known civilian. Unknown spacecraft were marked yellow. The visual display marked Gurand's squadron designation as they jumped into the system. Most of the craft already in the system were showing green. One screen showed an AMSF spacecraft blinking into existence after the jump. The Kiirkegaard's IFF recorded it as green and marked it as a spacecraft assigned to Gurand's wing. Suddenly, it flared and disappeared.

Misha watched in shock as she saw a blue civilian craft spew missiles at another AMSF craft. The blue pulsed, rotating through yellow, to green, back to blue and then settled into a deep red. Another spacecraft's green AMSF designation shifted to red, then another and then another as the Kiirkegaard's IFF system began sorting through the conflicting responses.

Misha shouted, "Britaine, do something. We are being fired on by human spacecraft. This convoy is going to be blown to bits if you don't do something now."

A dozen vessels from Gurand's Wing blinked out of existence before anyone else could react. Britaine glared at Misha as if she was the culprit blasting away at the AMSF squadron.

"But-" he started.

A voice blasted over the loudspeakers. "This is General Gurand to all wing spacecraft: Code Black. I say again: Code Black. You have your orders."

Chapter Thirty-Seven

Britaine pulled a multicolored glass-pack from a pocket sewn into his crash couch. His fingers fumbled and he almost let it slip from his hands before dropping it into the data reader on his console. He spoke with a quiver. "All hands: battle stations-condition red. Colonel William Britaine to Kiirkegaard Automated Systems: Code B-1. I say again: initiate Code B-1."

The spacecraft shuddered and jinked throwing everyone against their restraints or in the cases where they had unhooked themselves from their restraints: into bulkheads, chairs, consoles, trash cans, each other, and in one unfortunate case, across the vast area of a half empty cargo hold.

The inertial dampers whined audibly in an effort to keep up with the wild gyrations. The Kiirkegaard curled, curved and kinked until it finally completed a 180-degree maneuver facing the way it had come. All around them, Gurand's wing began taking fire. Spacecraft spewed atmosphere into space or simply exploded in a flash of light.

Britain squeezed his eyes shut and spoke again. His voice broadcast loudly to all parts of the vessel, even overriding the blaring klaxon of the condition red alarm. "To all aboard the Kiirkegaard: There is a Binder fleet in Gagarin. Hold fast. We are jumping out now."

Without human direction, the Kiirkegaard reacted to the orders embedded in Britaine's glass-pack. It laid in an automated series of turns to throw off any possible enemy tracking systems. Then it initiated a reverse jump back to the system it had just abandoned.

Britaine ordered an automated maneuver. It had to be automated as only an uncommon human could order a second jump following so closely behind the first. He knew he wasn't such a rare individual, so he had prepared a glass-pack with the orders preprogrammed. A wave of nausea swept over him. He could feel his gorge rise. He would be lucky not to lose what little was left in his stomach from his last meal with half of the command

and control crew spewing vomit over their consoles and their spotless uniforms. His eyes grew fuzzy and he began to lose his vision as blood rushed to his eyes. His guts began to churn and cramp.

Just as a jump through folded space acted on a human physiology like express atmospheric changes, repeated jumps without giving time for the body to rejuvenate was like a scuba diver's rapid ascent causing the bends. The problems began to compile and compound. Inertial dampers worked well keeping the body intact, but they didn't work well on the internal blood gasses, bacteria and toxins found deep within the body.

Britaine glared out of a fog. He could see that damned woman McPherson. She was staring at her console visuals, calling for updates and scans. She was watching the calamity going on around them, seemingly unaffected by the second jump churning through the spacecraft. Her skin looked flushed, but no more than if she had been through a moderate workout. Her uniform looked damp, but not soaked through as his felt. She seemed oblivious to the officers on either side of her. One officer was vomiting greenish bile; another had fainted.

As fast as the jump had started it was over. He saw rather than heard McPherson shout orders into his command console. He couldn't clear his thinking long enough to imagine what she was going on about. The enemy was behind them in the Gagarin System. They couldn't have followed the Kiirkegaard. They would not have known her course. A spacecraft could jump in an almost infinite number of directions, although it was normally star to star as the stars themselves provided navigation points.

He brought his attention back to McPherson as she slammed her fist against the console. He heard her cursing, but could not seem to get his eyes to focus enough to see her lips move. She slammed at the release buckles of her crash couch restraints setting herself free. He couldn't imagine why she would want to do that. He wasn't in any position to move and didn't want to. For all he cared, the Binders could just kill him right now even if they had managed to follow.

The next thing he knew McPherson was kneeling over him. He realized he was out of his crash couch and stretched out flat on the deck plates. His eyes were clearing and he tried to sit up. A huge hand attached to a thick wrist pushed at his chest thumping him back to the deck.

"Not yet, Colonel," McPherson said staring down at him. "Here drink this." She slipped a tube into his mouth. He sucked at it without thinking. He was glad he did. It was cold, clear and sweet. It began to clear his head and settle his stomach.

"What is…?" he tried to ask, but his voice faded away to a rasping rattle.

"Water," she said. "I am not much of a medic. All I know is that if it hurts, then put water on it or in it. Hydrate or die. Water seems to help most people when they get bounce sickness. That is what rookies get the first few times in combat armor. Nausea, stomach cramps, dizziness. Sound familiar? Yeah, only bounce sickness isn't quite as bad as you went through, but I don't know what else to do."

"Kiirkegaard?" he asked and was surprised to find his voice was working again. "What is the status of the Kiirkegaard?" He sat up. This time, he was thankful to note that McPherson kept her mitts off him.

"Whatever preprogrammed course has been set is what is happening. I don't know enough to try to change anything. We may be at a dead standstill for all I know or cruising full tilt into a sun. I can tell we were hit with one signal after the jump. It was the Binder anomaly. That anomaly is an IFF signal of Binder origin intended for human reception. I assume we didn't respond."

Britaine stood slowly and looked around him. Only a few of the crew were active. No one was moving beyond grabbing at cramped guts. He could smell someone or more than one someone had lost control of their bowels. He craved to be alone to check if he was one of the offending parties. He wasn't about to look and see if he had crapped his pants in front of this bitch.

McPherson smiled. "I'm going to check on the others as long as you are up, Colonel."

He nodded, "Your people?"

"I broadcast an order for them to water up. They'll get up and check on each other. They're APES. It's what we do."

Britaine snarled, "Oh, so you're better than we are? Spacers can't take this, but you grunts are immune? Is that what you are saying?"

McPherson turned away from him, ignoring his question. She went to help other officers. Britaine watched her for a moment and then crawled up to sit at his console. He began to call through his officer roster passing along orders whenever he got a response.

Some officers seemed to come through the ordeal better than others. He knew he had a superior constitution. He was a FAC pilot after all. Still, it was good McPherson had come to him first. It was always best for a commander to recover quicker. Morale would be higher when the others came around to find him still in charge. He was sure he hadn't needed her attention and that he would have recovered before the rest of his crew even without her help. As for her reaction to the rapid double jump, he knew that just proved she was a mutant of some kind.

As he made his comm calls Britaine watched McPherson unbuckling officers from their restraints and laying them out on the deck. As she went, she cleaned vomit off a few faces, even the blood from the nose of one young second lieutenant. He made a mental note have the man reassigned out of the CNC. He could handle the laundry or supply if he couldn't handle a little stress like a real warrior. He watched as McPherson collected water containers and began passing them around to his officers.

He thought to himself, "Freak. Definitely. Medical ought to do an autopsy to find out what makes her tick." He chuckled, forgetting completely his own reaction to the double jump. He said to himself, "Yeah, autopsy. I know she isn't dead yet, but would that be such a loss?"

"Say what, Muffin?" Britaine looked up and saw the First Watch Commander Major 'Nuke' Esteban's holo-image staring at him from the console.

"Nothing, Nuke. We are just clearing away up here," Britaine smiled. "Rough trip in the flight office?"

"Same-o, same-o, Muffin. Just another day in the life of a FAC pilot," Esteban said. Neither man mentioned the vomit stains down the front of Esteban's uniform.

Britaine smiled, "Same here." He glanced around. "We've got a few non-FAC jocks who seem to be unable to hold their mud, but everything seems to be a go. Sorry for the short notice on the jump."

"It is not a problem. I am zapping you a flash status report. We are still getting info from the rest of the watch on duty. I just talked with the XO in ops. He is getting a total ship status report for you ASAP."

Britaine said, "Continue at battle stations, condition red. Indications are there may be additional Binders in this system as well. I know we are not going to be fully manned very quickly. I doubt if very many of the enlisted crew can handle a simple double jump. I am not expecting speed records, but let's get it done as quickly as we can. It looks like Gurand walked us into a shit storm. We need to get ready for anything."

Britaine frowned as McPherson stepped through the open hatch into the corridor and began to undo the strap on the unconscious security spacer. He remembered he had ordered security to arrest her. He thought, "Well, all in good time. Let her putter around pretending to be useful. She isn't going anywhere; we'll get around to refrying her hash soon enough.

Esteban interrupted his thoughts, "Do you want me to have navigation lay in a course back into Gagarin?"

"Negative, Nuke. Are they functioning yet? Good. Navigation, lay in a course back to Heaven System with minimum rejuvenation time between jumps," he ordered.

"What?" Esteban said. "Wait. I know we can't jump back in until we are ready to go in with guns blazing, but we have to go back."

"Negative Nuke. Nav, respond." Britaine said.

He looked up to see McPherson standing at his side watching him. He shook his head. Couldn't he do anything without her hovering about like a lovesick cow! He decided maybe it was time for him to deal with her. Before he could call for security he was interrupted.

"Navigation here, Colonel. Please repeat destination."

"Heaven's Gate, Nav. I am not in the habit of repeating myself. Get the crap out of your ears."

Esteban said with an edge in his tone. "Come on, Muffin. We've got friends back in that fur-ball. We can't just leave them there."

Britaine shouted, "Can't? Since when do you tell me can't, Esteban? I've known you since you were a snot-nosed wingman who couldn't find his crotch with a whore's hands. It is not your place to say can't."

Esteban shouted back, "Damn you, Britaine. I say we go back as quickly as we can recover to do so. And we launch the FACs upon entry. We can smoke those weed-eaters."

Britaine snarled, "No. Negative. Not now. Not ever. Do you understand, shit-for-brains? Navigation, lay in the course as ordered."

He looked around at the shocked faces of his CNC officers. His voice rose in pitch as he shouted. "What? Do you want to give me an argument, too? I don't have time for this. Any more back talk and I will have the lot of you up on charges of insubordination. I don't need to explain myself to anyone here. I am in command, do you understand?"

A couple of officers stood with clenched fists. He didn't give a damn what they thought of him. He had ordered a course to Heaven's Gate and that was where they were going. He saw officers glance at him, up to McPherson and back down at him. He realized it might not hurt to have her stand at his back until he got this mess straightened out. He was sure the double jump had temporarily scrambled a few brains.

"Navigation?" he asked.

"No, sir," the navigation officer said. "Not me. I am not going to be the one to abandon the flight wing without firing a shot."

"Navigation, you are relieved of duty and confined to quarters pending insubordination charges."

The navigation officer replied, "Fine with me, Colonel Britaine. I would rather do time under arrest than go back to Heaven's Gate and be called a coward like you."

Britaine's voice cracked with anger. "Get out of my operations office. Nuke, get those co-ordinates input and do it now."

Esteban's face glowed bright red in his holo-image. His jaw clenched. "Not only no, but who the hell do you think you are no!"

Britaine said, "Comms off to flight operations. Kiirkegaard, voice print authorization: this is Colonel Britaine, lock off all commands from operations and the flight office. Full spacecraft control to CNC consoles."

He nodded to himself. That will fix them. He looked at his assembled officers. He spotted the second lieutenant who had been bleeding through his nose during the jump. The man was listening with his eyes wide open as his fingers picked at his uniform front, pulling off small chunks of vomit.

He said, pointing at the man, "You, go sit at the navigation overlay console. Set up the ordered course to Heaven's Gate. I know you are not nav qualified, but let the Kiirkegaard's systems do the math."

The man looked at the junior-grade major standing next to him. The major shook his head no and sat back in his chair. The young lieutenant shook his head no at Britaine and sat down next to the jg major.

Britaine exploded. "Kiirkegaard, command and control functions on my voice command only." He looked at the officers surrounding him. "Anyone here not willing to lay in the course to Heaven's Gate can get out of my CNC now. I will bury you all with insubordination charges. Get out now."

He watched in utter amazement as all of his officers quietly left the center. He felt a presence at his shoulder. He saw McPherson still standing at his back.

"Okay, McPherson. What the hell do you want?" She said nothing as she stood looking at him. "Of all of the people I would have expected to be insubordinate at a time like this, I would have chosen you, McPherson. What are you still doing here?"

She said, "Waiting, Colonel Britaine. I am just waiting."

He shook his head and turned back to his console. "Ops?" There was no answer. "XO? Major Paradise in the flight operations office, respond." There was still no answer.

"Colonel Britaine here: open communications to all levels of the craft. Security, send an armed detail to the operations office on the double. Second watch, report for duty. All first watch personnel are relieved of duty and confined to quarters."

He turned to McPherson, "Come with me to the flight office. There may be something wrong there and I am formally requesting your services per our contract for in-transit emergencies."

McPherson nodded, "Yes, sir."

Britaine thought, "Good. Damn good she didn't say anything else. I don't need a frustrated, frigid bitch to start in on me. Maybe she will make herself useful." He nodded and beckoned her to follow him.

McPherson stopped at the hatchway and spoke. "Colonel, if I may make a suggestion?"

"What is it now? Can't you see that we have a crisis to deal with?"

"Yes, sir, I believe it might be best if we seal the CNC hatch and put a voice lock on it "

"What? Yes, that is a good idea." He spoke the command into his comm unit and they watched the hatch slide shut without a sound. He voice printed the lock and turned to go. McPherson didn't follow him. He stopped and turned back to her.

"Now what?"

She pointed at the lone security spacer standing by the hatch. The man was a mess and he looked baffled at the activity around him. The spacer was a one striper. He was so new he still had packing material stuck to his backside, but Britaine realized the man might be useful whatever his state.

Britaine said, "Right. Spacer, follow."

The spacer looked almost panicked. "Sir, um…sir, I request to be allowed to go to sickbay."

McPherson shot out a hand and ripped the man's needler from its holster. She stuck the needler in a pocket. Then she put her other hand on his chest and gave a slight shove. The spacer collapsed to the deck.

"Sorry, Colonel, but I don't believe this spacer will be joining us."

The flight office overlooked the FAC ramp for take offs and landings, so it was not near the command and control center. The operations office was widely separated from both. The design prevented a missile attack from taking out more than one major center of control. It would make a long walk for Britaine and McPherson.

As a result of their hurried pace, Britaine was slightly out of breath when they reached their destination. He had been expecting to run into other personnel, but he did not see many. The crew he did see was still either working their way out of the jump nausea, or scurried out of his sight, ignoring his shouts.

The flight office was empty when they stepped through the open hatch. He sat at the first console he came to and checked the ship status. He saw McPherson shut and lock the hatch behind them. He couldn't imagine why she needed to lock the hatch. She would only have to open it when the second watch and security showed up.

He readily saw the Kiirkegaard was sitting still in space with all monitors on passive. That was good. The

Binders would have a hard time finding one small non-moving spacecraft in the vast volume of space, if they were in the system. His mind refused to lock onto the fact that some of the vessels firing at Gurand's wing had been human.

He commanded the Kiirkegaard to compute a course to Heaven's Gate, including the standard minimum time for personnel recovery. "Colonel Britaine to engineering," he said into the comm unit. The hatch chime sounded before he could get an answer from engineering. He thought it was about time the second watch showed up.

"Open the hatch, McPherson," he ordered. She hesitated, but he pointed sternly at the hatch.

Major Paradise stepped into the flight office. Britaine was surprised to see Paradise looking so calm and cool. With him were First Watch Commander Major Esteban and Second Watch Commander Major Chang.

"Well?" Britaine asked him.

"Colonel Britaine, the three of us need to speak with you. In all fairness, I will tell you that Third Watch Commander Junior-Grade Major Janasovich declined to meet with us." Paradise's voice softened. "Look Muffin, between Nuke, Waterboy and myself; we have a quorum without Tinker."

Britaine bellowed, "Quorum? This is not a democracy. There is no quorum."

"Come on, Bill. That is not what I meant. We all agree that given recovery time and enough time to lay plans, we should be going back to Gagarin to engage the enemy. We just want you to explain why you want us to go Heaven System," Paradise said.

"Explain? I can see I have been entirely too lenient on you three. I don't have to explain squat to any of you. This is my spacecraft, and it goes where I say it goes. End of discussion."

Paradise said, "No. It is not the end of discussion, Colonel Britaine. We respectfully request you reconsider your decision to leave the field of battle."

"No. I-" Britaine started.

Paradise interrupted, "Then, sir, we demand you relinquish your command to me. You are hereby placed under house arrest. Please leave the flight office and confine yourself to your quarters pending charges of cowardice in the face of the enemy. Come on, Bill. Don't make us order security to haul you out of here."

Chapter Thirty-Eight

Britaine was beside himself. His voice was so tense he sounded choked as he tried to speak. "Get out of the FO," he ordered. "Security to the flight office. I want Officers Paradise, Esteban and Chang arrested for mutiny and confined."

Chang said, "No go. Security is on our side. They're no longer following your orders. They're standing off waiting for our call. They aren't cowards anymore than we are. You are the only coward here, you gutless bag of turds."

Britaine spun on Chang just as Paradise and Esteban jumped at him. Before either man could reach him, McPherson stepped forward. A quick stiff arm into his nose dropped Paradise to his knees, blood gushing profusely. In the same fluid movement, she slammed the heel of her foot into the side of Esteban's knee. He fell to the deck screaming. Chang turned from Britaine to confront McPherson and found his forward movement impeded by a needler pressed against his right eyeball.

"Cease your actions, gentlemen," she said calmly. "Or someone is liable to get seriously hurt."

Esteban screamed. "Seriously?! You bitch! You broke my knee."

Paradise shouted around his hands holding his nose. "You stupid grunt, don't you realize you are nothing more than this coward's lapdog?"

Chang added, "You're in for the same thing as this coward. Don't you know he doesn't care anything about you?"

Britaine said, "Third-Level Commander McPherson. Please clear my flight office."

McPherson gestured with her free hand for Paradise to help Esteban to his feet and out the hatch. She then backed Chang out of the FO by pressure from the needler barrel. There was no security detachment in sight. She watched the three men limp away until the corridor stood clear and empty.

Britaine slumped back at the console, momentarily unsure of what to do. He shook himself like a wet dog. He called engineering, but there was no answer. He tried calling Tinker, the Third Watch Commander Major Janasovich, but there was no response.

"Sir?" Britaine looked up to see McPherson standing there. "Sir?" she repeated.

"What, McPherson? Just spit them out if you have more suggestions. We don't have time to dilly-dally about," Britaine replied.

"With all due respect, sir; time is all we have plenty of. We have that and my APES. You are the spacecraft expert, so you tell me if I am right. You have locked down all the navigation consoles from all three of the command centers. They are now slaved to your voice command, right?"

Britaine nodded, "Yes, but it seems Paradise, Esteban and Chang have gotten to the engineering staff. Without engineering we don't have the engines to go anywhere. Does that compute in your tiny little grunt brain: engineering and engines? Get the connection?"

McPherson smiled patiently. "Exactly, Colonel Britaine, they have the power and we have the controls. That is a stalemate. We aren't going anywhere and neither are they.

Britaine nodded, "So, then what? Do we sit locked in here until we starve, or they rig a bypass around the CNC controls?"

"Neither Colonel, my suggestion is that I take a squad or two of my APES and retake engineering."

Britaine nodded as if tasting something nasty, "Okay, then. Do it." He couldn't believe he had to trust this woman. She had been a pain in his side since she came on board. Still, he could have her busted from her command after she managed to get him back to Heaven System.

Chapter Thirty-Nine

Misha shook her head in wonder as Britaine closed the hatch to the flight office behind her. She was amazed such a fool had ever made it to colonel. She knew Britaine was not stupid, but he evidenced so little common sense. She remembered her father pounding into their heads that the problem with common sense was that it was so uncommon.

When she was sure the hatch cover was in the fully closed and locked position, she turned toward APES country and ran down the empty corridor in a ground-covering lope. She expected to run into a security detail at any moment or a group of officers, but all she saw was a few spacers and lower ranking sergeants wandering aimlessly.

She shouted at them to return to their duty stations and await orders from Colonel Britaine. Some of the spacers responded by turning and heading off, glad for any specific order to follow. Others continued to stare at her as if she were crazy. A few shouted profanities at her, calling out that they didn't take orders from grunts, ground-pounders, or whatever other things they could think to call her. None of the spacers attempted to interfere with her.

Misha ordered her comm unit to begin collecting intra-craft calls. She needed to pick up a few tidbits of information such as what was going on in other parts of the spacecraft. She was only mildly surprised to hear conversation after conversation about either giving the command to Paradise or about mutiny against Britaine. She was sure the only difference between the two was a minor difference in perspective. She was just as positive any court-martial would look upon both actions with equal distaste.

It would only take one ill-timed action and this whole mess would turn bloody. She wasn't sure anything could fix this mess. She just knew if she could get her APES ready in time they could stand between both sides. Maybe their presence would diffuse some tempers until they could come to a solution. Misha hoped that would work as she hurried to APES country. She fervently hoped that it wouldn't just put her people in a cross fire between two different groups of the same kind of stupid.

Chapter Forty

Broadcasting unit wide, Misha ordered, "This is Third McPherson to all Allied Protective Expeditionary Services. I am sure you know by now a mutiny is brewing on the Kiirkegaard against Colonel Britaine. Be prepared for action, but do not react except to defend yourself. I want all weapons on lock down now." She continued without breaking stride. "I want everyone in the squad bays. Communications using only by APES secure lines. Stay off Kiirkegaard's network. I am almost back into APES country, maybe five minutes out. We will deploy at that time to aid Colonel Britaine in the defense of his command. Save your questions for now. McPherson out." She hoped that would keep her command from jumping into the mess before she could set a clear course of action. Britaine needed help fast, but APES are trained to be lethal. No one wanted or needed dead crew.

Misha rounded a corner and came face-to-face with a security patrol. She expected some resistance from the crew, but she was surprised they waited to stop her when she was only one corridor away from the hatchway into APES country and her own troops. Any reinforcements she might need were only a shout away. She skidded to a stop, her soft-soled black jump sneaks squeaking against the deck plates. There were only four spacers in the security detail. Unarmed they would have presented a problem for Misha, but not an insurmountable problem. Four against one was doable. However, all four carried needlers, although their weapons were still in their holsters.

She held her arms open wide, spreading her hands to show she was unarmed. She still had the needler she had taken from the spacer outside of CNC, but it was deep in a pocket where it was hard to reach. Misha didn't want a shootout if she could avoid it. She was fast, but not that fast. The odds were against her in armed combat.

Misha smiled, "Let's be easy on the trigger fingers, okay? I am just trying to get back to APES country. There isn't any reason for anyone to get hurt." While she was talking, she reached up with one finger and slowly tapped her comm unit three times. That would reopen the channel to her unit and activate her locator beacon.

She recognized two of the spacers. Their names were stuck in her head, just at the tip of her tongue. They were two from the training bay incident. She thought, "How long ago was that? It seems like weeks, no wonder I can't remember their names." Still, she had to speak to send a message to her troops. She smiled and said to the short male sergeant, "Four armed security people seem like a bit much for an empty corridor, don't you think?" None of the four spoke or drew their weapons, but they were blocking her progress. She was pleased that none of them were facing the direction her reinforcements would come from. Suddenly, the names popped into her head. "Sergeant Williams and Spacer First Class Molinna, right?"

Both nodded sheepishly.

She smiled and took a step closer to them. "Good to see you again. May I pass by to get to my quarters?"

One of the unknowns, a man with a large drooping mustache, drew his needler nervously and pointed the muzzle in her direction. She could see his finger resting on the trigger guard and not the trigger. The other unknown was a young man with flaming red hair. He drew his needler as well. Red slid his finger onto the trigger, but pointed the muzzle at the ceiling over his head.

Misha smiled knowing Red would do more damage to himself than to her if he flinched and shot the needler at the ceiling. Needler ammunition would slice into human flesh with knifelike deadliness, but it wouldn't punch holes into the steel bulkheads. As a result, needler ammo tended to splatter and ricochet in a shower of flechettes.

Misha said, "No need for weapons, folks. I am just trying to get back to my squad bay. Let's keep our finger off the trigger, shall we? What do you say, Sergeant Williams?"

"I don't know, Third. I have orders to detain you; orders from Major Chang," Williams said.

"I can understand your need to follow orders, but Major Chang is wrong," Misha replied.

Molinna interrupted, "Major Change said you broke Major Paradise's nose and shattered Major Esteban's kneecap, and you threatened him with a needler."

Mustache said, "We ought to shoot the bitch now, just to be done with it." Red bobbed his head in agreement, his eyes wide.

Molinna said, "Shut up, you two."

Williams nodded. "It is true we don't know what is going on, but you know it really doesn't matter. Chang said Britaine has gone crazy, turned coward and is running from the enemy. Britaine is all over the intercom shouting about mutiny."

Misha smiled, held her hands wide and took another step toward the group. She was wondering why her squad hadn't arrived yet. She said, "I know it's confusing, but-"

Williams interrupted, "It isn't confusing and it's officer problems. I don't really care what they do. I'm just following orders." The other three nodded their heads in agreement.

Misha nodded in concert and took another step closer. "I can see how you'd think that, but whose orders you're obeying can make the difference between obeying the rightful commander and participating in a mutiny."

Red shouted, "You better shut up. We know you're just siding with your boyfriend Britaine." He shook the needler in his hand. He looked over at Mustache to make him brave.

"Everybody shut up." Sergeant Williams said. "I am sorry, Third. But, I have a job to do. We all do. As far I know Major Chang is an officer. I have to follow his orders. Why don't you come with us and talk with him?"

Molinna nodded in agreement. "I know you've had some problems with Major Chang, but I'm sure we can get this straightened out."

"Yeah," Mustache said. "And if Major Chang is right about that bastard Britaine turning coward and running, then the Major has a right to remove him from command, don't he?" This last, he asked Sergeant Williams.

Williams shook his head. "No, he doesn't. It means he should be removed from command, but that isn't up to Major Chang to decide, or Paradise or Esteban. But, if he went crazy, they'd have to remove him from command."

Misha took a step toward the group. She was now within easy reach of three of them. She still wouldn't be able to grab Red if it came to hand to hand. "Yes, Sergeant Williams. You are right as far as you go. However, if Colonel Britaine did go crazy, it still wouldn't be up to Major Chang would it? Wouldn't that be based on a report by the medical staff?"

Mustache said. "For all we know sick bay told Major Chang that Britaine was crazy. How the hell do we know what officers talk about? Besides, we know you're just siding with that bastard Britaine. And didn't we tell you to shut up? Dammit, Williams, let's just jam her in handcuffs and stuff her into the stockade until we get this straightened out." Still pointing the needler at Misha with one hand, he reached out with his free hand and grabbed her outstretched right arm. He tugged at her, trying to spin her around to have her back to them.

Misha let her knees bend a bit and ducked her right shoulder. This little bit of direction change shifted Mustache's balance, causing the man to turn slightly. His turn carried the muzzle of his needler away from her. She spun her right arm around and locked a grip on Mustache's elbow, bending it backwards. She braced her feet, tightened her muscles and she yanked him into her torso with a jolt. Her left hand shot forward and got a grip on his needler. A quick twist of her wrist and the needler was in her hand. She spun the gun around and slid her finger onto the trigger. She didn't fire. She still wanted to avoid major bloodshed if she could. Instead of shooting, she grabbed Mustache by the front of his uniform and threw him into Red. The two men went down in a crumbled pile. She dove forward, wrenched the gun away from Red, rolled into a ball and came up facing Williams and Molinna as they scrambled to pull their needlers from their holsters.

Misha had Mustache's gun in her left hand and Red's in her right, but she still held her fire. Ducking her head, she plowed upward between Molinna and Williams and slammed into Molinna. The tall spacer bent at the waist as Misha's forehead crashed into her stomach. Misha straightened quickly, mashing the back of her head into Molinna's nose. Molinna fell over backward, knocked unconscious.

Misha kicked her left leg straight back behind her connecting with Williams' chest. Pressed for time, she had used more muscle than she had planned. She heard bone crunch as some of William's ribs broke. The man went down.

Mustache and Red were untangling themselves and getting to their feet. Misha spun from the momentum of her kick into Williams, planted her left leg onto the deck plates and kicked straight out with her right leg. The sole of her book connected with Mustache's face with the sole of her boot. The man's eyes glazed over as his nose broke. He sank back onto the deck.

Misha stood over Red as the man froze halfway to his feet. She pointed both needlers at him, one muzzle for each eye, only a scant inch away from the eyeballs. From this distance, she was sure all he could see was the open barrels. She waggled the needlers in a motion for him to stand up.

She said, "Relieve Williams and Molinna of their side arms. Please move carefully and slowly, spacer. Now, give them to me. Good. Now tend to your comrades, call the sick bay to come and get them. Williams has broken ribs, Molinna has most likely suffered a concussion and your buddy with the mustache has broken his nose."

Misha left as Red frantically called for help from the Kiirkegaard's sick bay. She knew his next call would be to either security or to the mutineers, but she didn't have time to take care of the injured or take him prisoner.

Chapter Forty-One

Race Jackson cursed under his breath. He had hoped for more time. He thought four spacers would have at least slowed McPherson down.

"What do we do now, Race?" Sigget Donnellson asked.

Race shrugged, "What can we do? We have to take care of her ourselves. We have two whole squads here. She is tough, but she can't take out even a quarter of us."

Second Rice Bilideau said, "Right, Race. But, you heard her. She has all four of those needlers she took from those dipwad vacuum suckers. We aren't armed with squat."

Race snarled, "Shut up, Beans. I don't care if she is carrying a particle beam cannon. McPherson has sided with that coward of a boyfriend of hers. She forfeited the right to even be in the APES. As far as I am concerned that puts Second Moraft in command. We have both your Dawg Squad and my Foxtrot. Do you really think that twenty-two APES can't bust the head of a lone coward? Besides, Theda said to capture McPherson alive and that is what we're going to do. Got me?"

"Easy, Deuce. I'm on your side," Bilideau replied.

"It ain't my side or her side. We're APES and we came out here to fight weed-eaters. And no one, got me, no one is going to stop us. Not some cowardly vacuum breather or his girlfriend. I don't care whether she is APES, Marshal, or the gods on high."

Rice nodded, "Hey, I agree. I haven't ever run from a fight and I'm not going to start now. My question is: how do we capture her without getting shot full of needler ammo?"

Jackson said, "She will be here any second. We ambush. Dawg Squad goes into Able's squad bay. Singletary won't mind. Hell, we don't even know where he went off to. Foxtrot will split into two. We put half of us in Bravo's bay and half in Charlie's. Nobody moves until she is in the hatch to Able. Then we pounce. She won't expect us and we should get her before she gets a shot off."

While he was speaking, Jackson dispersed his squad. He was pleased the rookies were moving quickly. He hoped they had sense enough to stay out of the way once the action started. He needed his veterans. Besides, he wanted to get in a few licks of his own. He felt betrayed. She fooled him into giving her his loyalty, despite what others had been saying about her. He even defended her. But, she was running from those weed-eater bastards. She was running from a fight, taking sides with that ass hole Britaine. He didn't know what disgusted him more: her betrayal of his loyalty or her cowardice.

He crouched in the hatch to Bravo bay. He couldn't watch the corridor for McPherson. If she saw him, it might set off the ambush prematurely. He gestured for everyone to be silent as he watched her progress on a motion sensor. He smiled smugly as he thought how convenient it was of the bitch to turn on her tracking device.

APES country was not really a series of rooms and corridors. The design of the ship was for a large open space on one deck. The rooms were all the various combat components used by the Allied Protective Expeditionary Services. The mobility rooms lined up, steel wall to steel wall, with the hatches facing each other to form corridors or hallways.

Each component had a combat skid plate built into it. When deployed on a ship, they deactivated the skid plates and locked them onto the deck by tensor fields. When the APES dirt dropped, they took their squad bays, armories, kitchens, storage lockers and weapons bays with them. The skid plates would be activated and spacecraft would open up, blow free the tensor fields and disgorge the APES unit, dumping troopers and equipment in a mad rush. The squad bays, armories, kitchens, storage lockers and weapons bays would drop to the planet surface guided by automated systems. Once on dirt they would become bunkers, pillboxes, tanks, command center, and even mobile surgical hospitals. The armored troopers manually operated their individual skid plates for a controlled descent.

The standard configuration on board spacecraft was for the commander's day office to be the first room inside the hatchway of APES country. Next, the squad bays sat in alternating order forming a corridor. Able's bay was usually set directly across from the day office. Bravo bay was next to the day office and Charlie's squad bay across the hall from them.

However, Third Cans hadn't cared about the standard configuration. The day office was first inside the hatch. Able's bay was next to it instead of across the corridor. Charlie was directly across from the day office and Bravo was next to Charlie, across from Able.

Jackson silently thanked Third Cans for his don't-give-a-shit attitude. It made this ambush much easier. It might confuse things a bit during a drop, but not seriously. Normally, McPherson would have stepped through the main hatch, making a quick right turn into Able's bay. As it was, she would have to pass by Bravo's hatch and step through the second hatch on the left. This would put half of Foxtrot Squad behind her in Bravo and half of Foxtrot Squad at her back in Charlie's bay. She would face all of Dawg Squad as she stepped through the hatch.

Just as her signal blended on the tracking device with the hatch frame of the Able's bay, Jackson shouted, "Now!"

He barreled out of Charlie's bay, flying across the corridor. McPherson's back was to him as she faced all of Dawg Squad. She started to turn and retreat from Bilideau's squad. Someone crumpled at her feet, slamming into her ankles. Jackson left his feet and drove his shoulder into the small of her back. He felt more than saw Donnellson hit her high in the shoulders. Their combined weight buckled her knees and drove her to the deck.

He could hear McPherson shouting, but he couldn't make out the words in the tumult as two full squads tried to work out their frustration against the back-stabbing coward. Someone shoved a bungee cord into his hands. He braced against another body and wrapped the cord around McPherson's wrist, shouting for someone to hold her other arm down. Who did or how they did it, he didn't care, but a thick wrist came into view. He wrapped the cord around it stretching the bungee cord to its fullest extension. After he tied it off, he let go. It snapped tight.

Jackson pushed and pulled at bodies, shouting for people to clear away. Soon he could roll off McPherson and get to his feet. He found himself almost nauseous from having had to touch her. He felt contaminated. He looked at her lying at his feet. Someone had bound her legs tightly, from her knees to her ankles. He looked at the knots. They would hold. She lay glaring at him, unable to speak through a gag in her mouth.

Bilideau said, "What do you think of the muzzle, Race? I didn't think of it before, but the bitch tried to bite me. Plus, we have the added benefit of not having to listen to her whine."

Jackson nodded. "Good move. Now what do we do, Beans?"

Bilideau shrugged. "Damfino. I'll call Theda and see what she says."

"Where the hell did she go anyway? Shouldn't she have been here for this?" Jackson asked.

"Don't ask me. I ain't the guy with the answers. I'm just a lowly second. Somebody else does the thinking. She said she had somewhere more important to be."

"What is more important than being here to relieve her boss for cowardice?" Jackson asked.

"What are you asking me for, Race? I just work here. You ask Second Moraft."

"Yeah, yeah, yeah. I'm just talking. Go call Theda and see what she says to do with this bitch. I'm going to dump her in her office with the other goof we snagged," Jackson said.

He turned to his squad. He could see a few were going to be nursing bruises. He wondered how many of the punches were by friendlies. McPherson hadn't been unfettered long enough to do that much damage.

"Okay, Foxtrot will pick her up and get her next door."

Donnellson stepped forward and rammed his boot into McPherson's unprotected ribs. "That one is for good measure and to make sure you behave," he chuckled.

Jackson grabbed Donnellson by the back of his collar and slammed him face first against the bulkhead. He spun him around and stepped in nose to nose.

"Sigget, no wonder you never made second. McPherson may be a coward, but she is now an APES prisoner. Listen all of you; we do not mistreat our prisoners."

"But Race, she was deserting during a time of war," Donnellson whined.

"I don't care. She'll get what she deserves from a court-martial. We hold her, nothing more. Personally, I would just as soon kick her lying teeth out and shove her through an airlock, but that'll have to wait. Nobody touches her until they get the word to do so. Bilideau, that goes for you and all of Dawg Squad as well, got me?"

Bilideau looked up from his comm unit and nodded. "S'right by me. I don't want to get my knuckles anymore slimy than they already are."

Jackson pointed to Dashell, Foxtrot's medic. "You take two other guys and haul her next door. Check her over to make sure she isn't hurt. I want her healthy for her execution."

Chapter Forty-Two

Misha thought about struggling as the three men half carried, half dragged her to the day office. She decided it wouldn't do much good to struggle since she was still bound hand and foot. They unceremoniously dumped her in the middle of the deck.

Dashell leaned down and spoke into her ear; his breath was hot and stale. "I don't care if you do have injuries, Bitch. I hope you're bleeding internally and just die. Save the APES the money for your trial and punishment. Sleep tight." He patted her head. When the men left they shut and cycled the hatch.

Misha rolled and tried to sit up. She was surprised to see Forrester sitting quietly in a corner. He appeared to be unharmed, but was bound as she was, minus the gag.

Forrester smiled at her, "Well, well, well, what do we have here? Good to see you, Misha. No, no, don't get up on my account."

Misha succeeded in getting her back to the cold steel wall and inched her way up into a sitting position. She looked around and saw there were no sharp corners, edges or hooks she might use to pry loose her bonds. She knew there wouldn't be. Sharp corners would have been a safety violation on any spacecraft. But, something in her made her look anyway. She continued inching upward. She braced with her feet on the deck and her back to the steel wall. The difficulty was that her legs were tied together. This meant she had to drive upward with both legs, the easy part. Then she had to hop backwards and upwards with both legs at the same time, the hard part. By pushing and sliding she finally got herself into a standing position.

Forrester said, "Bravo. But, now what?"

Misha bunched her shoulder muscles and started to pull against the cords.

"No," Forrester stopped her. "Those cords will stretch." He continued through her glare, "I know you know that. But, they shrink back up when you release the stress. They will tighten. You may find yourself bound more securely than when you started. I know you are strong, but even your heavy-worlder muscles can't snap one of those bungee cords. Hop over here and let's see if I can work your gag loose."

The room was small enough it only took two small jumps before she was standing over Forrester. She looked down at him. She wanted to ask, "Now what, Mister Know-It-All?" But what came out around the gag was "Ow a, ir owia?"

"Humm?" Forrester said. "Definitely we have to work on the gag. I am unable to work myself into a standing position like you. Sorry, but you are going to have to come down to me." He turned to show her his wiggling fingers. "I have about this much mobility."

Misha put her back to the steel wall and slid with a thump to the deck. Getting the gag down to his hands was a simple matter of falling over sideways. She inched toward his back until she felt his fingers on her face. She hoped he could get a grip on the gag without digging too deeply into her skin.

"I think I got a hold of the gag just behind your ear. No, don't pull yet," Forrester said. "This is tight. I'm sorry, Misha but it feels like you might lose a layer of skin off your ears unless we go real slow, or I may be able to work it down around your neck."

Misha hunched her back and thigh muscles and hurled herself away from Forrester. It caught him by surprise and yanked him over, but he held onto the gag. She felt the gag slip around her ears. One side was loose enough it was partially blocking an eye. She thrashed her head and shook like a dog trying to work itself out of a collar. Finally, the gag slid off the top of her head. She breathed in sharply and let the breath out in a slow sigh. She rolled into a sitting position and hunched her way to lean her back against the desk.

Forrester lay on his side with his back to her. He rolled over to the steel wall and worked his way into a sitting position. They looked at each other.

Forrester said, "That was neither slow, nor did we work the gag down."

Misha smiled, "It got the gag off. That was the objective."

"Yes, but like I told said, you might lose some skin. You're bleeding down the left side of your face. It doesn't look deep, but you did scrape off a sizable patch of your hide."

Misha chuckled grimly. "It's just skin. I have plenty to spare. Thanks for the use of your fingers. Do you think you have enough range of motion to work on the knots on these other cords?"

Forrester shook his head. "No. I have the motion, but I don't have the leverage I would need to pull at a bungee cord. They have too much stretch to them. What about you?"

She twisted sideways so he could get a look at her hands. They were tied back to back. She had less range of motion than he did.

Forrester nodded. "Okay. We need to think of another way to get out of here."

"Let's see, we are locked in a room with steel walls and double thick hatches designed to withstand, not only the vacuum of space, but enemy artillery and weapons fire. We are surrounded by at least two dozen men and women trained to kill with their bare hands, and we are bound hand and foot. You must be some kind of special thinker if you can see a way out of this," she said sarcastically.

"I didn't say I had a plan. I just said we should think about it," he replied with a smile.

"While we think, mind telling me what you are doing trussed up down here?" Misha asked.

"Good question. I'm not sure. I strapped in for the jump," Forrester gestured with his head toward the private bedroom. "We didn't get the all clear signal, although we did have more time than normal. Then suddenly we jumped again. When I finally got enough of my feet under me to stagger to the hatch, your troops grabbed me, wrapped me up, and dumped me back in here. Do you know what's going on?"

"A bit more than you, but I am sorry to say not the whole story." Misha wondered where to begin. It seemed like such a long day. Much of what had happened started with classified information from both Guinjundst and from the Binder IFF. How much should she reveal to a Marshal Service sergeant? It would be an easy choice if it was a piece of information that might mean life or death. She looked at Forrester and wondered how much he really knew. She was sure he wasn't on the Kiirkegaard hitching a ride to an exotic vacation. He knew too much for that.

Forrester returned her stare. "Well?" he asked.

"I have way too much to tell and I don't know where to begin." She gave him a brief synopsis of the events of the day, starting with her discovery of the Binder IFF signal and ending with her being dumped into her office bound and gagged. She didn't omit any part, even those parts about human spacecraft shooting at AMSF craft.

Forrester whistled tunelessly. "Deep doggie doo doo."

Misha nodded. "That's the truth. We run or we support mutiny. Hell of a choice."

"I am baffled. Please don't misinterpret, but you aren't the type to run. I also know that you have no reason to like Britaine. Why are you backing his side?"

Misha shook her head. "That's something that I would've thought every APE, except the newest rookie, would have understood. I don't have a choice in this matter. I think Britaine is wrong. If Britaine has reasons for running, he hasn't explained them to me. However, he doesn't have to explain it to me. I think we should stay and fight, but my contract says I must, and I emphasize, must support the lawful commander of any spacecraft where I am deployed, in all such matters. To my sure knowledge, no competent authority has relieved Britaine. Only General Gurand as the wing commander can relieve him for cowardice or incompetence and only the head of the medical staff can relieve him for insanity. I've been with Britaine today, and only an idiot would declare him insane. Yes, he is an incompetent coward, but crazy? No." She looked at Forrester and asked, "Why are you here?"

Forrester snorted, "I just told you everything I know. Your guys grabbed me-"

Misha interrupted. "Knock it off, Sergeant Forrester. You know that is not what I meant. If you're just a bureaucratic data pusher, then I am a DropSix warthog shepherd. Who are you and why are you here? Come on, Gan. You show me yours and I'll show you mine."

"Okay, okay, I really am Sergeant Gan Forrester of the Marshal Service."

Misha smiled, "So far so good. Now tell me something that I don't know."

Forrester said, "You have to keep this between us. I really am going to Gagarin and I really did just catch a ride on the Kiirkegaard. However, I am a field agent and the service chose this spacecraft specifically because of you...and one other."

"Me?" Misha looked startled.

"Don't look so surprised. You're big news. Plus, you have some very special secrets locked away in your head. I was asked to find out from you what I could about the events on Guinjundst."

"Whoops," Misha said with a big grin. "That one remains secret for now. Not for much longer, I suspect. I still can't talk about it."

"Well, it's not much of a secret the Binders used biological and chemical weapons against our ground troops for the first time, right?"

"Well, I thought that was still a secret," she said with a smile.

"That was something the Marshal Service suspected before I was sent here. It was pretty well confirmed by the simulations you're using in the tri-wave. But, there's something else, isn't there?" he asked.

Misha just looked at him with a blank face.

He shrugged and continued. "I thought it was something to do with the Orion Confederacy joining the Binders."

Misha snorted.

Forrester nodded. "I know. They aren't much in the way of joiners. However, I know they still harbor an ill will against the Allied Systems for the beating we gave them over the incident at James Three. All of our indicators show they're not ready to begin taking us on yet."

"I'm surprised the Marshal Service is so well informed about what's going on outside Allied space. It was my understanding your charter is domestic criminal service only."

"Let's just say we find internal protection sometimes demands an understanding of external pressures."

Misha nodded. "But, I didn't even think the Orion Confederacy was considered enough of a threat to investigate."

"It is too late to investigate if we wait until someone becomes a threat. I like to call it preventative analysis."

"So, why did you think Guinjundst had something to do with the Orions?" she asked.

Forrester replied, "Because of the scenarios you were running in the tri-wave sims. Second Takki-Homi explained that for training purposes you had to pit yourselves against someone. The Binders do not present much of a challenge in training, or didn't before Guinjundst."

Misha smiled. "That's all too true. There isn't usually a lot of training necessary to take on a Binder attack. That used to be a stand off and shoot action."

"Used to be?" Forrester asked, quoting her own words back to her.

Misha shrugged. "Things change. So who is the one other?"

Forrester looked surprised. "One other what?"

"If I may quote, 'the service chose this spacecraft, specifically because of you and one other.' That is what you said, isn't it?"

"Oh, that one," Forrester smiled. "All I can say at this point is that the Marshal Service has an undercover operative on board the Kiirkegaard. No don't worry; it's not in the APES. I don't think Marshal Service command thought we needed informants or undercover operatives in the APES. Until now, that is. No disrespect intended, but it was thought the information gathered would be of low value."

"It's what you don't know that can kill you," Misha muttered.

"What? Yes, that should be the Marshal Service motto. Is that an APES saying?"

"No," Misha said. "That was what my daddy crammed into our heads from the first time we walked out the front door. DropSix is not like Heaven Three. Much of it is unexplored even after eleven generations on the planet. Strange things can still come out of the dark if you're not careful."

"I've heard the lower altitudes can be somewhat dangerous even for a heavy gravity world," Forrester said.

"True enough. You can only reach sea level by using high pressure equipment anyway. Standard atmosphere is only found in the high mountain regions. We've only sent a few drones into the oceans to see what or if any life exists in that chemical soup. But, there are still vast uncharted areas."

"Doesn't sound like a nice tourist spot," Forrester smiled.

"No it isn't. So, who is he?" Misha asked.

"Who is who?" Forrester looked puzzled.

"You know who I mean, Gan. You're good at changing the subject, but you mentioned an undercover operative."

"Yes, I did. But, it doesn't have anything to do with you. We were getting reports of pilfered equipment. It was nothing more than simple theft. So, the AMSF asked us to investigate to find who was buying. They felt they could clean their own house, but they wanted us to help nab any civilians involved."

"So, to catch civilians you put someone undercover on the Kiirkegaard?" Misha looked puzzled.

"Yep," he said. "It's easier to find the buyer if you watch the seller. And before you ask, AMSF command knows about our operative. Britaine doesn't. And no, I am not going to tell you who it is. I won't compromise this individual's mission."

"You know, Gan. I think I may be able to give you a new direction to take in that investigation. However, anything I tell you is fully recorded and forwarded to my command. This is all open exchange of data."

"It might be better if you keep our conversations just between us," Forrester said. "If you suspect APES are involved, you don't know how far up the line of command any corruption might have spread."

Misha nodded. "True, but I will not go around my leadership. There may be high level commanders involved, but I doubt it. I'll run this whole conversation past Fourth Ottiamig if we get out of this mess. This is just speculation, but we need to take a closer look at Trooper Singletary of my squad if there is any theft, black marketing or fencing going on."

"We?"

"Yes, we. Singletary is my responsibility. I have had suspicions from the start, but I haven't had time to investigate. I guess I need to make time."

"I can't do much right now, though," Forrester smiled and wiggled his fingers around his bonds. "Can you tell me why you suspect this Singletary might be involved?"

Before she could answer they heard the hatch begin to cycle open.

Chapter Forty-Three

Bound as she was there was nothing Misha could do to protect herself against anyone coming through the hatch. Never-the-less, her muscles tensed and she twisted her neck around to see who was coming through the hatchway. Half expecting to see Jackson or Bilideau, she was surprised to see Takki-Homi and Aardmricksdottir step into the room. She could see two other APES standing in the hatchway watching the corridor, but she couldn't swivel her head around far enough to see who was where.

Takki-Homi silently leaned Misha forward and tugged at her bonds. Without a word, he slipped a utility knife from his jump-sneaks and slid it between her hands. The blade slid cleanly through the bungee cords.

Misha started to say something, but he signaled her to be silent. He also shot a warning look at Forrester to keep quiet. He pointed at her glass-pack. Misha realized she still had an open comm line. She tapped the unit to shut down any outgoing comms while he quickly sliced along the cords cutting her legs free.

Vark said, "Comms clear. That was the only signal I see coming out of here. I doubt if anyone else had the sense to monitor your comm signal, but you never know." She smiled at Forrester, "Spies in the AMSF, huh?"

Forrester grimaced, but Vark smiled and said, "Not to worry, not my problem. I never liked Singletary anyway."

"Thank you both," Misha said to Takki-Homi and Vark.

Before she could say anything else, Forrester interrupted, "What about me? This deck is getting a bit uncomfortable for an old man and these cords are pretty tight."

Takki-Homi grinned at Misha. "What do you say, Trey? Should we cut him loose or just leave him tied up here where he won't get in the way?"

Misha grinned back. "I think in the spirit of inter-service relations, we should cut him loose. Hang on to him. I'm sure you don't want to have to rescue him twice."

Forrester said, "Hey! I can take care of myself."

Takki-Homi nodded, "Doing good so far today, huh?"

Misha faced her two seconds, "Okay. I need to know the situation, but first: are we secure here or should we abandon the day office for another location?"

Takki-Homi said, "With your permission, Third?"

"It's your op, Taks. I am just the rescuee at this point."

Takki-Homi nodded. "Then it is time to get the hell out of dodge before the bad guys come riding back."

Charlie Squad's Trooper Riffler stuck her head through the hatchway and rapped her knuckles lightly on the steel wall.

Vark said, "We've got to go now. Can you move, Third or do you require assistance?"

Misha said, "I can move fine. I wasn't tied that long. Forrester has been wrapped up a while. Give him a hand." She gestured for Takki-Homi to lead the way. She watched in amazement as Aardmricksdottir simply picked up Forrester and slung him over her shoulder.

She followed Takki-Homi into the corridor where Charlie Squad Trooper One Gaineretti waited to lead the way. Other than two APES from Foxtrot Squad laying face down on the decks, the corridor was empty. Takki-Homi signaled Gaineretti to move. The trooper checked the hatchway out of APES country and stepped through. He next signaled Aardmricksdottir to move forward with Forrester and Riffler to follow.

Takki-Homi grabbed one of the two Foxtrot troopers, dragging the man to his feet. Misha could see that it was Spaznitski. She looked down and saw the other was Trooper Seven Becker. Both men looked the worse for wear, but they looked like they would eventually heal. Takki-Homi stripped Spaznitski's glass-pack from his pocket and literally threw the man into the day office. He swept up Becker and repeated the process. He then dragged the hatch closed and spun the lock. He looked at Misha and spoke in a half whisper, "Might as well code the lock to keep them in there for now."

Misha nodded and spoke the codes to voice print the lock to operate only on her command. She set the lock to hold for the next hour, not as a permanent lock. If something happened to her, it would take a vibromolecular cutting torch to get the two men out. She followed Takki-Homi's direction and left APES country, hustling to catch up to Aardmricksdottir and the others.

Chapter Forty-Four

Aardmricksdottir set Forrester gently to his feet on the deck, smiling at the older man. He was smaller than she was, but he must have packed muscle somewhere because he was a lot heavier than he looked. She stretched her back and stepped out of the way so the others behind her could move into the small space.

Takki-Homi led their small team to an odd-shaped space. Due to the tiny variances between spacecraft and any deployed APES units, there were always a few odd-shaped spaces left over. This space was behind Easy's squad bay. With the front of the squad bay lined up with the others, it left a gap between its back steel wall and a metal bulkhead of the spacecraft. A hatchway led into this small space. She wondered how Takki-Homi had known about this particular space as the only hatch into it was through spacer country.

Vark knew such spaces existed, but usually they were unattainable, as there wasn't any hatchway to reach them. Sometimes the accessible spaces were not much bigger than crawl spaces left around the edge of an APES container or bay. Sometimes the spaces were large enough for APES or spacers to make private use of the extra room. Who used the room was often dependent upon which service had a hatchway entrance to the space. As she looked around it was obvious someone had been using the area as a private playroom. She blushed profusely and turned her head away from McPherson when the Third entered the room. Her pale complexion gave away her emotions. She could only nod at Takki-Homi as he slid the hatch shut behind him.

"Are all the outgoing comms still off?" Takki-Homi asked.

Everyone double checked their glass-packs and nodded. Vark slid behind Gaineretti's bulk. The man was shorter than she was, but wider by a long yard. Vark's mind kept saying, "Don't look at me. Don't look at me. Just let me slide into the cracks." She shook her head trying to clear it. She knew she shouldn't be here. She should be with her squad. She thought, "I tried to tell Taks to leave me behind." She couldn't help but replay the rescue of McPherson again through her head.

Takki-Homi assigned Gaineretti and her to take care of any guards in the corridor. She froze when confronted by Becker. The man was as close to an incompetent as an APE can be and still not have died in combat, but she simply froze. She had never frozen before, even in actual combat. Gaineretti stepped up to Spaznitski and simply head butted the man to the ground. Becker had almost reached his comm unit when Gaineretti reached around Vark and slapped the man to the deck. Gaineretti hadn't even looked at her as he stepped over the two bodies to signal all clear.

Vark cursed herself knowing she wasn't ready for command. "What am I doing here? Who was I kidding when I thought that I could lead? I couldn't even keep my squad together when the shit hit the fan."

She reached a hand up and put it gently on Gaineretti's shoulder. She wanted to apologize for her actions in the corridor, but she couldn't bring herself to speak. She wouldn't have been surprised if the long-time veteran had shrugged her hand off, but instead he reached up and patted her fingers. His head gave a slight nod, but he didn't speak or turn around.

Takki-Homi turned to McPherson, "Now what, Third?"

Before McPherson could speak, Vark spoke. "I'm sorry." She hung her head, hiding behind Gaineretti.

McPherson looked at her. There wasn't much room, so Gaineretti had nowhere to move to get out of the way. "Excuse me? Sorry for what? Pulling me out of the fire back there? You have a peculiar sense of what you should apologize for."

Vark shook her head. How could she explain to these people? She thought she might as well just confess and be up front. She stood up straight and slid past Gaineretti. "No, sir. I guess for all of it. I shouldn't be in a command position here."

McPherson looked at her baffled. "Why not, Second? If anyone's been making mistakes around here it's me."

Vark replied, "You don't know, sir. I froze back there." Gaineretti placed a strong retaining hand on her elbow. She shook her head at him. "Thanks, but I have to be clean about this. I froze back there trying to get you out. I don't know why. I just did." She tried to look in McPherson's eyes but couldn't.

McPherson nodded as if she understood. Vark couldn't imagine how this woman could understand. McPherson was a bonafide war hero. The Third said, "Am I still tied up in my day office?"

Vark didn't answer, thinking that surely this was just a rhetorical question, but Gaineretti answered for her.

"No, sir. Free and clear," he said.

McPherson smiled, "That's right and remember I like it that way. Were there any casualties on our team?"

"No damage at all to our team, tho' I may have broken a nail back there," Gaineretti reported.

McPherson looked at Vark forcing her to make eye contact. She spoke in a soft voice. "Vark, have you ever struck another APE with the intention of doing deliberate damage, other than in training?"

"No, sir, why would I do that?" Vark sputtered.

McPherson smiled, "Trooper Gaineretti, same question."

"Me, sir?" Gaineretti asked. "Why would you think such a thing of me?"

Takki-Homi snorted, "Maybe she heard you did stockade time for laying out those three spacers on Amos Station or the time on Thackery where they had to drag you-"

Gaineretti interrupted, "Wait a minute, Taks. As I recall you were with me on Thackery. And Riffler, do you remember when she put half a squad of drunken warehouse box wranglers down when they tried to see what was under her uniform that time on Bennigan Prime?"

Riffler held up her hands, "Leave me out of this. That was self-defense and you know it."

"Easy people," McPherson laughed. "My point to Second Vark is there are differences between throwing punches at someone you consider your own people and throwing high explosives at a distant alien. Deuce Taks, maybe it would be a good idea that no one ever gets promoted to a second-level commander without a few bar fights under their belts. Whadda ya think?"

Vark stared, "You too, Third? You've been in a bar fight?"

"Well, I wouldn't call them fights as much as physical disagreements. After all, a girl has to protect herself from drunken APES, right Riffler? We even have to protect ourselves from those who're wearing very thick beer goggles. Besides, I would've thought that a beautiful woman like you would have had your share of unwanted advances."

Vark was surprised. Sure there was always someone with a loud mouth or grabby hands but there was always someone else to take care of it for her. She didn't have to... then it hit her. Yes, someone always came to her rescue when she found herself in those situations. When she thought it through, her rescuers almost always seemed to try something with her later. How could she have been so blind? She caused bar fights, but had never had to deal with the consequences. Vark said, "It's not just that. I wasn't as ready for this command as I thought. I couldn't keep my squad together like Deuce Taks. I couldn't even get the armor ready for dirt drop without getting extra help. You're just going to have to relieve me of command."

McPherson said, "Nope. And I don't really have the time to dance around the subject with you. You will have to do what you can as best you can. Just try as hard as you can. We'll sort the rest out later. It's tough luck and bad timing, Second. It bites, but we've got bigger problems just now."

McPherson spoke to Takki-Homi. "Give me a sitrep."

Vark was sure a demotion was in her future as soon as this situation was resolved. She decided if she wasn't command caliber, then at least she would be the best trooper she could be. With the pressure off, she knew she could relax and focus on what was important to the situation. She listened carefully. Takki-Homi gave McPherson a rundown of everything he knew. He explained that as far as they could tell by comm traffic, Colonel Britaine still had the flight office locked. The XO, Major Paradise, controlled the engine room. He nodded at Aardmricksdottir when he mentioned Vark had put a lockout code on all the APES armories. She was pleased at McPherson's smile, but she knew it would be short lived. The manual of arms stated the only intention of the lockout codes was for use in her capacity as the senior armor repair technician. It wouldn't take long for another armor tech to crash through her codes.

Takki-Homi told McPherson they also put lockouts on weapons lockers and expendables storage. It should keep the number of weapons being used to a minimum if the APES couldn't get to their combat gear. They should be able to minimize casualties on both sides if they could keep the number of lethal weapons down.

"What about Kiirkegaard's crew?" McPherson asked.

Takki-Homi replied, "Most of the crew has gone to quarters and locked themselves in. It's confusing out there. I can sympathize with them not wanting to get caught between what they see as officer squabbles. Not that I agree with them. I'm just reporting what I hear. Most of the enlisted and non-flight officers dislike Britaine enough to not support him. They also fear what might turn out to be a mutiny enough to not support it."

"What about our APES?" McPherson asked. In spite of herself, Vark winced. She was trying not to feel guilty, but she knew some of her own squad had not followed her lead.

Takki-Homi looked at Vark, catching her grimace. "It's not good news, Third. Six squad leaders are supporting XO Paradise with most of their squads. They are Bravo, Dawg, Easy, Fox, Hotel and Kilo, plus a few individuals from various squads."

Vark raised her hand. "Some of those individuals are from my Joker Squad. That would be Spakney, Putinova, Dallas and Yorkvina. I couldn't convince them to stand down."

McPherson looked puzzled. "Where does Beaudry stand? I was sure he would pick any side that was opposite to me.""

"You know, I would have thought the same thing," Vark replied. "He surprised me, but he told Spakney to…well, politely put, he told Spakney to shove it rather forcefully, sir."

"Good for him," McPherson said. "Also, I wouldn't have expected Jackson to jump sides. You're friends, Taks, what gives?"

"Sir, he lost family on Guinjundst. I think he's let his anger at the Binders overcome his good sense. Target fixation, if you know what I mean." Some people in combat suffer target fixation when they lock onto an objective and miss the things going on around them. They would bear down so hard on the enemy in front of them that they would miss a flanking motion.

Takki-Homi continued, "He also seems to have personalized the situation. I think he blames you that he isn't killing Binders at this very moment, you know?"

Misha nodded. It was obvious to Vark that the Third dreaded asking about her own squad. Misha managed to squeeze out a strained question, "Able Squad?"

Takki-Homi shook his head, "We just don't know at this point. We haven't been in contact with all of them. We know Peace DeLaPax took your five rookies under her wing. She's a good trooper and we can count on her to do the right thing. Hell, all the DeLaPaxes are like that. There are more of them in the APES than Ottiamigs and we all know there is a ton and a half of those. Still, we don't have a clue about Singletary, Park, Juarez or Slezak. Those four plus a smattering of others seemed to disappear. They haven't answered any comms. Not that

264

Vark or I tried too hard. We've been keeping a low profile, but we've heard DeLaPax tried repeatedly to reach them over open comms. But, they didn't answer her or Second Moraft's calls when she tried to comm them."

"I imagine those four are following their own agenda," Misha said. "What about the other squads?"

"Well," Takki-Homi said. "Both Golf and India took a page out of the spacer's playbook and locked themselves in their squad bays. They say they aren't coming out until they have a clear legitimate chain of command to follow. Truthfully, they're both new seconds and I don't blame them one bit. I was tempted myself to hunker down until the air cleared. But..." He let the conjunction hang.

Misha nodded. She could understand how a second would not want to take sides in a jumbled mess like this. However, the APES manual and the resident AMSF contract stated clearly the APES must support Britaine. Inaction was obviously not support. She was sure any review or court-martial would view the situation in the same way.

"Who do we have, Taks?" she asked.

"As I said: DeLaPax and your five rookies, Vark and six of her squad, plus we have Charlie intact. Not good odds, but I think the majority of APES following Moraft and Jackson are doing so just because they are following their seconds and they haven't thought the situation through. I can't believe that their hearts are into mutiny."

Misha frowned. "We must believe they've whole heartedly given over to mutiny. Otherwise, if the time comes we might pull our punches. We can't take any chances. Everyone understands? Good. Where are our loyal APES?"

Takki-Homi shrugged. "We have more bad news, sir. Race Jackson and Theda Moraft locked them down in the training bay. The five of us, well six counting our marshal friend, are all we have to start with. Then again, forest fires often start with small kindling."

Misha smiled, "Ok people. Who's got a match?"

Chapter Forty-Five

Aardmricksdottir looked back down the corridor they had just walked. Forrester was standing next to her, their backs to the bulkhead. He smiled at her. Gaineretti was down the length of the corridor at the closest hallway junction. He hooked a thumbs-up in her direction. She would have rather had Gaineretti taking point on this operation, but she understood McPherson's point about where they needed his history of close quarters' fighting. Someone had to cover her back.

She stretched out on the deck. Keeping her face as close to the deck plates as she could, Vark scrunched forward until she could see around the corner. Two APES from Kranitchovich's Hotel Squad flanked the side hatchway to the training base. She recognized Trooper Three Bailey, but didn't know the name of the other trooper. Vark slithered back around the corner. She was sure the two guards hadn't seen her.

She wouldn't have much to do besides detain the two APES if things worked out right. If not, well, this time she was ready to break some heads. Vark gritted her teeth. She would just as soon start with Bailey as anyone else if she had to start a fight. The man always seemed to be watching her wherever she went. No, she corrected herself, not just watching, but full on leering and even a little ogling. Still, he never did or said anything that constituted harassment.

She steeled her resolve. It didn't matter. She wasn't going to take it personally. Bailey was standing guard as a mutineer. He was stopping good honest APES from doing their duty. She wished she had their sub-vocal communications headsets, but the locked weapons lockers held all of that equipment. Third McPherson didn't deem getting them worth the effort at this point.

Vark tapped her comm unit "dot-dot-dot-dash." Then she tapped, "dot-dot-dash-dash-dash". She had used the old earth style Morse code for "V" and then for the number "2"; V for Vark and two for the number of guards at the side hatch.

She wondered who Morse was and why he needed a special code. She didn't know why anyone would come up with a code so irrational and without any discernible pattern. The system of dots and dashes required memorization or as was her case, reading off the list on her glass-pack data files. None-the-less, it was what Third McPherson told her to use. It kept the signals to a minimum and kept voice commands off the net. That way, any intercepted signals required analysis before anyone could react. Hopefully, any reaction would be too late.

"Mill-Hooman," Vark suddenly thought. "Yes, that's the name. The two troopers standing guard are Bailey and Mill-Hooman." She remembered now, Cantha Mill-Hooman was a transfer from some other outfit. The woman didn't seem to fit into Hotel Squad or any other group for that matter. She was not attractive in any physical sense with her squat compact body. She seemed to try to match her fleshy unattractiveness with a personality to match.

Some other second obviously passed a problem trooper to Second Stanley Kranitchovich's Hotel Squad. Now that she thought of it, it looked like a lot of units had dumped their problems into the 1392nd. Third Can's could have stopped it, she was sure, but apparently he hadn't either noticed or cared. That must be what Third McPherson was talking about when she said that they would be taking care of their own problems.

Vark brought her thoughts back to the situation at hand. Her small three-man team had to hold the side hatch position. They were to block any of the guards from leaving the side hatch and block any reinforcements coming to strengthen the guard. She wasn't sure how many reinforcements Gaineretti could hold off behind her, but she was more than ready to take on Bailey and Mill-Hooman, with or without Forrester to back her up.

Vark felt, more than heard her comm unit bip "dot-dash space dot-dash-dot". That would be Amossitta Riffler's "AR" signal that she was in place. Riffler had wormed her way through an airflow conduit. She should be able to view inside the training room. She was the only one of their group with AMSF environmental experience. Plus she was the smallest, so she was the logical one to work through the maze of conduits.

Riffler would not be able to enter through the hard-sealed air duct grates, but the Third needed to know what was going on inside the training bay before making an assault to free her people. Riffler wasn't happy with the task and had expressed her desires to be at the sharp edge of the knife. As it was, once she made her forward observations she would have to crawl backwards to get out of the ductwork and miss all of the head busting activities.

Riffler commed, "dot-dot-dot-dot (H for hostiles) dot-dot-dot-dot-dash (4) dot-dash (A) dot-dash-dot (R) dash-dash (M) dot-dot-dot (S) ARMS.

Aardmricksdottir cursed herself for forgetting to use the 'H for hostile' code when she had commed. However, the news that the guards inside the training bay had weapons was not surprising. How else could anyone suppress even a small group of APES!

Takki-Homi signaled, "Dash (T for Takki-Homi) dot-dot-dot-dot (H for hostiles) dot-dot-dot-dash-dash (3)."

"Dammit," Aardmricksdottir thought. "I'd hate to have to use this stupid code for full sentences." Still, to someone outside their group, it might sound like static, unless they were listening specifically for the code. McPherson's rescue unit would need the element of surprise.

"Dash-dash (M for McPherson) dash-dash-dot (G for go)."

Vark let out a whoof of air and stood up. She saw Gaineretti scuttle backwards towards her position as he watched their six. Forrester stood up beside her. She nodded to him, grabbed his arm and thrust him around the corner.

Chapter Forty-Six

Misha did not wait to see if Takki-Homi was behind her. She just barreled around the corner, her legs churning as she rushed full tilt toward the main hatchway of the training bay. Misha wanted to roar a battle cry. It was the primal human urge to bellow her defiance in the face of the enemy or to shriek a victory cry as she pounced onto her prey. But, she held her tongue. Her jump-sneaks whisked quietly as she blasted full speed down the corridor.

"Three and a half seconds to go twenty-five feet," she thought. She knew she didn't have much time. A lot could happen in three and a half seconds, but she had to get to the guards outside the hatchway before they could cry out or signal for help.

The three guards were clustered near the closed hatchway. Two of them had their backs to her. The man facing her saw her racing toward them. He threw up his arms and pointed his palms at her in a signal to stop. His name came to Misha unbidden. She preferred her enemy to be nameless and unknown, but her time studying the unit roster was rushing back to her. It was YellowHorse from Hotel Squad. The two other guards began to turn toward her. She recognized Amma Ammok and Sven Tingler, both from Hotel Squad.

Misha left her feet in a driving leap directly at YellowHorse. Her broad shoulders stuck glancing blows as she slammed between Ammok and Tingler. Ammok spun wildly away, struggling vainly to keep her balance. Tingler was heaved aside into the bulkhead.

Misha arrowed into YellowHorse, using her head as the point of a spear, ramming into his chest. YellowHorse had turned slightly and braced himself almost by instinct just before she hit him. She felt the jar as her head made contact. The man was as tough as they come. He stiffened enough to stay on his feet. Still, she heard bones crunch. She grabbed the front of YellowHorse's uniform keeping the man close. Her feet dropped to the deck. Bracing her flexed knees she straightened quickly, mashing the back of her head into YellowHorse's face. She felt blood splatter across the back of her neck. She threw the man's body on top of Ammok just as the woman's body crashed to the deck.

Spinning on her left leg, Misha turned to Tingler. The man was just rebounding off the bulkhead. She drove her right leg shin high into his crotch. Tingler dropped to his knees, but he struggled to get up. Misha grabbed a handful of hair and clanged the back of the man's head against the metal bulkhead of the corridor. He dropped unconscious to the deck.

Misha turned to find Takki-Homi towering over Ammok. The woman was pinned beneath YellowHorse's unmoving body. Takki-Homi was standing on her right hand. He held up one finger of warning. Ammok froze with a grimace of pain.

Takki-Homi bent down and ripped the woman's comm unit off her uniform's velcro tabs. He flipped it over and manually turned it off, disconnecting it from her glass-pack. He repeated the process with YellowHorse. Misha turned and pulled Tingler's comm unit free and shut it down.

Misha tapped on her own comm unit. "Dash-dash" (M for McPherson) "dot-dot-dot" (S) "dot-dot-dash" (U) "dash-dot-dash-dot" (C) "dash-dot-dot-dash" (X). Success!

She heard a respondent "dot-dot-dot-dash" (V). She knew that Vark didn't have to send any more message than that. If Vark hadn't been successful in her own mission, she would not have been able to send any message at all.

Misha sent "Dash-dash-dot" (G for go.) Without waiting for any answer, she spun the locks on the main hatch cover and pushed it open. As soon as she stepped into the training bay, she could see her loyal APES scattered about the deck in small clusters. All of them faced one or the other of the hatches with alert eyes. Three guards stood with their backs to Misha and one other guard stood by the side hatch. All four guards had needlers in their hands. The noise coming from her loyal

APES was loud enough to drown out the noise of the hatch opening behind the guards.

The nearest guard was Second Stanley Kranitchovich. Misha grabbed his shoulder and spun him around to face her. She latched onto his flailing gun hand, wrapping a hand around his wrist. With a quick turn, she locked his arm at the elbow. She grunted slightly and pulled. She felt his forearm give with a sickening snap. She twisted the needler from his hand as he fell screaming to the deck.

The guard on her right turned to face her. It was Trooper One Suzuki. Misha kicked with the sole of her foot planted deeply into the Suzuki's chest. The woman was thrown backwards into a clot of APES who quickly subdued and disarmed the woman.

Misha saw Takki-Homi drag Ammok with him from the corridor. He stood facing a Hotel Squad trooper using the Ammok as a shield. The Hotel trooper shifted his needler from his prisoners to Takki-Homi and back again. Misha twisted around Takki-Homi and put two needler shots in the trooper's chest. The man dropped to the deck with a surprised look on his face.

The last guard was facing the side hatchway. A rush of APES was starting to close in on him, regardless of the needler in his hand. Misha couldn't tell if he was trying to escape from the rush of APES or if he was trying to keep the hatch closed on Vark's team.

Misha shouted, "Down." APES dove for the deck all across the training bay. The guard didn't turn. He continued to claw at the hatch controls, his needler still in his hand. She put three shots in the center of the man's back. She turned to Takki-Homi before the guard dropped to the deck. "Taks, take this needler. Collect the other three. I want four good shooters outside the hatches. Not inside, like these idiots, but outside where they can do some good. Get someone to drag YellowHorse and Tingler in here. Who's that down by the side hatch?"

Takki-Homi said without looking at the fallen man, "Trooper Theress, sir."

She nodded without taking her eyes off Takki-Homi and said, "Get that side hatch open. I want Vark's team in here. Get Theress over there with the others from Hotel, plus the two hostiles from the hallway. Do it now, Second."

Out of the corner of her eye Misha saw a couple of troopers leap to open the side hatch without waiting for further orders. She saw Takki-Homi point at two of his Charlie Squad troopers. He didn't say anything to them, as it was obvious to anyone within the range of Misha's voice what she needed and wanted to be done. Takki-Homi hooked a thumb over his shoulder in the direction of the corridor.

As the troopers trotted past, Takki-Homi tossed two needlers at them. He pointed at Trooper Ortiz. She was holding the needler she had wrestled out of Suzuki's grasp. He waggled his finger at the side hatchway. Ortiz took off like a hungry panther after a wounded gazelle.

Takki-Homi then pointed at Trooper Beaudry from Vark's Joker Squad and gestured towards Ortiz's back. Beaudry looked surprised, but he sprinted after Ortiz without a word. He scooped up the fourth needler from the deck next to Theress just as a cluster of APES undogged the side hatch.

Hotel Squad's Bailey and Mill-Hooman fairly flew through the now open side hatch and sprawled out on the deck. They appeared completely unharmed except Mill-Hooman was sporting a bloody nose. Two pair of APES quickly sat on them. Vark and Forrester stepped into the training bay at a much more sedate pace.

Misha glanced at the APES beginning to crowd around her. There weren't very many of them. She hoped it was enough to take back a whole spacecraft from mutineers.

She nodded at DeLaPax. "Peace, drag this scum over into a corner. Put all of Hotel where we can watch them. Keep an eye on Marshal Forrester, please. Furthermore, we need to de-comm the lot of them." She held up and waggled the comm unit she took from Tingler. "But, I want all of their glass-packs set on full record mode, got me? For that matter, I want everyone to stay off voice comms without direct orders from me."

Kranitchovich holding his shattered shoulder started to speak.

Misha waved a hand in his direction, "Shut up, Second. I suggest you save it for your lawyer."

DeLaPax had gathered up all five of the Able Squad rookies, plus Forrester and started moving Hotel Squad into a far corner. She grabbed Suzuki by the hair and dragged the woman to her feet.

Misha called after DeLaPax, "Peace, I don't want them talking, not even among themselves. And we treat them with extreme civility. That goes for everyone in here. Hold them, but no further injuries if we can avoid it. Got it, Peace?"

DeLaPax nodded. "Yes, sir, it won't be easy, but we can do that, right kids?"

Ottiamig smiled at Misha and then back at DeLaPax, "Yes, Mother, I think we can behave ourselves." He looked pointedly at the knot of Hotel Squad troopers. "That is, if they can behave themselves."

Misha looked at her Able Squad APES now guarding their ex-captors. "Trooper Cutler, you're a med-tech. Grab what help you need and do what you can for the injured."

She turned around to find Aardmricksdottir and Takki-Homi standing quietly next to her. "Seconds, that was good work, you two. Who are your medical technicians? Cutler is going to need some help with some of Hotel's people."

Takki-Homi said, "That would be Riffler in Charlie. Sorry sir, but we haven't heard from her since she called in her forward observations."

Misha frowned. "Find out about her. Keep comms to a minimum. Stay with the code if you can, but go to voice if you have to and get Gaineretti in here. We shouldn't need him watching our six with Ortiz and Beaudry armed and watching the secondary hatch. She watched his receding back, then turned to her other Second, "Vark, who is your med-tech?"

"That is Greggoria Putinova, but it seems she is no longer under my command. I don't know where she is. Sorry."

"Don't apologize for that, Second. It looks like you held more of your squad together than I did. Find someone out of this bunch to give Cutler a hand with the injured. No mistakes on this Vark. I want those people held without any mistreatment that could backfire on us at their courts-martial." Or mine for that matter, she thought to herself.

Two troopers raised their hands. Without specific orders, they jogged over to give first aid to Hotel Squad's wounds. Misha spotted a young woman in the shrinking cluster of APES without assigned tasks. The woman was sporting a rapidly discoloring eye and bleeding from a cut across one cheek.

Misha turned to Aardmricksdottir. "Okay, Deuce. Let's get a handle on these people. All of Charlie Squad: go hunt down Deuce Taks. Trooper Trammler, tell him that I want to strengthen our perimeter defenses. I've got Charlie Squad doing guard duty and medical, plus it looks like two of your squad went to help Cutler with medical, right?"

"Yes, sir, that is Troopers Lamsa and Everridge. That leaves me with three others: Garcia, Brown and Hassletanker."

Misha nodded at the three. "Good. That's very good. Deuce Vark, I want you to get your squad to work on getting us weapons of some kind. Lean towards finding non-lethal if you can manage it. We seem to have seven other troopers from various squads. I'll split them with you. This'll give us just about three full squads to work with. Set your group off over in the far corner, get them started and then high-tail it back to me. Go!" She pointed to a far corner and waved Vark off in that direction. Obviously glad for having a specific task to accomplish, the tall blonde woman trotted across the training bay deck, followed by her Joker Squad troopers.

Misha looked at the remaining troopers. She crooked a finger at the young woman with the bruised and bleeding face. The woman trotted over to her.

Misha asked so no one but the woman could hear, "You're Kelly from Hotel Squad, right?"

"Yes, sir, I'm Trooper Eleven Ethica Kelly."

"You're not in agreement with your squad on how to deal with this AMSF mess?"

Kelly snorted, then looked embarrassed, covering her nose with her hand. "Sorry, Third, that slipped out. No, I admit I don't understand everything that's going on, but I do know our contract with the spacers says we must stand by Britaine."

"You read our contract? Isn't that unusual for a rookie?"

Kelly smiled, "I wouldn't know about unusual, but you did make a point of mentioning the contract in our unit Q&A meeting. I thought I'd better become more familiar with it."

Misha smiled back at the young woman. "It is unusual for rookies to read the contract, although they all agree to be bound by it. It would seem it was rare in Hotel Squad for veterans and even second-level commanders to read the contract. How'd you get the strawberry under your eye and that cut?"

Kelly scowled and looked in the direction of the knot of Hotel troopers. "I would rather not say, Third."

Misha said, "Let's make it an order then. My glass-pack is on full record for an official statement. You have sustained damage, although not life threatening, it will require some medical attention. How did you obtain your injuries?"

Kelly said, "I will respond under protest, noting I have a right to non-self-incrimination."

"Barracks lawyer, huh?" Misha frowned, and raised her voice "I don't have time for this, but we can play it that way, if I have to. Objection understood and noted in my log. You will not be held accountable for anything you say. However, please note any glass-pack recordings of any other personnel present will be scanned for relevant data concerning the incident in question. And believe me, Trooper Kelly, someone's glass-pack picked up what happened. They always do. Speak up."

"Second Kranitchovich took umbrage at my refusal to obey an order, sir," Kelly said.

Misha stared at the young girl. "Umbrage?"

Kelly answered. "Umbrage: to take offense-"

Misha threw up her hands. "Stop. I know what it means. You really are a lawyer, aren't you?"

"I never practiced, sir. I just passed the exams, but my father is."

"Ah," Misha placed the name. "That would be Fifth-Level Ansel Kelly, APES Attorney General?"

Kelly nodded. "I didn't tell anyone because I wanted to make it on my own, you know?"

Misha nodded in agreement. "Secrets like that don't last long in the APES. Besides, there are a lot of APES with family in the service. We all make it on our own. Now to business: this order from your second; was it a lawful order?"

Kelly shrugged her shoulders, "I don't know, Third. I really don't. I still can't put it all together. I don't know enough about what's going on. It just didn't seem right to restrain APES without your say-so. You are the commander of the unit and all. As to getting smacked across the face: well, Second Kranitchovich said if Second Jackson could slap his people into line, then he could too."

Misha nodded. That was another mistake on her part, but it was one that Kelly had paid the price for. It hadn't really mattered whether Kranitchovich had hit her or not, or whether he had just ordered it done, or even whether it was with his consent. He was wrong. She was just as wrong for not punishing Jackson when he had hit Trooper Donnellson.

"Okay, Kelly. We'll take this up later. I recommend you discuss this with legal counsel at the first opportunity," Misha said. Then, she raised her voice for everyone in the room. "Get Trooper Cutler to put something on that cut as soon as he takes care of the more serious injuries. In the meantime, I want you to latch on to DeLaPax. Where she goes, you go. Understand? Hear me over there, Peace?"

DeLaPax waved back to her, "Got her, Boss. One more lost lamb for my flock. Come on, girlfriend. You can tell your Auntie Peace all about that famous father of yours. I hear he's single again."

Kelly glanced back at Misha with a bewildered and somewhat concerned look on her face as DeLaPax waved her off to the side.

Misha walked to the small knot of remaining APES and called to Second Aardmricksdottir to join them. She looked at them one by one waiting for the second to reach the group. Each man or woman starred back at her, some with calm eyes, some with resolution and some with anger, but no one blinked or turned away from her stare. She nodded her approval more to herself than to anyone else.

"All right, APES. I assume for each of your own reasons you aren't with your assigned squads."

One of the troopers interrupted, "Sir, I'm Trooper-"

Misha stopped the woman with a wave of her hand. "Yes, I know; Golf Squad's Trooper One Na'aranna. You're also the 1392nd senior weapons technician. I have a short memory, Na'aranna, but not that short. Didn't like your second's assessment of today's activities?" Misha remembered Golf's second had locked themselves down in their squad bay.

"No, sir, not one damn bit. Momma always told me that inaction was always the wrong thing."

Misha smiled, "My father always said the same thing. However, I think to accept that old cliché as an absolute would show a limited imagination. There are times when doing nothing is the right thing to do. But, I would agree with you this is not one of those times. In any event, it seems as if my squad's weapons tech has gone missing. I don't know why nor do I care at this point. I want to attach you to Able Squad for the time being. Do you have any problems with that, Trooper Na'aranna?"

"Hell no! Why should I?" the woman looked puzzled.

"Good enough by me. Any of you other troopers got a problem working with me? No? Good." Misha turned to Vark. "I hate to pull the veterans out of this group and leave you with the rookies, but I've already got far too many newbies on my hand in Able Squad as it stands. Do you have any problem with that, Deuce?"

Aardmricksdottir smiled. "As Na'aranna so aptly put it,'hell no! Why should I'? Besides Third, by my count you've got six rookies. I get three from this bunch with my own three and we run six each. On top of which, you are giving me Aarvan as a rookie, right?"

Misha looked puzzled. She didn't recognize the name and certainly wasn't placing it with any of the faces before her. "Aarvan?"

A tall, gangly young man raised a taut fist. "Sir, that would be me. Aarvan Kelly, formerly Trooper Seven of Bravo Squad. I am, sir, a rookie."

Aardmricksdottir laughed. "Like fun you are. Boss, he's the first cousin of that young lady developing the black eye you were speaking to. There are more Kellys in the APES than there is Otti-"

Misha finished the sentence for her. "Ottiamigs, and we all know there are a ton and a half of Ottiamigs in the APES." Misha eyed the young man. She could see the resemblance to Ethica Kelly she had sent off with DeLaPax.

Aardmricksdottir said, "Well, there's at least a ton of them around. Aarvan probably cut his teeth on APES training. Besides, he had the smarts to duck out on Theda Moraft. I'll take his smarts over longevity any day."

Misha smile, "Good. You take all three of your rookies. Give me about ten minutes and then report back on weapons availability. Take Na'aranna with you for your brainstorming session."

Misha turned to the last two unassigned troopers. She remembered Trooper One Aggie Raza, a tough, long-standing veteran. The only impairment to Raza's advancement was her lack of discrimination in choosing sexual partners. The other man was no more than a last name, a position and a face from the unit roster, Trooper Two Lamont. Both were from India Squad, whose second had taken his team to ground.

"Raza and Lamont." She looked at the two. Neither smiled nor batted an eye. "Good enough. We got work to do. Are you ready?"

Lamont jerked his head once in a quick nod but said nothing.

Raza winked back slyly, "I am always ready, Trey. It's game on!

Chapter Forty-Seven

"What do you mean she's gone?" Jackson bellowed at his med-tech Dashell. "I give you one small task to do: keep McPherson under wraps and healthy in the day office until we can get her moved into the training bay with the rest of those freakin' cowards. Ol' son, you're as worthless as feathers on a snake. So, don't just stand there, tell me what the hell happened?"

Dashell looked around for support, but everyone in the Foxtrot Squad bay averted their eyes. "Well, we had her trussed up real good, like you said, and we dumped her in the office, just like you said. We put a couple of guys, Spaz and the Dog Boy, in the hallway to watch the hatch. Next thing I know, I go to look and the bitch is gone."

"Man-oh-man," Jackson shook his head. "You left Spaznitski and Becker to watch over her? You left Spaz and the Dog Boy alone? Those two booger brains couldn't watch a mirror without getting confused. So where are those two dip wads now?"

Dashell shrugged. "Last I saw they were still unconscious in the day office. No real damage, so I just left them there. I suppose they're still there."

Jackson grabbed Dashell by the front of his coveralls and shouted into his face. "Think, will you! We need to know how she got out. Did she have help? If she had help, how many were there? Which way did she go? Did she take Forrester with her?"

Dashell whined, "I don't know, Second. I wasn't there." He tried unsuccessfully to pry Jackson's grip loose from his clothing.

Jackson shook his head and for good measure shook Dashell like a rag doll. "I know you weren't there. You'd be unconscious with Spaz and the Dog Boy if you were you there. Go wake them up and find out what they know."

Second Bilideau spoke up, "Okay. So, she is gone. Relax, she's Theda's problem. Oooooh, I like that

281

thought: cat fight! Anyway, McPherson is just one woman, Race. What can she do?"

"Yeah, Beans, but she is one tough woman," Jackson replied.

Beans Bilideau shook his head. "How do you know? All you've seen is training and all you've heard is rumor and propaganda. For all we know she can't stomach a real fight. We've both seen it before. Look it, she's runnin' from this fight, right? I'll bet she's off hidin' somewheres right now, shittin' in her diapers."

Jackson frowned, "But what about Guinjundst?"

Bilideau put his hand on Jackson's shoulder, "Think, man. She must'a run then too. You had family there, right? Well, would they a gone runnin'?"

Jackson shook Bilidieau's hand free, "Hell no!"

"Hell no is right. They stood and fought. Died like APES. So, how did McPherson live? I'll bet my last paycheck she ran then too, just like now. Your family died as heroes, not this tin goddess."

"Yeah. Hell, yeah!" Jackson slammed his fist into his other hand. "Gotta be. You're right, Beans. She is running now and she must have run then. But, you're wrong about one thing."

Bilideau arched an eyebrow.

Jackson nodded. "She is not Second Moraft's problem. She's ours. Theda told us to take her and hold her. We didn't." He turned to the men and women scattered around his squad bay. "All right, get off your butts and make yourself useful. Scatter around through APES country and look for McPherson and Forrester. Everyone partners up; go two by two and stay in comms with Second Bilideau. Don't underestimate McPherson. She's a coward, but then even a rabbit will attack when cornered, so don't get cocky." Jackson tapped his comms unit open. "Second Kranitchovich, this is Second Jackson. We need to talk."

When there was no answer, Bilideau arched his eyebrow again questioningly.

Jackson spoke again, "Stanley. This is Race. Quit dickin' around and answer me." There was still no answer. He looked at Bilideau, "Dammit, Beans. Get over to the training bay and see what's going on. Take as many of these yahoos as you can snag. With McPherson on the loose, we can't take any chances. She might be in hiding, but she might try to pick us off one at a time." He switched his comms to an open frequency broadcasting to every APE unit. "This is Second-Level Commander Race Jackson. I'm calling McPherson."

Silence came out of the comm unit.

Jackson continued. "Give yourself up to us. It'll be easier in the long run. There're a bunch of angry APES looking for you. They don't like running from a fight and they're all a little bit more than frustrated. We don't want you or anyone else getting hurt."

There was a long still silence from the comm unit.

"Look, McPherson. I can only protect you if you surrender to me."

The comms silence grew ever longer.

Finally, a female voice answered back. It was Theda Moraft. "That's enough, Race. Let her stew in her own juices. We got more important things to do than run to ground one little coward."

Chapter Forty-Eight

Misha looked at the two second-level commanders standing next to her. Their comm units received Jackson's broadcast. She shrugged as if to say she didn't really know how to respond to Jackson's veiled threats.

Takki-Homi grinned and said, "Whooo boy! That Race Jackson sure can be a hoot sometimes, can't he?"

Misha replied, "Taks, sometimes I wonder about your sense of humor."

"Who me, Trey? Well, I know that crying won't help, so we might as well just laugh about it."

Vark grinned soberly, "At home they always told me if you can't dance with the devil, you shouldn't laugh at his jokes."

Misha said, "I believe we can dance with this devil. You both heard him send Bilideau and some of Dawg Squad to check on Kranitchovich and the rest of Hotel Squad. They should be here soon. Are we ready for them?"

Takki-Homi nodded. "Ambush laid in. Beans won't take the long way around so I've pulled Chewie and Peanut off the main hatchway."

Misha looked baffled, "Chewie and Peanut?"

"Sorry, sir, that is Platzchewski and Trammler of Charlie Squad. We put all of Joker Squad with Vark's new weapons just inside the hatch."

"What weapons did we manage to scrounge up?"

Vark answered, "All we had in the training bay were batons, pikes and cudgels. We stripped the rubber tips off. They are still non-lethal, well...mostly anyway. But, they'll drop Dawg Squad in their tracks when they come through the hatch. I gave about half of what we worked up to Peace for guard duty on Hotel Squad."

Takki-Homi continued. "Ortiz and Beaudry are standing close watch on the side hatch. If Bilideau comes around that way, we're sunk, and they'll have to open fire with their needlers. We'll inflict major damage, but it can't be helped."

284

"I agree," Misha said. "Did you get Peanut and Chewie holed up somewhere?"

"Broom closet, I think that's what it is, anyway. I set those two in place to act as pushers if any of Dawg Squad goes doggie and falls behind."

Misha looked at Takki-Homi, "Doggie?"

"Cowboy talk for a straggler. Guess I can't help it; the old home-town lingo comes back when I get excited."

Misha nodded. "Time enough for that story later. We should be ready anytime now. Vark, keep your squad on their toes. Let's take them down fast, but let's try not to kill anybody, okay. But, I need your intelligence and communications specialist with me. Who've you got?"

Aardmricksdottir said, "Great duo: Tree and the Greek."

Misha shook her head. "I'm going to slap you two. Remind me to have nicknames entered into the unit database."

"That would be Everridge and Lamsa, sir. You already have them. They're the two working with your med-tech Cutler on Hotel's damage."

"Good. Send them to me and get ready for Dawg."

Aardmricksdottir turned in agreement and sprinted to the hatchway. On the way, she let out a low whistle. All of Joker Squad's heads popped up and swiveled in her direction. She held up five fingers, then flashed six fingers, pumped her clenched fist once and pointed at Misha. She reached her squad and began spreading them out without bothering to watch the reaction of her troopers five and six. Everridge and Lamsa sprinted to Misha.

Misha asked the two, "How is Hotel's medical situation?"

The shorter of the two spoke up. "I'm Trooper Lamsa, sir. You'd have to confirm with Trooper Cutler, but it looks pretty good for what supplies we've got. For a rookie, Bear is a nice hand with injuries."

"I'm Trooper Everridge, sir. Everyone looks stable, even Theress, if we can get him to sickbay within a few hours. Those needlers cut badly, but they don't cut deep. You put a needler smack into the middle of their hatch watch's chest, but it hit his breastbone and shattered. It made a mess out of muscle, but didn't hit anything major."

Lamsa nodded in agreement.

Everridge continued, "The worst looks to be Kranitchovich. His arm is shattered in about a dozen places. The elbow looks twisted. It'll need major surgery, but he'll live. And frankly, serves him right."

Misha interrupted, "Okay. I want you two to stay near me. Which of you is the communications tech?"

Lamsa held up his hand.

Misha said. "You would be the Greek?"

The man blushed deeply, "Yeah, but sir, it isn't like it sounds. It's not about a sexual thing-"

Misha interrupted. "I don't think it matters at this point. Greek, what I need is for you to make sure no one sends any signal out on our comms. Put a block on them." She reached over and slipped his glass-pack out of his pocket. A few quick taps on the pack and she handed it back. "I just gave you my command override. I want our signals squeaky clean on the outbound. Furthermore, I want a constant inbound ear out for any comms traffic from anyone else. That includes AMSF and APES."

Misha turned to the other man, "Okay, you would be Tree, then. Good. What I need is for you to analyze the traffic Lamsa intercepts and give me situation reports. I need clear and clean sitreps to give me a view of what is going on and where it is happening. I need it fast and I don't have time to handle it myself. Got it?"

Both men responded with, "Roger that, sir."

Misha turned to Takki-Homi. "Deuce Taks, what's the word on Trooper Riffler?"

"Good news, Trey. She just got stuck backing out of one of the enviro-vents. She maintained voice radio silence, but she was tapping code like crazy. Gaineretti

286

said she was really pissed by the time he picked up her signal. I sent him with two others to pull her out."

"One last thing, Deuce: where is Bilideau? He should have been here by now."

Chapter Forty-Nine

Wilderman watched Bilideau's back as they trudged down the hallway. He was sure Beans dragged him along on this wild goose chase as punishment. He thought, "All I was trying to do was squeeze out the back hatch to meet up with Singletary. Clearly, this is an opportunity for profit. Mutiny is a thing for command level APES and AMSF officers to worry about, not me. Money is my line. I'd rather be checking in with Gates and company; not being here with this group of chumps checking another group of chumps."

Wilderman slowed his steps again, trying to put distance between Bilideau and himself. He thought if he could get far enough behind, then he could duck out and still meet up with Singletary. However, every time he slowed down, so did Bilideau. They were almost at a crawl and they were almost to the hatchway.

The group rounded the last corner. Wilderman was surprised to see Deuce Kranitchovich hadn't put anyone on guard duty outside the training bay hatchway. The hatch was open to the inside. Kranitchovich was lazy, but he wasn't stupid.

Wilderman watched the first two of their six-man party disappear through the hatchway. He saw the next two hesitate, but arms reached through the open hatch and yanked them into the training room. Bilideau turned to shout. A very compact female body crashed into Bilideau and with a wild fury drove him to the steel deck, driving a knee into his solar Plexus.

Wilderman heard a whoosh of air escape from Bilideau and turned to run. Instead of moving, he froze. The barrel end of a needler snuggled onto the tip of his nose. His eyes crossed momentarily as he stared at the weapon. He refocused onto the face of Chewie from Charlie Squad.

Chewie smiled sweetly. "In the training bay, if you please."

Wilderman began backing toward the open hatchway while the needler stayed connected to his nose.

He wanted to back away quickly, but was afraid to make any sudden moves. He knew Chewie well enough to know the man was crazy. Out the corner of his eye Wilderman saw a melee of wildly swinging arms, claws and teeth, it was as if the woman on top of Bilideau was trying to shred him. Wilderman paused, not knowing which way to turn.

Chewie said, "Hey Peanut, go ahead and kill the S.O.B., I don't care, but you have to explain it to Taks; not me. As for you, Wildchild; just back around this mess on the deck. We are having a little party in the training bay. The pleasure of your company is required."

Wilderman felt the needler push against his face, causing him to move backward toward the hatch. He slowly moved around the two tangled bodies on the deck, until Chewie's body blocked them from view. He felt more than saw, two bodies rush around him. He hoped they pulled Peanut off Beans before she killed him. The man was a cretin, but he didn't deserve to be minced like last night's roast beef. His heels stubbed the base of the hatch and he crashed backward through the hatchway into the training bay.

Chapter Fifty

Misha looked at the small group around her, wondering for the umpteenth time if she was doing the right thing by dividing her forces. She knew it was a classic mistake, but she couldn't see any other way. There were too many things to do that all needed doing at the same time.

She debated with herself on how to divide those forces. It was a no-brainer to leave Charlie Squad intact. They were already a well-formed unit with strong leadership. She gave Takki-Homi two of their four needlers as they had the farthest to travel across the spacecraft. Charlie Squad was the least of her worries although their mission was critical by contractual standards. She doubted Second Takki-Homi would fail.

She wanted to leave all the rookies behind to guard Hotel and the pieces of Dawg Squad that they had captured. Misha's part of the plan was a dangerous task even for veterans. But, there were not enough veterans to go around.

She had needed Second Aardmricksdottir for a special task that would take her and three others from Joker Squad out of the training bay. Vark took Joker Trooper Six Garcia, and Jokers' two newest rookies, Trooper Ten Brown, Trooper Eleven Hassletanker and Kilo's Trooper Eleven Smith. Although, Vark's task was better undertaken stealthily, Misha had still insisted they take one of the remaining needlers.

Strangely enough it was Trooper Beaudry who had given Misha a solution to the prisoner problem. He suggested they put the twelve healthy prisoners in the tri-wave sim couches and send them on a long vacation to a quiet beach somewhere. They wouldn't pose any problem to whoever was guarding them. He also, with a malicious smile, suggested they program the tri-wave to instruct their captives in the APES manual, various contracts, and legalisms involved in inter-service relations and mutinies. He suggested he would be able to keep watch over the four remaining injured prisoners if she left him with one other person. She could see his mind working as he also suggested that to keep everyone safe, they should lock the training bay hatches from the inside and the outside. Over his protest, she had given him her last needler and left him with Trooper Aarvan Kelly. She would rather have Kelly with her, but the other two unassigned rookies were Oberman and Ramirez. Both had formerly been in Dawg Squad. She was pretty sure of their loyalties, but didn't want to test them too hard by having them guard former squad mates.

In the end, she had no choice but to keep Able Squad together as a unit with the four replacements she had culled from the earlier group: Ethica Kelly, Na'aranna, Raza and Lamont. Plus she commandeered Greek and Tree to continue monitoring and reporting on communications traffic. Finally, she had the two ex-Dawg rookies. It was a large force for intra-craft action, but it wasn't a team by any stretch of the imagination.

"Okay, you APES. We're going to take back engineering. Frankly, if we don't, then we don't go home."

Chapter Fifty-One

Misha crouched in a closed hatchway. She was passing through Kiirkegaard's officer country. They found many of the hatches closed and locked from the inside. She could hear movement on the other side of this hatch, but she doubted that whoever was inside would come out. Many of the crew, including a large number of officers locked themselves in quarters to avoid either a charge of cowardice or a charge of mutiny. She felt sorry for their predicament, but a review board would most likely find that by disobeying Britaine's calls for help, they were guilty of failing to obey an order, if not worse. Still, she kept one eye on the hatch and one eye on Aggie Raza and Ethica Kelly. The two women were on point. They had reached a major intersection in the spacecraft's maze of corridors and hallways. Both point men were flat on their stomachs peeking around the corners, keeping their heads as low to the ground as possible, each looking in a different direction.

It was a dangerous way to look around a corner. Misha would have been happier to jump around the corner blasting away with needlers. Or, if they had been suited, they could have slid an opti-cam cable around the corner and broadcast the view of the hallway to everyone's HUD display.

They had only managed to commandeer two additional needlers from stray AMSF Security. The team of Ottiamig and Lamont, the veteran from India Squad and her Able Squad rookie found an unlocked hatch. They quietly slipped the hatch open. Ottiamig was just about to step through the hatchway when Lamont grabbed him by the collar and yanked him backwards just in time to avoid a hail of needles.

Misha grimaced when she realized she had been almost directly across the corridor from the open hatchway. The needles spanged off the bulkheads and peppered her face and arms. The ricochets did little damage as the needles shattered and spent their energy before flying back at her.

Everyone froze where they were. Misha needed those weapons, but it would be a difficult task to flush out armed and trained men when her team wasn't carrying anything deadlier than a large stick. Misha moved to stand across the hatch from Lamont. Ottiamig looked ashen at his near miss, but he stood gamely behind Lamont, ready to rush the room if Misha called for it. Trying to talk the men out would have been the best course of action, but she ruled it out right away. First, she didn't know anything about who was in the room, how many there were or on which side of this mutiny they found themselves. Second, she sucked at diplomacy and negotiation.

Misha ducked down toward the deck and stuck her head into the room. She quickly whipped it back. There were two men in the room. Both men aimed their needlers at the hatchway. Both fired at her, but both shots were high. Neither man fired wildly. Each shot was a short controlled burst, neither wasting ammunition nor energy. Stealth wouldn't work. Misha didn't see any other way into the room. A direct frontal assault would be disastrous. She was sure she could reach them before they could cut her down. The APES who followed would surely be able to wrestle the weapons away from the two men, but Misha would be seriously injured or dead.

She looked at Lamont. He only shrugged as if to say he didn't have a clue how to proceed. She glanced at Ottiamig and saw him nod back to her, signaling he was ready to rush the two men. Lamont reached back and patted him on the shoulders. Without a smile, he said, "Down, pup. We can die later."

Na'aranna sidled up to Misha, peaked around her shoulders, and then ducked back before the men could fire. She whispered to Misha, "What we need is a concussion grenade."

Misha nodded back and then called loudly enough for the men inside to hear, "Na'aranna, bring me that canister of grenades. I'd like to take these men alive, but I don't have time for delicate negotiations."

Na'aranna frowned as if she did not approve of bluffing, but said loudly, "I've got a couple of CT-906 shrapnel grenades that'll shred everything in that room to little more than dripping slime on the chandelier and greasy spots on the carpets."

Misha said loudly, "No. No. I don't think we need to do that. I'd like to be able to allow medical to identity the bodies without having to do deep DNA scans. I think if we just toss in a CY-2 cyanide grenade and pull the hatch shut, we could move on and not worry about these two bozos. Be quicker, don't you think?"

Na'aranna said coldly, "Not really quicker, plus the CY-2 takes so long for them to die; burns from the inside out. Shredding is more merciful."

Misha all but shouted, "I'm not much in the mood for mercy. I've got better things to do than mess with these two vacuum suckers. They shot at me first so let them try breathing cyanide." She took her cudgel in both hands and snapped it over her knee. She looked up to see Lamont as he raised an eyebrow at the feat. Misha flashed the hand gestures. "Follow close behind me." Lamont nodded. She called out, "Okay, team. Put your breathers on and be running, just in case we don't shut this hatch quickly enough." She stifled a smile as Lamont, with deadpan seriousness, jerked an imaginary breather out of an imaginary side pocket and settled it over his face. He wiggled his eyebrows alternately and then wiggled his ears, but he pumped his fist as the signal, he was ready to go.

Misha called out. "On the count of three, I'll toss in the CY-2. Then Lamont grabs the hatch and slams it shut. Then we can get on our way. Everybody got that?" She held up one finger to Lamont and received his nod of understanding. Misha said, "One!" She then tossed in both halves of the cudgel sending them skittering to opposite ends of the room. She uncoiled her muscles and leapt into the room expecting to have to cover the distance before the men could react. She knew the distraction of the fake grenades would only give her a heartbeat to reach them before they could fire. She was surprised to see they were rushing towards her with panic on their faces. Misha shot out her right arm and clothes-lined the first man. Using the momentum of the contact she pivoted on her right foot. Spinning, she drove the heel of her left foot into the second man's stomach. She heard a whoosh of air as the man collapsed to the deck.

Lamont reached the first man and with only a brief struggle twisted the needler out of the man's hand. The second man dropped his needler. He was on his hands and knees gasping for air. Misha picked up the man's weapon. For the first time, she saw a third person in the room. There was a young woman strapped to the bed, gagged and blindfolded. She was stripped completely nude. Misha tossed her needler to Na'aranna who was standing in the hatchway. "Block the hatch. Do not let anyone else in."

Na'aranna looked past Misha to the bed and said between clenched teeth, "Roger that." She turned her back on the room and stood cross armed. Misha could see the back of her neck was turning bright red.

She turned to Lamont, "Find something to tie these two up. Make it tight."

"I will use their intestines if I can't find anything else," Lamont replied. From his expression, Misha couldn't tell whether he was serious or not.

Misha turned to the woman on the bed. She grabbed a sheet and spread it across the woman to cover her. The woman flinched at first, but she relaxed minutely as she realized what it was. "Don't worry," Misha said. "I'm not going to hurt you. Give me just a sec." Misha got the blindfold pealed back and smiled at the woman. "There you go. Let's see if we can get that mouth muffler off." She reached across to work at the knot rather than pull the gag off. She kept talking to the woman in quiet soothing tones. "I've had one of these on recently and I know they are uncomfortable. I should have this off... there you go."

"Thank you, thank you, and thank you. I am-" The woman blurted out.

Misha interrupted. "Hold on. First, are you going to need medical attention?"

The woman snorted, "Nothing a hot shower won't cure. That and taking a ball-peen hammer to their nuts. I probably will need trauma therapy once things settle down, but I'm not... well, no medical anyway. I just got enough of a rush of adrenaline and anger to get me through until things settle down around here. Thanks."

Misha finally got the bands loosened enough on the woman's wrists, so she could sit up. She did so, letting the sheet fall to her waist. She didn't slow down enough to pull it up as she reached for her own ankles to untie her feet.

Quickly enough, the woman got to her feet. Ignoring the sheet completely she walked to the closet and pulled out an officer's utility jumpsuit. Dressing, she unceremoniously stuffed her breasts into the suit and slid the tabs closed from navel to neck. She turned to Misha and stuck out her hand.

"You're McPherson, right?"

Misha, nodding, shook her hand. "And you?"

"You were right, doesn't matter." She looked down at the two men tied up on the deck. "It's just enough to know that two cretins favorite wet dream, precisely at this very moment, turned into a cold, dark nightmare." She looked up at Misha. "You know, I almost wet the bed when I heard those grenades hit the deck. Say, so you suppose you could give me one of those needlers to take care of these two?"

Lamont said to the woman, "Ma'am. They are tied good and tight, they aren't going anywhere." He looked at Misha, "Unless you want I should drag them somewhere for you? Like the trash compactor."

Misha shook her head. "Sorry, I've got to keep the needlers and I really don't have the people to spare to give you a hand with these two."

"Not to worry. I can take care of them now. I could have handled them before, but they jumped me in my own cabin, plus they had needlers, you know?"

Misha had hated to leave the woman alone with the two men, but she really didn't have weapons, people or time to spare. She imagined that she should worry more about the two men than the woman, but it was hard to work up any sympathy for the pair.

They were getting close to her first planned destination, far past AMSF officer country and into a cluster of offices and workrooms. They were moving slower and with ever increasing caution. Misha looked up the corridor at Raza and Kelly. Neither of whom had needlers. Misha believed if the action of the man on point required stealth that he was less likely to expose himself if he was unarmed. Misha had given one needler to DeLaPax, who with Metzler, was watching their backs. She left the other needler in Na'aranna's hands. As the senior weapons tech, Misha assumed her familiarity with weapons would give the team the best chance if this outing turned into a full-blown firefight. She knew they would meet resistance before they took back engineering, but they needed more time to gather intelligence and more weapons.

She looked around at her team. Everyone carried some weapon. She made Steinman and Qualls trade the pikes they had been carrying for cudgels before they left the training bay. These hallways were too close and tightly packed to try swinging a seven-foot spear with a hook on the end.

Raza signaled from up front, "All clear."

Misha nodded and signaled for her to proceed along the right hand hallway.

Raza flashed an "OK" signal and tapped Kelly on the shoulder to get her attention. Raza pointed at Kelly's eyes and then pointed down the left hallway. The older veteran turned and slid silently along the right corridor.

Misha twirled her fingers above her head and pointed down to where Kelly still stood. With a quick twist of her wrist, she shot her hand to the right, held two fingers up and stretched both arms in the direction Raza had disappeared. Misha could see Kelly still at the intersection with her eyes glued to the left corridor. Her team slid silently forward and turned the corner to the right, dividing into two parallel columns moving along each bulkhead of the wider corridor.

Ottiamig slid in next to Misha. He signaled for permission to speak.

Misha said softly, "Question? Spit it out now while we have time."

"Sir," Ottiamig began and then hesitated.

"Go ahead, Tuamma. I won't bite your head off." She smiled and added, "This time."

"Well, I haven't ever been in this part of this spacecraft, but I served on one that was similar. There should be a shortcut through to engineering back the other way."

Misha glanced behind her, just in time to see DeLaPax and Metzler relieve Kelly of watching the left passageway. Kelly turned and sprinted by Misha and Ottiamig with just a whisper of sound from her jump sneaks. She quietly watched her until she regained her position next to Raza at the far end of the corridor. She nodded at Ottiamig. "Shortcuts are nice, but the spacer crew knows them better than we do, right?"

Ottiamig looked crestfallen. "Sorry, Third, I didn't think about that."

"Not to worry, Tuamma. That's why I get paid the big bucks. Spacer crew probably has all of the necessary corridors blocked and guarded. Engineering is the focal point of this whole mess. We're at a stalemate that can only be broken by our taking back engineering if Britaine stays hole-up in the flight office with the command and control locked out. The spacers know that. So does Theda Moraft. She is likely to put her own guard around engineering before she tries to take the flight office away from Britaine. Going the long roundabout way may have us coming at engineering from a direction they are not expecting and consequently, might have a lighter guard than any shortcut or direct route. Plus, we need to keep looking for additional weapons, tools, personnel and whatever else might help us take back engineering without getting hurt. Besides, I've got a stop to make on the way."

Lamont eased passed the two. He patted Ottiamig on the shoulder. "Come on, pup. Let's get our grunt brains back on the job at hand and leave the heavy thinking to the lady with the triangles."

Raza and Kelly signaled all clear at the next interception.

Misha pointed at the team of Na'aranna and her attendant rookie Bear Cutler. She pointed her hand at Raza and gestured to the left. She clenched her fist in a downward motion. Misha wasn't worried as much about voices here in the office section as she had been in officer country, but she knew from experience when she got excited her voice had a tendency to get louder and louder. She knew it was best for her to use hand signals.

She turned and waved to get DeLaPax's attention. She pointed at where Kelly still stood watching the right hand corridor. Misha pointed at her own eyes, at DeLaPax's eyes and back to Kelly. She then clenched her fist and held it down. She had signaled for DeLaPax to relieve Kelly of watching the right corridor.

Without waiting for DeLaPax's response Misha jogged silently to the end of the corridor to stand near Kelly. She looked back as the rest of her team worked their way down the corridor. At each hatchway, a team of two would quietly test them. They passed it by if it was locked. If the hatch was unlocked, a tense moment would pass as the duo slid the hatch open, toggled the lights on and scanned the interior.

Only twice had they encountered spacers in unlocked rooms. Once they found a knot of very scared spacers praying around some kind of altar Misha hadn't recognized. They had quietly closed the hatch and left the group alone. The second time they discovered those two spacers who had generously, but without any graciousness whatsoever, given up their needlers.

Misha didn't want to take the time to check each hatch, but she knew it must be done. These corridors were too tight for a fight without leaving a force behind her. Besides, finding the two extra needlers made the whole effort worthwhile. She would be happy if they could secure a few more serious weapons.

Able Squad slid along the corridor. She surprised herself thinking of this team as Able Squad. Only seven of the fifteen-member team were from Able. That was less than half. Still, they seemed to be integrating well. She placed them in two-person teams, trying to match veteran with rookie. But, she hadn't split up Everridge and Lamsa as her intelligence and communications team, and she had tasked them with keeping track of Forrester. She had two teams comprised of rookies only. Even though they seemed to be working well, she planned to keep a weathered eye out for them.

Everridge and Lamsa were exempt from checking hatchways as they took every opportunity to huddle together. Lamsa would jabber away quietly while Everridge would input notes furiously into his glass-pack. They often stopped to check hatch numbers or double check a room against the data on Everridge's glass-pack.

Misha was surprised that Everridge had a complete schematic of the spacecraft downloaded into his data sets. It was strictly classified material. That is, classified by the AMSF, but not by the APES, so she wasn't worried about any breach of security. She was just surprised he had it. She hadn't been able to find such a thing until he downloaded his map into her glass-pack. As they had done every so often, the duo approached her. Everridge pulled her glass-pack out of her pocket without asking and quickly tapped it against his own glass-pack, activating a link. The information download completed faster than the sound of the connection could reach her ears. Everridge handed her glass-pack back.

Misha tapped it quickly to review the download. She pointed the edge of the glass-pack at a clear bulkhead and squeezed two points together. The glass-pack broadcast the picture on the bulkhead in vivid color. She asked, "Tree?" and pointed to a few red spots on the craft's schematic overlay.

Everridge shrugged. "Sorry, Third, there is not enough data to go on. The Greek is doing miracles to pull this much raw comms off the air. This information is about as much guess as it is real intelligence."

Everridge had been using red to mark possible positions of hostile APES, yellow to mark hostile spacers, green to mark friendly spacers and blue to mark positions of loyal APES. He said, "Something is going on over in the flight squadron's enlisted quarters. The Greek caught some conversation about APES being there, but not enough for me to make more than a guess."

Misha said, "Enough of a guess that you marked it in red."

"Yes, sir, I thought at first it was someone Moraft sent to work on the crew to get things back to operational status, but it may be somebody else."

"It may be somebody else? Come on, Tree. You can do better than that."

"Yes, sir, it could be Singletary. I don't know what he is up to, but chances are it won't interfere with our operations. It will most likely have something to do with his finding a way to get off this spacecraft. That is, get off with his stash of cash, his contraband and his ass all intact."

"Good work, you two. Stay on this." Misha hesitated. "What else have you got?"

"We've got a report from Beaudry and Kelly back in the training bay. Everything is clear, cold and quiet."

Misha frowned. "How could they send a situation report without opening comms?"

"The Greek locked down all the outbound he could, but there is no way to lock everything out. Besides, the message came by way of Aarvan Kelly to his cousin Ethica. He piggybacked it on a low frequency that is normally for data transmissions only. They apparently used some kind of family code. The Greek and I both heard the transmission, but it was nonsense to us. I doubt if we could ever decode it, because there isn't enough to go on, and it used metaphors only family would understand."

"All right, see what you can pick up on this area." She pointed to an area of the map where Aardmricksdottir should be located.

Lamsa said, "Don't worry too much about Deuce Vark, Third. Tree and I have been with her for as long as she has been with the APES. She is one hot troop," Lamsa stopped and blushed.

Everridge said in mock horror, "Greek, I think that is the most sexist thing I have ever heard you say."

"Wait a minute," Lamsa stuttered. "I didn't mean she was hot that way. I mean, she is hot that way, you know, but that is not what I meant. I meant that she had good moves…" Lamsa squeezed his eyes shut and clamped his mouth closed.

Misha looked at Everridge.

He looked back and said, "You know what he means, Third. He just gets a little tongue-tied around pretty women."

Misha smiled. "I image Deuce Vark brings the worst out in him. Maybe we should put him in another squad?"

Both men looked at her in shock. Lamsa tried to speak but only a grunt came out.

Everridge said, "Hell no! I mean, excuse me, Third, but the Greek looks at Vark like she is his baby sister. She isn't his problem." Lamsa punched Everridge in the arm. But, before Everridge could continue Steinman trotted up.

"Sorry to interrupt, Third," Steinman said, "but we got a couple of unlocked hatches up here that you need to check out."

"Okay, Israel," Misha said to Steinman and clicked off the glass-pack's view. "Did you find weapons or people?"

The man beamed at her use of his first name. "We sort of found both, sir."

"Are the people hostile or friendly?"

"More neutral, I think," Steinman said. "They are more than willing to give up their weapons, but not to join us. Lamont and Ottiamig sort of helped them to give up their weapons, if you know what I mean?"

"I think I understand."

"Has anyone tried that hatch?" She asked pointing to a big solid looking hatch.

"Yes, sir. Oberman and Ramirez from Dawg tried it, but they said it is locked tight from the inside. I don't know what they would lock up that tight, but it must be important. We don't have anything with us to break through that hatch, do we?"

"Nope," Misha said. "But, I may know a way in, anyway. Israel, you take whomever you need to help you with what you found. Confiscate all weapons. Search them all. Right now, I don't trust anyone but our own people. Put all the spacers in one room until I get there. Tree, you and Greek have Na'aranna check all the weapons and distribute them. Have her reinforce both ends of this corridor. I want a free space in through here."

Misha spared one quick look at the point and the rear guards, both teams looked ready and rock hard. She turned and walked up to the vault hatch. Tapping the hatch comm, she announced herself and waited. Silently, the vault hatch handle cycled. While she waited, Misha glanced behind her. Steinman was staring at her with a questioning look.

He pointed at the hatch and asked, "How?"

Misha smiled. "Open sesame. No, it's not magic, Israel. Sometimes you just have to ask."

Misha turned back to the open hatch and stood face to face with Chief Master Sergeant Elizabeth Brown, more accurately, eyeball to muzzle with Chief Brown's .45 caliber pistol. She held her hands wide to show she was unarmed. Chief Brown stuck her head out the hatch, looking both ways, she turned back to Misha.

The Chief nodded. "It is a damn fine thing, you showing up here unannounced and all. You should'a called, at least give me time to put the coffee on and straighten up the place, I got a million and a half piles of crap scattered all over right now." She looked around Misha's broad shoulders and shouted. "Hey! You grunts be real gentle with my people, you hear? Or, I'll rip you a new one, got me?" She looked back at Misha. "Well, you just going to stand here or are you coming in? You're letting all the flies out."

Misha waved hello to Major Krandiewsky. Two other AMSF intelligence crewmen glanced at her, but both quickly returned to focusing on their displays.

Brown saw her glance at the men and said, "We are doing both inside and outside scans. Buzz has got Cuffs running copy on all internal comms he can find. I got Jimmy listening for any signals outside. We haven't heard anything of our Binder friends."

Misha looked at the two and said, "Might not have been Binder."

Krandiewsky said, "Excuse me? I thought that was what all the fuss was about earlier? You're telling me that we didn't intercept a Binder signal?"

"No," Misha said. "It was a Binder signal. Identify: Friend or Foe. IFF. I am positive of it. But, it might not have been a Binder spacecraft." Misha took a few minutes to explain that she had been with Britaine in the CNC when they jumped into the firestorm at Gagarin. She described watching the display views as human vessels began attacking other humans and broadcasting Binder coded signals.

"Damn," Misha heard from Jimmy behind her. "Then I've been workin' the wrong outside freqs. Hey, Chief. Better call Clancy in here to help me crank this P.O.S. to read for magnetic radiation signatures. If we got human bogies out there, they are dog silent. Maybe we can pick up on engine leakage."

Brown looked at Misha. "Well?"

Misha wrinkled her brow. "Well what?"

The older woman pointed around Misha to the corridor. "Most of those are my people you've taken prisoner. Can I have some of them back?"

Misha nodded, "I'll trade you. You can have your people if I can keep some of their weapons. I plan to take back engineering for Britaine and get this hunk of junk moving again. We are going to need all the firepower we can get."

Major Krandiewsky nodded and said, "Deal. Done and done."

Brown spun her pistol and offered it to Misha butt first. "You take care of my baby. I want her back when you're done. And I want her back cleaned. Don't worry about punching holes in the Kiirkegaard's hull. I got this puppy loaded with glass shot. It will knock a Bermuda Buffalo on its butt, but it shatters on a hard surface. And take these three extra clips. That should give you plenty of knockdown power. Watch out for the red tipped ammo. It is a special hydrate load: explodes four inches after contact. Plus, are these all right, Buzz?" At the Major's nod Chief Brown handed Misha two small grenades. "These are old-style thermite magnesium burners. We have them in case we get overrun and have to melt down the intel office. These things will slag this office to melted butter, but it won't react on the hull plating. It gets hot and messy really fast, so watch yourself."

Brown bellowed in a command voice. "All right, you cretins. Get your buns in here. We got a shit-pot full of things to do, and you're wasting my time."

Misha said as she gave back the handgun. "I don't want to leave you unprotected here. You had really better keep this popgun. I've never shot one of these before and I might do more damage than good. And as you might need to melt down this place anyway; I shouldn't take all of your goodies."

Brown did not smile, "Nor are you, child. I'll take my hand-warmer back. I miss her already, but the grenades come a dime a dozen, you keep them, but I suggest you don't use them if you don't have to; they are not very discriminate about what they burn. We still got a whole six-pack to toss around in here, if the time comes to that."

Misha nodded her thanks as she watched the intel crew stream past the APES and into the intelligence office. Clancy patted her on the shoulder on her way past to speak to Jimmy, who was frantically waving at her to come to him.

Forrester strolled into the room as if nothing out of the ordinary was going on. "Hey all, are you having a reunion without me?"

Brown shook her head in resignation, "I knew things were bad out there, but if you got saddled with that old geezer, then I am sorry for you, Third."

"Well, we all have our bears to cross," Misha said. "I need one more thing if you can?"

Krandiewsky said, "What would that be, Third?"

"Can you get a covert signal to Colonel Britaine in the flight office?"

"Not a problem, Third. At my desk, use the headset and punch the yellow button. It is a hardwired direct line to the FO."

Britaine answered the call almost immediately. Misha could hear a buzz of irritation in his voice.

"Dammit, Third McPherson, where the hell have you been? I've been locked down here too long. That prick Paradise has got his mutinous buddies banging on the hatch every few minutes trying to get in. I thought you went for help."

"Sorry, Colonel Britaine," she replied. "But, we ran into a bit of a problem with my people as well. It seems that neither one of us is very popular right now."

Britaine shouted, "I don't give a muskrat's pooter about popularity. I want my spacecraft back. I can keep Paradise out of navigation and craft controls, but we can't go anywhere without engineering. Get up here and help me lock down the flight office. Then you and I will go to engineering and light a fire under those lazy bastards."

"Colonel, I think you should stay put. You've got to keep Paradise out of navigation and control. I'm not entirely alone. Neither are you. You've got some good crew here backing you up."

"Who? Get them up here to help me."

"I am in the intelligence office with Major Krandiewsky and Chief Brown."

"Oh, Cripes! You have office weenies? Damn, bring them up here anyway. I need help with these systems and I need somebody on guard at the hatch. And you, McPherson, get into one of your little tin-can suits and blow your way back into engineering. Get me some propulsion."

"Colonel, I will do that if you order, but I think that might be a mistake. I've got some effective teams available and working. I don't think it would be wise to turn loose anyone in a combat suit inside this delicate spacecraft. One tiny mistake and we could rip holes in the hull big enough to drive a small moon through. To fit them through some hatchways, we would have to rip holes in the bulkheads. Those suites are just too big for most of these corridors. Plus, those suits have already been prepped for dirt drop and planetary combat. They are full of ammo, and by that I mean high explosives. I think I can re-take engineering with little or no loss of life or most importantly, no damage to the engines."

There was silence for a moment. "Yes. Above all, I don't want damage to those engines."

Through the headset, Misha heard a pounding in the background.

Britaine muttered, "What the hell are they trying to do now? It sounds like they plan on knocking the hatch down."

Misha said, "Colonel? I sent some of my people up there; APES that I trust. They should be there by now. They can guard you and give you a hand until Major Krandiewsky can get some of his people up there. Colonel, are you all right?"

"Yes, I'm fine," he snapped. "How the hell do I tell if it is your APES out there and not more of Paradise's stooges?"

Misha rolled her eyes upward, glad the signal only carried audio. "Try the hatch intercom, Colonel."

"Do you think I'm stupid, McPherson? I shut it down earlier, and um...I shut it off rather forcefully. I got tired of listening to the lies and false promises of Paradise and his followers. Now, all I get is a buzzing noise when I open the comms."

"Well, Colonel. Go to the hatch comm. Ready? Press the buzzer to get a long dash. Good now do a short dot and a long dash. Okay. Then a dash-dot-dash. Last one is a dot-dot-dot. That spells TAKS. It's a special code for Second-Level Commander Takki-Homi. He's the one I sent up to help you."

"Okay, Third. I did that. Now what?" His voice sounded as if he thought the whole episode was a foolish waste of time.

"Colonel, did you get an answer?"

"Yes, I got an answer," he replied with a sneer to his voice.

"Well?" Misha asked. She was struggling to keep the irritation out of her voice. The man had developed such a pattern of keeping information to himself it was a habit. It was obvious he still did not recognize that his inability to share relevant data had brought about the present situation.

"Well what?" Britaine asked.

"Well, what was the reply?"

"Oh," he said. "I heard a dot-dash-dot, then a dot-dash-dot, and then a dot-dash-dot."

"Are you sure the middle set wasn't dash-dash-dot?" Misha was sure that the reply had been RGR, but Britaine was reporting it as RRR. Still, it was close enough.

"Yes, I'm sure, dammit. I wrote it down so I would be sure. So, what the hell do I do?"

Misha smiled, "Colonel. I would open the hatch and say hello to Second Takki-Homi."

Chapter Fifty-Two

Misha looked around at the people gathered in the intelligence office. Officially Major Krandiewsky was in command, but he was just standing there looking back and forth between her and Chief Brown. As an APE, Misha didn't have any authority other than her force of personality over any spacer staff regardless of rank. She was sure the Major would do whatever she ordered, but she was equally sure that she could not run roughshod over Chief Brown. No enlisted person ever reached that rarefied rank without an understanding of what the organizational chart said, plus a true knowledge of who was really in charge.

Misha nodded to both, "Major, I suggest you split your forces. Chief Brown doesn't need all, or even have room for all three of your shifts to run the intel shop, so you could take a few of your people up to the flight office to give Colonel Britaine a hand. What do you think, Chief?"

Chief Brown replied, "Sounds right to me, sir. You know Colonel Britaine would be much happier with you up there than a mere enlisted person. I doubt if who you take with you much matters. Just leave me Clancy, Cuffs and Jimmy. As long as we are dead in space, there isn't that much outside intel to gather."

Forrester lowered his voice so that only Misha, Chief Brown and the Major could hear. "Just between us; I don't get this whole mutiny thing. This spacecraft is jam-packed full of highly trained, well-disciplined military people. How can they just ignore all that and commit mutiny against the rightful commander?"

Misha smiled, "Spoken like a real civilian and an investigator at that."

Forrester frowned, "What is that supposed to mean?"

"Most civilians get the wrong idea about the military. They think that we're all just killing machines who always toe the mark and blindly obey every command. And as an investigator, you're used to thinking a situation through to its logical conclusion. The military is made up of people who are neither robots nor exceptionally logical."

Brown nodded, "Amen to that! I think about thirty percent of any group, the military included, thinks with their crotch. Mostly, that would be the thirty percent that are men. Thirty percent of any group only thinks with their emotions. Again, mostly that would be the women part of the group. And thirty percent only follow the crowd, caving to peer pressure."

Misha smiled, "Sounds about right. That would leave about ten percent of any group of people thinking logically. But, even logical thought doesn't mean their course of reasoning will lead them to the right series of actions, because everyone's train of thought is colored from the beginning by their own agenda and desires."

Major Krandiewsky said, "Chief, I know we already discussed this, but are you sure we shouldn't stay out of this command mess? I mean, what if Paradise is right? Wouldn't logic dictate that we keep to our own jobs?"

Brown snorted. "Okay, Buzz. Look at it this way; it doesn't matter if Paradise is wrong, right or completely indifferent. He doesn't have the authority to relieve Britaine under any circumstances. Only the chief medical officer on a vessel can certify the commander is unfit for duty either physically or mentally. Doctor Dimms has made no such announcement nor has Paradise even claimed he has. I doubt that Paradise has asked him to make a certification. Puke would be risking more than his military and medical career to pronounce a commander mentally unfit. Do you know how many times a flight surgeon has made a psychologically unqualified certification in all the eight hundred years of the Alliance?"

The other three shook their heads.

"Well, I do," Brown continued. "I looked it up. It has happened just once, about 750 years ago. A court-martial pronounced him guilty of mutiny and he was hung along with everybody else who did not give active support to the legal commander."

"Hung?" Misha was startled. "You mean with a rope."

Brown smiled, "Yep. That is a pretty picture, huh? And that is still the standing punishment for AMSF mutineers."

Krandiewsky shook his head, "But, what if a commander is unfit? Surely the medical staff has some discretion."

Brown said, "I'm sure they do. There are a lot of cases where a commander is relieved of duty because of physical damage. Plus there are a butt load of cases where a commander is relieved of duty because of mental defect. But, and this is a bigger butt than Spacer Third Class Masterson down in environmental has got, every case of mental defect has documented and I mean a bushel basket full of documented physical and chemical imbalances that a doctor can see, measure, photograph and chart. Even then, except for that one time, it was only done when the spacecraft was at a base, using multiple base doctors and base facilities."

Misha said, "That's really a moot point. Major Paradise hasn't said Colonel Britaine was crazy, just a coward. I don't like siding with anyone running from a fight, but I like the sound of being hung with a rope even less."

Brown reached out a hand and squeezed Misha's bicep. "Don't worry, Third McPherson. I'm sure they couldn't find a rope to hold you. They'd probably have to use a docking cable."

Misha gave Chief Brown a sweet smile.

Brown continued, "I don't like supporting a coward either, but unless the command stalemate gets broken, we're all truly screwed because this spacecraft isn't going anywhere fast. And speaking of going: Misha, can you provide Buzz with a couple of your grunts to help him get past any of Paradise's people?"

Krandiewsky waved his hand dismissively, "No. I'm sure that wherever Third McPherson is going, she'll need all the hands she has available."

Brown said in a voice everyone in the room could hear, "Oh, better leave Rickie and Sticks here, too. Those two idiots don't know when to keep their mouths shut and they're liable to get us all in hot water if they are around Colonel Britaine for too long. I can put them on some internal monitoring."

Rickie looked at everyone in the room with mock horror. Sticks blew an old-fashioned razzberry.

Brown smiled and said. "By the way, Misha, how do I contact you if I run across internal information you need to know? You seem to be using some special APE code."

"Well, Chief. You need to talk to my intelligence staff, Troopers Lamsa and Everridge. You can rig up a secure comms line between the three of you. Let me go find them and you can get something secure set up."

Forrester spoke up before she could exit the hatch to look for Everridge and Lamsa. "Hold up, Misha. You've got better things to do than be a liaison between APES and AMSF intelligence staff. This sounds like a task specifically designed for an old Marshal Service data pusher."

Misha said, "Thank you, Gan. Tell them I said to do it double time. We've got places to go, things to see, and people to do."

Chapter Fifty-Three

Race Jackson shouted down the corridor in frustration. "Dammit, Taks. You're on the wrong side of this. We should be fighting the Binders and not each other. Come on and answer me, you stubby little bastard."

Sigget Donnellson looked at his Second. "I don't guess he's going to give up without more of a fight."

Foxtrot Squad clustered at the corridor intersection. Jackson had backed up until he had two blind angles between him and Taks' squad defending the FO. He lay on his stomach, peering around the first angle. This gave him a clear angle of fire for anyone coming around the other angle ahead. The double corner also gave him cover against any ricochet fire from Taks.

Race spit onto the deck plates, causing a nearby trooper to slide a little closer to the bulkhead. "Dammit, Sigget. We have both Foxtrot and Kilo Squads against just a couple of guys from Taks' Charlie Squad. We know Kranitchovich's Hotel Squad has got half of Charlie locked down in the training bay. Even if he hooked up with McPherson, we've got a lot better than three to one superiority."

"Yeah and we have at least twice as many needlers. We know they don't have more than two weapons."

Race snorted, "How do you figure that?"

Donnellson replied, "One to fire at us this way and one to fire on Kilo from the other direction. I'm not stupid, you know. I only heard two needlers going when first bumped heads and they shot at us and took down a couple of your rookies." He glanced behind him as their med-tech Dashell worked feverishly over a prostrate form.

Race said, "Yeah, but you know how Taks works. He was scrounging for weapons all the way here. Just because he didn't commit them in our first brush doesn't mean he doesn't have them. But, it doesn't matter, Second Moraft said to get Britaine out of the flight office and give control of the Kiirkegaard to Paradise. We've got to figure a way in there."

"I am not going down this corridor into the spray from even one needler," Donnellson said. "That's suicide without armor."

"Yeah, but we don't have armor, do we? Hey wait! We don't need combat suits. All we're getting from Taks in needler fire. We can stop that with any metal shielding. Go grab a couple of tabletops from somewhere. Rip them out of the walls for all I care. Take a couple of troopers with you."

Race thumbed his comm unit on. Static blasted his ears. Someone was jamming communications. He ordered the glass-pack to squelch any interference and search for an open channel to anyone in Kilo Squad. He would have to send a runner around the long way to let Kilo Squad know what he was planning if he couldn't get through to Second Cauton by comms. Both squads needed to use shielding and attack at the same time to get at the FO. Takki-Homi was defending and could hold against a superior force. The edge always went to a well dug-in defender. Surprise was no longer in the equation. Race had lost one trooper already and he had one wounded. He did not mind losing rookies to Taks needler fire; he just did not want to join those rookies any more than Siggit did.

Race looked behind him at Dashell and mentally updated his count to two dead in their first encounter with Takki-Homi. It surprised Race that Takki-Homi had gotten his defenders in place before Race could get Foxtrot and Kilo to the flight office. "Dammit," He said to no one in particular. "Theda was right. We spent too much time looking for that bitch, McPherson. Now Taks has got the high ground on us."

The trooper next to Race said, "High ground? What gives, Deuce? This is on the same deck. It's level."

Race shook his head, "It's a figure of speech, numb-nuts. It means he has the upper hand in terrain. Don't look so frightened, rookie. No fight is perfect. He may have the high ground, but we have numbers superiority in personnel and weapons, plus we have mobility. With a coordinated attack between Kilo and us we can hit him at the same time from two directions."

Jackson's comm unit beeped as it signaled a channel through to someone in Kilo. He tapped his unit open. "Second Jackson of Foxtrot calling anyone from Kilo. Who have I go?"

"This is Trooper Eleven Smith," a young woman's voice answered.

"Good. Smith, you tell Deuce Cauton that we've got Takki-Homi flanked. Grab a couple of metal shields from somewhere to use against the needlers. Tabletops should work if he can get them free. We do a coordinated attack on the flight office in exactly thirty tics. Exactly, on my time hack! Got it?

"I got it, Mr. Jackson. I will relay the message right away."

Chapter Fifty-Four

Trooper Eleven Smith looked at the tall blonde woman crouched next to her, "I would guess that Mr. Jackson still thinks I'm with Kilo Squad, huh? Well, that's one message that won't get through."

Second Level Commander Aardmricksdottir smiled, "Both Jackson and the glass-packs seemed to be confused about where your loyalties lie. But, you're wrong. That message needs to get through. Not to Kilo because they won't believe a thing you tell them since you left their squad, but try to punch a signal through to anyone in Charlie Squad. When you get one, let me talk to Second Takki-Homi."

Chapter Fifty-Five

Race Jackson crept forward as he crouched down behind the tabletop. With this protection, they should be able to crush Takki-Homi's team between his squad and Kilo. They were close enough for hand to hand combat where his superior numbers could quickly overwhelm any flight office defenders.

"Hey, Race."

"Not now, Sigget. Get your mind on the job."

"I just had a thought, what if Taks sees us coming from both directions, then ducks back into the flight office and locks the hatch."

Jackson shook his head sadly, "You are a putz. Do you know that? Then, at least he ain't shooting back at us, right? So we punch a hole in the hatch or the bulkhead and shoot our way in. Hell, at the same time, maybe come in through the ceiling from the deck up above. Now pay attention, Sigget. Check that hatch there." Race pointed to a hatch they had just passed. It was in no man's land. No one had gone into or out of the hatchway since their first contact with Takki-Homi's squad.

"Already did, Race. It was locked up tight. Hey, do you think this tabletop is really going to stop needlers?"

"Damn, you're a worrier. Yeah, it will stop needlers. I guarantee it or your money will be cheerfully refunded."

"Okay, but what if they got something other than needlers?"

"Shut up, would you? Look, if Taks had something else, he would have used it earlier, right?" His voice was confident, though he didn't believe what he was saying. "His team took some hits from us, too. Remember? We damn near took them the first time. He wouldn't have held much in reserve and if he had something, we would have more dead than we got. Not to worry, chicken-breath. This'll be a cake walk in the park."

317

Foxtrot Squad moved ahead until they were almost at the last angle of the corridor. One more slide forward and they would have Takki-Homi in their needler sights.

Jackson said, "Everybody, listen up. They know we're coming. We aren't the quietest bunch, but with us here and Kilo coming the other direction, we'll get them in a crossfire and burn their butts. The curve of the hallway will cut down on friendly fire coming in from Kilo to us, but stay down behind this shield anyway."

He looked around at his squad. Two rookies were dead. He had already forgotten their names. They were gone and he hadn't even gotten to know them; which was for the best. Trooper Eleven Portman was off to who-the-hell-knows where. Probably with his buddy Singletary running some scam. That left him with eight effectives. Two of them, Spaz and Dog Boy were hanging back. Both had been complaining about headaches after McPherson's day office escape. He shook his head and motioned them to move forward next to him in the front. He would give them real headaches when this was all over.

"Last thing: the word we were given is that all we have to do is get to Britaine and take him down. The Kiirkegaard's computer will record the coward's death and then automatically roll command to Paradise and we can get this bucket of crap back into the game so we can kill some weed-eating S.O.B.s."

He glared at Spaz and Dog Boy. "Okay pivot, and I do mean pivot, this table around the corner. Keep your heads down because Takki-Homi is a damn fine shot. Go!"

Spaz held the edge of the table against the left bulkhead. Dog Boy inched the right edge out and around it in an arc creeping along behind.

Jackson snorted. He expected to come under fire when they first came into view, but nothing happened. He peered cautiously over the table top and ducked back down. Halfway down the corridor he saw a small barricade built by the open FO hatchway. Takki-Homi must have had the same thought he did and used the conference table as a barrier. But, there must have only been one table, because he saw two needlers pointed in his direction over the barricade. Both shooters had their backs to the open corridor where Kilo Squad would approach.

He glanced at his timer and then scanned the faces of each of his troopers. His gaze came to rest on Donnellson's face. Something wasn't right. It felt too easy. The only thing at their backs was that one hatchway, but they had watched it constantly since they moved into position. No one could have gone in there and no one had come out. Besides, the hatch was locked, wasn't it?

Jackson said, "Hey, Sigget. You said that hatch was locked, right? Was it locked from the inside or the outside?"

"Damfino, Deuce. Locked is locked, ain't it?"

"Go back and check it again. Stay focused," Jackson ordered.

Before Donnellson could move to the hatch, it flew open, slamming with a loud clang against the bulkhead. Jackson watched in horror as a table dropped into place across the corridor. He saw Gaineretti, some trooper he didn't recognize and that crazy Peanut Trammler drop into place behind the covering shield. Quicker than a heartbeat and before he could react, three needlers popped into sight and began spraying a hail of needles into his squad.

At the same time, a barrage of needles began splattering across the bulkheads and ceiling around him. The shots from Takki-Homi's position weren't deadly, but their ricochets were shredding any exposed skin. Taks' team to their rear was cutting into his troops like crap through a golden goose. In fractions of a second half of his squad lay bleeding.

Jackson shouted, "Cease fire. Foxtrot surrenders. For Mama's sake, quit shooting." He threw his needler down and put his hands up over his head. Only three others could follow suit. When the shooting stopped,

Jackson thought his best hope was that Kilo could catch Takki-Homi from the rear and turn the tide of the battle.

Gaineretti's head popped up and looked Jackson straight in the eye. Gaineretti's needler pointed directly at his head.

"Easy there, trooper," Jackson said. "I'm not going to try anything."

Gaineretti shouted, "Clear."

Jackson swiveled his head slightly, expecting to see Kilo Squad swarming Takki-Homi from behind. Instead, he saw half a dozen troopers vault over their shield and put their backs to him. Now they were facing the direction Kilo would come, if they ever did.

Jackson wondered why Cauton hadn't ordered Kilo into action, but Peanut cut his thoughts short as she leapt over her barricade and moved in among his squad, tossing weapons back to the other two. Gaineretti and the other trooper moved to the open side of their barricade. The muzzle of Gaineretti's needler didn't leave Jackson's face even when the man climbed over the table top.

At a quick gesture, the other trooper turned his back on Jackson's squad and began watching the open corridor. Two AMSF enlisted people stepped cautiously out of the hatch and began sliding the table down the hallway to the blind corner, setting it up as a forward watch point. The two spacers hurried back to Peanut and gathered all the surrendered weapons. They tossed all but two each back into the hatchway and slammed it shut, but did not spin the dial to lock the hatch. One of them rapped his knuckles on the hatch. Even from his distance, Jackson could hear the mechanism spin and cycle closed to lock from the inside.

Chapter Fifty-Six

Misha sent a short blast of needles bouncing off the metal bulkhead, around a corner and into a cluster of troopers from Moraft's Bravo Squad. She was both satisfied and horrified at the same time to hear screaming coming from around the corner. She didn't want to kill APES. She knew the ricochets would lose their lethal effect, but the needler would still shred skin. She dodged back into a hatchway off the corridor. Return fire splattered against the bulkhead where she had stood.

She stepped into the corridor and re-leveled the needler for another blast when the weapon suddenly clunked empty and spanged the blank cartridge onto the steel deck. Misha stomped her foot and re-aimed the gun. She realized what she had done and ducked back through the hatchway, looking sheepishly at Trooper Na'aranna beside her.

Na'aranna said, "A bit frustrated are we? I think we may be able to find you a spare cartridge."

Misha tried to control the deep red blush blossoming across her face. "Frustrated at the situation, but not with the needler," she admitted. "I was trying to activate the mass driver induction feed on my suit, but I guess I am not wearing my suit, huh?"

Na'aranna said in a matter of fact tone, "I have seen that a hundred times. If you put a bunch of veterans without their suits on an unarmored firing range, they begin stomping their feet so much it looks like a chorus line."

Aggie Raza tapped Misha on the shoulder and dropped a fresh needler cartridge into her hand. "I don't know what you two are talking about. That's never happened to me."

Na'aranna snorted, "You dance around so much you look like you're having seizures, or in your case, in the middle of an orgasm."

"Moi? Sorry, Nana, but ain't nothing that ever moves me more'n sex!" Raza replied with a mock look of shock.

Misha slammed the cartridge into the open needler, "I get the point, ladies. All kidding aside though, I don't think we're going to get past Bravo Squad from this direction. Do you have any suggestions that don't involve us ending up in a med bay or the morgue?"

Raza grinned, "Well, maybe if we just ask them nicely they will surrender. I mean, you don't get if you don't ask, right?"

Na'aranna snorted. "This is coming from a woman who has never said no in her life."

Raza laughed, "Come on, Nana. I say no all the time."

Na'aranna replied, "Yeah, but only when someone asks if you've had enough."

Misha looked at Raza and then at Na'aranna. "Okay," she shrugged. "I don't think it'll work, but it won't hurt. Trooper Na'aranna, see if you can get Tree and Greek to blast through this comm signal jamming and get me either Moraft or Paradise."

"What?" Raza asked with a real look of shock on her face, "I was just kidding. Really, I didn't mean it as an honest suggestion."

Misha nodded. "I know, but as you said, if you don't ask then you don't get. Plus this way may be cheaper and only slightly less painful than trying to fight our way in."

Na'aranna after a brief conversation with Everridge said, "Tree says Greek will be able to do a round-about patch and you'll be up in a tic." The jamming had been getting worse with each passing hour.

Misha replied, "Thanks. Oh, did he mention anything about the source of this communications interference?"

"Sort of," Na'aranna said. "It was something to the effect of shoving glass-pack comm units into strange orifices on the guy responsible for messing up his airwaves. He and Greek are still baffled about the comms jamming. It doesn't seem to be localized around any one particular spot, but they are both sure it is internal jamming."

Raza said, "My guess is that it's XO Paradise because it sure as hell isn't us. That crap is more of a pain to us than a help."

Misha shook her head. "I don't know what is causing it, but it's as much a hindrance to Paradise and Moraft as it is to us. Codes and secure links are all that should be necessary for any conflict this fluid." She snorted. "Sound like a textbook, don't I? All I know is that we aren't causing the jamming and it doesn't make sense for Paradise to do it either. But then, mutiny doesn't make sense either and the S.O.B. is doing that."

Everridge signaled he had a patch through to Moraft.

Misha took a deep breath and tapped her comm unit open. "Mr. Moraft? This is Third-Level Commander Hamisha McPherson. You are participating in an illegal action. Stop all hostile activity, order all APES under your command to stand down and surrender to my legal authority."

Moraft's voice squeaked out of the comm unit sounding tinny and distant. "Look, McPherson. APES are warriors, we don't run from fights. I won't side with a coward whatever the reason."

Misha nodded as if Moraft could see her. "Theda, I understand how you feel. Wait, let me finish. I know you don't know me and you have no reason to respect or feel any loyalty to me."

"Damn straight!" Moraft interrupted.

Misha continued as if she hadn't heard. "But, I'm an APE just like you and I've been put here by higher command. You should respect and have loyalty to their decisions."

"Yeah, sure! They left that dickless piece of pond scum Cans in charge so long that this unit is only one step above a pack of wild dogs. Since you haven't seen fit to lead us into this war, I damn well will."

"You know, Theda. I agree with everything you just said," Misha nodded.

"You what?" Moraft's voice sounded baffled.

"You're right. Cans was dickless. And if I can't lead us through a dirt drop then you should. But, most of all, I agree that this unit is only one step above a pack of wild dogs. Considering all of that, Theda, do you think that even if we did get to dirt drop into an LZ we would be in any condition to fight and win?"

Moraft all but shouted, "We would drop and fight. We are APES. That's what we do."

Misha said, "You're right with one exception, Theda. We drop, we fight and we win. That's what we do. Are you so sure we could win?"

"I'm not afraid to try, dammit."

"Neither am I. You and I would probably come out of it alive. We're survivors. We're veteran warriors. But, we are also supposed to be leaders. How many APES would die because you and I are at odds?"

"Then get out of my way, McPherson."

"I can't do that, Mr. Moraft, anymore than you can just quit. We have screwed the pooch on this one. I suggest we call a truce, get this overpriced gas bag of vacuum-breather's nuts and bolts back to Heaven's Station and let the big brass figure out who's right and who's wrong."

"I ain't running from a fight, dammit."

"You wouldn't be running, Theda. The whole op is flushed. We go back together. What do we care who drives this bus?"

"I don't know, Third. It just-" Moraft started.

A man's voice blasted over Moraft's signal. "Shut up, both of you! I am in command of this vessel and it goes where I say. And I say we damn well head back to Gagarin. You APES may turn tail if things go bad, but I'm an AMSF officer and I do not leave my people behind."

Misha sighed, "XO Paradise, I presume?"

"Major Paradise to you, and I'm no longer the executive officer. I have assumed command of the Kiirkegaard. And as such, I order you to stand down and surrender for arrest."

Misha said, "Major Paradise, I figure you're not in command anymore than Colonel Britaine is at this point. And personally, I don't care which of you pretends to be in command. At this point, going back to Gagarin is a waste of effort. Theda, you can see that, can't you?"

"I don't know, I guess-" Moraft started.

"Shut up, Moraft," Paradise shouted. "You do what I damn well tell you to do. You're not paid to think. You're a grunt, you're paid to do what you're told. And you, McPherson, you bitch, how the hell can you call going back a waste of time? There were spacers and APES dying back there!" Paradise shouted.

Misha said, "Yes. But 'were' is the appropriate verb, sir. What was going down in the Gagarin system has already happened! If the Allied forces won, then all we could do would be to help clean up. If the Allied forces lost, well then going back won't change it."

Paradise snarled, "So, you still advocate turning tail and running? Are you asking me to relinquish my command back to that coward Britaine?"

Misha rubbed her forehead and looked at Raza and Na'aranna. "Major Paradise, I'm not asking anyone anything except to look at our situation. Right now, we are not going to Gagarin or to Heaven's Station. We're dead in space. As long as this stalemate exists then we'll stay here until we run out of air, food or heat, whichever comes first. Sir, I agree with you, I'd rather die in battle than become a corpsicle in space."

Moraft said, "Major Paradise, I think she's right. Any battle at Gagarin is already in the history books and we aren't going anywhere."

Paradise's voice crackled through the comm unit. "Shut up, Moraft. One more word and I'll have you shot and tossed out an airlock with the rest of the garbage. Do you hear me, grunt? I will not give the command back to Britaine."

Misha said, "I suggest we agree to a truce. You keep engineering and we leave Britaine in the flight office. Let's get back to Heaven's Station. The higher command can decide what to do with-

Paradise shouted, "Enough! This conversation is over. Moraft, go do your job and clear my corridors of that coward's girlfriend and her yellow-bellied stooges."

Chapter Fifty-Seven

"Hey, Chief?" Clancy called across the intelligence office. "We aren't getting squat monitoring internal communications. Where the hell is this jamming coming from?"

Chief Brown looked up from the readout on her glass-pack. "Damfino where it's coming from. Did you run a diagnostic on jammer signal strength?"

Cuffs said, "No, Chief. Why would we do that? I mean we can't pinpoint the location without a good triangulation."

Brown snorted, "Hunh? Are you sure about that? Did you try a shooter or a bump and run? No? I didn't think so. What do you think the DIRT file is for?"

When she got blank looks from everyone in the room, she sighed. "Okay, kids. Remember way back on your first day aboard we downloaded onto your glass-packs a bunch of files for you to study? Yeah? Well think harder. DIRT stands for the Dummies Intelligence Reference Text. I personally wrote it for you dummies, because there are things you need to know and I won't always be here to hold your hands."

Clancy smiled, "Yeah, I read part of it. It was mostly checklists and odd bits of information about obsolete equipment. Sorry, Chief, but it was pretty dry stuff."

Brown smiled back with genuine humor, "Yeah, it is dry. It's a working reference guide not a romance novel."

Cuffs scanned data on his glass-pack, "What was that? A shoot and run or a bumper? No, um, wait a tic. Here it is. And I quote 'of the three methods for locating a signal generation point, best is the triangulation method.' We know that one from technical training. This goes on a bit, let's see, yada yada yada..."

Brown snarled, "Excuse me, spacer. I wrote that and I distinctly remember writing clear and concise instructions. I do not blather on or write 'yada, yada, yada'."

"Yeah, I know Chief, just trying to get to the salient points." Cuffs said without looking up at the hooting and woofing going on around the room. "What?"

Brown laughed, "Salient points?"

Cuffs said, "Um, yeah you know, Chief. Salient: the important, the prime-"

Brown laughed harder, "Damn, Cuffs. I know what it means. We're just surprised you know what it means and we're even more surprised that you could use it in a complete sentence. You've been sandbagging us? No. No. Don't deny it, just get back to reading. I love it when I get my own words quoted back to me; just get it right without the yada parts."

Cuffs nodded. "Yes, Chief. Okay, 'a shooter is when a signal is piggybacked along the incoming jamming signal. By sending a signal shooting along the incoming signal, using varying strengths and duration, a technician can monitor the shooter signal return signature or running bounce back, thus determining the strength of the jammer signal. Plotting the strengths along the signal line and matching it to the attached chart you should be able to locate the general vicinity of the jammer signal generation point.' Wheew! That's a load."

Brown snarled, "A load of what, spacer?"

Cuffs replied, "Sorry, Chief. I meant a mouthful. But, yeah I can see where that'd work, somewhat, I think?"

Brown shook her head, "Clancy, why won't this work?"

Cuffs said, "Won't work? I thought you said-"

Brown shook her head and pointed at Clancy. "Speak up."

"Well, Chief. I think we may have too many bulkheads in the way. This would be wonderful to try in space, but in the confines of a vessel, well, the interference factor would be too high to provide reliable data. But, what the hell; it beats nothing. Let's try it."

Brown said, "Don't get your knickers in a knot, girl. Hold on." She pointed a finger at Cuffs and said, "Read on."

"Okay Chief. It says a bump and run is when the searching signal is bounced off a stationary object, such as another spacecraft, a planet or a moon, to provide an additional signal line for the location of the jammer generation point."

"That won't work either," Gan Forrester said.

Startled, Brown jumped. She had forgotten he was sitting quietly in the corner. She thought, "Damn that man is so grey he can hide in plain sight." She said, "Okay, Marshal. Fill us with your wisdom."

Forrester smiled back. "It won't work for the same reason as the other method, there are way too many bulkheads causing interference. That's also why we only have intermittent jamming. Even a jammer signal can't be transmitted cleanly through this maze of steel walls and metal bulkheads. Both methods would only have application in open space or near a planetary orbit."

"Correct, Marshal," Chief Brown smiled. "Everyone get that? Good."

Cuffs said, "Damn it, Chief. Why did we have to go to all this trouble to read it if you knew these methods wouldn't work?"

Brown stood up, stretched, and looked Cuffs in the eye, "First of all, spacer, don't cuss at me. I am old enough to be your mama, so talk to me civilly. Second. I am not here just to make you snot-nosed brats do your job, I'm here to teach you how to do your job."

"Sorry, Chief," Cuffs apologized. "I didn't mean to cuss. It just slipped out."

"Damn right it slipped out. So don't let it happen again. No cussing in this frakking office, hear me?"

A chorus of raucous calls rang out.

Brown nodded. "Good, just so we have some sort of understanding. Now if we can't do a shooter or a bump and run, what is left? No guesses? That leaves us with a triangulation, doesn't it?"

"Okay, Chief," Cuffs said, "I'll bite on this one. We are in one place. To triangulate we need to shoot the jammer signal from two locations."

Brown slapped her forehead, "Why me, Lord? Why me? Think, all of you. Are we really all in one place?"

Clancy said, "Yeah, Chief. Except for a couple of guys we have sleeping across the corridor, but that isn't a wide enough distance for triangulation separation."

Cuffs said, "Yeah. That's it, except for…oh, shit, Chief. I mean, damn. Sorry, what the hell am I thinking?! The Major and half our crew is up in the FO. They can shoot the second leg of the triangulation from there. Gods, I am stupid today."

Brown smiled broadly and gave Cuffs a thumbs up. "Good thinking, spacer."

Clancy said, "Yeah, it was good mental work. But you knew it all along, didn't you, Chief? Why didn't you just say so?"

Brown said, "You all have to learn to think on your own. If someone is always there to give you the answer, then the day when that someone isn't there, subsequently you will be well and truly frakked. My goal is to get you all to think three dimensional or to kill you trying."

Cuffs said, "I know what they have in the FO. It can't run a triangulation. I mean Buzz is smart and could probably budge things together, but I don't see how he can put it together without a 3c914MTc module in their comm gear. Hey! We've got a spare across the hall. We could get someone to run it up there."

Forrester raised his hand, "I can do that, Chief. If you just get someone to show me what is the 3C9er thing is."

Brown nodded. "That works for me." She pointed at a pair of young spacers. "You two run the man across the hall and make sure he gets to the flight office. Then shag your asses back here. Hey! Take those." She pointed to a couple of weapons lying on a desk by the hatch.

The spacers picked up the sunburners, short blunderbuss-like guns with a large bell-shaped opening. They were non-lethal incapacitating weapons. Officially, they were TVOTs, (pronounced Tee-Vots) or temporary visual obstruction tools, because they shot a blast of broad-spectrum light temporarily blinding an opponent. Unofficially they were sunburners because of their obvious after affects.

The two spacers cycled open the hatch and stepped into the corridor. Marshal Forrester pulled a needler out of his shoulder holster and stepped through the hatchway while checking the magazine for load. A torrent of needler fire almost cut the two spacers in half. Forrester took a hit high in the shoulder. He managed to use the momentum from the shot to spin himself back into the intel office and crash to the deck.

Brown bellowed. "Everyone duck and cover. Weapons hot. Clancy, freeze!" She stopped the woman from jumping into the corridor. "You can't help those two and you can't help me if you get yourself killed. Get armed and get on that hatch. You and you, back her up. Don't lock down yet."

She looked about the room. "Cuffs, do what you can for Forrester. Don't argue with me. I know you're not a medic, but you're all he's got, so do something."

Brown looked down and saw that her .45 semi-automatic pistol had jumped into her hands of its own accord. She flicked the safety switch off as she stepped to the vault hatch. Exposing only her arm, she pointed the gun down the corridor and rapidly boomed out half a dozen shots. After the quiet pfft of the needlers, the mini-explosions of the gas propelled slugs fired from the handgun echoed off the metal bulkheads causing everyone in the room to jump. Stepping quickly into the corridor and taking a classic shooter stance, she pumped the remaining dozen rounds into the retreating backs of a small group of security forces. Only two made it to the corner to retreat to relative safety.

The slide mechanism on the .45 shot back in the open and locked position. Brown calmly thumbed the magazine release button dropping the empty clip to the deck. She expected to hear it clang as it hit the deck when she slammed a second clip into the magazine, but the expectant clang didn't happen. She fired two shots into the metal bulkheads near where the retreating security forces had fled. The glass bullets made a satisfying 'whang' as they ricocheted off the bulkhead. Without turning her head she said, "Clancy, watch my six. You other two, watch the eleven and one o'clock positions."

When the three were in place she looked down. The spent clip hadn't bounced on the metal deck because unbeknownst to her, Brown stood straddle-legged over a spacer's body like a mother bear protecting an injured cub. Her face twisted in a bear-like grimace of rage. Both of her spacers were obviously beyond help. Not bothering to suppress or hide her tears of grief and fury, she reached down and patted each lifeless body on the head. She tried to find the words to tell them how sorry she was, but the words choked in her throat.

The hatchway across the hall opened a crack. She could see of her intelligence spacers. They had been sleeping in the room. Both had hidden under the bunks when the shooting started and had warily opened the hatch a crack to look out once the shooting stopped.

With a strength that belied her age, Brown grabbed the bloody bodies by their utility uniform collars and dragged them out of the corridor into the newly opened room. She dumped them unceremoniously in the middle of the deck. "You two get your butts into the office. Now!" Following the two, she stepped back into the corridor. Shooting a questioning look at Clancy, she received a shake no in response. No one had poked their heads around the corner, so she waived the other two spacers back into the intel office, leaving only her and Clancy exposed. Clancy looked nervous, but held her ground with fierce determination.

Brown's command voice bellowed and echoed off the metal bulkheads, "All right, you sons-of-bitches! Speak up now or forever hold your piece, because I will hunt your asses down to the last man."

A voice answered, "Chief Brown? Is that you?"

"Who the frak do you think it would be, you pinhead? You storm into my corridor, blast away at my people, and you expect someone else to be here? Who the hell are you? Speak up, dammit, before I come down there and send more of you punk-ass security cretins to eternal damnation."

"Tech Sergeant Wilkins, Chief. Hold your fire? Can we can check our wounded?"

"Let them frakking bleed to death, Wilkins. What are you doing shooting at AMSF people? And don't shout at me around the corner. Step out like a man with balls instead of a thick-minded stobor in jerk off mode."

"Okay, Chief. Don't shoot. I'm coming out, okay?" The man spread both hands wide and stepped around the corner. "I'm unarmed, see?" He glanced behind him and motioned at someone out of sight to put their gun down. "Hells bells, Chief, your guys startled us and all, jumping into the corridor with those sunburners at the ready. It was just a reaction. I hope they're okay?"

"They're dead, Wilkins. Who else have you got with you?"

"I have just one other guy. He's an FNG, a frakking new guy named-"

Brown interrupted. "I don't want to know his name. That way if I kill you both I only have to remember your name in my prayers. Get the FNG out here to check on your people. Do it now, Wilkins!"

Wilkins desperately waved the new guy into the hall and pushed him forward to check on the still bodies before him. It was easy to see, even for non-medical people, that none of the security forces had survived.

The FNG said, "I think they're all dead, Sergeant Wilkins. What do we do now?"

Looking at Wilkins, Brown said, "Yes, Wilkins. What do you do now?"

Wilkins said, "I don't know, Chief. I never saw anyone dead before."

"What were you doing in my corridor?" Chief Brown asked.

"Major Chang said there was a mutiny on board and we were to clear the corridors of all personnel."

"Major Chang?" Brown asked.

"Yeah, Chief. And he said to be armed and on our toes because hostiles were trying to take over the ship."

"So, Wilkins, your idea of clearing the hallways is to shoot first?"

"Oh damn, Chief. It's like I said, they just jumped out all armed and everything. We didn't mean to kill them. It just happened."

The FNG said, "Yeah, besides Chief, if you guys aren't with the mutiny, why are you armed? Hell, you shot at us."

"Shut up, son," Brown said quietly. "If you don't say another word to anyone except your lawyer you might not hang for mutiny or get a lethal injection for murder."

Wilkins turned pale, "Come on, Chief. Mutiny and murder? We were just doing what Major Chang ordered us to do."

He turned even paler when Brown said, "Major Chang is part of the mutiny, so what would you get for aiding and abetting, Wilkins?"

"Dammit, Chief, all I know is the officer in charge of my section tells me what to do and I went and done it. Now I'm sorry for your guys, but I am loyal to the AMSF. Frak no, I am not involved in any mutiny."

Brown shook her head, "Where the hell have you been all day, Wilkins? Don't you know what is going on around you?"

"Um, well. Me and the boys here, um…got into a batch of homemade pruno and, well, I guess we got a bit shitfaced. I didn't know anything from nobody until a little bit ago when the Major found us and put us on duty. Look Chief. I know we aren't supposed to get drunk on deployment, but we weren't on duty or nothing. If you report that, then my career is screwed."

Chief Brown shook her head sadly, "Drunk on deployment is the least of your worries, you idiot. You better heed the advice I gave your young friend to shut up and talk to no one except legal counsel. The two of you clear this corridor and put these bodies in that room with my men. You will both submit to my authority and confine yourselves with the bodies until I say different. Got me?" Both men, very subdued, nodded and began moving the bodies. "Leave all weapons on the decks." She told the men.

Brown called to Clancy over her shoulder. "Okay, pick up all of these weapons and get everyone inside the vault. Call Buzz in the flight office using the secure phone."

From inside the intelligence office, Cuff's called out, "Hey, Chief. Forrester's hit pretty bad. I got the bleeding contained, but I think we gotta get him to sick bay pretty quick."

"Can he walk?"

Forrester answered. "Yes, I can walk."

Cuffs replied, "Maybe."

Brown didn't want to leave the intelligence office to get the man to sickbay. With Buzz in the flight office that would leave Clancy in charge. Not that she had any problem with putting Clancy in control. She was a sergeant, a fine supervisor, and she could keep things in line. The truth be known, Clancy was probably better with people than she was. Someday she might even make a great officer. But, at this juncture in Clancy's career, she didn't have as much experience as the Chief did, and if something went wrong, she didn't want to leave Clancy catching the short end of the stick. More than anything, Brown was loathe to send any of her people into a hostile situation. If security was patrolling the corridors, more of her people could get killed. She knew she would have to go herself.

Wilkins stood up after helping move the bodies and said, "Let me help him, Chief. I know it won't erase my screw ups, but maybe I can help get him to sickbay."

Chief Brown nodded. "Okay, Wilkins. You're with me, unarmed and technically under my arrest. Cuffs, get everyone back on the comm boards and intel monitors or get quiet and stay out of the way. Let's get back to business."

Chapter Fifty-Eight

Misha looked around at her team. Na'aranna and Raza stood next to her. Everridge and Lamsa were huddled in a corner. Ethica Kelly and Bear Cutler were sitting quietly but alertly with their backs against a bulkhead. Across the corridor, she could see Lamont and Ottiamig peering out the hatchway of a room holding the two-man teams of DeLaPax and Metzler, Steinman and Qualls, and Oberman and Ramirez. It was a large corridor designed for engineering use, for hauling huge machines and components back and forth to the various shops along the hallway. It was easily five meters wide and just as tall.

She pointed a finger at Lamont and crooked it to her. She held up four fingers and pointed to her feet, saying nothing. Since she hadn't worked with Lamont before she was not certain he would understand her hand signals. But, she was sure if she called out, her voice would carry far enough down the corridor for Bravo Squad to hear. Even if she spoke softly and her voice didn't carry, they could be using enhanced eavesdropping equipment. It didn't make sense to broadcast her intentions. Her team would be open in the corridor and vulnerable to gunfire.

Lamont waved a hand behind him and stepped into the hallway. Most men would have ducked and sprinted across the corridor, but Lamont patted Ottiamig on the shoulder signaling him to stay put and sauntered as if strolling through a park, except that he held a needler poised in each hand pointing down the corridor in either direction. He paused briefly in the center and sent a hail of needles showering Bravo's position. During which time, Able Squad Trooper Four DeLaPax darted past him. He calmly continued his stroll across the corridor and into the room. The return hail of fire, including the blast of a low-yield grenade, narrowly missed him.

He said without smiling, "You called, Third?"

She gave a low whistle to get everyone's attention and pointed at Tree and Greek. They came over to her and waited quietly. "Kelly and Metzler, on the hatch. Watch both directions." She called across the hall to Ottiamig, "Tuamma, get someone else on the hatch with you. Watch both ways." She stood waiting while Ottiamig turned and spoke to someone in the room. In a flash, Oberman appeared next to him, dropped to one knee and peered studiously back up the corridor. She would have preferred to let everyone in the squad know what was going on, even if it only meant broadcasting to them over a squad comm unit frequency, but the jamming made that all but impractical. She would have to rely on her veterans to fill in the rookies as they went along. "Greek, blast us some white noise to cover our conversations. Furthermore, see if you can get an enhanced ear on any talk coming from up or down this corridor."

"Roger that, sir," Greek replied, his eyes glued to the glass-pack and fingers dancing across the small pad.

Everridge added, "He's too modest to say so, but he has already been listening down corridor to Bravo Squad. We're not getting anything much from them except the general 'get off my foot' kind of stuff."

Misha smiled. "Good initiative. We need to conceal our backsides, covering our own talk and listening up our six, also."

Everridge nodded, "Yes, sir. Guess I didn't think that far. That must be why they pay you the big bucks."

Lamsa looked sheepish and elbowed Everridge in the ribs.

"Oh, and Greek wants to know if we can bring Tammie on board with some of the communications work. She's been hovering over our shoulders at every opportunity all day. We might as well show her some tricks of the trade, you know?"

"Tammie?" Misha looked confused.

"Yes, sir. Sorry," Everridge replied. "I mean Able Squad Trooper, what is it… Ten? Tammie Qualls, your communication tech? You know, Jigsaw? The rookie you have teamed up with Bear Cutler. She's one of the most eager rookies I've ever met. She constantly wants to learn more, once she got over her being nervous about screwing up. I've got to tell you, she had an extensive comms background with the Heaven's Three Police Force, but she's still hungry to learn everything we have to teach."

Misha shook her head. "I'm an idiot, guys. I guess I don't know my own people well enough to know their first names yet. Sorry, everybody, I can guarantee that by our next op, I'll have my own scoobies together.

"Not to worry, boss," DeLaPax smiled. "I'm sure Jigsaw won't be offended. Like Tree says she's a good kid. For that matter, even with this patched up squad we got a better team than I ever saw under Third Cans."

Misha nodded, "Okay, Tree. You commandeer Jigsaw whenever you can. Keep in mind that I don't want to lose any gun hands. We're all APES here. Comms is secondary, got me?"

A chorus of 'roger that' rang out.

Lamsa raised a finger and nodded. "White out affective."

Misha said, "All right, team. We seem to be in a stalemate here. We can't get into engineering and they can't get out. We can snipe at them and they take potshots back at us until there isn't anybody left on either side. Their defensive position will cut us to shreds if we rush them. The same thing happens to them if they rush us. Input?"

Immediately Tree spoke up. "First off, I have more bad news. It's very hard to tell from what comms we are able to pick up, but we caught a scrap of information leading us to believe another squad of APES is moving in this direction. Our only guess is that it's either Foxtrot or Kilo."

Misha frowned, "Doesn't matter which, either one will chew up our backsides while Bravo Squad claws away at our front. Other input? None? Okay, first: Tree, can you and Greek find some way to shut off the lights along this section? And I mean, without permanent damage to the Kiirkegaard? It's our only ride home, remember? Oh, and go ahead and tap Jigsaw for on-the-job training."

Lamsa nodded vigorously, but Everridge only shrugged and said, "Can try to get the lights out, Third."

"No," Misha ordered, "Can do. Get to it. Here's what I need from everyone else." In short order, Misha had everyone lined out and moving into position. She moved the point of her ambush back up the corridor taking most of her squad with her. She didn't want to leave too few troopers to defend against any possible outbreak from Moraft's Bravo Squad, but she didn't know how many APES were in the force about to slam into her from behind. She combined two teams, giving Raza nominal team command over Kelly and the rookies Oberman and Ramirez. She left them as the cookies or the bait with instructions to sound like the whole squad was still in place. But, with only four troopers, they would also have to hold back Bravo Squad if Moraft tried to break out. They would be desperately short handed if something went wrong and anyone got past her ambush.

Misha could hear the soft pfft of a needler spitting out its glass shards and the whiney ricochet as they bounced off metal bulkheads. She heard shouts when the return fire bounced back. With all the shouting and banging about the four were making, she would have thought a whole third-level command was in place.

She divided the remainder of her squad into two groups. One group consisted of troopers Metzler, Steinman and Ottiamig under the leadership of DeLaPax. They were placed in a room a long way up the curving corridor toward the oncoming APES and out of sight. She admonished DeLaPax that under no circumstances were they to spring the ambush until everyone had gotten past them. Otherwise, her small team could be quickly overwhelmed.

Misha placed herself and the remainder of the ambush team about midway between Raza's team and the curve. She had the majority of her veterans with her, believing she would be bearing the brunt of the oncoming force. If Raza's team failed to keep Bravo Squad bottled up, Misha's group would be sandwiched between two opposing forces.

She looked around for Everridge, Lamsa and Qualls, but they were not in sight yet. Unfortunately, there were no rooms or even alcoves in this part of the hallway. Her team was huddled behind the few chairs and boxes they had found. Nothing they had would stop any serious weapons. She spread her people out as much as possible in case anyone had more grenades.

Her three teams were far enough apart they couldn't see each other, but the curve would also eliminate friendly fire casualties. Misha still had room to back her team up if pushed by the oncoming force, but she didn't want the reinforcements to get close enough to shoot into the backs of Raza's team while they worked to contain Bravo Squad. More importantly, she could not afford to have the two squads hook up or let any reinforcements reach Moraft.

The soft swish of jump-sneaks brought her around to face Everridge, Greek and Jigsaw. She glanced up, the lights flaring brightly. "No go?" she asked.

"Greek has the switch ready to shut the whole thing down all at once, but Qualls plugged in a subroutine that'll let us shut off what you want, when you want it. I told you she was a good trooper. Once Jigsaw got over her shyness and worrying about screwing up, she became a whirlwind. She's wearing me out just watching her. Anyhow, we're ready on your command, sir." Everridge said.

Misha said, "Good work and a big attaboy to you, Jigsaw. That's good thinking. When I give the word I want us in pitch black all the way back to Raza's team. I want it as bright as Angorra daylight at the point of that curve ahead of us and make it dark from DeLaPax's team as far down the corridor as you can go."

Qualls asked, "Not just dark where DeLaPax is?"

Misha shook her head. "No, I don't want anyone suspicious if they come across a dark spot. I want them groping in the dark for a long way, then they'll cruise past DeLaPax to get to a bright spot, just like the light at the end of a tunnel. Can do?"

"Roger that, sir," Qualls said. "The way Greek showed me this set up, all I have to do for a shut- down is slide my finger along the blueprint diagrams when I want something off or when I want it turned back on."

"Nice work," Misha said. "Now, I want you back-to-back with me. Two reasons: one, I'm a better barricade for you than these boxes and two, I want you to watch our backsides in case Bravo Squad breaks past Raza. You shout a warning and hit the lights above them if you see anyone coming from that way. Got it? Good! Now lights out, it's show time." She was disappointed to see the corridor did not curve enough to hide her team in total darkness while still lighting up the ambush kill zone. Even before her eyes adjusted, she could see her team. The engineering corridor was wide enough to put all six of her shooters side-by-side. Instead, she had them quickly move all the boxes and chairs to either side of the corridor. The hostile force would be looking from the light into the darkness and with a little luck they might see an open hallway with a clutter of boxes stacked in the corridor for temporary storage.

Misha had Lamsa lay on the deck next to the bulkhead using a few chairs as camouflage. Everridge mirrored Lamsa as he stretched on the deck along the other bulkhead. She took a kneeling position behind Lamsa stacking as many boxes as she could in front of her without blocking her line of fire. She brushed up against Lamsa's leg, reaching down she patted his calf in reassurance. She felt him jerk and pull away.

"Well," she thought, "he doesn't have to like me to do his job." She felt Qualls lean into her back. She thought that at least Qualls didn't find her repulsive to the touch like Lamsa. But then Qualls is a woman and probably doesn't look at other women the way a man like Lamsa would. Looking quickly behind her, she saw Lamont in a standing position along the bulkhead behind a large stack of boxes. Across the corridor, Na'aranna mirrored Misha's kneeling position. Opposite Lamont was her last trooper, medical technician Bear Cutler. She fervently hoped they wouldn't need his services after this skirmish. She knew her team was too exposed and Cutler could be very busy, very soon.

She worried the ambush around in her head, not thinking of another way to settle the matter until she saw the reinforcement point men come into view. Two men skittered around the curve and slid to a halt at the edge of the darkening shadows.

"Hold it," she thought. "Just hold up a bit until your tail end catches up. Hold it." She only vaguely recognized either man and didn't know their squad designation.

As if listening, both men stopped and turned to look behind them.

Misha heard the taller of the two men say, "Damn, I hate the dark."

The short man replied, "What's the matter? Momma's little boy afraid of the dark?"

The tall man answered without embarrassment, "Nope, I'm just afraid of the things that live in the dark. You would be too if you grew up on a planet like Nightshade. Should we move forward?"

The short man shook his head, "Nope. Let's hold until we have someone to give us cover before we move into that mess. Shit, looks like those AMSF clowns just left stuff stacked all over down here. We're most likely to trip over something and break a leg."

"How much farther is it to engineering? Hey, how is Bravo Squad going to know not to shoot us when we hove into view?"

"Don't know. That is not my problem. I suppose when we get there they'll shout a warning and we answer."

Second Cauton came around the corner stopping next to the two men. Misha did a mental adjustment. She knew she was facing Kilo Squad.

Cauton said, "Damn, I hate the dark." Both men looked at each other, but said nothing. "So what are you two lame excuses for troopers doing just standing here?"

The short man said, "Just waiting on you, Deuce. I figured you'd want to cover us as we move out of the light again."

Cauton replied as more of the rest of the squad bunched up in the light, "Yeah, well you've got all of the cover you're going to get. Move it out!"

Misha did a quick count, seeing only eight bodies. She knew that one of Aardrmicksdottir's makeshift squad had come from Kilo, but she couldn't remember who it was. It didn't matter which, because the eight in front plus her one still left two Kilo troopers unaccounted for. Even though Cauton was the least experienced second-level commander in the outfit, surely she had ample sense to have two troopers as a rear guard. Misha had to try and hold her fire giving Kilo's rearmost guard enough time to get past DeLaPax.

All eight Kilo APES moved forward as one. No one hung back, although they did stretch out a bit. Almost unconsciously humans huddle closer together in the dark. Misha's team would hold their fire until she shot first. She hoped to hear DeLaPax open fire as a signal that all of Kilo had gone past, but when the small knot of bodies became nothing more than silhouettes against the light at the corridor curve, she opened fire aiming directly for the shadowy middle mass of Second Cauton. "Fire," she shouted. A storm of needler shards, small metal pellets and polypropylene capsules rained down on Kilo. Second Cauton pitched over backwards and lay still on the deck. Half of Kilo collapsed, either injured or dead in the first volley. Only the clustered bodies of their comrades kept them all from dropping in the initial round.

A split second later the rest of Kilo Squad dropped to the deck. As if to announce they were still alive a round from one of Kilo's guns spanged off the deck above Misha. Involuntarily she flinched, even knowing that ducking was a waste of time. The shot was long gone by the time the sound reached her ears.

She heard a grunt behind her followed by Lamont's voice. He sounded calm as if he were ordering lunch,

"Well, shit. That ain't right! They gone and ruined a new uniform." But, she heard his pumper blast and saw its bright muzzle flash. The pumper used a gas propellant to spray exploding capsules down the darkened corridor.

She threw her arm across her face as a flood of glass needler shards showered her and Lamont, hearing the shards whack into boxes and ricochet off the bulkheads all around her. She felt a small sting along her right side and what must have been pieces ricocheting off the bulkhead peppering her arm.

"Lamont," she shouted over her shoulder. "Cease fire. You'll give your position away. Everyone shift to position Blue-12!" She fired back into Kilo Squad, unable to tell what or whom she was hitting, but she didn't move. There was no position Blue-12. If Kilo believed her team shifted, they might not shoot the same spot they had hit before. It was a wide corridor, but not that wide. Still, anything that was a miss was better than the alternative.

"Tammie," Misha said forcing calmness into her voice so as not to rattle the rookie. "Light up Kilo Squad, if you please."

"Roger that, Third." Suddenly, a blaze of light illuminated Kilo, but they were so close the light washed over Misha's team, leaving them very exposed.

Misha shouted, "Fire at will, Lamont." But, there was silence from behind her. She wanted to turn and check on the India Squad veteran, but instead she continued pouring fire into the remainder of Kilo Squad.

She felt Qualls slam an elbow in her back. The rookie shouted, "They're coming in from behind. I'm lighting it up now." With weapons fire echoing off the metal bulkheads and decks, Misha didn't hear the commotion coming from behind her. Bravo Squad must have broken past Raza and was now threatening her team. She heard Lamont's pumper roar behind her. She swiveled her head and saw him jack another round into the chamber with one hand. His other arm hung limply at his side. Cutler also turned and furiously shot at Bravo Squad peering around the curve.

Qualls shouted, "Incoming." Misha spun back to face Kilo. In the time it took to check on Lamont and Cutler, a female Kilo trooper had risen up and tossed a grenade at them. It was too late to stop her throw, but shots from Lamsa, Everridge, Na'aranna and Misha all impacted in neat precision on her torso. Qualls leapt into the air, twisting her body horizontal to the deck and caught the grenade before it hit the deck. She seemed to rotate and spin, throwing the grenade in a straight line further along the corridor towards the advancing Bravo Squad, where it bounced off the metal bulkhead and dropped around the curve. Qualls hit the deck and slid to a crumpled heap at Cutler's feet.

The whump of the explosion was muted, but a wave of concussed air passed over Misha. In the muted silence after the explosion, she could hear cursing and running feet as Bravo Squad pulled back into engineering. She turned her aim to Kilo Squad, but before she could fire she heard metal tearing and felt a vibration rumble through the deck.

"Hold fire." She shouted. "Everyone, hold fire. Kilo Squad, drop your weapons and surrender."

A voice shouted back, "The frak you say. We got you trapped in the open between us and Second Moraft. You surrender."

Misha thought about DeLaPax's team. Even though the firefight had only been seconds long, it seemed a lot longer. Unless, Kilo's rear guard had DeLaPax trapped, she might be able to move up and box Kilo in tight. Doing so would expose her team at the lighted corner where she would be very exposed.

Suddenly, five Kilo troopers leapt to their feet and raced back up the corridor. They stopped suddenly as an APES combat suit lumbered around the corner into the light. The short man who had been Kilo's point man, slid to a stop within arm's reach of the suit, his head about navel high on the massive suit. The suited APE reached out, grabbed the man delicately by the front of his utility uniform, and tossed him with a flick of a finger against the metal bulkheads. The man oozed to a heap on the deck.

The remaining four Kilo Squad members turned to escape. Misha took aim to prevent the men from getting past her. A sound from the combat suit froze everyone in their tracks. The suit ratcheted a huge load of ammo into its mass drivers. She didn't know who was in the suit. It was a rookie suit without any of the usual veteran's personalization or artwork decorating it. In the long run, it didn't matter whether it was a rookie or a veteran in the suit; if they opened fire with their mass driver, it would sweep the corridor of everything and everybody. Normal mass driver ammo configuration was armor piercing rounds. The shots would not stop until they were well into the vacuum.

A metallic voice boomed over the suit's loud speakers. "All hostiles will drop their weapons and surrender to Able Squad. They will do so now." The four remaining Kilo effectives dropped their weapons as if they were scalding hot.

Misha said, "Everridge and Lamsa. Pick up all weapons. Na'aranna, cover them. If anyone moves, shoot them." She turned to check the rest of her team. Lamont was still covering any possible Bravo Squad approach and Cutler was bending over Qualls with a first-aid kit open. The woman croaked something she couldn't hear. "What did she say?" Misha asked as she moved quickly to Lamont.

Cutler smiled, "Something about finally catching the perfect double-play ball, whatever that is. She's going to be all right. She just had the wind knocked out of her. But, it looks like you'll need a bandage or two."

Chapter Fifty-Nine

Misha looked down to see blood trickling from a small puncture on her right side. It was not a bad wound, but her left arm was slashed and ripped with enough that it looked like she had been in a wrestling match with a tangle of DropSix warthog razor-wire and lost. "What do you know!" she exclaimed. "It doesn't hurt yet. I don't think I am going to bleed to death anytime soon. Lamont, how are you holding up?"

Lamont was still on his knees. His pumper pointed resolutely in Bravo Squad's direction. The man replied calmly without any hint of emotion or humor, "I got my uniform dirty. Sorry Trey, but I can't seem to make my left arm work. I must have a malfunction in the gears or somethin'."

Misha heard a slight slur in his speech as if it was taking too much of an effort to form the words. She expected Cutler to step up, but when she looked over her shoulder, Cutler was already bending down checking on Kilo Squad's wounded, dying, and dead. She started to call him back, but Lamont stopped her. "He's doing triage, Trey. He has to work on those who need it more. You and I are still standing, so we wait for medical attention. Right?" His voice was quiet and a bit slurred, but he spoke in a professional tone as if discussing a hypothetical situation.

"That is a-one thinking, trooper. Keep an eye on our six for a bit, okay?"

"Roger that, Trey," the man slid to the deck. "I think I'm going to keep watch from down here if it's okay with you. It seems the air is a tad bit less hazy down by the deck."

Misha laid a comforting hand on the top of his head. "We'll get a medic to you soonest. You hold here and keep an eye on Jigsaw."

Qualls croaked. "I ain't bleeding and I ain't dead yet." The woman rolled to a kneeling position next to Lamont. "You do what you gotta do, Third. We will hold here, right Lamont."

"Frakking A, little sister," was all Lamont could manage to squeak out.

Qualls smiled weakly, "Lock and load, big brother."

Misha walked away from the two as they traded cliques, some older than Earth trench warfare. She walked past Cutler working on a bloody trooper, past Everridge and Lamsa stuffing weapons in a huge carry-all and straight up to the combat suit. She reached up with her left arm and winced at the pain. She switched arms and rapped her knuckles on the suit's chest. She could only image the damage the ship had taken when the suit ripped its way through hatches and smaller corridors. Without a sound, the face shield slid back out of the way to reveal Aardmricksdottir grinning at her.

"Vark, reporting for action, Third. Sorry it took so long to get here. Per your instructions, we had to make sure the armor bays were locked down tight."

Misha nodded. "What weapons do you have in there? I want to make sure we do not gut this puppy into open space."

Vark grinned, "You know, Third. I haven't ever tried to breathe vacuum and I don't intend to start. This suit's been stripped bare. It's an old spare we keep around to train new troops. All we have is the armor shell with muscle enhancements."

Misha said, "That's not exactly standard equipment for deployment, Second. As a matter of fact; I've never seen a stripped out model."

Aardmricksdottir nodded, "Yes, sir. We kind of reported it scrapped for parts. Third Cans never seemed to care and it seemed like a good idea to me. The tri-wave simulators are decent for suit training, but nothing equals real time grunt work."

"Roger that. After this is over you send the specs up the chain and let the big boys bat the idea around. And next time, let me know about things like this. I'm too young to die from a heart attack. I almost had one when I saw you crash around the corner."

"Yes, sir," Aardmricksdottir said with a chuckle.

"Now, let's get back in the game. Did you strip out the comms in there?" All combat suits had enhanced communications circuitry that should cut through any interference.

"No. We have the wires to tap into the Kiirkegaard's comm system, but all spacecraft internal comms are completely down now."

Misha looked around the suit to check for DeLaPax's team. She saw Peace looking back. "All right?" she asked.

"No casualties, boss. We hung back as long as we could, holding for rear guard, but none showed up. Vark came by before we jumped into the fray. Anyone hurt beside you?"

"Lamont took a hit. It looks bad. We've got to get back into this quick. Raza's team got overrun and Moraft jumped up our backside."

Vark rapped her steel knuckles on the bulkhead with a clang. "Then pardon me, Third, but get your ass out of my way."

Misha nodded at DeLaPax. "Peace, you follow behind Vark." She banged her fist on the suit's chest. "Judiciously, Vark. Let's do this very judiciously so as not to damage our ride home."

Aardmricksdottir flexed her arms in the suit and shot her hand sideways. With a screeching clang, she dug steel fingers into the corridor bulkhead, closed her fist and grabbed a handful of twisted metal. She yanked backward tearing loose a strip of the metal bulkhead. Calmly she said, "Yes, sir. Very judiciously. I won't tear open anything that isn't holding air. But, I assume everything else is fair game?"

"No more personnel damage than is absolutely required. These are still Allied personnel. Got me?"

"Yes, sir."

"Good, we're going to back down this corridor to the next set of hatchways. That was where Raza was making her stand. We'll check on her team and from there you'll take point. We're going to take engineering back, but I don't want damage to any machinery. I am not walking home from here and I cannot afford to pay for a tow truck for this distance, got me?"

"Roger that, sir."

Misha turned to Everridge and Lamsa. "Get your butts back on intel. See if you can hack into any open communications signal."

Chapter Sixty

Second Moraft shouted at Trooper Nine Kranich. "What the hell is with you? You're supposed to be some hot weapons expert and you can't clear that corridor so we can get reinforcements in here?"

"Dammit, Mister Moraft. We ran into a shit storm out there."

Moraft turned to her Trooper One. "What went down, One."

The woman grimaced holding a bandage to the side of her face. "We ran flat into Raza from India Squad. Clearing her took all of Kranich's special explosives. We expected to get all of McPherson's people when we blew into them, but she wasn't there."

"What do you mean she wasn't there?"

"She'd pulled almost everyone else back down the corridor. She left Raza and some rookies in place. That bitch Raza is more of a heller in a firefight than she is in the sack. We damn near didn't get past her. She took out three of our people in the firefight. I got the bitch in the end; bloodied her myself. I saw her fall before some snot-nosed little rookie pulled her into a room and locked the hatch."

Moraft snorted. "Did you dig her out?"

"I didn't see any need. We kept moving down the corridor. We still needed to get McPherson cleared out. We found her, but got shot to pieces trying to get to her. Sorry, Mister Moraft, McPherson has a lot more help than Jackson told us. That's where we lost our other trooper. I couldn't get a count of how many there were."

"What are they using for weapons?"

"A whole damn arsenal, Theda. They even tossed a grenade at us. Bloody hell, Theda; I would have stayed on the attack but I saw her call in a combat suit just before I had to bug out."

"A combat suit?" Moraft asked in amazement. "We are well and truly frakked."

"Roger that, Theda. They are going to eat our lunch and still have room for two desserts and a bowl of prunes."

Trooper Three's three-man team raced into engineering. Turning, they slammed the big double hatches closed and clamped them shut. All three of them scrambled away from the hatch and ducked behind huge banks of machinery. He shouted, "Incoming, Deuce. We can't stop a frakking suit with these popguns."

Moraft turned to Kranich. "Well? You're the expert, what've we got that will open up a combat suit?"

"I've got nothing that won't open up the Kiirkegaard to naked space at the same time," he said. A booming clang rang out as if someone was pounding sledge hammers on the steel hatchway.

Trooper Three called out, "Hey Deuce, someone's knocking at the hatch. I think it's for you."

Major Paradise ran up to Moraft. His face was beet red and his hair was sticking out every which way. He grabbed Moraft by the shoulder and spun her around to face him. She shrugged slightly and his hand slid off. He shouted into her face. "What the hell are you doing in here? Get your team out there and defend these engines."

She looked into his eyes, then looked at Trooper One and said, "I should've taken retirement. I'm too old for this."

Paradise spit, "I am ordering you to get out there and clear those corridors."

Moraft said calmly, "No, Major Paradise. I don't take orders from you or any of your kind. We're done here. I've lost over half of my squad. I am not losing any more. McPherson was right. This needs to be over and done with."

An amplified voice boomed out, "This is Second Vark. I'm in a fully functional combat suit. I am prepared to rip this hatch open and tear you some new assholes. However, Third McPherson tells me that I've got to give you the opportunity to surrender without more APES dying. Come on, Theda. It isn't worth it anymore."

352

Trooper Three shouted to Moraft, "That's the straight skinny, Deuce. This is one for the history books. We're done here."

Paradise shouted, "You are not done until I tell you that you are done. Moraft, get your ass back out there and do your job."

Second Moraft shook her head, "No. I don't think so. I hate like hell to lose, but it's suicide to go out there. Troopers, we call it a day. Weapons down and open the hatch."

Paradise screeched, "No." He pulled out his weapon and before anyone could react, he put half a dozen needles through Second Moraft's brain. He had the lightning fast reflexes of a FAC pilot. It was too late for Moraft, but Trooper One slammed Paradise's arm sideways, knocking the muzzle away and in a fraction of a heartbeat chambered a round and put a needle into Paradise's chest. As fast as she was, hers was the third round to hit Paradise as Trooper Three and Trooper Nine Kranich both blew holes in the man.

Chapter Sixty-One

Misha sat quietly in her day office. It had been a busy four days since they took back engineering. They made adjustments and completed the fastest jumps possible to Heaven's Gate. The last jump was six hours behind them. It put them well into the Heaven's System. Britaine had ordered a navigation jump as close to the station as safety protocols allowed.

She expected to get a message from him at any moment announcing the time of their arrival. She expected it to be a hand delivered message. He was using lower-ranking spacers from the intelligence office as couriers. Communications was still inoperable. They had learned since jumping into the Heavens System that most of their external communications were down as well.

Misha replayed the whole deployment in her mind, re-working and re-thinking every action and decision from the time she stepped aboard the Kiirkegaard. She knew from her perspective, she could not have done anything differently given the circumstances. She did what she believed was right. However, what she thought and what higher command thought might be two entirely different trains of logic. At times, she was convinced that no one in the 1392nd would come away without charges, whether it was failure to obey a command, cowardice in the face of the enemy, or simple support of a mutiny. Other times she was sure she had taken the only logical and legal course of action.

Colonel Britaine ordered all non-essential personnel locked down in quarters. Normally, that would have included all APES, but Britaine didn't trust anyone who hadn't actively supported him during the aborted mutiny. The continued breakdown of communications convinced him there were still mutineers underfoot. Misha assigned Takki-Homi's Charlie Squad to secure the command and control center. Britaine continued to blockade himself. Britaine was so paranoid he refused to believe the death of Major Paradise had completely broken the back of the mutiny.

Takki-Homi came through the mutiny with his squad intact. It was a true testament to his leadership and command style. Misha thought, not for the first time since the mutiny, that Takki-Homi would make a better third-level commander than she ever would.

She had Aardrmicksdottir's Joker Squad and her own Able Squad doing continuous security duty throughout Kiirkegaard. She tried to do complete sweeps from one end of the vessel to the other, but with only two squads, it was practically impossible in a spacecraft this large. Plus, she needed to have APES security posted at sick bay for the wounded and injured, as both loyal spacers and mutineers were bedded there.

Britaine also insisted she guard all mess staff during the preparation and delivery of meals to any personnel locked down in their quarters. Furthermore, she was tasked with watching over the engineering department, placing security in environmental controls and a dozen other places, and guarding people that Britaine insisted she try to watch. Misha would like to use the extra APES from Golf and India Squads, but she wasn't sure she trusted any second-level commander who had done nothing during the mutiny. She wondered if she was becoming as paranoid as Colonel Britaine.

Misha ordered the rest of her unit locked down in APES country. She accepted promises from all surrendering troopers that they had truly ceased all hostilities. She did not lock anyone into quarters nor did she post any guards. She left APES country open and clear. As a third-level commander, she wanted to separate those who had supported the mutiny from those who fought against it and from those who did nothing. However, she didn't have the space or the loyal troops to enforce a separation. Also, she was still not convinced that any side of the conflict would be free from repercussions.

Some changes were necessary, even though they were temporary and subject to change by higher command. She temporarily attached Na'aranna to Able Squad rather than send her back to Golf. She didn't want to put a good trooper under the command of a second who couldn't decide whether to climb a tree or cut it down. Na'aranna was an excellent trooper and an outstanding weapons technician, but she needed stronger guidance than Golf's second was willing or able to give. Hard feelings were becoming evident throughout her command. She had suspended all normal APES activities. Without training and physical exercise, the confined quarters caused tensions to rise in a few short days. Misha felt she had all the internal conflict she needed for right now, without breaking up fights between Na'aranna and her old squad.

She cleared both Foxtrot and Hotel squad bays of all healthy APES. There seemed to be a pitiful few. The APES medics were using both bays for hospital beds as the APES standard combat medical facility was woefully inadequate for the number of wounded.

She removed the three Joker Squad troopers who had joined with the late Second Moraft. She slotted Trooper One Spakney, Trooper Eight Dallas and Trooper Nine Yorkvina temporarily with Bravo Squad. Misha left Bravo as it was, not putting a new second in command, leaving trooper three in temporary charge. Bravo's trooper one was confined to the hospital as her facial injury was more critical than it first appeared. Without the medical facilities on Heaven's Gate, the woman would most likely lose her eye, APES medical bays were not able to grow new ones.

Misha had mixed emotions about adjusting some troopers on the official organization chart, but she was not upset about changing their designations. That fell well within her prerogatives as the third-level commander, but she knew they were only cyberspace data work changes.

Troopers Kelly, Lamont and Raza were both confined to medical. Organizationally, she placed all of them in Able Squad. Both Kelly and Lamont claimed they were fit for duty. But, Lamont still had only limited use of his arm and Kelly could barely move without a limp. Trooper Raza was in very serious condition. She hadn't regained consciousness since Kelly pulled her to safety and locked them in the room off the engineering corridor. Cutler said if she woke up, she would probably survive, but she would never again climb into a combat suit for a dirt drop.

In her daily logs, Misha noted that as they were being overrun by a superior force, Kelly pulled Raza to safety. Neither of them would be alive if she hadn't exposed herself to incoming fire to save a comrade. It had been Kelly's only valid option even though it did expose Misha's rear to enemy attack.

Misha's own wounds hadn't healed, but she refused to confine herself to the hospital. Her refusal stuck as there were no higher-level APES on hand to countermand her decision. She ordered Cutler to pull out any shrapnel and bandage the wounds. He had remarked that her dense muscles had kept the shards from doing any severe or permanent damage. Her left arm felt stiff, but her right side only bothered her when she twisted in a particular direction. She quickly learned not to twist in that particular direction.

She officially transferred Dawg Squad's Trooper Oberman and Trooper Ramirez to Joker Squad. It was only another data exercise since both troopers were residing in the morgue. Misha bit her tongue to keep from crying when she designated Kilo's squad bay as a temporary morgue for APES who died during the conflict. The occupants of Kilo's bay were double and triple stacked, but they made no complaint. Displaced troopers bunked wherever they could find an empty bed.

Her only concern with her squad was they were unable to locate a number of APES. The Kiirkegaard was too small to hide in forever, however, with the demands placed on her by Colonel Britaine and her own limited resources, she was unable to locate what she thought of as Singletary's squad. Singletary had dropped off the map. Also, on the list of missing were Able Squad's Jem Li Park, Miguel Juarez and Aimee Slezak.

Further, they were not able to locate Foxtrot's Clark Portman and Joker's Greggoria Putinova.

With the occasional help of Marshal Forrester and as time permitted, she interviewed others about Singletary. Most interviews pointed to Dawg's Trooper Wilderman. He admitted to being one of Singletary's associates before the mutiny, but denied any knowledge of what Singletary was up to now. Wilderman steadfastly maintained that all he ever did was follow the orders of Dawg's Second Bilideau. He said he was sure Singletary had a plan to get off the Kiirkegaard because the man had contingency plans for everything.

Misha was ready for a confrontation with Singletary. She wanted it and was eager for it, but she was frustrated in that she couldn't find the man. She knew if Singletary was as smart as Wilderman gave him credit for, then her ex-trooper one would know that he would lose any face-to-face meeting with her. She had greater resources and manpower. So, the man went rabbit: running and hiding in small places. She remembered that her father always said you can want all you want, but you don't get just because you want.

A knock at the hatch interrupted Misha's thoughts. She looked up to see a young spacer from the intelligence office standing at attention. "Hello, Sticks. Welcome back to APES country. You've been down here often enough these last few days that we might as well get you drafted into the APES and make it official."

The young man paled and stuttered, "You can do that?"

Misha laughed, "Of course not. We only take volunteers. And relax; we don't do that coming to attention thing when you're reporting. So, what's up?"

The spacer tried to relax, but ended up looking more uncomfortable than before. "Colonel Britaine is in the CNC with Buzz, I mean Major Krandiewsky. They would like you to join them on the double, or I mean, as soon as conveniently possible, ma'am."

Misha smiled and said, "Right. Okay kid, here's the deal. You can call me sir, you can call me Third

McPherson, you can call me third, trey, Misha or even just 'hey you'. But, you call me ma'am one more time and I will rip your larynx out. Do you copy me?"

"Sir, yes sir," Sticks answered snapping to attention again.

She just smiled at the young man and gestured for him to lead the way. She had meant it as a joke, but now it was almost as if Sticks was afraid to say anything at all. It was a quiet walk to the command and control center. Along the way, the corridors were empty and all hatches were shut and locked. At the CNC hatch, Misha nodded to Charlie Squad Trooper Four Trammler who was standing guard. The woman had a sunburner held at the ready, but she looked comfortable and relaxed. From what Misha had heard of this young woman, anyone foolish enough to think Trammler was truly relaxed was in for a world of hurt.

Misha said, "Thanks for the escort, Sticks. You didn't get us lost even once."

Trammler choked back the snort of a laugh, but there was no response from the Sticks, so Misha shrugged and said, "Peanut, how goes it?"

Trammler replied, "Cool beans, Trey. Not a creature is stirring, not even a mouse."

As Misha stepped through the hatchway, she nodded at Takki-Homi and Riffler who were resting in chairs. She looked around the room, spotted Britaine and Krandiewsky and called out "Good afternoon, gentlemen."

Colonel Britaine waved her over to where he stood at one of the consoles. The man had been agitated since they left Gagarin and seemed to be getting worse every time she saw him. "What the hell is going on, McPherson?" Britaine demanded.

"Something is always going on somewhere," she replied curtly. "I don't really know and I am not in any kind of a mood to play games with you. So why don't you tell me what the problem is and I'll see if it is possible to give an answer at the level of intelligence that even you can understand." She was on the verge of shouting, but she no longer cared. "If you don't like it, then that's tough, because I have had about all the crap I'm going to take from you and yours. Do you understand me?"

"How dare you talk to me that way!" he shouted back. "This is my spacecraft and I am in command."

"That is a load of donkey dust and you would know it if you had half a brain," she replied with a chill to her voice.

"What?" he said. "I will have you brought up on charges, you stupid grunt."

Misha held up a hand to stop Takki-Homi and Riffler from rising out of their chairs. She stepped up to Britaine. Standing nose to nose she said in a voice like cold steel, "You're in command of this vessel only because I say so and for no other reason. You want to bring me up on charges? Fine. Just get in line, Colonel. Otherwise, from this point forward you can talk to me like a rational adult with status equal to yours or as Buzz is my witness, I will drag your ass into the middle of Heaven's Gate Commons and pound your arrogant ass into a mound of useless slag."

Britaine just stared back. She wasn't sure whether it was a look of amazement or incomprehension. She didn't really care. "Don't think I can do it? I don't care. Test me, you worthless piece of human FOD. I've spent the last few hours writing letters to families of dead APES. Good men and women who died because you couldn't lead a hard-on to an orgasm even if you had a cold beer and a Cameraan hooker as a guide."

She turned to Krandiewsky, "You got something to say, Major? My glass-pack is recording, so might as well get it said now so they can bring it up when they press charges."

Buzz smiled back and winked, "You know, Third McPherson. I think you're showing remarkable restraint under the circumstances. In my opinion...," these three words he emphasized clearly and spoke in the direction of his own glass-pack. "In my opinion, the human race and the Allied Mobile Space Force would have been much better off if Mrs. Britaine had just given the senior Mr. Britaine a blowjob that night all those years ago."

Misha turned back to Britaine. "Now that we have an understanding, Colonel, why don't you tell me about the bug you've got up your shorts?"

Britaine stuttered back, "Yes, ma'am. I mean yes, Third McPherson. It is the communications."

Misha waited, but he didn't continue. She prompted him, "They're still down, right?"

Krandiewsky answered, "Sort of down and therein lays the problem."

Misha asked, "I'll bite, what problem?"

Krandiewsky said, "It's the IFF from Heaven's Gate. We can't approach the tarmac, or even get within missile range without the appropriate codes. Once we send the appropriate code, the station locks us onto their command and brings us in on autopilot. So, since we don't have an operable communications system we were planning to sit out here until they noticed us and sent someone to investigate."

Misha nodded. "I figured as much. So we have to wait a bit longer to get off the Kiirkegaard. What are a few more hours after all the time we've already spent cooped up?"

Krandiewsky nodded. "Therein is the problem. Someone has already sent the appropriate codes. Since we are so short handed, we didn't have anyone on constant communications and navigation monitoring. It took us a while to notice we were not sitting still. We're going to hit the tarmac in less than an hour."

"Singletary." The name almost blasted from her lips. "He's planning to get off this ship and disappear onto the station before anyone on station knows what has happened on board."

Krandiewsky asked, "Singletary is your missing APE?"

Misha nodded, "A schemer and a scam artist." She looked around her. She noticed Sticks standing still in the corner. She pointed at him and said, "Sticks, get a move on and find Marshal Forrester. Do you know where he might be?"

Sticks nodded, "Yes, ma'am. He's in sickbay with Chief Brown."

Misha looked startled, "I thought he'd been released from sickbay. Has he had a relapse?"

Sticks said, "Oh no, ma'am...I mean, sir. Chief Brown just went down with him to get his bandage changed and to talk with his wife."

Misha blurted, "Wife? What are you talking about? Whose wife?"

Sticks grinned. "Oh, I guess you haven't heard. It turns out that Med-Tech Staff Sergeant Jèsusa Rezzi is really Mrs. Gan Forrester and she really is a Marshal Service operative."

"Huh and double huh. Were you listening to our conversation?"

"Yes, sir, but only those parts about the communications problem. I didn't hear anything about your threatening the Colonel."

Misha smiled, "You had better find both Forrester and Rezzi. Brief them on what's going down. Let them know their pigeon is getting ready to fly the coop and the hatch to the cage is open."

She turned back to the two men, "I hate to ask the obvious, but have you tried to piggyback a signal on the IFF?"

Krandiewsky nodded, "That was the first thing we tried. But, whoever has been setting up this jamming anticipated that and all we get is feedback."

"I suppose I can use my three squads to secure all hatchways until we can get a message to station security."

Britaine shook his head vigorously, "Two squads. You can't use Tackyhummer's squad. I still need them. In fact, I need for you to order his whole squad up here for guard duty. You may think this is the work of this Singletary, but I think there are still mutineers who're going to try to take this spacecraft away from me. They

362

could use the landing procedures confusion to overcome just a few guards."

Misha said, "I don't think that's very likely, Colonel Britaine. They would have nothing to gain at this late date."

Britaine shot back, "I don't care what you think." He winced when he saw Misha's face cloud up, but he continued on, "I believe there's still a possibility of attack. That is enough for me and for your precious contract. See, I looked it up too. Now, I insist."

Misha nodded, "That's indeed your call, Colonel." She spoke across the room. "Second Takki-Homi, please make your squad at the ready." She turned back to the two officers. "Well, I can try to cover all the exits with two squads."

Britaine snorted, "You have to do more than try. I can't allow any of these mutinous bastards off my spacecraft. I want them all caught and punished."

"I agree anyone who gets off this vessel will probably duck into the station's population and be gone before station security knows we have a problem. But, all I have are two squads to work with."

"Won't work."

Krandiewsky nodded, "I hate to agree with the Colonel, but he's right on this. There's more than a half a dozen deck hatches in addition to the main hatchway. There're also fifteen maintenance bay hatches, plus about a dozen specialized logistics ports, missile tubes and gun bays. That's too many for two squads to cover."

Suddenly Britaine said, "We also tried to piggyback messages on the other signals."

Misha said, "What other signals?"

Britaine snorted and then looked furtively at Misha, "Sorry. There are other signals that automatically transmit. If they weren't sent, they would alert Heaven's Gate to a potential problem and we wouldn't be allowed to dock."

Misha waited, but the man didn't continue. Finally, she asked, "Well?"

Britaine snarled back, "You may threaten me all you like, but I am not here to instruct you in AMSF procedures."

Misha replied, "Fine by me." She turned to Krandiewsky, "Buzz, may I ask what signals we're talking about?"

The major nodded. "Three basic signals are always transmitted from any returning spacecraft in addition to the IFF. The first is the data download from our stores and inventories. It's a data dump into the station's main supply chain for replenishment. The second is an automated download of any damage that tells the yard dogs to prepare for repairs. The third is an accounting download; payroll, invoice payment, that kind of stuff."

"Did we try a piggyback on any of them?" she asked.

Krandiewsky nodded. "We tried on all of them. The messages are being slammed back by a filter. It appears any message that mentions security, Marshal Service, mutiny and a whole load of other words isn't getting through."

Misha thought for a moment and pulled out her glass-pack. Quickly, she typed up a message, dropped it in the reader and called it up on a display monitor. She called Krandiewsky over and said, "Take a look at this. This is a trick I learned recently from a couple of rookies named Kelly. We'll just use open unencrypted messages instead of the special Kelly family codes. We need to try to get this message into the accounting data stream. It's back-dated to before I ever arrived on Heaven's Gate, so it should generate a response. What do you think?"

Krandiewsky frowned in thought, "Looks like an invoice."

Misha nodded. "That's the point. It shouldn't look any different than any other accounting message traffic. We need to make sure it's coded for immediate payment and forwarding."

He asked, "Do you think they're going to react and do anything?"

Misha said, "I think so, but we need to get as many messages like this into the system as we can. Who do you know on the station?"

A short time later she left Krandiewsky and some of his intelligence staff as they slid their messages into the accounting data stream. She only had a few minutes to track down as many of her two squads as possible to cover as many of Kiirkegaard's exits as she could.

Chapter Sixty-Two

Misha stood in the main hatchway foyer. The wide room had a dozen corridors and ladders converging onto its open space. She held a needler in each hand. Ottiamig stood next to her. He had a sunburner held at the ready. Misha had decided if she couldn't cover all the ways out of the Kiirkegaard, she would try to cover the most obvious exits. She was also not of a mind to let any APE stand guard alone; ordering everyone to pair up.

The only other occupant of the large room was Clancy. The intelligence sergeant held an oversized maintenance glass-pack to read the landing manual for hatch opening. Occasionally, she scanned through a few pages in either direction and then glanced up at the hatchway's console for confirmation. Britaine didn't trust any of the maintenance crew near any hatches.

Misha felt, more than heard, the station's landing clamps grapple and lock onto the spacecraft's stanchions. She saw a light turn green on Clancy's console and Misha felt a subtle change in airflow as the environmental systems switched over to station control. She saw another light turn green and heard a small hum generating throughout the deck plates signaling they were off internal power and locked into the station systems. A third light turned green.

Two spacers raced around a corner and into the main foyer. Both men froze in their tracks when they came face to face with a brace of needlers and a sunburner.

Ottiamig cleared his throat loudly and gestured with the muzzle of his weapon, sending both men scurrying back the way they had come. Misha looked at Ottiamig without expression. He shrugged, "Sorry, Third. I was not in the mood to shoot more of our own people." Before she could agree with him, Takki-Homi, Trammler and Riffler burst into the room. Their weapons were held at the ready. Colonel Britaine followed. The bulk of Charlie Squad blanketed him like a cocoon. Gaineretti and Toxix brought up the rear. At a command from Second Takki-Homi, his squad fanned out and brought their weapons to bear on every entrance into the room.

Only when this was complete did Colonel Britaine speak. He pointed to Clancy, "You, on the hatch. Get it open!"

Clancy looked at Misha and grinned. Theatrically she pointed her index finger at the console and as if stabbing with a sword, she punched one button and the hatch began to cycle open.

Misha turned to face the opening hatch and was momentarily blinded by glaring white lights. A booming voice shouted, "Station security. Drop all weapons and keep your hands where we can see them." Misha dropped her needlers to the deck and held her arms out wide at shoulder height. She heard the clatter as Ottiamig and all of Charlie Squad followed suit. The voice boomed again, "Colonel Britaine and Third McPherson only, please step forward onto the tarmac. No one else move."

Misha moved forward without waiting for Britaine to respond. Before she reached the ramp, Britaine pushed past her. She heard the rattle of heavy weapons fire vibrating through the deck and froze. Britaine dropped to the ramp, covered his head and shouted, "It was the Code Black orders requiring me to report to the station. I wasn't running away. Don't shoot me."

Misha stepped over him and continued down the ramp. Once past the initial glare of lights, her eyes began to adjust. She could see station security covering the deck area in force. They had emptied the tarmac of all other personnel, except for one lone small figure standing off to the side.

An AMSF major stepped up to her and said, "Third McPherson?"

Misha nodded.

The major stepped past her and walked up to Britaine. Misha put the major out of her mind as she turned to the lone figure. It was Fifth-Level Commander

IvanYetta Vaslov. The diminutive woman waved her over.

"Fist Vaslov, I don't know how to tell you how glad I am to see you."

Vaslov nodded, "Good to see you too, McPherson, even under whatever these circumstances are, and I hope you have a good explanation for all of this excitement."

Misha said, "Yes, sir. I hereby formally surrender myself and my entire command for arrest."

Vaslov shook her head grimly, "I thought something serious had gone wrong, but hold off on that 'formal' garbage until I know more."

Misha said, "Yes, sir: mutiny, murder, theft, insubordination, violation of contract, cowardice under fire." She looked back at Britaine still cowering on the Kiirkegaard's ramp and continued, "Well, maybe and maybe not. I recommend everyone on board be arrested and let the lawyers sort it out."

Vaslov grunted. "I hate to arrest our own people for a spacer's squabble."

Misha shook her head sadly, "Not this time, Fist. There's enough mud to be slung about for some of it to fall on everyone. We had APES supporting mutiny, others who did nothing and we have more than a few dead, killed by our own troopers."

Vaslov spat on the deck and said, "Dammit, McPherson, we can't afford this crap.

Misha nodded, "Yes, sir. I know that as commander, I'm held accountable for the actions of my command, all of them. I submit myself for arrest on charges of mutiny and for taking violent actions against the mutineers."

Vaslov shook her head. "No, I said to hold off on that and I mean it. You're damned either way if we go that route. When I say we can't afford this crap, I mean we can't afford to take more APES off the front lines of this war. It's heating up and I have my orders. This is bad enough, but you're the only APES unit to come back from Gagarin."

"What?!" Misha all but shouted.

Vaslov nodded looking far away. "We've had a couple of other spacecraft General Gurand sent back as special couriers under his Code Black orders. We've gotten images and reports from the snafu there, humans siding with Binders and all. The most painful thing is that we have reports that all the units with Fourth Ottiamig have either been captured or killed." She held up a hand to stop Misha's response. "Look, I don't know everything that went on aboard that spacecraft and I'm sure I don't want to know. I have more problems to resolve today than your screwed-up command. That's for the lawyers to hash out if, and I mean a big if, we can't cover up any APES involvement. We're going to make this go away if we have to invest in a whitewash factory. You best glue your lips together until you talk to APES counsel, all of your involvement is APES business only, got me? And you'll tell your people the same thing, all of your people. Feel free to toss any other lawyers out the nearest airlock, if that's what it takes. Um... only airlocks when you are docked. I think most lawyers deserve a little extra time in vacuum, but let's not put whipped cream on a shit pie, okay?"

Misha nodded in relief. She had been sure her career was doomed, but Vaslov just handed her a get out of jail free card, a pardon and a pass all rolled into one. By legal standards, she was guilty of supporting the mutiny and for taking active and deadly action against those same mutineers. She was even guilty for not doing anything about the mutiny as some of her command did nothing. She was guilty of allowing everything Singletary had done and at the same time guilty for not stopping him. She was also guilty of participating in Dawg Squad's attack on Britaine in the flight office even though she had not even been in that part of the ship. Vaslov was right. It was a mess for lawyers to solve and best leave it for them to handle. However, if APES higher command wanted APES involvement to disappear, then she would do her best to make it go away like a morning mountain mist in the hot sun.

She asked, "I heard gunfire. Do you know what's going on?"

Vaslov shook her head. She turned and called to a spacer second class. Brianna Morin trotted up with a big grin. The young girl hugged Misha and then said, "Oh, I guess they don't do much hugging in the APES, huh, Trey?"

Misha laughed as she blushed at the unexpected friendship, "Not in my experience. No. But, it is good to see you."

Fifth Vaslov asked, "Brianna, what is the word on the gunfire?

Brianna said, "Security comms said some people were trying to jump to the station from the Kiirkegaard through a logistics port. It sounds like it took some persuading to make them surrender. There wasn't any word on casualties on either side, so there probably wasn't much more than a few warning shots." She held a finger up as she listened to communications in her ear bud. She looked at the APES, "It was a small group of APES. Some guy named Singletary and a guy named Park both got shot, but it doesn't sound serious since we are using non-lethal bullets. Ohhhh, Singletary took a stray hit in the crotch and might need an icepack for a few days. They were turned back into the ship and not allowed off."

Misha laughed and with a shake of her head said, "Singletary? Well, at least I know where he is now." She said to Vaslov, "Singletary is an APE who-"

"Shut it, Misha," Vaslov interrupted. "Save it for your never-to-be-published memoirs."

Misha turned to the young spacer and said, "So, Brianna, it looks like your duty station isn't as dull now as you thought it was."

Vaslov said, with a slight smile, "Brianna and I have had a few busy moments lately."

Brianna said, "I got your invoice requesting urgent payment for the flute I bought. Since it was dated before I even bought the flute, I thought something was wrong. I tried to tell my commander, but he said it was just a computer glitch, so I punched up APES command and Fifth Vaslov answered the call."

Vaslov nodded, "Brianna was hot and raising such a ruckus I took a few minutes to listen to her story. The whole thing sounded fishy, so we started making some calls. I couldn't get any reaction from station security until the wife of some major, a Buzz something or other, started raising all kinds of hell about getting an invoice from her husband for sexual favors. So, between the three of us, we finally got someone at station security to listen."

Misha smiled, "I didn't realize Buzz had that kind of sense of humor. Well, maybe not. Maybe he just knew what would send his wife over the edge."

Brianna nodded, "Whatever it was, it finally worked. We managed to get enough people to cover every possible exit."

Vaslov smiled at the girl, "Good job, too. It seems you have excellent instincts."

"Thanks," Brianna said. "Sorry, but I've got to get back to work. I'll talk to you both later, okay?"

Vaslov said, "I would like that, but it will probably be a while before Third McPherson can get away. She has a command to quietly reorganize, a lot of reports to bury, and from what I've seen so far, she'll have more legal depositions to avoid than gnats on a buzzard's butt.

The two APES watched Brianna rush back to her duties.

Vaslov nodded, "That girl told me she was going to be an APE someday, just like you. With our losses in this AMSF fiasco, we may have to ramp up our enlistments, so she may switch quicker than normal. But in spite of that cheerful little girl, this is a bad day for APES."

Misha frowned, "Sorry for the mess, Fifth, I wish-"

Vaslov interrupted, "No more about that from you." Before Misha could respond, she said, "Get all your people reorganized and informed about their non-involvement in any AMSF investigation. Explain that there is and will be no APES investigation. It is not our mess and we have no comments to make without our own lawyers present. Get your command formed up and prepare for deployment. Let me know ASAP what you need in replacements. I don't know if we'll have to leave the 1392nd on the Kiirkegaard or move you to another spacecraft."

Without expecting a reply the small woman continued and ticked off her fingers, "One: we can't afford to lose more APES to some AMSF screw up. Two: right, wrong or indifferent, you've lost your first two commands in remarkably short order. The APES and I agree that's not an attribute in a commander that we look for, however... however, the situation is so frakked up that we're going to have to overlook and ignore this. We can't demote or discharge someone for something that we deny ever happened." Vaslov shook her head and said, "And three, because of our losses, now we have to promote you to fill Fourth Ottiamig's position. Congratulations, Quad McPherson."

The End

Cast of Characters

Aardrmicksdottir, 'Vark' – 1392nd Joker Squad Second-Level Commander & Armor Repair Technician

Ammad - 1392nd Charlie Squad Trooper Seven & Expendables Clerk

Ammok, Amma - 1392nd Hotel Squad Trooper Six

Baily - 1392nd Hotel Squad Trooper Three

Bambi - Kilo Squad Trooper One (Battle of Guinjundst)

Bammorou - 1392nd Charlie Squad Trooper Ten & Skid Plate Repair Technician

Barrett - Spacer First Class, AMSF Kiirkegaard

Beaudry, Bennett - 1392nd Joker Squad Trooper Three & Skid Plate Repair Technician

Becker, 'Dog Boy' - 1392nd Foxtrot Squad Trooper Five

Bilideau, Rice 'Beans' - 1392nd Dawg Squad Second-Level Commander & General Supplies Clerk

Boozer - Kilo Squad Trooper Three (Battle of Guinjundst)

Britaine, William 'Muffin' Park - Lieutenant Colonel, Commander of the AMSF Spacecraft T/E-716 Kiirkegaard

Brown - 1392nd Joker Squad Trooper Ten & Weapons Technician

Brown, Elizabeth 'Dead-eye' - Chief Master Sergeant, NCOIC of Intelligence, AMSF Kiirkegaard

Bruce, Twiller – Master Sergeant, Steward, AMSF Kiirkegaard

Cans, Hamilton - 1392nd Third-Level Commander (retired), former Commander of the 1392nd

Cauton - 1392nd Kilo Squad Second-Level Commander

Chang - Dawg Squad Second-Level Commander (Battle of Guinjundst)

Chang, 'Waterboy' - Major, Second Watch Commander, AMSF Kiirkegaard

Clancy - Staff Sergeant, Intelligence, AMSF Kiirkegaard

Cochran, John – The Sixth (highest rank in the Allied Protective Expeditionary Services)

Cuffs - Sergeant, Intelligence, AMSF Kiirkegaard

Cutler, Bear - 1392nd Able Squad Trooper Seven & Medical Technician

Dallas - 1392nd Joker Squad Trooper Nine

Dashell - 1392nd Foxtrot Squad Trooper Three & Medical Technician

DeLaPax, Peace - 1392nd Able Squad Trooper Four & Armor Repair Technician

Deavereaux - 1392nd Charlie Squad Trooper Nine & Communications Technician

Dimms, Richard 'Puke' - Major, Doctor Flight Surgeon, AMSF Kiirkegaard

Donnellson, Sigget - 1392nd Foxtrot Squad Trooper One & Weapons Technician

Esteban, 'Nuke' - Major, First Watch Commander, AMSF Kiirkegaard

Everridge, 'Tree' – 1392nd Joker Squads Trooper Five, Intelligence Specialist

Forrester, Gan – Sergeant, Allied Marshal Service

Gaineretti - 1392nd Charlie Squad Trooper One & Intelligence Technician

Garcia – 1392nd Charlie Squad Trooper Six & Medical Technician

Geleann, 'Gee' – Civilian & Misha's baby sister

Gubcza, Aric 'Goober' – Easy Squads Second-Level Commander (Battle of Guinjundst)

Gurand – General, AMSF Flight Wing Commander

Hassletanker – 1392nd Joker Squad Trooper Eleven & General Supplies Clerk

Ivanov – Spacer First Class

Jackson, Race – 1392nd Foxtrot Squad Second-Level Commander

Jackson, Richard – APES Third-Level Commander (Battle of Guinjundst)

Jacobis – Spacer Second Class, Fighter Maintenance Technician, AMSF Kiirkegaard

Janasovich, 'Tinker' – Junior Major, Second Watch Commander, AMSF Kiirkegaard

Juarez, Miguel – 1392nd Able Squad Trooper Five & Weapons Technician

Kelly, Aarvan – 1392nd Bravo Squad Trooper Seven & Weapons Quarter Mater

Kelly, Ansel – Fifth-Level Commander, APES Attorney General

Kelly, Ethica – 1392nd Hotel Squad Trooper Eleven & Expendables Clerk

Kosimov – Hotel Squad Second-Level Commander (Battle of Guinjundst)

Krandiewsky, Hiero 'Buzz' – Junior Major, Officer in Charge of Intelligence, AMSF Kiirkegaard

Kranich – 1392nd Bravo Squad Trooper Five & Weapons Technician

Kranitchovich, Stanley - 1392nd Hotel Squad Second-Level Commander & General Supplies Clerk

Lamont – 1392nd India Squad Trooper Two & Quarter Master

Lamsa, 'The Greek' – 1392nd Joker Squad Trooper Seven & Communications Technician

Lorenzo – Kilo Squad Trooper Four (Battle of Guinjundst)

McPherson, Hamisha (Misha) Ann - 1392nd APES Third-Level Commander & Able Squad's Intelligence Technician

Mendo – Kilo Squad Trooper Seven (Battle of Guinjundst)

Metzler, Oouta – 1392nd Able Squad Trooper Eleven & Power Specialist

Mill-Hooman – 1392nd Hotel Squad Trooper Nine

Molina, 'Mo' – Spacer First Class, Security, AMSF Kiirkegaard

Moraft, Theda – 1392nd Bravo Squad Second-Level Commander

Morin, Brianna – Spacer Second Class, Security on Heaven Three Space Station

N'Guakkano – Joker Squad Second-Level Commander (Battle of Guinjundst)

Na'aranna, Nana – 1392nd Golf Squad Trooper One & Weapons Technician

Ng - Hotel Squad Trooper Ten (Battle of Guinjundst)

Oberman - 1392nd Dawg Squad Trooper Six & Expendables Clerk

Ortiz – 1392nd Charlie Squad Trooper Five & Armor Repair Technician

Ortiz – Spacer Second Class, Spacer, AMSF Kiirkegaard

Ottiamig, Kema Wallace, 139th APES Fourth-Level Commander

Ottiamig, James 'Jimmie' – 1151st APES Second Level Commander

Ottiamig, Tuamma – 1392nd Able Squad Trooper Eight & General Supplies Clerk

Papadoropoulis, 'Papa' – Joker Squad Trooper Two (Battle of Guinjundst)

Paradise, 'Digger' – Major, Executive Officer (XO), AMSF Kiirkegaard

Park – Charlie Squad/Second-Level Commander (Battle of Guinjundst)

Park, Jem Li – 1392nd Able Squad Trooper Two & Skid Plate Repair Technician

Platzchewski, 'Chewie' – 1392nd Charlie Squad Trooper Six & Power Specialist

Portland – 1392nd Easy Squad Second-Level Commander

Portman, Clark – 1392nd Foxtrot Squad Trooper Eleven

Pushkin – Kilo Squad/Trooper Three & Medical Technician (Battle of Guinjundst)

Putinova, Greggoria – 1392nd Joker Squad Trooper Four & Medical Technician

Qualls, Tammie 'Jigsaw' – 1392nd Able Squad Trooper Ten & Communications Technician

Ramirez – 1392nd Dawg Squad Trooper Nine

Ramirez, Sheila – 1392nd Easy Squad Trooper Nine & Medical Technician

Raza, Aggie – 1392nd India Squad Trooper One & Skid Plate Repair Specialist

Rezzi, Jèsusa – Staff Sergeant, Medical Technician, AMSF Kiirkegaard

Rickie – Spacer Second Class, Intelligence, AMSF Kiirkegaard

Riffler, Amossitta – 1392nd Charlie Squad Trooper Three & Medical Technician

Rittenhaus – 1392nd Charlie Squad Trooper Eight & Quarter Master

Rodriguez, Juanita – Joker Squad Trooper Four (Battle of Guinjundst)

Rodriguez, Juanito – Joker Squad Trooper Six (Battle of Guinjundst)

Saheed – Second-Level Commander (retired) Misha's former leader
Severin – Kilo Squad Trooper Six (Battle of Guinjundst)
Singletary, Gates – 1392nd Able Squad/Trooper One & Quarter Master)
Skeller, Packet – Civilian & Misha's DropSix ex-fiancée
Slezak, Aimee – 1392nd Able Squad Trooper Six & Expendables Clerk
Smith – 1392nd Kilo Squad Trooper Eleven & Power Specialist
Spakney – 1392nd Joker Squad Trooper Eleven
Spaznitski, 'Spaz' – 1392nd Foxtrot Squad Trooper Four
Steinman, Israel – 1392nd Able Squad Trooper Nine & Cook
'Sticks' – Sergeant, Intelligence, AMSF Kiirkegaard
Suzuki – Bravo Squad Second-Level Commander (Battle of Guinjundst)
Suzuki – 1392nd Hotel Squad Trooper One
Takki-Homi, Suzuki 'Taks' – 1392nd Charlie Squad Second-Level Commander & Cook
Theress – 1392nd Hotel Squad Trooper Seven
Tingler, Sven – 1392nd Hotel Squad Trooper Eight
Toxix – 1392nd Charlie Squad Trooper Eleven & General Supplies Clerk
Trammler, 'Peanut' – 1392nd Charlie Squad Trooper Four & Weapons Technician
Vaslov, IvanYetta – 13th APES Fifth-Level Commander
Wang – Spacer Second Class, AMSF Kiirkegaard
Wilderman – 1392nd Dawg Squad Trooper Five
Wilkins – Technical Sergeant, Security, AMSF Kiirkegaard
Williams, 'Bill' – Sergeant, Security, AMSF Kiirkegaard
Yamara – 1392nd Kilo Squad Trooper Eleven (Battle of Guinjundst)
YellowHorse – 1392nd Hotel Squad Trooper Four
Yorkvina – 1392nd Joker Squad Trooper Eight

ABOUT THE AUTHOR

Alan Black is a #1 bestselling author on Amazon and Kindle for Metal Boxes, a young adult science fiction military action adventure. He has published seven novels, with five still in print. Black is a self-published multi-genre writer. His main goal is to write story driven novels. His scifi novels are character and action driven rather than focused on science. His historical novels are story driven, not history lessons. His literary fiction is entertainment based.

Alan Black's vision statement: I want my readers amazed they missed sleep because they could not put down one of my books. I want my readers amazed I made them laugh on one page and cry on the next. I want to give my readers a pleasurable respite from the cares of the world for a few hours.

I want to offer stories I would want to read.

More information at
www.alanblackauthor.com
https://www.facebook.com/pages/Alan-Black-Paperback-Writer/259372705810

METAL BOXES

The best of new space adventure!

One of the best books of the new breed of scifi writers. Have been a fan of space adventures for the past 40 years and this is by far one of the top ten reads! I cannot remember such a fun and memorable read...thank you!

By FD Chandler, January 4, 2014

Very good book

Great action. Fine characters. Rollicking adventure and great humor. Don't miss this one! I look forward to more from this writer.

By James P. Ruff, Jr. (Altos de Yerba Buena, San Jorge III, Casa 8, Chia, Cundinamarca, Colombia, South America), December 12, 2013

Great read, could not put it down!

A very riveting book! I could not put it down. The anticipation to see what was going to happen next was awesome. Great technical detail along with enjoyable entertainment. The story was easy to follow along with as well as having great detail and intrigue...

By Larry Wright, November 18, 2013

CHEWING ROCKS

A strong female character you can't help but love

Alan Black paints an out-of-this-world picture of young Sno busy outside her spacecraft in her EVA suit, by herself, mining asteroids for rock and hopefully, a rare metal or two. When she returns to her home base in Arizona City on a small planetoid called, Ceres, she gets in a barroom scrap with 4 fellow miners from a competing operation. Without harming so much as a fingernail, she puts them in their place and then shortly after blasts off into the asteroid belt again to work a claim.

It's what happens when they chase after her that makes Chewing Rocks so much fun to read. Great action, wonderful word visuals of the planetoid city, the spaceships and the mining operations along with a multitude of colorful characters made Chewing Rocks hard to walk away from...

By James Paddock, January 26, 2014 (author of *Deserving of Death*)

CHASING HARPO

CITYSunTimes, Scottsdale, Arizona at news.CITYSunTime.com

When an orangutan goes on the lam, anything can happen. Chasing Harpo, by Arizona author Alan Black hosts an intriguing cast of quirky characters you'd like to visit with longer. Including the star, Harpo -- an orangutan who believes humans are here purely for his entertainment and, of course, to deliver his food.

A fun ride and a great adventure for all ages, as Harpo and his trusty servant, Carl, try to outwit the zoo security team, the police, the attorney general and a gang of drug dealers.

By Melanie Tighe, October 1, 2013 (Anna Questerly author of *The Minstrel's Tale*)

Clever humor

I found it thoroughly entertaining. The humor is of the bizarre or zany variety. Black has a way of creating a turn of phrase or a situation that made me chuckle many times. I found myself liking the characters, all of whom where colorful, exaggerated stereotypes (a way of actually challenging those stereotypes by making me laugh at them). They were individuals that were easy to keep apart. This book is entirely written tongue in cheek but with an underlying serious message about our treatment of the environment and animals, especially in zoos. The story itself was a rollicking romp that included a fair bit of suspense without ever taking itself too seriously.

Seeing the world from the point of view of Harpo, the orangutan in some chapters made for a hilarious outside look at us as humans and made for some of the funnier aspects...this was a fun book to read and I recommend it for when you need to look at life a little less seriously for a bit.

By Yvonne Hertzberger, January 2, 2014 (author of _**The Dreamt Child**_)

THE FRIENDSHIP STONES (BOOK ONE OF AN OZARK MOUNTAIN SERIES)

Growing up in the Ozarks in the 1920s

An engrossing coming of age story set in the Ozark Mountains right after World War I. The heroine, 12-year-old LillieBeth Hazkit, lives with her parents in a two-room rented cabin. Work is scarce in the mountains, and her father, who was gassed in World War I, has to take a job far away at a charcoal burning company and is able to come home only on the weekend. The work does his damaged lungs (_no)_ good.

 LillieBeth cheerfully does a round of chores that would make a grown man blanch today. She also "harvests" small game for dinner with the family's .22 rifle. She can go to school in a one-room schoolhouse only once a week because it's so far from home. She brings the rest of the week's work home to do there. With her cozy home and her parents she feels rich. After all, doesn't she have two dresses, one for work and one for Sunday?

From a Sunday sermon she learns that God wants everybody to love all people, even the unlovable ones, so she sets out to befriend an old recluse, Fletcher Hoffman, a man who rode with Quantrill's Raiders the Civil War and did his share of killing afterwards. He just wants to be left alone.

380

The story revolves around LillieBeth's attempts to befriend Hoffman and the actions of a pair of violence of a pair of louts who attack Lily Beth and are have enjoyed raping women in the neighborhood for years, destroying their lives and any possibility they could marry. It's the women's word against theirs. They always say the women wanted it.

In addition LillieBeth's landlady orders them to leave their cabin so that her son and his wife and his family will have a place to live. This will leave the Hazkit family homeless, and LillieBeth will be forced to leave the only home she has ever known.

LillieBeth's emotions are becoming more complex as she grows into womanhood. She is confused by her conflicting emotions, wanting to do the right thing—to follow Bible's injunction to love her neighbors, but she finds it hard to love the men who attacked her and the landlord who is evicting her family.

Black gives us a vivid description of life in the Ozark Mountains in the 1920s. He also gives us believable characters which we can love or hate as the story requires. Highly recommended. And when you finish reading it, give it to your 12-year-old daughter to read.
By Marilynn Larew, November 25, 2013 (author of **_The Spider Catchers_**)

A great story - first in a series!
It follows the story of LillieBeth Hazkit and her family, in the 1920s mountains in Missouri. It's a hard-to-categorize book - young adult, Christian, historical fiction - but thoroughly enjoyable.

The book is very descriptive in the period detail - clothing and hairstyles, the one-room school house/church, the run-down cabin where LillieBeth and her family live, and the post-Civil War unemployment.

The setting felt very familiar to me since I lived near the Ozarks years ago, and spent many summers camping in the hollers and picking up pebbles on the riverbanks. Because of some slightly mature subjects in the book, I wouldn't recommend it for anyone under about 12 years old, but there is nothing to offend anyone older than that. And even the mature parts are tastefully done.

LillieBeth is a 12 year old girl, right on the cusp of womanhood. She still loves playing in the woods and giggling with her girlfriends, but during the span of the book she is forced to grow up and take on more responsibility, including guarding a friend's dark secret and facing down men who would harm her family. She spends months befriending a difficult, angry neighbor, and starts to find her place as a young woman in her community. I won't spoil the ending for those who are considering buying the book, but I will say I'm looking forward to the next book in the series so I can find out what happens next.

By **Lisa Kearns** North Carolina, USA, February 5, 2014

THE GRANITE HEART (BOOK TWO OF AN OZARK MOUNTAIN SERIES)

I bought this yesterday!
Again, this book, the second in the series of Ozark Mountains, is so refreshing. I was sad that it ended. I look forward to the "next" book. (It's coming soon!) I shared with my sister, that Alan has expertly woven God in the storyline. She has now bought "The Friendship Stones" (See my review on this book) in the Kindle version at Amazon. The fact that a mother and son could team up together and give us high quality AND fun reading, it's just absolutely wonderful. The glossary at the end of the book is great learning. Made me laugh at how many I knew!

By **Fran Villa**, March 11, 2014

Made in the USA
San Bernardino, CA
29 June 2014